PRAISE FOR

Chasing Shakespeares

"[A] remarkable achievement, a thoroughly enjoyable book that gets subtler the more you think about it. Beautifully written, it blends history and fantasy, past and present, ideas and emotions, into a seamless whole which is as entertaining as it is thought-provoking."　　　—Iain Pears, author of *An Instance of the Fingerpost*

"A brilliant and moving work! Sarah Smith gives Josephine Tey a run for her money, revealing vividly a slice of history we never knew we could believe in, intertwined with engrossing modern characters."　　　—Ellen Kushner, author of *Swordspoint* and host of PRI's *Sound & Spirit*

"By page five I forgot I was reading to comment and began reading to devour. *Chasing Shakespeares* is breezy, erudite, never ponderous, a love story about how we make our heroes, and how they make us."　　　—Gregory Maguire, author of *Wicked* and *Mirror Mirror*

"Romance, intrigue, and the literary whodunit of our time—*Chasing Shakespeares* is a romp and I savored every moment of it."　　　—Hallie Ephron, author of *Delusion*

"Wonderful! In trying to solve the mystery of the authorship of the plays, Sarah Smith has provided an intellectual treat for all Shakespeare lovers. Guaranteed to enthrall, excite, enrage and enlighten in equal measure."　　　—Edward Marston, author of *The Bawdy Basket*

"A deft mixture of scholarly research and romance, plus a mystery for the ages. Raise a glass to the Earl of Oxford and toast the marvelous Sarah Smith. This one's a keeper!"　　　—Linda Barnes, bestselling author of the *Carlotta Carlyle* series

"Frothy romantic mystery for English majors . . . Marjorie Garber meets Reese Witherspoon." — *The New York Times*

"[Makes] the Shakespeare authorship controversy as riveting as any film noir plot bursting with bodies. . . . A complex book about attachment and ambition, the clash of class and culture . . . a worthy addition to Smith's already impressive output." — *Publishers Weekly*

"Engaging. . . . [Smith] might convert the reader . . . but you can enjoy *Chasing Shakespeares* just as much if you prefer to go on thinking that the Bard was [Joseph Fiennes]."
— *Detroit Free Press* (four stars)

"A smart literary thriller . . . full of the real fun of scholarship. . . . Smith can give A. S. Byatt a run for her money around the globe — or the Globe." — *Christian Science Monitor*

"A delicious literary mystery. . . . Great fun." — *Baltimore Sun*

"Both a fun read and a highly literate introduction to the intricacies and challenges of historical research. One comes away entertained and enlightened." — *St. Louis Post-Dispatch*

"[An] exhilarating, fast-paced roller-coaster of a novel. . . . Smith weaves a wonderfully elaborate and intriguing tapestry. . . . [Her] masterful storytelling makes us experience this epiphany in all its tortuous delight." — *Providence Sunday Journal*

"*Chasing Shakespeares* instructs and entertains and, ultimately, raises more questions than it answers, which is why it is so intensely interesting." — *Virginian-Pilot*

"A first-rate literary detective story." — *Shakespeare Matters*

"Fabulous . . . poetic . . . [with] a lively cast of characters, including Oxfordians, some of whom are wonderfully caricatured as wild-eyed zealots and cranks." — *Chicago Oxford Society Newsletter*

SARAH SMITH

Chasing Shakespeares

A NOVEL

WASHINGTON SQUARE PRESS

NEW YORK   LONDON   TORONTO   SYDNEY

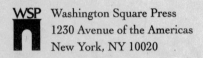 Washington Square Press
1230 Avenue of the Americas
New York, NY 10020

ISBN: 0-7434-6482-6
        0-7434-6483-4 (Pbk)

First Washington Square Press trade paperback edition May 2004

10 9 8 7 6 5 4 3 2 1

For information regarding special discounts for bulk purchases,
please contact Simon & Schuster Special Sales at 1-800-456-6798
or business@simonandschuster.com

To the only begetter
of these ensuing
Joanna Wexler

———————————————

and to Otto Penzler and Michele Slung,
who first thought it might be a book

———————————————

but most of all
to our ever-living poet
(under whatever name)
William Shakespeare

———————————————

omnia mei dona Dei

A Note on the Names

Most of the Elizabethan characters had titles, and many of their titles changed during their lifetimes. Edward de Vere, for instance, was successively Viscount Bulbeck and the Earl of Oxford; William Cecil became Baron Burghley; Robert Cecil went through other titles before becoming Earl of Salisbury.

This is the sort of thing that drives readers mad, especially Americans. And for the purpose of this book it was important to know who was related to whom.

So, with two exceptions, the titled characters are referred to here by their family names. The two exceptions are Edward de Vere and Henry Wriothesley, who are usually called by their titles, Oxford and Southampton.

Though some of the characters here are based on historical characters, they are used in a fictional sense.

The rest of the evidence is pretty much real. On the Web site for this book, www.chasingshakespeares.com, I've included notes on the times when Joe cites incomplete or wrong evidence, as well as much other useful and amusing information like a genealogical table, short biographies of the Elizabethans, a time-line, a map of London, and a selection of weird Shakespeare sightings. That's www.chasingshakespeares.com, also reachable through www.sarahsmith.com. Enjoy.

*T*hat day I was just about to lose my vocation, my job, my good sense, probably my mind, but what I thought I was losing was Mary Catherine O'Connor.

"You shouldn't go," I said to Mary Cat. We were in my truck, stuck in traffic on the Southeast Expressway on the way to Logan; I had one more chance to tell her all the things she hadn't listened to before. "You don't want to do this, it isn't your life."

"They want me," Mary Cat said. "I'll be of use, Joe."

"You *are* of use—" I ground gears, cut off a Toyota that wanted to pass me on the right, and switched into the airport lane. One thing about driving a pile-o'-shit truck with the truck bed full of broken windows, people get out of your way.

"This is the way God means me to be of use."

She was putting on her gentle voice, settling into being a postulant already. She'd worn her worst clothes for the trip, tired-out jeans and a faded orange kerchief over her red hair, and that red parka I hoped she'd have taken out behind the barn and shot. Mary Catherine O'Connor, the most beautiful girl in Boston, was trying to look plain.

She wasn't my girl. Just my friend, my study buddy, my co-researcher at the Kellogg. I'd met Mary Cat my first week of graduate school. We'd been the only two students in Rachel Goscimer's seminar on Elizabethan research, me and this stunning red-haired girl. She wore no makeup at all and cheap striped jeans and a faded sweater and a patched, stained, feather-leaking red parka that looked like she'd got it out of the charity bin at Saint Mike's. But I'd been pretty taken with her, and I'd asked her out before I realized the kerchief over her curls and the little gold cross she wore meant she wanted to be Sister Mary Catherine.

"You were the one who applied to the Society of Mary," I said. "God didn't fill out the application. Mary Cat, you can tell them no. At least you should be applying to someplace you can use your education, not making coffee for pissy old drunks," I said.

I didn't say she should be applying to a teaching order. And she didn't have to say what we both knew, they'd never let her teach. But there was a silence while we both didn't say that. I negotiated the tunnel ramp. Traffic was bad in the tunnel and we crawled forward, breathing fumes, watching a futile road of red brake lights in front of us.

"You'd stay if there were anything good in the Kellogg Collection," I said.

"I wish I weren't leaving you with the Kellogg."

"I don't mind that, I can do the rest of it alone. But you'd stay, wouldn't you?"

"I have to do this," she said.

"You would stay."

She didn't say anything, just nodded, not agreeing, just showing she'd listened.

"Then don't you see you're not going because God called you, you're going because you're pissed off?"

"That's ridiculous, Joe," she said hotly, not like a nun at all.

"Just wait a while," I said. "Finish your Ph.D."

I carried her backpack from the parking lot and waited with her while she stood in line for check-in. I hoisted her backpack up on the scale to be weighed, watched while the baggage handler tagged it, LHR, London Heathrow, and looked after it as it slid away. She was going. She was going after all. We walked together toward the security check.

"Keep in touch," I said. "Write me a letter, e-mail, something."

"If I can," she said. "Come to visit in London. Sister Mary Joseph says we've plenty of room for guests."

"I sure will come to London. I'll make you write your thesis," I said. "I'll stand at the door, frighten the winos, make them give you some peace. Get Sister Mary Joseph to give you afternoons off, go to the British Library."

She laughed at that.

"I mean it. You're too good to throw away. Please."

She looked up directly at me, clouded green eyes. She took my hands in both hers. Hers were as rough as mine, not a scholar's hands. "All I can do is go where I'm needed," she said. "I can't bargain what I'm needed for. Joe, you're the researcher, you'll find something in the Kellogg, I know it. I'll be praying for you. And when you do, and you have your first book planned and you're on your traveling fellowship, come to see me on Docklands Road and tell me all about it." She hugged me, a quick nun-like hug. "I've got to go now."

I watched her go through the security gate. Then I went out and found my truck in Central Parking, and kicked the tires once or twice, and sat in the cab and picked off the seat a couple of feathers from her red parka. Go figure; the feathers were what almost made me cry. I swore a while to make myself feel better.

Didn't help a bit.

My grandfather farmed. My father came back from the Vietnam War, sold the farm, bought a hardware store. Me? I wanted to write Shakespeare's life.

I remember reading my first lines of Shakespeare. I was nine years old and had the measles. Itched like a wool sweater. I'd read everything in the house, comics, an old Reader's Digest Condensed Book, Dad's supply catalogs, and there was only one book left, a big ratty falling-apart paperback mended with duct tape. It fell open to *Macbeth*.

Double, double, toil and trouble . . .

If you're a kid, two plays can start you on Shakespeare, *Macbeth* or *Hamlet*. I goggle-eyed my way through witches and murders and ghosts, having as much fun as if it was Stephen King. And then I got to the end of the play. Lady Macbeth is dead, and Macbeth is so torn up he can't even realize it, all he can do is wish it were sometime else when he could sit down and work up to grieving her. And he realizes he's got forever because she'll be dead forever.

Tomorrow and tomorrow and tomorrow —

That speech took me somewhere a nine-year-old kid had no business going. It was a place that could swallow me up and not even notice. Like the woods beyond where the roads go, where grownups get lost. I put my head down on my arms and cried, and it wasn't just I had the measles, I knew that place was out there. But I knew, when I got there, I'd recognize the place and I'd know a man who had been there too.

That was the first Shakespeare I really read. I've never forgotten. And from then on, I guess, Shakespeare was something that was going to happen to me, a part of my future, something that was going to happen when I grew up.

It must have been then I started wondering who Shakespeare was, but I never thought about Shakespeare being my work until ten years later. It was the summer after my junior year in college. I'd just begun installing windows to get money. Window installers go through jeans like toilet paper; I was picking up a pair on the cheap in the Salvation Army in Montpelier, saw a paperback, *Young Man Shakespeare,* bought it because it was about Shakespeare. There's a divinity that shapes our ends. I read it that evening, bouncing around in the back of the truck with a houseful of old windows. I read about Shakespeare in Stratford and I looked up, saw the sunset light through the road grit and the wind, and Donny and Ray Lavigne were joking at me from the cab of the truck, sharing a beer and seeing who could belch longest. *Some book you got, Joe, ain't even got tits and ass on it, what's it good for?*

Shakespeare. A guy eighteen, already married, I knew guys like that, a few years later they were pumping gas and the best thing in their lives was their kid was playing Little League. But Shakespeare? He was going to go places other men couldn't even imagine. What happened?

How could you not want to know?

So I wrote Roland Goscimer and told him how much I'd liked *Young Man Shakespeare,* and got a letter back from Rachel Goscimer; and a year later I walked into Rachel Goscimer's seminar on Elizabethan research, and the only other person in it was a smart, fine-looking girl named Mary Catherine O'Connor.

And then Rachel Goscimer had pulled off a coup and got Frank Kellogg's collection of Elizabethan books and manuscripts, and got all of us the right to publish what we found there. But Rachel Goscimer was dead now, and Roland Goscimer was mourning her, and Mary Cat was in London washing winos' feet, so there was nobody left to face the Kellogg but me.

~⁓

That day I found six forgeries in the Kellogg Collection, which was a record, but not by much.

I had been working with the Kellogg Collection seven months, and at four in the afternoon on the Ides of March I cataloged my three hundred and fifty-seventh forgery; do the math, that's about a fake and a half a day. Opening one of Frank Kellogg's archival envelopes had started to be like putting your hand into the potato barrel and feeling something furry. You might not know what it was, but you knew it wasn't good.

The Kellogg Collection had its own room in the basement of Northeastern. The computer I was using to catalog it was brand-new. The room was new; the whole Northeastern library was new. The big library exhibit so far was an elephant tusk carved into a hundred Buddhas. The Kellogg Collection had been going to be the second big thing, Northeastern's exhibit for the new millennium.

The Kellogg wasn't all bad; no collection is. Kellogg's aunt had bought Elizabethan costume books, and we were going to be pretty well set on Elizabethan history and politics. But that wasn't what we'd expected from the Kellogg. We'd wanted the manuscripts.

And we had 'em, all right. Faded brown ink, ragged paper, letters sealed with ribbon and with fragments of wax. Boxes of them. Letters from Mary Queen of Scots, from Queen Elizabeth. Six Shakespeare letters, one with a sonnet attached. I was scanning them all, for the catalog, and I'd started to amuse myself by printing them out and posting them on the bulletin board in the room. The Wall of Sin.

I tacked the printout of the latest forgery to the board and stared at the rest. Shakespeare, Jonson, Marlowe, Queen Elizabeth, Sir William Cecil, Mary Queen of Scots, the Duke of Norfolk.

Frank Kellogg, the Midwest Discount King. At the Warrenton County Agricultural Fair in 1895, his mama Mary Steuart (age thirteen) learned from a gypsy that she was the direct descendant of Mary Stuart, Queen of Scots. Ignoring clues to the contrary, for instance that her father wasn't king of England, Mary married a department-store heir and started collecting. She lassoed her husband and sister in, and eventually her boy Frank, and they bought everything they could find on Mary Stuart, Queen Elizabeth, and the Catholic-Protestant wars.

For years people had talked about that collection. Passed on rumors about it. Wanted it. Sure, the Kelloggs had been a little odd; sure, nobody had really seen the manuscripts; but a collection of Elizabethan materials going back a hundred years? There had to be amazing stuff.

Rachel Goscimer had got the Kellogg for Northeastern. Even the last time she'd been in the hospital, dying, she'd worked on Frank Kellogg. "Dear Mr. Kellogg," she'd whisper, sitting up in bed holding the phone, "we have two of the most marvelous young scholars here, they are so eager to write about your collection!" Kellogg died a month before she did, so she'd known he'd left the collection to Northeastern; but she never knew what was in it, so she died happy.

The difference between the right word and the almost right word, Mark Twain said, is the difference between the lightning bug and the lightning. For seven months I'd been hearing thunder and swatting bugs.

And Mary Cat had been right here with me; but now she'd given up. I wondered whether I ought to give up too. But at least Mary Cat was going to what she thought she wanted; and what I wanted would have been this, if a word of it had been real.

I stood glaring at the Wall of Sin. William Shakespeare writing to Richard Field about printing *Venus and Adonis*. The Earl of Southampton writing to Shakespeare, thanking him for a sonnet. Queen Elizabeth sending ten pounds to Shakespeare. Biographies are lives made comprehensible, beginnings, middles, ends, solid as post and beam. Forgery is rot in the beams. Forgery is a bulldozer, an ax, a fire. Forgery kills the heart. Forgery makes good Catholic researchers decide they're wasting their time in graduate school and go off to London to serve the poor. I started pulling the print-outs off the board one by one, balling them up and seeing if I could hit the wastebasket with them. I was doing okay, getting myself a little Antoine Walker action going, and if I was missing Mary Cat I was doing pretty good at fooling myself I wasn't, when the phone rang.

For a moment I thought she'd missed the plane, she'd changed her mind. But the voice on the other end of the phone was no one I recognized.

"Is this like Joe Roper?" Breathy Marilyn Monroe kitten voice. Whoever it was, she was on a cell phone; the connection had that drainpipe sound. But the voice went with the March weather, rainy, a little sweet, with an undertone of spring.

"Yeah."

"This is Posy Gould? Roland Goscimer told you about me? I knew Frank Kellogg? I want to see the Kellogg Collection?"

I looked across at the half-bare bulletin board. Goscimer was sending someone here?

"I like just finished my orals in English? And I'm going to work on Sir William Cecil?"

In the Kellogg Collection? A grad student. She sounded like a Valley Girl but she'd pronounced Cecil right, *Sissel*. Cecil was a funny choice for a thesis in English. Was she a biographer too?

"You knew Frank Kellogg?" I asked. That would mean she was rich. Something in her voice sounded that way, like private schools and private jets.

"Frank was just like sort of a friend of Daddy's."

Yup, rich.

"Are you going to be at Goscimer's reading?" she asked. "I'll meet you. What do you look like?"

Um. "Brown, brown, glasses, six feet, built like I used to play hockey. How'll I know you?"

"Oh," said Posy Gould. "You'll know me."

~

I hung up the phone and called Goscimer. "Posy Gould?" I said.

Goscimer's chuckle quavered over the line. "Ah, Miss Gould."

"Has anybody told her what's in the Kellogg Collection?"

"Pride goeth before a fall, Joe, and an upright spirit before destruction. I don't believe I mentioned it. Miss Gould has been very persistent."

"Why'd she want to see the collection?"

"Her friend Frank Kellogg told her there were amazing things in it. Miss Gould is rather amazing herself. She is supposed to have a tattoo of Queen Elizabeth's signature, Joe. Somewhere upon her body. Do young people ever still say 'hubba hubba'?"

"Hubba hubba," I said dutifully. "Is she any good as a researcher?"

"A tattoo," Goscimer sighed, as if that explained everything about Posy Gould.

Over the phone there was a moment's silence.

"I'm sorry," Goscimer said. "About the collection, I mean.

About Mary Catherine's leaving. I'm—so very sorry to leave you with it, Joe."

"Well," I said, "maybe this Gould girl wants to help me catalog."

"You could do an edition for your thesis. Editions are very useful and respectable."

"I'll give it thought, sir."

I hung up. An edition, I thought. Editions are new publications of old plays or poems, all cleaned up and accurate, with up-to-date footnotes and a scholarly introduction. A good edition would only take a year. But editions were for people who didn't have anything to say or couldn't prove it, so they collated copies and variants and spaded the ground for better scholars. An edition wouldn't get me a job, wouldn't put me on the path to being one of Shakespeare's biographers.

What I'd been looking for in the Kellogg was a new sense of Shakespeare, a new way of understanding him and his times. What I'd dreamed of finding was not a manuscript (well, I'd *dreamed*) but a new fact. It could happen, it had happened; the Wallaces had gone through the entire Public Records Office and found Shakespeare's deposition in the Mountjoy case. If the Kellogg Collection had really been about Mary Stuart, there might have been something about Shakespeare and the Catholics.

I wasn't going to find anything.

I sat down again at the computer, opened a new catalog record, reached into the box to get the next item, and brought up—*shit*—one more of the familiar slick archival envelopes.

Inside the envelope was another envelope, a sheet of old parchment folded over itself in the eighteenth-century way. The seals that closed the envelope were missing, nothing left but a blood-stain of reddish-brown wax. There was no address either, only an inscription in a dashing loose hand. "An abominable Forgery." Probably faked, though for a change it didn't look it.

I unfolded the parchment and had the letter in my hand.

⁓

It smelled; that was the first thing I noticed. Not a stink but strong: the smell of wood fires, of dust, of horses, of smoke and fog and the hard-to-reach neglected shelves in libraries: the smell of centuries. The paper was rag stock, thick and strong, but the ink was oak-gall, which is acidic; it had browned the paper and on one corner, where the ink had blotted, the words had been eaten away. The hand was piss-poor, small and barely legible; the lines straggled down the page in waves of effort, painful regular letters becoming tired shakes. Sweat from the writer's palm had blurred the ink.

I could put my hand on the paper and see and feel the guy writing it, four hundred years ago.

And halfway down the page was a phrase I could make out, "the plotte of ye Playe."

This is it, I thought, this is something, and turned it over to look at the signature.

Ah, fuck, *screw* it. I stood up, stomped around the room, kicked the desk. *Shit.*

William Shakespeare.

Up on the wall, screwed on the wall the way they do with benefactors' pictures, hung a photograph of Frank Kellogg. I thought pretty seriously about putting a pry bar through the glass, unscrewing the frame, and throwing Frank Kellogg out with the trash. It was a good warm healthy thought.

And then I dug the printouts of the other Shakespeare forgeries out of the trash and looked at them together with this one. This one that had felt real to me.

Most forgeries don't hold up five minutes; the paper's wrong, they're written in ballpoint, something. They're short, because the forger doesn't want to deal with facts. "Let Mrs. So-and-so pass to visit her son, A. Lincoln," that sort of thing. They're easy to read, because what's the point of a forgery you can't read?

This letter was written in Elizabethan secretary hand, the fast script that sixteenth-century professional writers used. Secretary hand, even faked, is a bastard. I could read the salutation, something about a horse, and halfway down the first page, a joke. "Whence cometh thy name, knowest thou?—Marry, my lord, from my father, says I."

One sentence I could make out well enough. It was probably the one I was meant to read.

"Those that are given out as children of my brain are begot of his wit, I but honored with their fostering."

A letter from Shakespeare, saying he didn't write the plays.

When I was a kid, I used to go out in the woods around East Bradenton and try to find the old deserted farms. Ruins of a chimney in the grass, a hole filled with stones, the skeleton of an old truck, bits of stone wall in the underbrush. By the wall, fragments of a blue-and-white cup. I'd wonder who threw the cup against the wall and why. Ruins were like lives, but with sunlight and smells and dirt to dig in. The more mysterious it was, the more fun.

A clever forger would make his forgeries like a deserted house or a rusty truck in the woods. Mysterious, full of facts you couldn't check and could only imagine about. This letter would be a puzzle for someone, and make someone want to boast and show it off and make a fuss over it, and be tempted to think it wasn't a forgery.

I was dealing with a clever forger.

Shit.

And all those nuts who thought Shakespeare didn't write Shakespeare? They'd love this.

I took off my glasses and squinted at the letter.

It was addressed to the poet Fulke Greville. Cute. Greville had been a courtier under Elizabeth and James I. Lived near Stratford. Not the first person you'd think of; well-documented; somebody the forger could find out about. The letter's first paragraph said something barely legible about Salisbury dying. Good detail; Robert Cecil, Earl of Salisbury, was Greville's worst enemy. The joke was wrong for Fulke Greville; he was a melancholy, serious man, not the sort you'd send old jokes to. But that mistake wouldn't prove this letter was a forgery.

There are scientific methods to tell whether a letter is a forgery or real. Most of them involve chemistry and time and money. I had the others, and I tried them. I smelled the paper, trying to sniff chemicals or new ink under the smoke and dust and cinnamon. I magnified it letter by letter with the loupe. I scanned it, both sides, and zoomed in on individual words, individual letters, trying to decide whether the trembling in the handwriting was forger-shakes or an old man's palsy. The signature didn't copy any of the six Shakespeare signatures, but looked similar. The formation of letters was like Hand D's in *More*, which could be Shakespeare's hand. The signature had a flying tail. The writing was small—forged handwriting often is—but Shakespeare's real signatures are small too. I held the paper up to the light to check for maker's marks or distinctive wirelines: nothing. The ink wasn't blurred except from "Shakespeare's" sweaty palm, so this wasn't new ink on old paper unless the paper was coated some-how. Most coatings show up under UV; I dug in the closet for the UV light before remembering Roy had borrowed it.

Shit again.

Roy Dooley was my boss on this job, one of the research librar-ians at Northeastern and now librarian of the Kellogg Collection. It had been a big promotion for him. The first few days he'd fussed over the unpacking of every box, every item. And then he'd gone off and cried.

Roy wanted something good to come out of the Kellogg.

What was he going to do with this?

I put the letter and envelope and all in the middle drawer of the desk and went to find Roy.

He was in his office, just leaving for the night. "Hey, Joe, what's up?"

"Same old stuff; a copy of Baker's *Shakespeare Commentary*, some more costume books — Roy, do you have the UV light?"

"Karen from Circulation has it, she's having a Grateful Dead theme party." One of the problems with being a biographer is you start thinking that way about people you know. Roy looks like a hamster; Karen is a babe; Roy adores Karen. I knew that Roy would wear a tie-dyed T-shirt to Karen's party, go around all night saying "Groovy," get pissed on Bud, tell Karen he loved her, and spend Sunday wishing he was dead.

Roy was the kind of guy that needed to make an impression.

"Anything interesting?" Roy asked hopefully.

I could have said right then, standing at the door of his office, "Roy, I've got this fucking letter," and maybe everything would have come out fine. I was only imagining things about Roy; it was the Roy I'd made up I didn't trust. Biography does you wrong;

you use imagination to fill in what you don't know, but then you go on as if it's true. So the life you're writing always is your own. You forget that.

"Nah," I said finally. "But bring back that UV light Monday?"

My computer had a CD burner and a local hard drive, where I'd been storing the scans. I copied the scans of the letter onto a CD, wiped them off the disk, put the original letter and its covering back in Kellogg's archival envelope, and locked the whole thing in the center drawer of the desk, wishing I had Mary Cat to talk it over with.

I was set up for Posy before ever I met her.

⁓

If there had ever been a good time to find a Shakespeare forgery, it wouldn't have been that week. The Goscimers' biography of Shakespeare was coming out.

Their second biography, after *Young Man Shakespeare*.

If you've ever read *Young Man Shakespeare,* you know why March 16 is important. March 16, 1946: Roland Goscimer had just got out of the Army. He was in London, writing for *Army Times,* wondering whether he ought to go back to graduate school. He had a theory that Shakespeare had gone to Italy. At a bar one rainy Saturday night, March 16, 1946, he'd told the idea to a secretary at the American Embassy. March 16, 1946; they remembered the date like I remembered reading my first lines of Shakespeare. The secretary's name was Rachel. "Let's go to Italy and find out," she said.

Young Man Shakespeare had been published on March 16, 1965. And now, thirty-five years later, fifty-four years to the day after they had met, their second book was going to be published on March 16. Their second book, and their last.

Their biography of Shakespeare.

Shakespeare whom they loved as much as I did.

Shakespeare who, according to the letter I'd just found, didn't write the plays.

The morning of March 16, Dad came down from East Bradenton to celebrate the publication with me.

Dad believes in hardware. As soon as he arrived, he started scouting around the apartment, looking for dripping faucets, checking door hinges. "There ain't screening on that window, son. It's March, you goin' to get black fly here. I could pick up some screening."

"They got no black fly in the city, Dad."

"Don't mind, is what I'm saying."

Dad had showed up early to do just this, and he was going to do it. I corrected freshman English papers while he trotted out to his truck, came back with screening, took out the old corroded screening, and fit new into the frames. Every March at home Dad went around to all the houses in East Bradenton and fixed the screens. Every night in March from as long as I can remember, Dad would be out in the back of Roper & Son Hardware, his fingers pricked dirty by the mesh. All the old ladies in East Bradenton dated spring by when Henry Roper came round to spruce up their houses.

"You got yourself something to write about from that collection?" Dad asked, sliding a screen back into its channel.

"Not yet. I'll work it out. Don't you worry."

"You'll do fine, son, I ain't worried."

Since the mall opened on the highway, East Bradenton barely existed. On Main Street, Woolworth's closed years ago, Dandee Foods had closed, the old town hall had dwindled into a state relief office, and the only places not sporting For Sale signs were the VFW, two consignment stores, and a place that said it sold antiques. The only thing that kept East Bradenton alive was my father.

"What you doin' for lunch? Thought you and I could go to Mr. Bartley's in Cambridge before I got to get back north. Maybe we could invite that Mary Catherine."

"She's gone to London," I said, and explained.

"Well, that is a waste," Dad said. "Nice gal like that."

"I got one thing to do after Goscimer's lecture, got to meet a woman who called about the Kellogg. Won't take a minute, though, I'll make an appointment with her for later. Then we'll go to Bartley's."

"No need, if you're busy," Dad said.

"I ain't busy, Dad." He'd driven four and a half hours to get here. Ought to know he could make claims.

In Search of Shakespeare was on my desk, an advance copy I'd used to double-check the footnotes. Dad looked at it curiously. "Good for you, you working on that book and all."

"You coming to his lecture?" Of course Dad had come down for just that, but he wasn't going to mention it until I did.

"All the smart folks going to be there? Your teachers and all? I'd stick out like a whore at a revival, old guy from up north."

"Plenty of whores at revivals, Dad. You come along. Just don't you wear no short skirt."

When I'm with Dad I drop into talking the way I grew up with. It has its own rhythm. You can say things in it you can't in graduate-school English. It's a language to use when you work with your hands, when you frame in walls and set windows. *You mucker, you horse round there and get yourself set, naow. You take care, that whoreson plaster bucket's heavier'n a dead minister.* English graduate-student language has pretty words for it. Concision. Eloquence. And I'm not ashamed of that way of speaking, no more than I am of being Dad's son. But I wouldn't use it around Goscimer, and Dad knows.

"If Goscimer's the kind of man I hear tell," Dad said, "might be he'd mention your name, say he was beholden to you. I'd be glad to hear that. Suppose I hang round the back."

"You sit up front." He wouldn't. Dad was shy of even visiting me.

I went into the bathroom, grimaced into the mirror, opened the bathroom cabinet, looking for aspirin. The door whined and stuck halfway open. Sometime today, before he went back north, Dad would find this too and spend two or three minutes carefully dripping oil into the hinge, and the bathroom cabinet would purr like a mangy cat.

I could have fixed it. I hadn't. I could have taken this bathroom cabinet, wire-brushed it down, sprayed it with a couple coats of Krylon Epoxy White Enamel, it'd have looked like the day it was made.

I swallowed two aspirin, dry.

Nowadays all the screens are made of fiberglass mesh and plastic. They come all in a piece. One's broke, you throw it out and get a new one. Ace has them cheapest; Ace buys them fifty thousand at a time. The old hardware stores are dying.

I could get a job being superintendent of a set of apartments. Realty companies are always looking. Teach part-time maybe. Freshman English. Or I could go back to Vermont. Coleman Hardware, the Ace over at the Bradenton Mall, had been looking for an assistant manager since September. I had taken accounting and finance with my undergraduate English courses. I could tell a shave hook from a scraper. I could have run a hardware store, made a better living than I was ever likely to by teaching, and not made Dad feel he had to stay out of my life. Take over the Coleman franchise someday, rename it Roper & Son. Put in a shelf of old tools. Overprice 'em. Talk broad V'mont for the tourists. Ayuh.

I could imagine the sort of person who'd be content with that. But though I could imagine him, could conjure him out of mesh and Dad's fingers and a rusty bathroom cabinet, I kept on trying to be Shakespeare's biographer, the way Mary Cat kept on trying to be a nun, the way Dad kept on at East Bradenton.

Northeastern's biggest lecture hall was full by the time Dad and I got there. Almost every seat was taken. Museum School pixies in black perched on the elbow rests, Cambridge ladies in suits and duck boots stood at the side of the room, bearded men with book bags sat on the floor in the aisles. Almost the whole Northeastern English department was here. Helen Vendler and Marjorie Garber were here from Harvard. Everyone in the world had come to hear about the new biography from the man who wrote *Young Man Shakespeare*. There was one seat left in the front row; one of the other Shakespeare teaching assistants had saved it for me.

"Dad, you sit here, I'll stand."

"Not me, ain't sittin' in front lookin' bored, I can tell you." Dad retreated toward the back of the room. I looked after him, feeling guilty because he would have to stand. We should have got here earlier. I shouldn't be sitting while my father stood.

Goscimer wasn't here yet. I should have gone over to the Goscimers' apartment, too, and walked over with him. I hoped he was okay. He wouldn't be late for a lecture, but he was a shy man.

The television was here. The TV camera was right in the middle of the center aisle, behind us. Their arts reporter was murmuring into her microphone: "Roland Goscimer, author of the classic *Young Man Shakespeare* . . ."

"Are you Joe Roper?"

And there was Posy Gould, standing in the aisle. She'd said *You'll know me.* Oh yeah. For a moment all I could see of her was an impression of color and richness. A black lamb jacket, a lime-green dress and purple stockings; orange hair cut square; bright parrot eyes, big black irises circled with gold. Big pearls around her neck, big pearl earrings, smaller pearl on the ring through her nose. She shrugged off her coat as she looked down at me; she was wearing a sleeveless dress, in New England in March. At the edge of the low-cut armhole, I saw a flash of red bra.

Hubba hubba.

"I'm Posy Gould? From Harvard? I called you?"

Harvard? That she hadn't told me. "Yeah. The Kellogg." For a moment I had a vision of myself and Posy Gould in the cataloging room in the library basement, not cataloging—

License my roving hands, and let them go
Before, behind, between, above, below . . .

I'd had a long dry time, working in the same room with a smart girl I liked who wasn't available. Posy, I figured, was available. But rich, so not available to me.

"Would you move?" Posy said to the teaching assistant next to me. She settled into the seat as if all good seats belonged to her. "Daddy knew Frank Kellogg," she said. "I so wanted to get first crack at the collection. I'm really jealous of you."

"No need."

"Can we look at it tomorrow morning?"

"Yeah, that's good."

She made a note in her Palm Pilot. I got another glimpse of that red bra.

"So you're working on Cecil—" I started.

Suddenly people in the auditorium were clapping; there was Goscimer.

He was carrying an old-fashioned green book bag with a big square shape in it, and he looked thin and feeble and grey. He had somebody with him, a woman from his publisher, but she was talking to the TV reporter. He hesitated at the bottom of the stairs. I stood up and went to help him up on the platform. Under his coat his arm was trembling. He smiled at me distractedly as I helped him take off his coat.

"Oh, don't leave me, Joe, I don't want to do this." He'd always hated lecturing.

"You'll be fine, sir."

Goscimer slowly shuffled over to the lectern and slowly unwrapped the book. He held it up and let the audience see it for a moment before he laid it down carefully, two-handed, on the surface of the lectern. People applauded and some student gave a two-fingered whistle. I helped him turn his mike on and faded toward the side of the stage where I could see him, be there if he needed someone. When Goscimer got good and started, I'd slip down into the audience again.

The chairman of the English Department introduced him. "Helen Vendler has called *In Search of Shakespeare* the 'Shakespeare biography for the new millennium,'" he said. Down in the auditorium Helen Vendler smiled. *In Search of Shakespeare* was doing incredibly well. It seemed like everybody who had ever read *Young Man Shakespeare* had bought it. The *New York Times* had put it on the front of the *Book Review*. It was being published in England next week; Goscimer was flying to London to be interviewed for the BBC. "I give you Roland Goscimer," the chairman ended grandly. Goscimer hunched his shoulders and looked embarrassed. Out in the auditorium the students cheered and waved at the camera.

"This all began, of course, with *Young Man Shakespeare*," Goscimer began. "For three years, my dear wife and I searched for records of Shakespeare in Italy . . ."

Privately, I knew, they'd never been sure Shakespeare didn't go to Italy; but they'd never found proof. There were no records of Stratford glovers visiting Italy to learn the new fashions, no "Guglielmo Shakespeare" in Florence or Rome. They had written instead about the search, the detective work of literary scholarship, piecing together the information they had about Shakespeare, walking the streets of Genoa and Mantua.

"After our work on *Young Man Shakespeare*, we thought it would take ten years to write this book," Goscimer said. "We thought that we knew everything about him!" He looked around at the audience and smiled, an unexpected sweet ironic smile I hadn't seen since Rachel Goscimer died. "That is where scholarship starts, thinking one knows everything . . ."

It had taken the Goscimers thirty-five years to write their second book. Thirty-five years, Roland and Rachel Goscimer, working day after day in the library or in their tiny book-crowded apartment, researching, speculating, tracking down, polishing the book line by line.

"What a pleasure it was to spend one's life with two people one loved," Goscimer said, "Shakespeare and my Rachel. What a quality of mind she had. She cared for facts. For truth. The love of *life as it is* was the quality of Shakespeare's mind that impressed us both. Shakespeare was never content to understand anything *approximately*. His genius encompassed all ways of life, all of mankind, and not in generality, but in every specific of their lives. He knew the special terms of every profession. He not only understood lawyers, kings, astrologers—doctors, gardeners, barmaids—but understood them as people. The world was his university, the streets of London his book, and he never tired of reading. He loved life not only as he imagined it but *precisely as it is*."

It was a famous line from *Young Man Shakespeare*. I thought of me in the truck, reading that phrase.

"How could his biographers do less than know everything about him? We had so much to learn. I could have done nothing without my dear Rachel. A lesser woman would have quailed before the task. To learn heraldry, English history, hawking, hunting; to learn everything about English Renaissance music, the theater, military terms; she had the persistence for all of them, and the wisdom and *imagination* to see through detail to the man himself."

That first day I met Rachel Goscimer, she'd got me talking about Dad's old drinking buddies at the Bradenton VFW; then she'd asked me what I knew about Elizabethan soldiers, which had been not much. "Use your imagination." I'd balked a little. I was more comfortable with facts and dates.

"One must imagine something before one can research it, Mr. Roper," she said.

So I tried. "They'd have that stare," I said. "And their own slang," *dinky dau*. "Words in Spanish, French, Dutch. And their own ways of dressing," those old Army camos, "they'd sling their capes under one arm to leave their sword-arm free. The backs of their necks would be chapped from wearing armor. They'd joke whether God was Catholic or Protestant." Behind her hung the Walter Hodges drawing of Shakespeare's Globe. "They'd go to the Globe but when it came to the history plays, the soldiers, they might not cheer, they'd just sit there and know."

Shakespeare was important to them. Shakespeare had been there too. "You think he was a soldier," she said.

"I think he'd been in every dark place that is."

Neither of us said anything for a moment after that. I was sitting there wondering where the fuck that had come from, some fine-haired jerkoff speech, making stuff up out of my head. But at the same time I was thinking, yeah, Shakespeare could have served time in the army, I wonder if anybody's looked for him in muster rolls, pay records.

She had started teaching me even then.

"My Rachel barely lived to see this book completed—"

She taught me to use my imagination and then to check it. She taught me that the person who writes a book isn't always the one whose pen touches the paper or whose name is on the cover. She taught me secretary hand and self-confidence, gave me a whole collection to work with. And then she died.

And left me a promise to keep.

I went to see her the day before she died. I had brought flowers, yellow chrysanthemums. She held one in her fingers, and then put it in *A Midsummer Night's Dream,* which was lying open on her lap, and closed the book on it. She was so thin, no more than eyes and cheekbones on the pillow, but she was smiling. I talked. Told her about reading *Young Man Shakespeare* the first time. I told her about the Kellogg Collection arriving, this was before I'd seen what was in it so I didn't have to lie to her. I talked and talked so I wouldn't have to say goodbye.

And then she held up her hand and she said five words. She could barely whisper and I could barely hear her. But "Shakespeare *did* go to Italy," she'd said, and looked at me as if to make sure I'd understood. "He did," she whispered, not even whispered, just made the shape of it with her mouth. "Imagine."

And I made her my promise.

"I'll find out," I said.

She'd reached out and taken my hand, and smiled, and held it for a long time, and neither of us had said anything more.

Dad was standing on the other side of the hall, at the back, with his John Deere wool hat on and his shoulders square. He was holding his hand in front of his mouth like a man smoking down to the butt of his cigarette. Shy of showing his missing teeth. Dad was a good man, stuck to it, never gave up, and most of what's good in me I'd got from him. But when I thought of starting in East Bradenton and ending up writing Shakespeare's life, when I asked myself whether it was possible for a man to go that distance, it was Shakespeare and the Goscimers I thought of, not Dad. I couldn't believe, or even fantasize, that Dad's son would write a Shakespeare biography. I could only imagine.

I'll find out. Me? I hadn't even said *I'll try.*

"And now," Goscimer said, suddenly unsteady, "now we have finished. Now our task is done." He paused, a long tremulous pause. "My dear Rachel," he said. "As *Shakespeare* drew to its end, she failed. She wished to keep on with the task of checking our sources. It grew beyond her power. Our dear young friend Joseph Roper helped us finish." Caught by surprise, I ducked my head. "Today I thought I would have read something from our book, the death of Shakespeare. The last words she and I worked on—shall ever work on." He stopped again. "But instead I shall read Shakespeare's words."

He opened it and read the dedication. "To Rachel," he said:

Since brass, nor stone, nor earth, nor boundless sea,
But sad mortality o'ersways their power,
How with this rage shall beauty hold a plea,
Whose action is no stronger than a flower? . . .
  O none, unless this miracle have might,
  That in black ink my love may still shine bright.

And then he stopped.

He couldn't go on. Where could he go? His silence filled the auditorium. The visiting professors and the Cambridge ladies, the bearded men with book bags and the Fine Arts undergraduates waited, looked at him, looked at each other, looked back at him, dismayed. The lecture hour wasn't over. They wanted to cheer for him, but not yet. Their hands were hovering close to each other, wanting to break out in applause, but not yet. Here were these famous people in Renaissance studies; here was Roland Goscimer who'd finally finished his big book; and the last thing they wanted to hear was Shakespeare didn't mean anything to him beside his dead wife.

"I don't know what to say," Goscimer said, holding his hand over the microphone, turning away from the podium. "There is nothing left to say." I went up and stood beside him, took his arm, but I didn't know what to do either. "I can't—" Goscimer turned away from the audience. Now no one was at the lectern. The professors were looking at each other.

There was a stir in the audience, and the person who got up was Posy Gould.

She bounced like a dancer up the stairs to the lectern, distracting every man in the place. She plucked the microphone away from Goscimer, held it like a singer would, moved with it away from the lectern. I saw her back, the curve of her hip, the red swinging vibration of her hair.

"Hi, I'm a friend of Joe's from Harvard? I met Rachel Goscimer once." Posy's breathy little Marilyn Monroe voice echoed around the room. Goscimer sniffled, looked up, listening to anyone who'd talk about his wife. "She was such a brilliant woman." She started telling anecdotes from that one meeting. Some of Rachel Goscimer's Cambridge-lady friends started nodding. Posy Gould glanced back at Goscimer, saw he wasn't ready to lecture yet, and stepped down into the auditorium. (Everyone was craning to look at her.) Now she was talking about discovering Shakespeare herself through Goscimer's lectures and *Young Man Shakespeare*, and then she turned to face Goscimer, telling him how much she admired him.

"But all of us can say that just as well," she said, and looked around and handed the microphone to a man in the auditorium. He looked confused but he played along, stood up and started telling Goscimer how moved he'd been by his advance copy of *In Search of Shakespeare*. The critic passed the mike to Helen Vendler, who said something about the Sonnets and passed the mike to the president of Northeastern. Marjorie Garber took the mike and said "What do I mean to Shakespeare? What does my presence, as a reader, mean to Shakespeare?" and passed the mike to a girl who blushed and said "I read this great play about witches and I decided to take Shakespeare and *he* liked dogs and *I* like dogs and

I'm really enjoying your class" and passed it to an old lady about eighty, who quavered a Shakespeare sonnet and passed it to Laurence Senelick from Tufts. The mike circled the auditorium; everyone wanted to say something about Goscimer or Rachel Goscimer or Shakespeare. Goscimer blinked and collected himself and made his way back to the lectern; someone passed the mike back up to him. He stood holding it. And then, without him saying a word, people began to stand up, to cheer and applaud.

All of a sudden the hour was over and everyone was looking around, blinking, realizing it had been a great moment. No one wanted to leave. A crowd pressed around Goscimer. There was another crowd, of course, around Posy Gould. I stood in a corner looking at her, wondering whether she was a phenomenon or a menace.

"That was fine," Dad said.

Posy Gould would move to fill awkwardness. She had grace. Or she was just pushy, Harvard pushy, thinking no matter what she did it had to be intelligent and interesting.

"Colorful as a Burlington streetwalker," Dad said, looking at her; it might have been disapproval or secret admiration. "You did good, standing up with him like that."

It was Posy Gould who'd done good for Goscimer.

"Let's get out of here," I said.

We ate at Mr. Bartley's Burger Cottage. It was right across from Harvard, from the walls and the gates of Harvard. Next day, Posy Gould was going to come and see the Kellogg Collection. I was jealous of her, I guess, her opportunities, her assurance. She didn't think she had to go wash winos' feet, didn't have to install windows. I wished I had her freedom.

Posy Gould was working her way into my imagination.

At ten o'clock the next morning I went to meet her on Huntington Avenue. She arrived in a taxi. Today she was wearing pink and black: pink sweater, pink tights, short tight black skirt, and the black vintage lamb jacket. All the pearls again. She hadn't dressed up for the Goscimer lecture, this was her ordinary getup. It was a cold March Friday morning, raining. The colors on her were like a spotlight saying *here's Posy Gould.*

"Yesterday," she said, "was it okay I said you were a friend of mine?"

"Sure."

I led the way to the library basement. Her shoes made a clatter like tapdancing down the stairs. "I just need to look at what Frank found, he told me he found *amazing* things."

I let her go in first so she could get the full effect of the Kellogg Collection. Piles of catalogued books waiting to be shelved. Cardboard boxes full of more books. I'd set out a little show for her on the desk. Samples.

She looked at them, picked up a book. *Great Mary,* a novel, by Rose L'Heureux. On the cover, a blond Mary Queen of Scots with bazooms like Dolly Parton was shrinking away from a gigantic muscled masked man with an ax.

"You're kidding."

"That would have been his aunt, bought that. Try the pamphlets, in that box."

The pamphlets were real. She looked at the top two. *An Account of the Treasonable Behavior of the late Q. MARY of Scotland, including True Proofs of the Plot against the Life of ENGLAND'S True Queen, ELIZABETH. The Tryall and Martyrdom of our most holy and Catholick Queen Mary, Queen of Scotland and Rightfull Queen of England.*

"Harvard has both of these," she said.

"I expect Northeastern won't throw them out."

She shuffled through the rest of the pamphlets and shrugged uneasily. "And there are scholarly books." She leaned to look at a pile of them. "This is it? They collected for like a hundred years and this is all?"

"No," I said. "They bought a lot of amazing things."

"So show me."

I dropped my backpack in the corner. I'd put old Frank's prize items in a box under the desk. As I brought it out, my forehead almost brushed the locked center drawer.

"Start with Queen Mary's sleeve," I said. "That's just about my favorite."

"Queen Mary's sleeve?"

"Worn by Mary Queen of Scots at her execution. Stained with her blood."

I took out its case, an elaborate Victorian plush-covered presentation box, and opened it like a waiter showing off the specials. Inside there was a mess of old fabric, dull maroon brown stained with a stiff darker brown. A big silver plaque told whose the sleeve supposedly was. I handed Posy case and all.

She put it down on the desk and studied it. I turned on the desk lamp for her and watched her. In the dim research-library light, with her red hair and pale face, she looked like an Elizabethan beauty.

"All Queen Mary's clothes were confiscated and burned or washed after her death," she said, frowning and looking up at me. "To keep people from making them relics?"

"Yeah," I said. "It's fake."

She touched the material, delicately, with the tip of one finger.

"So thanks for showing me a forgery," she said a little defensively.

"Yeah, well, I'm sorry, there's more. Want to see a letter from Christopher Marlowe?" I fished it out of the box and tilted the letter toward the desk lamp so the light raked across it. "See those scratches? Quill pens are too soft to scratch paper. This is a steel pen nib, invented two hundred years after Marlowe died. Want to see Mary Queen of Scots' love letters to Norfolk? We've got three."

Her jaw set.

"There's no kind way to say this. Your dad's friend was a forger's mark. He bit every worm went by." I rapped my knuckles on the box. "The collection has truckloads of this sewage. Every piece of it had to be checked. It's taken me and a friend seven months so far, when we should have been working on our dissertations. My friend quit. Left grad school."

"*You* checked them?" she said. "I mean—" She looked around the bare new room.

"You mean somebody who knows better than I do should check them," I said, "from a better place than Northeastern?"

"Frank Kellogg was a *very good businessman,*" she said.

"I expect he was."

She sat on the edge of the desk. Her thigh brushed the front of the locked center drawer. The idea was flooring her, the whole idea that a friend of her father's could have been taken. "There can't be nothing," she said.

There could be nothing, but that wasn't something Posy Gould would know. Her big pearls looked real.

"Look through the box," I said. "Help yourself."

She did. She lifted the first forged letter out of the box, carefully brought out paper after paper, laid some aside, put others in a pile. Then she went through each paper in her good pile, one by one, slowly. She was methodical and her choices were pretty much the letters I'd had to check. And slowly, one by one, she laid each on the bad pile, until there was nothing left.

"Shit," she said finally.

"He wanted to be important," I said. "I think it was mostly him who bought them; the forgeries look modern."

"Shut up." She drew up one of her long legs and hugged it, knee under her chin.

"Believe me, I'd be happy they were real."

"Just shut up!" she said. "Frank was always coming out to L.A. He was going to finance a film about Mary Queen of Scots— Daddy's a producer? Frank got me interested in Mary and Cecil and he'd give out these little hints about his collection. So I finish my orals and I fly out to Chicago to see him? And there he is, dead."

Dead she said like it was a personal insult to her.

"Did you find the really big thing he had?" she asked.

I wasn't prepared for that. I thought of the letter and tried not to think of it. "He had all sorts of really big things."

"He always said he had one great piece in his collection. Better than anything else. He was going to sell it to make his movie as soon as he found the perfect Mary Queen of Scots. He was look- ing at Cate Blanchett."

"Maybe he meant the sleeve."

"No," Posy Gould said. "It was a manuscript. Something to do with Shakespeare. He found it by accident."

My mouth went dry.

"Frank said it was going to be huge. It was going to totally change everything."

"No kidding," I said. "A Shakespeare letter written in ballpoint pen."

And she looked up at me, and I knew I'd slipped.

"Not a manuscript," she said. "A letter? A letter by Shakespeare?"

"Or a play," I said. "A poem. Part of a play."

"You said letter." She crossed her arms below her breasts and looked at me. "Okay," she said. "You can drop the whole *Good Will Hunting* act and show it to me."

"I don't know what you're talking about." I sounded like a line from a bad movie.

"Yeah, right." She looked over at the boxes, and dismissed them. She looked up at the ceiling tiles. She walked over to the desk, pulled at the side drawers and then the center drawer, turned around, and held out her hand palm up.

"Key."

"That letter's a forgery," I said.

"Then why isn't it in the box with the others, duh? Key." She looked up at me. "I've seen the letter. I know it exists. So don't even try."

I shoved my hands down in my pockets, where the key was. "Why isn't the letter in that box?" I said. "Because of that lecture you went to yesterday. Thirty-five years Professor and Mrs. Goscimer worked on that book, I worked on checking facts for them, and it may not be by any fucking Harvard professor but it's fucking good and it took two people's lives to write. Mrs. Goscimer died the day after it was finished."

"And this letter's so exciting I'd just have to tell everybody and spoil everything?" Posy said.

"Remember Don Foster's Shakespeare eulogy?" I said. A

few years ago, Don Foster from Vassar found what he thought was a new Shakespeare poem. In my opinion Shakespeare wouldn't have written that poem if he was dead, but it had made the front page of the *New York Times*. "There's a whole shit-ass little industry around finding new Shakespeare stuff. People get excited about 'Shakespeare manuscripts' even though they're all forgeries or mistakes. And you know what the letter says. I'm Goscimer's student. I don't want those fucking anti-Shakespeare nuts down on him when he's just publishing the book."

"You *read* the letter?" Posy said. "What does it say?"

"You didn't read it?"

"Frank Kellogg was a lech. I had dinner with him one night at his house in Chicago, and after he asked me to get Daddy to introduce him to Cate Blanchett's agent and before he made a pass at me, he showed me the letter. I had like five minutes to look at it while he was breathing down my boobs. It looked great but I didn't get to read it."

"It was supposed to look great," I said. "That's the idea."

"I can be totally like a bitch over this. I can call people at the *Times*. They will be so all over you. But notice how I didn't say a word about it to Goscimer or anybody? Like I want to make a fuss about a forgery? I kept quiet for a whole year until I could see it again."

Bitchy, privileged, pushy: Posy Gould. But I remembered that moment of grace when she stood up to rescue Goscimer. And she'd spotted all the forgeries.

"It looks good but it isn't. Get out of my way."

I unlocked the drawer. She pulled the desk lamp forward. The letter was in the drawer all by itself, the old paper on top of the eighteenth-century parchment. The drawer was new, still spotless, like a display case for the letter. She looked from it back to the pile of forgeries on the desk.

"Wow," she breathed. She picked it up in two hands, carefully, by the edge, brought it toward her face. "Smell." She held it out to me.

"I can smell. The paper came out of an old book in a library," I said, irritated.

"The writing looks old."

She stared at it, with that long careful analytic stare she'd given all the other forgeries. She held it up near the lamp and squinted at it. I gave her the loupe. She turned the paper over and looked at the signature. Then she put the letter down, not with the other forgeries, but in the center of the desk, by itself, with the lamp shining on it like a spotlight; and then she looked up at me.

"I think this one is real."

~

"What does it say?" she asked me.

Posy Gould of Harvard couldn't read secretary hand. One for Northeastern and Rachel Goscimer.

"I've only been able to make out bits of it," I said. "There's an apology for his handwriting, he says he's not used to the pen anymore. He says when he was young he met a nobleman. He held the guy's horse and told him a joke. He became the nobleman's servant. And there's something about Robert Cecil—the Earl of Salisbury; I can't read it all but it looks like Shakespeare says it's safer to talk about something now Salisbury's dead."

"Wow. And?"

"He says," I didn't want to tell her this, " 'Those that are given out as children of my brain are begot of his wit, I but honored with their fostering.' That part's clear enough to read. He specifically says the noble wrote *Hamlet*. And that's why it's a fucking forgery," I said. "That's the oldest Shakespeare slander in the book, that he didn't write his own plays."

"Right, sure, people have said it for years. *I wonder why,*" Posy said.

"Because they're nuts or snobs or assholes." I waved Posy toward the chair; she shook her head. "Because they're conspiracy theorists. Because they want Shakespeare to be amazing, the way Kellogg's forgeries are amazing. Because people who think they have past lives never think they were an ordinary man, always a king."

"And you're sure Shakespeare wrote the plays?"

"Fucking A I am," I said, "and the letter's a fucking forgery because everything Kellogg bought was a fucking forgery. Don't you tell me Shakespeare didn't write the plays." I was venting months of frustration. "Look, I know you wanted the letter to be something special. It isn't, that's all."

She picked up the letter, very carefully, very gently, and turned it and laid it down again on the desk, signature side up. *From my house in Stratford, William Shakespeare.* Carefully, tenderly, she put out one finger and just touched the signature, once. They used to let people do that in Stratford, touch a signature on Shakespeare's will, once. She looked up at me.

"So," she said, "what are you going to do? Bury it at the bottom of the forgeries and hope nobody ever finds it?"

"For now," I said. "Yeah. Pretty much."

"That's dumb."

"Until I prove it's wrong."

"By yourself? How?"

I just scowled, not having any other answer. Except for the UV light, I'd done my tricks.

"Come have coffee with me," Posy said.

⁓

It was eleven A.M. and beginning to sleet. The guard at the library entrance looked up from his Tony Hillerman, checked Posy's pink plastic purse and my backpack, and waved us through.

The Curry Center is basically a food court: Burger King, Pizza Hut, D'Angelo's. Posy looked around like I'd taken her to Mars.

"What are we, like on the highway?"

"What kind of coffee you want?" I asked.

"Mochaccino, skim, with cocoa and cinnamon?"

"Coffee, decaf, hazelnut, or breakfast blend," I said, "that's what they have."

"What's in the breakfast blend?"

"Coffee."

I stood in line waiting to pay for two coffees, watching the students scattered around the food court. Most of the green-house part of the food court was deserted because of the cold. At a table by the window, a man scowling under greasy gray curls was playing chess with himself, swearing against invisible opponents. A woman, maybe forty years old, was asleep on one of the benches, with a kid asleep in a stroller beside her. Her daughter? Granddaughter? Northeastern students fight some long odds.

Posy had grabbed us an empty table near the fountain under the stairway. She'd set us up facing out, with our backs to the wall, like gamblers.

"Let's talk about this whole Shakespeare authorship thing?"

she said as I sat down. She whipped out a notebook and a pink Hello Kitty pen. "I mean you're totally wrong that everyone has always said Shakespeare is Shakespeare. Emerson, Whitman, Mark Twain, Henry James? Twain made fun of him. Whitman said Shakespeare couldn't have been a common man because his sympathies were with the nobles."

"Posy, the people who say Shakespeare didn't write Shakespeare are the same kind of people who wrap their heads in tin foil so the aliens can't read their thoughts."

"Like Henry James?"

Henry James wrapped his head in tin foil. It explained a lot. "I've read about the anti-Shakespeare people. Delia Bacon started corresponding with Shakespeare's ghost. George Batty glued all of Shakespeare's work into a roll and wound it round a hose reel; he just kept cranking and cranking and rolling out messages only he could understand. Who was the guy wanted to divert a river because he thought Shakespeare's manuscripts were buried under it? These people are short some spark plugs. Read Schoenbaum or Matus."

"Or Gary Taylor, sure," she said impatiently. She could play Top This Reference. "But you can *so* see why people think Shakespeare isn't Shakespeare. Here he is, born, married, these mysterious lost years when he isn't *anywhere*, then like abracadabra, famous playwright." She dipped into the big pink purse and brought out *In Search of Shakespeare*. "Your professor Goscimer thinks he went to London in the lost years and was an actor, but that whole part of the biography is so *conditional*, Goscimer starts writing about the theaters and the playwrights because he just doesn't have anything to *say* —"

"It was four hundred years ago. Evidence disappears."

"In *Young Man Shakespeare* the Goscimers thought he went to Italy."

"Until they never found anything," I said.

"Why didn't they just keep looking?"

It was an infuriating way she said it, like she'd never had to think about how much European trips cost. "They ran out of money. They're not rich." To her, not rich probably, meant they had to count the number of times a year they went to the Bahamas.

"They could have got a Fulbright. You're not answering me. Why did the Goscimers think Shakespeare went to Italy?"

"What does this have to do with the letter?"

"You tell me, I'll tell you."

I shrugged. "He probably read some Italian; his Italian sources weren't all translated. He knew details of Venetian law, like the liberty of strangers, and knew Padua was under the protection of Venice but Mantua wasn't. He had the right distance between Padua and Belmont. He used Italian phrases like 'by the ear' and 'sound as a fish.'"

"Cool."

"Doesn't mean anything. Shakespeare got it all in London, reading in Richard Field's shop." Richard Field, born in Stratford, went to London and printed translations of Italian books.

"Shakespeare's got sources in Spanish and French too. Did Richard Field print Spanish and French books?"

"Yeah, actually, he did."

"Oh, right, Shakespeare read *Italian for Dummies* and went right on to Montemayor's *Diana.*" Posy clicked her pen and wrote *Italian? Spanish? French?* "Okay," she said, looking up. "So Shakespeare knows more languages than his biography explains. It's true with law too, right?"

"No. Read Clarkson and Warren."

"Shakespeare writes whole plays about the law and he uses every one of his legal terms correctly. Read Phillips."

"Shakespeare read books about the law. *You* read Phillips, that's what he says."

Posy ignored me and Phillips and scribbled down *Law.* Posy Gould must have got into Harvard by ignoring anyone who said she hadn't got in.

"What else?" she thought aloud. "He liked jousting. Hunting, archery, falconry. You don't get those things out of books."

"Heywood got them out of Gervase Markham," I countered.

"And Heywood is just so bad by comparison." *Hawking,* she wrote. "Shakespeare's favorite book was Ovid's *Metamorphoses* in Arthur Golding's translation *and* in Latin. He liked music and dancing. Madness and medicine." She was writing these down too. "This is what the anti-Stratfordians say, right? They list all these things about Shakespeare and they aren't true of Shakespeare of Stratford?"

"They are true," I said, "because he wrote the plays." Yeah, I knew it was a circular argument. But most of what we know about the man comes from the plays.

"Shakespeare of Stratford was a wool dealer and a money-lender," she said. "Shakespeare of the plays doesn't care about money. 'Who steals my purse steals trash.'" She took a sip of her coffee left-handed and licked her upper lip. *$$$,* she wrote.

"Sure, he lent money at interest, so did his father, so did most of the people in Stratford who could. That doesn't prove he was Shylock."

"What about all those battle scenes and military stuff?"

"They don't prove he was a soldier."

"But he knew military stuff. *And* law. *And* medicine. *And* he had an interest in madness. *And* astronomy and astrology and he learned it all in the seven lost years." Posy's list now covered most of a page. She clicked her pen to change colors and wrote *AND HE WROTE PLAYS!!!* in big orange capitals and held it up and shook it at me.

"He was a genius." Man, I hated that genius argument and I was using it on her. "He was," I tried to say it better, "he could look at people better than anyone else who ever lived. He must have worked fucking hard at looking."

"Right, and he was a chameleon too. Nobody noticed him," Posy said. "He sucked knowledge in, so wouldn't you think somebody would give him a scholarship to college? No. He wrote poems, so wouldn't his friends tell people about this great new poet? No. The only one of his patrons we know about is Southampton. Who loaned Shakespeare his library so he could read all the things he did? Who helped Shakespeare?"

"Richard Field," I said.

"Excuse me, where does Richard Field say 'I gave Shakespeare his start'?" Posy held her hand up to her ear. "Is that your final answer?"

"Posy," I said, "don't you believe in Shakespeare? Are you anti-Shakespeare?"

She raised her shoulders in an exaggerated shrug. "I don't know, no, but— Richard Field is such a crock. Shakespeare used, what, nearly two hundred sources? How many books did Richard Field print a year? Twelve maybe. Two hundred sources, that's like a big chunk of a major Elizabethan library. Shakespeare had to have known a noble. Where did somebody let Shakespeare read Montemayor's *Diana*, in the original? And whose land did he fly hawks on?" Shakespeare's always comparing people to haggards and eyases, as if he flew hawks. "You need like miles of land; I have friends who hawk in England and they all have huge estates."

I bet they did. "Huge estates," I said really quietly, "had servants. You may not think servants count. My grandma was a hotel maid. Shakespeare probably worked for some noble."

She sighed, big dramatic sigh, and looked across the plastic table at me. Nobody accuses Curry Commons of being a high-class place; in the plastic chair, with her elbows on the plastic table, holding a paper cup of cheap coffee, Posy looked expensive and exotic beyond belief. "Excuse me for existing," she said, "but hawking, law, all those expensive books, modern languages, travel, *I* know what it sounds like."

"It's someone picking up how the court talked because the court was a fat audience for plays."

"Don't go all stony on me. It's a nobleman's education. It sounds like a noble who's been to Italy and is showing off. In other words," she said, "you could say Shakespeare's biography is weird because *it's the wrong man's biography,* duh."

Posy Gould of Harvard, grabbing Shakespeare for herself and her friends who had big estates. The pearls made soft gleams around her neck. "I've just spent a year fact-checking *In Search of Shakespeare,*" I said. "I know who Shakespeare was. We know who his parents were, who his family was, we have records of his business dealings, we know more about Shakespeare than about almost any other playwright of his time. And he is no fucking noble."

"Except do we know how he learned to be Shakespeare?" she said. "Isn't that what you want to know, how 'young man Shakespeare' got to be Shakespeare?"

I stared at her.

"Duh, you *are* working on the lost years?" She looked at me exasperated. "You thought I wouldn't find out what you were working on, after you grabbed the Kellogg from me? You want to prove he went to Italy. Or find out what he was before he was Shakespeare. I want to know too," Posy said, and suddenly she was serious. "I want to know— Especially after that letter."

And for a moment our eyes latched and locked like two puzzle pieces finding each other.

"What are you working on, really?" I said. "Not Cecil."

"I *am*," she said. "I'm working on Shakespeare and Cecil. The whole connection between Shakespeare and the Cecils, the spy network—I've got some ideas. So I think it's really interesting that this letter mentions the Cecils? Let's try to work out what the letter says. We can't do it here. Come on."

Posy Gould lived in Davis Square, the new chic neighborhood for Harvard students. Her apartment, up carpeted stairs, was an expanse of silky parquet floor, a kidney-shaped zebra-striped sofa, a wide bay window that gathered light out of the rain. It smelled of Posy: muskiness, perfume, wet wool sweater, her hair, soft luxurious things. She kicked off her shoes and padded across the perfect wood toward the kitchen. She turned on lights and I saw built-in cherry bookshelves, top-line Hadco windows. The kitchen fittings would have driven Dad crazy with joy.

"Why are you looking at my windows?"

"Nice view," I said.

"Daddy bought the building just before real estate went through the roof. It has been so profitable—"

She looked at me and stopped talking about buying buildings.

I took off my boots, self-conscious about my shabby damp socks. Posy's feet made heel-and-toe marks on the floor. She was small, and the place was built small and delicately. Built for her, maybe. By "Daddy." By the window there was a computer desk. She turned on the desk lamp and the computer, a tiny expensive toy.

"Type out what the letter says," she said, as if it were that easy.

Posy's computer desktop was a portrait of Queen Elizabeth in fluorescent pinks and greens. Posy'd lined all the software icons up as jewels on Queen Elizabeth's sleeves. Microsoft Office, Cite, the *Oxford English Dictionary*, the *Encyclopaedia Britannica*. I printed out the two sides of the letter, different magnifications, fanned them out on the table beside the laptop, and folded myself down into the chair to decipher the letter.

Five minutes later I hadn't even made out the first word past the salutation. It might have been *minded*. Or *whereas*. Or *rugrat*. Secretary hand is a whore.

"I need a pad of paper."

I wrote out the letter line by line, leaving spaces where I couldn't make out the handwriting. The page was mostly blanks. I got one more detail; the letter seemed to say Greville knew the nobleman's daughter. For a forgery, that was uncomfortably specific, the sort of detail that could be checked. But Greville, courtier for forty years, must have known everybody, so the forger would get away with that too.

I did what I could with the first side and reached for the second page, and, with it in my hand, I really looked at it.

From my house at Stratford, William Shakespeare.

For a moment, Goscimer's book or no, I wanted it to be true. I wanted to be holding Shakespeare's letter.

Which said he wasn't Shakespeare. I put the printout down.

"Do you want like a beer or something? And I'll order something in. What do you want?"

"Yeah. Whatever you're having."

Just seeing Posy's place told me why she liked Shakespeare's being a noble. Over the zebra couch, on the red walls, Posy had hung big framed posters lit by baby spots. Queen Elizabeth on the right, her wide lips firmly closed, wearing a padded dress like white armor studded with pearls. On the left, another beautiful woman with the same red hair; her cousin, Mary Queen of Scots. Between the two women, a preacher-faced man with a long, stabbing, iron-colored beard, William Cecil. Lit by the baby spot, he had deep, dark, remarkable eyes, calculating, spiritual, the eyes of a fanatic. The most powerful man in England, the man who would save Elizabeth and murder Mary.

Shit, the picture wasn't a reproduction. It was a painting. William Cecil, Queen Elizabeth's right-hand man, the most important politician in the Elizabethan age; a portrait of a major Elizabethan figure, and sure Posy was studying the man, but she *owned* this?

She saw me looking and grinned, sugar-sweet. "It's a copy. You can't tell?"

"Hoped it was, but it's pretty good." Shit. I was done to death with forgeries.

"Ooh, it had you going," she said. "Nicky will be so pleased. He painted it himself. Nicky adooooores me."

"Nicky's your boyfriend?"

"He wishes. Pizza's going to take like an hour to deliver. You want to go out?"

"Sure."

I helped Posy into her black lamb jacket, and she and I talked about her Cecil theory while we walked over to the restaurant, ducking our heads against the March rain and wind.

"I think Shakespeare worked for Cecil," she said.

"How come?" Cecil wasn't a literary patron.

"I think in the lost years, Shakespeare was a spy."

That got my attention.

"Cecil is Elizabeth's chief spymaster, right? Where do plots against Elizabeth come from? The Catholic countries. Spain and *It-ta-ly,*" Posy enunciated. "Cecil and Walsingham hired spies all the time. Particularly travelers and actors."

England in Shakespeare's time was at civil war between Catholics and Protestants. Elizabeth's father, Henry Tudor, King Henry VIII, had divorced his first wife to marry Elizabeth's mother, Anne Boleyn. England had been Catholic then, but the Pope had excommunicated Henry and had declared Elizabeth illegitimate, so Henry had broken with Rome and made England a Protestant country. Now, with Henry dead, the new Protestants were loyal to Protestant Elizabeth. But England was still full of Catholics, practicing their religion secretly.

Philip of Spain was the leading monarch of Europe then. He wanted to control England, either by killing its queen or marrying her. He couldn't marry Elizabeth. But if Elizabeth died, her most legitimate heir was her cousin, Mary Stuart, Queen of Scots—the same Mary Stuart the Kelloggs had formed their collection around. Mary Stuart was Catholic and a widow.

Spanish money was financing the Catholic resistance. If the Catholics won, England would be nothing more than a Spanish colony, a Catholic backwater under a puppet queen.

William Cecil, the smartest man who ever stood behind a throne, had to make sure the Catholics lost.

"Cecil wants to make people loyal to Elizabeth. He turns her into this fantasy figure who represents England. She's like the Madonna and she'll never get old and she'll never die."

I nodded.

"Cecil stages like her whole reign, like a play. Even on Elizabeth's accession day, she's playing a part. She hangs around in Hatfield Park dressed up like a nun in black and white, sitting underneath a tree, reading a book, so when the courtiers ride up with the Queen's ring, she can pretend to be surprised and do this whole *thing*, Latin prayer and all." It's a famous story: Elizabeth carefully put a bookmark in the book, rose as the courtiers bowed to her, accepted the ring that wedded her to England, and knelt to say an appropriate prayer, not too Catholic, not too Protestant. "Like she was just having a picnic under that tree," Posy said. "In November? I so believe that." She ducked her head against the wind, wrapping her black lamb jacket around her.

"So Elizabeth plays the Madonna in front of the curtain," she continued, "but everybody's spying behind the scenes. Christopher Marlowe was a spy, and when English acting companies went abroad, they were spying."

"You think Shakespeare was a spy? There's no evidence Shakespeare ever worked for Cecil."

"There totally is. Have you read *The English Romayne Life?*"

We'd reached the restaurant. She waited for me to open the door for her. It was a big crowded café full of thin artsy people. The walls were painted red and blue, the people were all dressed in black, the coffee was designer, and at least five tables were being hogged by one person writing the Great Millennial Novel on a laptop. All the sandwiches but one were vegetarian. I ordered the turkey.

"And two Vietnamese coffees," Posy said before I could order plain coffee. She handed her sandwich and mine to me and led the way past a couple of red-covered pool tables to a couch at the back of the café. We put down our sandwiches on a table that, under a Plexiglas surface, was made from a giant hardware sorting bin. Washers, chain, faucets. Dad would have loved it.

"*The English Romayne Life,*" Posy said, digging a book out of her purse. "By Anthony Munday, you've heard of him?"

"Bad playwright, Shakespeare maybe wrote a scene for his *Sir Thomas More?*"

"He ended up a playwright, but he started out a boy actor and then he decided he was going to write. He wrote tons of really bad poetry and dedicated it to everybody who wasn't fast enough to get away from him. One of his patrons told him 'If you want to study literature go to Italy,' but didn't give him any money, so Munday and a friend of his turned themselves into fake Catholics."

Posy handed me the book and took a neat little bite out of her veggie wrap, cupping her hand to protect the futon.

"They went to Paris," she said, swallowing, "and told the Jesuits they'd seen the Truth and wanted to go to Rome and study to be priests. The Jesuits gave them money. Munday went to Rome and learned Italian and studied at the English College for a few months, but he got thrown out for being drunk so he came back and told Cecil the names of all the Jesuit priests who were studying with him."

I remembered Munday as I leafed through the book. Mary Cat had talked about him, not flatteringly.

"Munday spied to get to Italy," Posy said. "So what about Shakespeare? Shakespeare would have wanted to go study the Renaissance in Italy, right? And there is *clearly* evidence he was working for Cecil."

"What evidence?"

"The Sonnets," Posy said. "By 1590, William Shakespeare is writing his first sonnets for William Cecil. I can prove it."

⁓

"I can prove it" you don't hear very often, not in Shakespeare biography. "You can prove this," I said, "and the Goscimers didn't notice it?"

Posy pointed a daintily chewed end of wrap at me. "The Sonnets are about the Earl of Southampton, right?"

"They could be."

"They're totally about Southampton and they start in 1590. The year William Cecil started trying to dictate who Southampton would marry." She folded her legs beneath her, enjoying her story. "In 1590 Southampton came to court. He was eighteen and rich, Cecil's granddaughter was sixteen, and Cecil ordered Southampton to marry her. Southampton didn't want to; he was—" Posy broke off and pointed her chin discreetly toward the entrance. "He was *that.*"

A boy was standing at the entrance to the café, hipshot like a model, posing in the light from the window as if Posy had ordered him up for an illustration. His blue jeans fit like paint; his blond hair reached his waist, rock-star-length, and he had studs in both ears. He was looking around for someone. Around the café, men and women were quivering like dog's ears, hoping he'd notice them.

"Southampton was like totally gorgeous and *not* eager to marry,"

Posy said. "Too young, too cute, too gay. Men wrote poetry to him. *Narcissus. Venus and Adonis.* Marlowe wrote *Hero and Leander,* describing how gorgeous Leander was, just like a girl. Southampton never cut his hair, he wore it in long curls trailing over his shoulder."

"Shakespeare's patron," I said, looking at the kid. You forget, even when you work with lives, how your subjects once were *people;* how they were eighteen for just one year and wanted to make the most of it, how they posed and flirted and stood in the doors of cafés, not knowing their love affairs would be famous. Now Southampton is a name on a dedication, but, yeah, once he was eighteen.

"Not the patron of the Sonnets," Posy corrected me. "The man they were being written to, at least the first ones. Shakespeare started writing sonnets about an only child, just come to court, who was supposed to marry but admired himself too much. 'From fairest creatures we desire increase, That thereby beauty's *Rose* might never die . . .' "

Wriothesley, Southampton's family name, is pronounced Rosely.

"Cecil's secretary wrote exactly the same thing about Southampton in *Narcissus.* So who is Shakespeare writing for, at least at the beginning of the Sonnets? Cecil. Cecil's practically *speaking.* Get married, produce an heir."

The boy had found the man he'd been looking for. They were standing at the counter, elbow to elbow, half leaning against each other. The man was ordering for both of them. But the boy was flirting with the girl at the bar.

"Southampton was interested in women too," Posy said. "He got married eventually. Not to Elizabeth de Vere. He kept her dangling five years and then married somebody else. But in the meantime Shakespeare fell in love with him."

"If you think the Sonnets are nothing but biography—"

"So we know Shakespeare was either somebody working for Cecil or a nobleman," Posy went right on. "And that's why the letter you have, that mentions Robert Cecil and a nobleman, that's why it's really, really interesting?"

⟋

I thought it over, and tried the sugary, milky coffee Posy ordered, and grimaced. "You're arguing against yourself if you say William Cecil hired Shakespeare. Cecil didn't need to hire anyone. He was Southampton's guardian. He could just order Southampton to marry the girl." He could; that was the way guardianship worked. "And once Shakespeare started calling Southampton 'the master-mistress of my passion'? William Cecil was the most powerful man in England. He'd just have had Shakespeare put in prison. Or killed."

"But he didn't, so Shakespeare must have been important. A nobleman, not an actor."

I had her. "A nobleman more important than William Cecil? More important than the Lord Treasurer, Elizabeth's private secretary, the head of the secret service? Who was more important than Cecil except Elizabeth?"

"I don't know yet," Posy said.

"There wasn't anybody. Not by 1590. William Cecil was the king behind the throne and his son Robert was his heir."

Posy made a face.

"So the letter's a forgery," I said.

"The Sonnets aren't a forgery." She wrapped her arms around herself, pulling up one leg and resting her chin on her knee. Her thinking position, I guessed. I leaned forward and put my coffee mug down on the table, letting my eyes just brush across the dim view under Posy's microskirt.

"Do you think the Sonnets are in the right order?" Posy asked. I hauled my thoughts back to business. "I don't know."

"Just give me this," she said, "Sonnet 80 comes after Sonnet 1." In Sonnet 1, Shakespeare's introducing himself to the young man. In Sonnet 80, he's jealous of another poet who's also writing to the young man. "I'll give you that."

"Okay. In Sonnet 80, Shakespeare's saying he has a rival. A rival poet.

> *O, how I faint when I of you do write,*
> *Knowing a better spirit doth use your name*
> *And in the praise thereof spends all his might*
> *To make me tongue-tied. . . ."*

It was the first time I'd heard her quoting poetry. She knew how to speak lines. She took a swallow of her coffee and went on. "But even Shakespeare has to admire the other poet:

> *Was it the proud full sail of his great verse,*
> *Bound for the prize of all-too-precious you,*
> *That did my ripe thoughts in my brain inhearse,*
> *Making their tomb the womb wherein they grew?*

"So what poet would Shakespeare think was better than he was? Almost the only modern English poet he quotes . . . And Shakespeare talks about this poet and 'spirits'? This has to be Marlowe."

Was it his spirit, by spirits taught to write/Above a mortal pitch, that struck me dead? "Yeah, you can have Marlowe."

"Totally Marlowe," Posy said. "A great poem, that's *Hero and Leander*. Shakespeare's writing his own poem at the same time, that's *Venus and Adonis*. Which Shakespeare dedicates to

Southampton, April 1593, and Southampton totally ignores it. So Sonnet 80 was written around April 1593."

It was a pretty fair theory about Sonnet 80; but there are a lot of pretty fair theories about the Sonnets.

"And just afterward the other poet disappears from the *Sonnets*. Marlowe dies."

Christopher Marlowe, author of *Dr. Faustus*, was murdered May 30, 1593, age twenty-nine. One of the saddest things that ever happened to English. His death worked for her chronology, I had to give her that.

"So," I said, "Shakespeare killed Marlowe?"

"Nooo," Posy complained. "Shakespeare *met* Marlowe when they were both working for the Cecils, Shakespeare spying for William and Marlowe for Robert Cecil, before Sonnet 80, before April 1593."

"I don't buy it. According to you, Shakespeare and Marlowe were both spies, and they were both in love with Southampton. Marlowe was the better-known poet. Why not hire Marlowe?"

Posy frowned. She leaned against the back of the futon sofa, picking at the cover. "Shakespeare's—older. Steadier. Doesn't it strike you Shakespeare writes as though he's older than Marlowe?"

"He is older. He has three kids."

"No, you know what I mean:

That time of year thou mayst in me behold
When yellow leaves, or none, or few do hang
Upon those boughs which shake against the cold . . .

"He sounds like he's bald and trembly and stuff. An old man."

"He's only twenty-six."

"Maybe he isn't. 'When forty winters shall besiege thy brow.' When you're forty. Maybe even 'shall besiege *thy* brow,' when you're forty like I am. Oh wow," she said suddenly. "What if he *was* forty?"

"What?"

"What if the *real* Shakespeare was forty in 1590?" she repeated. "Forty, so he'd be born about 1550, and he knew Cecil. If he was noble— There weren't that many Elizabethan nobles. We could look that up."

"In Cecil's biography?"

"On the Internet!" She got up, leaving her coffee. "Come on."

There was a bookstore next door. By the time I'd caught up with Posy, she was leaning across the counter talking to a woman at the bookstore's computer. "—look up something on the Internet? It's really important. Open up Britannica.com and type 1550 AND CECIL?"

The woman gave her a look but didn't resist. The articles popped onto the screen like answers in a Magic 8-Ball. William Cecil, 1st baron Burghley. Edward de Vere, 17th earl of Oxford.

"That one," Posy said.

She put her finger on the monitor screen. I looked over her arm.

OXFORD, EDWARD DE VERDE, 17TH EARL OF (b. April 12, 1550, Castle Hedingham, Essex, Eng. —d. June 24, 1604, Newington, Middlesex), English lyric poet and patron of an acting company, Oxford's Men, who became, in the 20th century, the strongest candidate proposed (next to William Shakespeare himself) for the authorship of Shakespeare's plays.

The Earl of Oxford. The nut cases' favorite Shakespeare. "Ah shit," I said, quietly so as not to offend the lady at the counter. "Posy—"

But Posy was typing her password in and reading the rest of the article. " 'Oxford lived for eight years as a royal ward,' " she read to me in a very quiet voice. " 'Under the care of William Cecil . . . *and in December 1571 married Burghley's daughter, Anne Cecil.'* "

"And I suppose their daughter was Elizabeth de Vere," I said. "So we know what the forger wanted to prove."

She pulled me away from the desk, toward the bookshelves in the back of the store, into a deserted aisle. "Don't you see it?" she said in a low voice, looking up at me with odd shining eyes. "Cecil didn't have to hire Shakespeare to write the Sonnets. Shakespeare wrote to Southampton about marrying Elizabeth de Vere because *Shakespeare was Elizabeth de Vere's father.*"

"Nobody believes in Oxford, Posy, nobody."

"We don't have to *believe.*" She was laughing but Posy's face had gone white; the mascara round her eyes was quivering like feathers round the eyes of birds. "Joe. Joe. We have the *letter.* It's not a forgery. We have *proof.*"

~

We walked back to her apartment in cold silence. I just wished she'd never seen the letter. Shakespeare was writing love poems to his own daughter's fiancé? It was like Jerry Springer.

Posy knelt by her bookshelves and started pulling out books. I watched her angrily, then fired up her computer again and typed "Oxford Vere Edward" into Google. There was a good-sized site proving the Oxfordians wrong.

"That just means people believe in Oxford," Posy said, looking over my shoulder. "Download the site. Is there a site for people who do believe in Oxford?"

"Yeah," I said grimly. There were two.

"Download them too. Look. Here he is."

She'd found a picture of the Earl of Oxford. In the portrait he was maybe my age, and he looked like a snob. He had one eyebrow raised, la-di-dah; one side of his mouth was half-smiling, a little angrily. He was the Earl of Oxford and you weren't. Most Elizabethan portraits look at you; the Earl of Oxford's eyes looked to the side, not interested in anything but himself.

He was wearing an elaborately cut and slashed jacket and a flat cap like a beret. Italians have always been big on fashion. He'd been to Italy.

"It all hangs together," Posy said, leaning over my arm to look at him. "Cecil didn't kill Shakespeare because Shakespeare was his son-in-law. Didn't you say Shakespeare had to be important?" She knelt beside me, looking at the picture on the screen. "He's handsome, isn't he?" The glow of the screen made her pearls neon-white against her skin.

"Shakespeare wasn't a noble," I said, "and I for fucking sure don't think anybody I admire could have fallen in love with his own daughter's fiancé; and the letter is a forgery."

"Prove it, then," she said, turning to look at me.

"It'll fail a good chemical test."

"So test it."

"Unfortunately, experts charge for tests."

She sat back on her heels. "Is that a problem?"

I had about seven hundred dollars in the bank. Sure as shit, lady, that was the problem. I could ask Roy Dooley for the money, but then I'd have to tell Roy about the letter.

She stood up with a rustle of tights against skirt. "I'll ask Nicky to test it."

"Nicky?" I remembered. The boyfriend. The guy who'd painted the picture of Cecil.

"Does the name Nicholas Bogue mean anything to you? Okay. Nicholas Bogue. Nicky. He's a manuscript dealer in London," she said. "I mean, he's good. He could tell whether that letter's real. Could you go to London with me?"

Could I what?

"I don't believe in Oxford," I said. What I meant was I didn't have the money to waste on craziness.

"You are such a—" She looked up at me, long, appraisingly, but almost vulnerably too. "Are you just trying to *lose* this letter? You're supposed to be smart, I can't believe you're being this stupid. We just *found Shakespeare*. I knew Shakespeare knew Cecil, you knew Shakespeare went to Italy, a lot of people think Shakespeare didn't write the plays, and now we have proof, *and I want to know all about this letter*. Why did Shakespeare write it to Fulke Greville, and did Greville know Elizabeth de Vere, and—I can't believe you don't want to know about this."

"Read the anti-Oxford site and just calm down. Oxford can't be Shakespeare."

"Why not?"

"Oxford died in 1604." I was paging down the anti-Oxford site. "Shakespeare kept writing plays until 1613."

"You'd have to redate the plays," Posy mused.

"Stop it."

"I won't stop it, I think we're right."

"There's no *we* here. Think about the paleographic critics, Maunde Thompson and J. Dover Wilson. Or Foster's database,

SHAXICON. You'd have to explain them away, and everything in Schoenbaum and Irvin Matus . . ."

Posy leaned over my shoulder, her bare arm against my cheek. "Okay," she said. "If Nicky finds out the letter's a forgery, cool, okay, that's the end of it. But if not—You're smart. I'm smart. Come to London with me. Let's see what we can find out."

I could try to talk someone into doing the tests for seven hundred. I could sell my truck, which would mean I couldn't get to installation jobs. I could forget my teaching job and the Kellogg work and zero my bank account and go to London with Posy Gould.

She laid her hand on mine, laced her fingers with mine. Posy Gould was as different from me as a woman could be from a man; but I knew what she was saying the way I'd never known anyone before, a way I couldn't even put words to; and we'd only met each other yesterday. Who was I kidding? Shit, if the woman had believed in Shakespeare, I would have followed her like a dog.

"I knew from nineteen years old I wanted to write about Shakespeare." I untangled my fingers from hers. "But it's Shakespeare I want to write about. The real Shakespeare. You've got some good stuff. Go with the Cecil connection and fuck the Earl of Oxford."

"Come with me to London," Posy said. "Bring the letter. Give it to Nicky to look at, or somebody else if you want. Daddy will pay for everything. Nicky will say it's a forgery, you can come back and show Nicky's report and that's it. But I want that letter looked at and so do you. If you don't want to prove it right, how about proving it wrong? Give Nicky a couple of days on this. I'll help you prove it wrong."

"It is wrong."

"I asked about you," she continued. "I mean, I had to find out about you, right, you got the Kellogg Collection away from me? You're like this phenomenon out of nowhere. You wanted to write Shakespeare's life since forever. The Goscimers had you working for them before you were even officially in grad school. You're Mr. Shakespeare. I'm no Shakespeare scholar, I just like walked into this from knowing Frank and thinking about the Sonnets, but I feel like I can't miss it, if I missed this I'd miss my whole life, I've just got to be part of this. And you're going to walk off and leave this letter on the floor? Can you do that?"

And she was right, of course. I'd never been to London. I needed an expert. Daddy would pay for everything. I could prove it wrong. But the bottom line was, and she knew it, I would be thinking about this letter until I knew.

The right words are lightning.

"Does your friend Nicky have a Web site?" I said. "Or some way I can check him?"

Nicky Bogue had a Web site; listing in a British society of pale-ographers; articles about him. He was legit as far as I could tell.

"I teach," I said finally, "and I work on the Kellogg, and I do other work on the side. I need the money. If I can cover my hours, I'll go. But you'll have to pay my expenses and my substitute, and I won't believe in Oxford for you."

"Sure, and charge whatever you should charge for research. Daddy won't mind." Posy reached into her purse, pulled out a platinum Visa card, moved me aside, and started clicking keys. "Window or aisle?"

We took a taxi to the Northeastern library. I left a note for Roy. "Borrowed, one Elizabethan letter, suspected forgery, for analysis." I took the letter, the eighteenth-century envelope, and the manila envelope.

I'd taken forgeries out of the library for checking before. Roy didn't mind. I wasn't doing anything wrong.

The guard didn't even look up to see us leave.

One of the other Shakespeare teaching assistants could take my classes; we made a deal over Posy's cell phone while I stuffed clothes in my backpack. I phoned Dad from the airport and left a message, speaking slowly for his old answering machine. "Dad. I got a chance to go to London. I'll be back in a few days. Everything's fine."

I didn't tell Dad why I was going to London, or that I was going with Posy.

And I didn't mention the letter.

*O*n the plane, Posy fell asleep. I was too wired. I had my passport, shaving cream, good jacket; I'd taken five hundred dollars out of the bank. I felt like I'd left something behind. My underwear. My caution.

"Glass of champagne, sir?" When Posy bought the tickets, she'd asked me window or aisle but not economy or extravagance. We were flying first class. First-class passengers had deep thick-padded seats, individual choices of movies or video games, shrimp cocktails, a complimentary dark blue padded toiletries kit. It made me feel both privileged and patronized, these half-useless comforts that came from being with Posy Gould, the rich girl. Dad would have told me to quit fussing and enjoy myself.

Air and machines hummed around us. Posy was asleep, cuddled up in the big recliner next to me. The letter was in the padded pocket of her Vaio case, in a big purple plastic envelope with the printouts and my CD. I reached down for the envelope and my hand brushed against her right ankle. She murmured in her sleep as I fired up the computer and started working on the letter again.

Two glasses of champagne and three hours later, I'd made out most of the *Hamlet* anecdote. On one of the summer feast days "in the xxv. Elizabeth," 1584, "William Shakespeare" saw a play, from his description a version of *Hamlet*. (Way too early for *Hamlet*.) "Shakespeare" saw the nobleman on horseback and held the horse's head, to speak with him. The nobleman was intrigued by Shakespeare's name. *Whence cometh thy name, knowest thou? — Marry, my lord, from my father.*

He said he would have such a name, and live retired, and not go stately. And I, says I, would go to London and wear satin.

Then come to me in London, the nobleman said.

Sounded like a fine forged story to me.

Come to London, Posy had told me. I looked sidewise at her.

What would prove this letter wrong? The dating of *Hamlet;* whether *Hamlet* could have been performed in Stratford in 1584. Whether Oxford "lived retired." I'd have to look up Oxford in the British Library.

The British Library. London. I was going there. *London*.

Maybe I'd look up Mary Cat on Docklands Road, I thought, then figured I shouldn't.

Last year, when Mary Cat had first visited the Society of Mary, she'd brought me back an Elizabethan map of London. I grubbed it out of my backpack and unfolded it.

London was small then. The center of the city was the Thames, wide and mud-yellow and crawling with boats. South of the river there was still almost nothing but fields. Between the river and the fields lay the city.

Westward, upriver, where the river water was still clean, a clot of buildings surrounded Westminster Abbey and Westminster Palace. Beside Westminster Palace spread a gigantic medieval tilt-yard, longer than a football field, where knights still jousted for the Queen. Elizabeth's standard was flying from the palace flagpole; the Queen was in residence. The government would have been with her; the court and government revolved around Elizabeth.

Eastward from Westminster, houses with walled gardens ran in a narrow road along the Thames. Somerset Place, Durham Place, Suffolk Place, Norfolk House, tall houses with little towers of their own, but like farmsteads: kitchen gardens, outbuildings, stables, landing stages for boats, places for rich people who still spent most of their time in the country but wanted to have a house near Westminster.

Eastward of the nobles' houses was London.

The City of London was only maybe ten blocks across, a warren packed inside huge medieval walls. Old Saint Paul's Cathedral loomed over its western half, and at its eastern edge spread the Tower of London, half royal residence, half political prison. Red-tiled house roofs jammed the space between, and church towers spiked the air.

On the map it was summer. Tiny sketched cows were grazing in the fields outside the walls; men were shooting at an archery butt; wash was drying on the grass. Shakespeare's London was supposed to stink so terribly you could smell it five miles to windward, but I knew how this city would have smelled on an early June morning, when the fires were long banked and the roosters just beginning to crow, cool and sweet and with moistness edging the air.

London Bridge was the only bridge. On the Southwark end of the bridge the mapmaker had drawn pikes and tiny heads of Catholic traitors. Instead of bridges, a hundred little insect-boats scurried oar-legged up and down the river.

South of the river spread a huddle of houses, Southwark, a muddle of shops and lodging houses and brothels. And just at the edge of Southwark, right by the river, loomed two big circular arenas, for bear-baiting and bull-baiting.

Bankside, they called that neighborhood.

History is an act of imagination, a map drawn before airplanes, before balloons, by a man who had to think himself into the air, above the rooftops and church spires. History is an imaginary point of view. Posy Gould's history had nothing in it but important people, Cecils and earls and spymasters. Flattering and intoxicating, like free glasses of champagne. On my mental map, the center of London was a neighborhood of brothels and mud streets. Bankside.

North of the city, barely visible on the map, I could see two smaller ring-shaped buildings. One was the Curtain, one the Theatre. The Burbage family, which owned the Theatre, would pull it down in a few years and haul the timbers south of the river, to Bankside, to build the Globe.

Posy peered over my shoulder, yawning. She put her finger on an enclosed field and a little church among the great houses: "Here's Daddy's flat in Covent Garden. Right by"—she moved her finger a little south—"William Cecil's house." A block of a house with pointed towers. Orchards. A big open yard for Cecil's wards to practice fencing in.

"Is Cecil's house still there?" I asked.

Posy shook her head. "There aren't many Elizabethan buildings left in London."

"Shame."

"I think it's great, all the building," Posy said. "When Dad started buying property in London, seventeen percent of London houses still didn't have indoor plumbing? And even now Internet access is still charged by the minute?" Apparently, to Posy, no Internet access was like no toilet. "I mean, it took the millennium, but *finally*. You should get some sleep. Do you want melatonin?"

I shook my head.

"You'll be such a wreck tomorrow."

She fell back asleep as easily as a kitten. Her sweater rode up a little, showing an inch of sweet plump stomach. If she had a tattoo of Queen Elizabeth's signature, I couldn't see it.

On one of the video channels, a travelogue of London was playing. Come visit Millennial Britain. Cool Britannia. Madame Tussaud's.

The London Eye, the Millennium Dome. The new Globe. When it was over, I tried to sleep too, and I'd almost nodded off when I thought of something that brought me uncomfortably awake.

Goscimer thought the Sonnets were probably about Southampton. But if they weren't, Goscimer thought the Fair Youth was William Herbert, the Earl of Pembroke. I'd fact-checked this part of *In Search of Shakespeare,* and I remembered very well, uncomfortably well, that Cecil was also trying to persuade this second "W. H." to marry a Cecil granddaughter.

Whose name had meant nothing to me until this moment.

Bridget de Vere.

Probably another daughter of the fucking Earl of Oxford.

Coincidence, I thought, and tried to sleep.

ou should have taken melatonin," Posy said.

In the middle of the night the sun came out over Heathrow Airport. I stumbled behind Posy down corridors lined with strange ads. SORTED FOR THE WEEKEND? Posy bounced up and down on a long black rubber moving walkway. She looked like she was on an exercise machine. "Don't do that," I muttered.

LEFT LUGGAGE CLOSED DUE TO BOMB THREATS. The Catholic-Protestant war was still going on after four hundred years.

We stood in line to have our passports stamped. "Purpose of your visit?" the guard asked me. *Pu'pus of yer viz'it?* I was caught by the cadence of his English. "Tourism," the Englishman filled in for me, "right you are, my darling."

My darling?

"Research," Posy said. "Want to see my notes?" and waved the purple envelope of printouts. The guard smiled at her. She smiled at him. Posy was a girl with nothing to hide.

WAY OUT, said a sign.

Heathrow, like Logan, was under construction for the millennium. None of the escalators were working; I trudged up endless metal flights of stairs, slumped under my backpack, following the bouncing Posy.

"We'll take a taxi into London," Posy said; but I'd seen a sign pointing to the London Tube.

"Can we do the Tube? The map," I explained. "I have a T-shirt with the map."

"You are such a tourist."

"Yup."

England: the white cliffs of Dover. England's green and pleasant land. Hedgerows. People saying "luv." My first sight of England was the upholstery of the Piccadilly Line. Blue, white, red, black, blips and strips and worms of color crawling across the seats. The subway smelled sharp and sweet at once, a little airless, foreign. The passengers were foreign too, not the subway crowd you'd see in Boston. A tall, fat black woman in African dress. Buddhist nuns. Two Asian kids leaning against each other. The girl had long greasy greeny-black hair and sharpened ninja fingernails, and she was wearing a fake airline-stewardess uniform. In Boston she'd have been Eurotrash; I didn't know what she was here. At the end of the car a big thuggish guy with a beard was eating a thick greasy dripping sandwich. The smell of bacon wafted through the air. I figured he was English. Everyone was looking at him curiously.

"Mind the gap," murmured a soft robotic voice.

All the ads were different. TOWER BOOKS-RECORDS-MUSIC NOMUSICNOLIFE, strange bands, Soulwax, Vengaboys, January, Mary's Giant Schnauzer, Shut Up and Dance. MOUSE TO MOUTH RESERVATIONS—BOOK2EAT.COM. WELCOME TO THE FUTURE. EATMYHANDBAGBITCH.COM. HOW WILL YOU MEET YOUR SOULMATE IN THE NEW MILLENNIUM? HOLIDAYS ABROAD: prices in pounds for beaches in Spain. VENUES FOR HIRE. The phone numbers were a digit too long. TEN THINGS YOU MIGHT NOT KNOW ABOUT SMINTING.

Sminting. A candy. A sport. Something financial. I couldn't even guess.

Opposite me, a man was reading something that looked like the *Herald*, but right on the front page was a big color picture of a naked woman with boobs you could have hiked on.

I'd thought I knew England. I didn't know shit. Just opposite us was an ad with some English-aristocrat-looking guy standing in a veldt, holding a hawk in one hand and a bottle of beer in the other.

"Asahi Super Dry," the text read. "Chris Quentin. Masterly with Distinction. Striking Also." The rest of the ad was in Japanese.

The train whooshed out of the tunnel; immediately the light got colder, damper, grayer. Through the window, rows of yellow brick hobbit houses gleamed dully in the mist.

England.

I leaned hungrily forward and looked through the window at wash lines, scraps of garden, motorcycles parked by sheds, until we went into the tunnel again.

Covent Garden was our Tube stop, Posy said. At least here I knew what was coming; Covent Garden had been in *Young Man Shakespeare*.

The Goscimers liked opera and ballet, and they'd haunted the Royal Opera House, Covent Garden, for the cheap standing-room tickets: "We waited all night in the cold," they had written, "talking about Shakespeare, and around us the trucks hauled in vegetables from the country. The city streets smelled like fresh loam. At seven in the morning we bought our tickets and cele-brated with a big hot breakfast, tea and eggs with HP sauce at the café across the street, talking to the market gardeners. Three and six for the tickets. Forty-two cents. We were groundlings."

The thumping of a bass line hit us as we got out of the station. The crowd was a jostling and shoving New York nightmare of people, a mosh pit. A black woman wearing a Hard Rock Café T-shirt from New Orleans was standing in front of a woman mime covered in silver paint, who was pretending to be a statue of Eliza Doolittle. A brittle blond Japanese woman in a fake leopard-skin coat was snapping a picture of them both. Two

Indian men walked past talking about some business deal. "Convertible debentures, I say, Patel—" Everything was scrubbed, clean, new, millennial. A second Eliza Doolittle walked past in lacy Victorian dress and a big hat. "Bai me flahrs?"

"What happened?" I asked Posy.

"What do you mean what happened?"

"There was a market here. For hundreds of years."

"Like it made sense to sell vegetables in central London? Do you know what the per-square-foot is?"

The market buildings were full of little souvenir shops, crafts stalls, antiques. I smelled hamburgers and hazelnut coffee. Posy led us past green spun-sugar Disney market buildings toward a street of renovated white office buildings.

"Is the Royal Opera House still here?" I asked.

Posy took my shoulders and swiveled me. My eyes were two feet from a poster: the Royal Ballet was dancing *Romeo and Juliet* in a new millennial production. I looked up at window boxes of red geraniums, balconies, bright new signs, down the street at white shops where I was never going to find a café serving tea and eggs with HP sauce. I missed something I had never seen.

Posy had gone ahead toward one of the white buildings. I read the three discreet brass plates by the door.

Gould Holdings Ltd.
Corunna Entertainment LLC
Mr. Edward Gould

The door opened onto a modern hall and an elevator, a square waiting area, a door into a big white office. Three pretty women were scurrying around with cell phones, papers, coffee, oohing and aahing and giggling and Yes-Mr.-Gould-ing, and into view walked a tanned actor-looking man holding a cell phone to his ear.

"I told you that?" Posy's father was saying. "You were at a party, you were high on crack, Miles, you heard me in your dreams say that. You got to get a hold of yourself. Take a break. Betty Ford. Whatever they got for Betty Ford in England."

Shit, we'd gone to Los Angeles by mistake. *Variety* and *People* lay on the table in the waiting room. Pictures hung on the walls, all signed; one of them was Ronald Reagan standing with his arm over Posy's dad's shoulders. While Posy's dad was talking, he was smiling at the three secretaries, mimicking a man laying a line of cocaine across a mirror and snorting it up with a straw.

"Tommy doesn't know from shit what his contracts say, Miles, he's an *actor.*"

Posy's father was a big man, but even if he hadn't been he would have taken up a big space. His watch was a thick gold coin on a gold band; his suit was brown-grey, an odd expensive color, with a faint dusty green stripe that brought out his green eyes. He looked like the kind of guy who only had to smile to make a deal. No wonder Posy didn't know what logic was.

"Honey!" Gould flicked the cell phone off, waved away another phone, and wrapped his arm around Posy in a big hug. He was happier to see her than Dad could have acted if I'd been elected president. But I saw Posy's shoulders square a little.

"Hi, Daddy," she said. "This is Joe, who's working with Frank Kellogg's stuff at Northeastern?"

Gould looked at me a little frostily. "So you're the kid who stole Frank's collection away from my daughter." He stuck out his hand anyway. I put out mine, conscious of travel dirt, armpits.

Gould looked me up and down, so open about it that it wasn't really personal, and smiled like a salesman.

"What brings you to London, Joe?"

"His professor," Posy answered for me. "Joe's professor has a radio interview on the Beeb a week from tomorrow. Joe's been letting me look at Frank's stuff, and I had a couple of things I wanted to look up, and Joe wanted to come to London to do some research anyway, so I said he could stay with us."

"Great," Gould said. "We'll put you downstairs, the garden room." He gave me a friendly dismissive smile. I'd got the same look, the same smile, from fathers when I'd showed up to date their daughters with my hands cracked from stuffing insulation. *You won't last.* Serious dates, real men, don't work with their hands.

We gathered up Posy's luggage and my backpack. The entrance to the Gould apartment was down the back of the hall. "Tommy?" Gould's voice still reached us as we waited for the elevator. "Tommy, how many times I have to tell you, never talk contracts with Miles? You know the guy's crazy, talking about business makes him crazy. Leave it to your buddy Ted, okay?" The elevator arrived with a soft hiss of foreign-smelling machinery; as I fit Posy's luggage in, I could hear Gould snapping the phone closed. "Leave the thinking to me, dumbass," Posy's father muttered as the doors slid shut behind us.

Posy let out a little breath of relief.

"We're not telling your father about the letter?" I asked in an undertone.

"Wait until we talk to Nicky."

The garden room actually had a garden outside the window, a scrap of dug-out earth glowing with Gro-Lites and spring flowers. I figured out how much wattage and gardening and water-pumping it took to keep those things going, and figured I ought to be impressed. The chairs were leather, the bedspread had tassels; in the bathroom were fifteen kinds of soap and lotions and more mirrors than a barbershop, and there was another copy of *Variety* on the bedside table. There were signed pictures here too, actors and actresses who'd stayed here, people a heck of a lot more important than me.

Shaved and showered and smelling expensive, I went back upstairs to find Posy. The living room was all white with a palm tree in a pot and a couple of big modern pictures over the couch. In the middle of the space, a steel-and-glass sculptural-looking staircase led upward to the bedrooms. To one side there was a dining room with a big steel-and-glass table and breakfast laid out on an all-glass sideboard. Egg-white omelets and fresh fruit.

"Don't have coffee," Posy said, "you'll screw up your metabolism? You shouldn't have coffee until tomorrow. Get some sleep."

"We need to phone Nicky," I said.

"Whatever." Posy trailed toast crumbs across the white rug to the library.

Ted Gould's library had a broadband connection, a fax machine, and a couple of big computers as cool and silent as bankers. On the walls were hung old London movie posters and a big velvety-looking engraving of David Garrick as Hamlet. Right next to it was a framed note from Garrick. The bookcases were more glass, steel-and-glass shelving with glass doors, and the books were on display facing out. *The Grapes of Wrath, Gone with the Wind*, famous books, all perfect: perfect dust jackets, not a dinged corner nor a turned-down page.

Every one of them, I realized, somebody'd made a movie of.

"Nicky?" Posy was talking on the phone, quietly, looking out to make sure her father wasn't around. I went back into the living room, wondered what was going on with Posy and her father, looked out the window down at the tourists in the street below. At the corner of the street I could see a policeman. A London bobby. *London.*

"We're going to see Nicky at noon," Posy said. "Sleep until then and you'll be okay by tomorrow."

The heck I would. "I'm going for a walk." London, London, it was London down there; and Nicky would take one look at the letter and see what was wrong with it, and we'd go home. I would be back in Boston tomorrow. "You tell me where you and this Nicky are going to meet, I'll get there."

Unexpectedly, dazzlingly, Posy smiled, a real smile. "I'll come with you."

"You don't have to."

"Yes, I do. You should see your face. It's like you're getting your first kiss. You're being such a tourist." She hesitated. "I mean, can I come?"

⁓

"I know where to take you," she said.

We took a London taxi to Trafalgar Square: Nelson's Column, the fountains, the four gigantic stone lions, traffic swirling mirror-wise, LOOK RIGHT stenciled onto the street, and pigeons cooing, flapping, rising. We made it across the traffic to the central island.

"Here." She bought me a cup of pigeon feed. "Be a tourist."

"Nah, you do it." I've never got used to pigeons. City birds, rats with wings. She scattered the feed lavishly. The pigeons made a flurry around her. Her hair swung as she threw the feed into the air. Her black jacket and yellow skirt, and the greedy birds, grey with hints of rainbows: I wished I had a camera. No need. I'd remember.

"I love London, and I like never get to be a tourist," she said.

"Why not?"

"Oh, you know, it's dumb. Feeding the pigeons."

"So this is your first kiss too?" I said casually.

She looked up at me. A moment passed. A pigeon, flapping, flicked my head with a wing. "Fucking bird," I said, startled.

"I'll show you something totally touristy. We'll go on the Tube, because it'll be better seeing it when you come out of the Tube."

"What?"

"Like it would be a surprise if I told you?"

We got out at Westminster. I knew Big Ben was at Westminster, but as we came out from the Tube station into the sun, I saw it, the Houses of Parliament, Westminster Abbey, and just as we came up the stairs Big Ben began to beat out the hour. I could feel the chimes on my skin, *bom* bom *bom* bom, in my bones, vibrating my throat and my tongue, like language. A red bus passed, and behind it stood the Houses of Parliament, the tall Gothic tower and the enormous clock: England.

"Okay, Kodak moment. But that is not where we're going," said Posy. "Close your eyes." She turned me around. "Okay, now you can look. Cool Britannia. England 2000. The London Eye. Is that great or what?"

We were facing the river, the Thames. But we were standing in an enormous circular shadow. Over us, as high as Godzilla, stood a gigantic Ferris wheel. It rose like a mouth over Big Ben and the river, blue and white and silver and glass, fanged all around with sharp glittering points.

"Isn't it great? Come on," said Posy.

Me, me, me, the monster said, like Posy's henna hair and fluorescent clothes, with none of Posy's grace. "Shit, what is that?"

"The Eye."

The Greeks believed in hubris, the kind of pride that goes before a fall, the sin of building just too fucking big. The Elizabethan image for that kind of tragedy was a wheel. Go up with the wheel, you forget it's going to go down.

"They call it the Eye because you can see all of London." Posy was wheedling two people near the front of the line to sell her their tickets. "You can wait another hour," she told them as she paid them ten times the value of their tickets and pulled me in. Shit. We inched up white modernistic stairs in a crowd of tourists and stepped into a slowly moving pod.

"Tickets are so hard to get, it just opened the beginning of this month. And we jumped the line," Posy said, gloating.

"Yeah."

"I shouldn't have done it? You wanted to see London—"

Privilege. She was in it so deep she didn't even know it. She assumed it: the rich go first, the rich get champagne, the rich are smarter and better and ride to the top of the wheel; the rich are Shakespeare. I looked down at her hurt face. Posy'd meant to do something nice for me.

"Yeah," I said. "I mean thank you."

We rose above street level. The pod was football-shaped, glass but for the floor and a few struts, like Ted Gould's apartment, all glass. It was full of Japanese tourists clicking digital cameras and big blond Nordic tourists squinting through binoculars. Posy leaned outward, spreading herself on the glass like film. I found a viewing place, wedged my backpack with the purple envelope carefully between my feet, and looked down. The crowds at the ticket office already looked like ants.

"Look at the boats," Posy said. On the river, the barges were miniaturized into waterbugs, like on my map.

We were above the buildings, above Big Ben. I could see the pattern of the streets now. "That's Westminster Bridge down there." *Earth has not anything to show more fair,* Wordsworth wrote about the view from Westminster Bridge. It was an ordinary bridge, an ordinary traffic jam with the shadow of a big wheel over it. On the banks of the Thames, as we rose higher, I saw office blocks, intruding toward the gritty sun. *The City now doth, like a garment, wear/The beauty of the morning . . .* London had been magic for me a moment ago. Now it was sour. I shouldn't blame Posy.

"That's the Millennium Dome," Posy said, pointing toward a huge white pillow transfixed with spikes, far in the distance.

We were rising toward the top of the wheel. Through the steel struts I could see the city broken apart. Far below, the streets crazed millennial London into fragments, as if the office blocks and construction sites had been glued together badly. Toward the east it was as though a rock had been dropped on London. Ripples of breakage spread out semicircularly. And then I knew what I was seeing, and the hair rose along my arms.

"Posy, there's the London Wall. There's the City of London."

"There isn't any London Wall," Posy said.

I could see its semicircle as clearly as the shadow of the Eye. I dug in my backpack and spread out the map Mary Cat had given me. The office towers faded into church steeples, the buildings dwindled into red-tiled roofs. London Wall rose in a half-circle, a high gray wall with massive gates: Newgate, Ludgate, Bishopsgate. There was London Bridge, the Tower of London, there were the boats on the Thames. Downriver of the Eye stood the palaces, Somerset House, Durham House, Norfolk House, with their long green gardens and their pointed roofs. Below us were Westminster Hall and ancient Westminster Abbey, a wedding cake in a patch of sunlight, the same four hundred years ago and today, and beyond that, where a long street was now, stretched the tiltyard and the Palace of Westminster with Queen Elizabeth's standard flying from the roof. For a moment our pod was higher than anyone else's. I leaned forward too, my breath fogging the glass, looking into the sun downriver toward Bankside, and through the dazzle of sun and fog I saw the insect boats heading toward the bearbaiting ring, the bullbaiting, and Shakespeare's Globe.

London is a manuscript, a square mile scribbled over by two thousand years of Londoners; it is parchment scraped clean and used again. But around London Wall the streets still curve, and the Tower and Westminster Abbey still stand. And Shakespeare is as big as the London Wall. Shakespeare left traces.

Let me find them, I said silently as the wheel began to descend. Let me find him.

⁓

"Right," Nicky Bogue said, spreading the letter out with long, fastidious fingers. "Lovely, isn't it."

"So?" Posy said. "Is it real?"

"Well, hardly, darling."

I was relieved, which surprised me. Posy was disappointed. "Nicky! Why not?"

"Too good by half."

We were sitting in Nicky Bogue's private office. Downstairs, in the showroom window (extra-thick ultraviolet-shielding armor-plated glass), were two beautifully framed autographs, a letter from Dr. Johnson and a bar bill signed by Elvis. While we'd been waiting for Nicky, a sheikh had come in and spent ten thousand pounds. Either Nicky was dealing the hard stuff out the back door or he knew what he was doing.

"One of Frank Kellogg's." Nicky didn't bother to put the question mark in. "He could never resist. There'll be a real Mary Queen of Scots signature in the collection somewhere; I'll give you a description of it before you leave. Just a rent receipt, I'm afraid."

"Got it already," I said.

"Good. I'd hate it to go missing."

Nicky Bogue had very pale blue eyes, the eyes of a forgery-finder. He probably wasn't more than a few years older than I was, and handsome-faced in an English way, blond hair, slightly chapped lips. He ought to have been on a veldt with a hawk and a dog and a girl and an Asahi Super Dry. But he was barely five feet tall. Something had gone wrong with his back, even his tailored suit didn't quite hide it, and a silver-headed cane leaned against his desk.

"Frank wanted the glory of collecting," Nicky said. "Very important people collect manuscripts, they always have. It helps them to feel more important. Rather a voodoo thing, don't you think? They don't simply have a bit of paper with some words scrawled on it, they own a bit of Churchill or Abraham Lincoln."

"Or Elvis?" Posy said.

"There is a rather famous lead guitarist, you cannot even guess the name, who has a signature of Elvis mounted inside the case of his favorite guitar. It makes that guitar play better, he says. I don't ask, I merely sell. The clientele for manuscripts are pathetic people, in the Greek sense. They are not simply collecting paper and ink. They buy Elvis's mana, his immanence, the Elvis nature. Catholic, really. Relics. Saint George's fingerbone in Henry V's spear. Catholicism meets paganism, meets Elvis's bar bill, framed."

"And your point?" Posy said.

"My dear, here you have a major religious difficulty. Here is, let us momentarily hypothesize, a letter of Shakespeare." Nicky tented his fingers and touched his mouth. "William Shakespeare, greatest poet of the English language, he was not of an age but for all time, et cetera. There are no known Shakespeare letters. Two words on the will, 'by me,' and six signatures. *Possibly* a page and a half of *Sir Thomas More*. And now one has a letter, an autograph letter, signed, two sides. Containing major biographical revelations. What you have, my dear Posy, is the dream letter. If one could find only a single letter in the world, one would ask for this."

It was lying on Nicky's blotter, in a new clear protective envelope.

"But what does the letter say?" Nicky continued. "Oh dear. 'I am not Shakespeare. I am this Oxford bloke.' Material for a religious war, Pose my lovely. Oxfordians versus Stratfordians. Orthodoxy and heresy. Martyrs. Virgin sacrifice."

"Nicky, just don't be protective," Posy said.

"I shall protect you the only way I can, by making elaborately sure the letter isn't real."

"It might not be fake?" Posy said.

"I don't mean that," Nicky said. "I mean I shall spend quite a lot of your father's money proving it's not. Chemistry, philology, biography. Chemistry," Nicky Bogue held up one long finger. "Is the paper right? Is the ink right? Has it been improved with gum Arabic? Does it fluoresce blue under ultraviolet?—which means the forger's browned the ink with ammonium hydroxide or sodium hypochlorite and we can all go home." Posy shook her head impatiently. Nicky went on talking. Posy stood up and pointedly looked out the window; she wanted him to help her but she didn't want to listen.

The walls of Nicky's office were jammed with framed signatures, photographs, good stuff from what I could see. One whole section was Franklin Roosevelt. Nicky liked to collect bits of power himself.

"Philology," Nicky said. "Are the words of the right period? Are they words Shakespeare would use, and use at this period? Unfortunately Don Foster's SHAXICON database is going to be of very limited use as we've no other Shakespeare letter to compare with it. We're left with external evidence. Shakespeare's biography."

"Usually a forgery's short and general," I broke in. Nicky looked at me like the furniture had spoken. "This one's specific," I said. "Makes it easier to check facts. I checked the facts for this period on a new Shakespeare biography." I was taking particular care not to speak V'mont, but at the second *facts* I slipped up; it came out broad A, *faaa'cts*.

Nicky's vowels were so pure you could have tested metal with them.

"Right," Nicky said. "Convenient. If you don't mind, you, Mr. — Roper, is it? — will tramp round the B.L. for us and fact-check once we decipher the letter. I'll have one of my men doing it as well. I want to double-check everything here."

It wasn't the accent Nicky'd caught, or not just the accent; it was the difference between his suit and my jacket, the scars across the back of my knuckles. Nicky looked across his desk at me. He had to look a little up as well, tilt his head back into his crooked shoulders, but from his expression, he was looking down.

"I haven't tried ultraviolet," I said. "You better do that." Reminding him that, after all, he was taking money for doing this, just like I was. I should have been grown up enough not to play those games.

"And what do I do, Nicky darling?" Posy said. "While Joe is doing all the interesting work?"

"I'm sure you'll find Mr. Roper's work so interesting that you'll help him," Nicky said, and his mouth twisted a little.

I pitied the man and wanted to kick him, pretty much the same thing. The whole office, the business, all these signatures, beautifully framed, tasteful, things people wanted: bits of power. I thought of Franklin Roosevelt. Powerful, rich, loved—crippled man. I remembered Posy saying "Nicky adooores me" and wrinkling her nose.

"May I show you what I want you to do, and then I will tell you why." Nicky picked up the phone on his desk and punched in a number. "Bring in the Ogburn books, will you, John?"

His assistant brought in two thick identical books and handed them to Posy and me. I hefted it; had to weigh five pounds. *The Mysterious William Shakespeare*, by Charlton Ogburn.

"This is the standard biography purporting to prove Oxford is Shakespeare. Appalling stuff. Ogburn's facts, however, are largely reliable if you can separate fact from special pleading. I will send you the text of the letter and you'll double-check the facts, if you don't mind."

If you don't mind.

"May I ask how you would conduct your fact-checking?" he asked me.

"Start with whether there's any connection between Shakespeare and Fulke Greville. I don't recollect any, apart from their both living in Warwickshire."

"Fulke Greville's father was honorary recorder of Stratford when Shakespeare was a boy." Shit. Did we have that in the biography? No. There was no reason why it had any relevance to Shakespeare, but if Nicky knew it, I wanted to know it too. "I shall provide you with a transcript of the letter as soon as my man can make it out. Meanwhile you might read the Greville biographies in the B.L."

Shit. I should have known about Fulke Greville.

"We should explode this letter as quickly and if necessary as publicly as possible, in spite of your sentimental loyalty to your professor, Mr. Roper. Should I say why?"

"Apart from the fact that it'd totally rewrite English literary history, Nicky?"

"First, yes, completely rewrite literary history, Pose, darling, you don't realize nobody cares about literary history. Second, Mr. Roper did steal it from Northeastern." My stomach twitched; no, I hadn't, but I wasn't best pleased I'd taken it away without consulting Roy. "It's not as if you'd stolen it from Harvard, Pose, but it is the sort of thing they notice. Third," and he paused.

"Third," he said, and his voice turned a little sharp. "If this were a real letter, you'd have been criminally careless with it. You've been carrying it around in"—his long hand found the purple plastic envelope in the trash—"in this, in, let me guess, Pose, your purse? No more. It stays in my safe."

"Are you sure you don't think it's real, Nicky darling?" Posy asked sweetly.

"No chance," Nicky said, a faint line between his eyebrows. "Sorry, Pose my love. But Frank Kellogg. I'd say this letter was created in the 1920s or early '30s. Just the time the Oxford mania began. It reeks of gullible collector. As Frank immutably was. The man was attracted to dreck.

"It merely—gets my wind up." I knew what he was saying there. "I don't want my name to be associated with it. I care about *my* reputation." He opened his desk drawer and got out a sheet of paper and the kind of pen that nobody uses except in the movies. It looked like a silver cannon. He unscrewed the pen top and wrote. "I am describing what I am keeping in my safe," he said, "as a letter purporting to be by William Shakespeare, belonging to the library of Northeastern University, brought to me by Joseph Roper for authentication. Value, there's some value in forgeries, Tober used to collect them, shame he's dead. One could sell it to Delaware, I suppose, it's rather a good one. Five hundred pounds?"

"Nicky! Five hundred?"

"It's not real," Nicky said.

"Then why are you putting it in your safe, Nicky?" Posy pointed out.

" 'If a forgery. If real—' " Nicky shrugged, and his shoulders moved oddly under his tailored jacket. He laid his hand over the plastic protector of the letter, held it there a moment like a cold man feeling warmth, took it away.

"At auction," he said half to himself, "not that I'd bid, the bidding would start at between ten and twenty million. Perhaps ten times that. . . . Posy darling, I would not know what to write. I would not know how to put a price on it." He looked up. His eyes were brilliant blue. He was smiling. For a moment he looked as handsome as he wanted. *"Who chooses me must give and hazard all he has.* I wonder who would want it, at that price. There would be someone."

⌒

"So that's Nicky," Posy said explosively as we walked down the Strand. "I hate him. I just hate him."

"Between ten and twenty million," I said. "Fuckin' A."

"Don't you wish we'd stolen it when we had the chance?"

"Shit, no."

"I think Nicky thinks the letter's real. He just doesn't want to admit it."

I let that pass. For now I was free of the letter; it was Nicky's problem. I felt the weight of heroism slide off my shoulders.

And Nicky would need maybe a week to run all his tests, and Posy meant to stay until he was finished. My classes were covered, and until Nicky's man deciphered the letter and I needed to start checking facts, my time was my own. In London.

"Do you think Nicky would steal it? No. It'll be worth millions to him if it's real." Posy was counting her chickens. "You'll bring it back to Northeastern with Nicky's authentication, Northeastern will decide to sell it, Nicky will broker the sale and be famous forever and so will I be and so will you. No, if it's real he'll want everyone to know."

"Don't worry about that," I said.

"He just so thinks that if I were smart I'd adore him. His fingernails are too long." Posy shivered under her black lamb jacket. "G-d. Let's get coffee and something to eat."

"No," I said. If I was going to live off this girl for a week, I might as well live right. "They still serve food in pubs?" I had an agenda.

Posy grinned at me like she knew something I didn't. "You want to eat in a real English pub?"

The Rose and Crown was decorated in red-and-purple plaid. Over in the corner some fuchsia-haired guy in short pants and dog-stompers was playing Super Mario Brothers on a console; on the TV, which was up loud, guys were playing soccer and a crowd was screaming for blood. At the bar and the tables men were shoveling in lunch: slick-suited beef-faced Englishmen, raincoated smooth-faced Englishmen, turbaned men I supposed were Englishmen too. Everybody was smoking.

I read the chalked menu over the bar. "Steak and kidney pie," I said.

"You know what kidneys do, right?" said Posy.

Steak and kidney pie, I'd read about it for years, Dickens on a plate, a thick rich stew of *Christmas Carol* and Sherlock Holmes. It arrived: globs and hard bits in a greasy crust with a slice of carrot glaring out of the middle like an eviscerated eye. It tasted like carbonated Gravy Master.

Posy had ordered chicken biryani. She silently took my spoon, dipped it into her pile of spicy rice and chicken, and handed it back to me. "You don't have to suffer. Never eat anything British but breakfast and tea."

In Elizabethan times the rich folk ate beef, mutton, fish, oysters, venison, and birds of all sorts, including swan. They soaked up the gravy with manchets of white bread. They spiced everything, to give it more taste, and sugared everything to preserve it. I took a swallow of beer and worked a little longer on my mystery-meat pie. If I shook some sugar and cinnamon over it, I'd be eating like a rich Elizabethan. I shoved the whole mess aside and helped Posy with her biryani, and we filled in the corners with a second round of beer. Beer is Elizabethan.

"So what do you want to do now?" Posy asked when we'd finished. "Do we go back to Daddy's and read our big books like Nicky wants us?"

"I want to see the City."

"What are you, like the Energizer Bunny?"

"You've been here before, Posy," I said.

"As if I wanted to go home. You haven't even met Daddy's mistress yet. She and I so do not get along."

We walked eastward along the Strand toward the City, stopping every so often to check my map. "Look," Posy pointed. "Surrey Street, Norfolk Street, Howard Street. This must be where Norfolk House was." I looked up at street signs. Norfolk House had been the London seat of the Howards, the greatest and most treachery-ridden family in England. Two of Henry VIII's wives were Howards; so was the last Elizabethan duke. Henry Howard, Earl of Surrey, was the first English poet to write sonnets and blank verse. Most of them died beheaded. I looked up at an ordinary modern office building. *Brittle beauty*.

" 'Brittle beauty, that nature made so frail—' " Posy was quoting the same Surrey poem I was thinking of. We kept on together, " 'Whereof the gift is small and short the season.' " We smiled at each other.

We walked down from the Strand to the river, two city blocks of narrow streets. The Howards' private garden had been two city blocks long. It put those little pointed roofs on the map in perspective. Just along the river walk were the Temple gardens. On Mary Cat's map of Elizabethan London the gardens were long lawns knotted with groves of trees. In the new millennium, what we could see behind the Temple Gardens fence was a much smaller lawn and a new gravel parking lot.

But in the middle of the lawn, in a pool of astonishingly green grass, stood one huge surviving tree, vase-shaped, oak or elm, ancient and gnarled with galls, and behind it was a building with pointed roofs. Not red tile but blue slate, four pointed towers crowning a five-story cube of brick and white stone. It probably wasn't old. But for a moment, smelling the cool greenery off the lawn and the muddy tang of the river behind them, half salty, half chemical, I was as if I had just stepped off a waterman's boat at Temple Stairs. I saw Norfolk House, a nobleman's garden with its great trees. To one side, soldiers were practicing at an archery butt; I could hear the thump of an arrow hitting the bull's-eye. It wasn't quaint at all, the archery, the sword fighting. It was soldiers keeping in practice in the middle of London, because there was a war on.

Shakespeare wrote that the Wars of the Roses started in the Temple Gardens. Shakespeare had walked here; Shakespeare had seen this very piece of ground. I once read that in every breath you take is an atom of oxygen once breathed by Julius Caesar. I leaned my forehead against the fence, overcome, sighing like an Elizabethan melancholy gallant, breathing the air Shakespeare breathed.

"Do you want to stop for coffee? You're looking totally glazed."

"I was thinking," I said.

"We'll go up to Saint Paul's. There's a café inside."

We dodged across a complicated intersection. "Ludgate Circus," Posy said. Lud Gate. We were inside the vanished City walls. I smelled diesel fumes, cigarette smoke, urine from an alley, burning meat from a hole-in-the-wall selling shawarma: I smelled packed malodorous Elizabethan London, smoky fires, sheep and cattle driven through the streets, horses, and, still, urine and burning meat. In front of us loomed Saint Paul's Cathedral.

"What are you thinking?" Posy asked.

"This is Saint Paul's Churchyard," I said. "Right here. Where all the printers were."

In millennial London a kid on a skateboard was jumping the steps of Saint Paul's Churchyard, but through him I could see black-and-white half-timbered buildings with splashes of color over their doors, gaudy Elizabethan printers' signs creaking in the March wind. Andrew Wise at the Sign of the Angel. Thomas Heyes, the Green Dragon. Richard Field at the White Greyhound. Books lay open on shop counters like maps of new kingdoms. Some of the publishers sold from taverns. I could see a tavern: servants shoving each other and talking about girls; old soldiers with gunpowder-tattooed faces drinking and arguing; and in the corner by a tray of books, a guy making his pint last, listening to conversations, turning over pages, trying to stuff as much as he could into his brain or his notebook before he had to pay for more beer or leave. Bright's *Treatise of Melancholy*, Ovid's *Metamorphoses* and *Fasti*, North's *Plutarch's Lives*, Sir John Harington's English *Orlando Furioso*. A servant maybe or a young actor with a family in the country, reading like a starved man, in his lost years.

"Coffee," Posy said firmly and steered me into Saint Paul's.

In the coffee shop in the crypt, I spread out my map and anchored it with packets of Demerara sugar. Posy got us fancy coffee with cinnamon and whipped cream.

"Field lived right here," I said. "By the old Blackfriars monastery buildings." I set a packet of sugar on the place. "Shakespeare lived here in Bishopsgate, less than a mile away"—another packet of sugar—"and later he moved even closer"—I slid the packet. "Shakespeare didn't need William Cecil's library. He had Richard Field's."

"Wrong," Posy said. "He *could* have had Richard Field's." She picked up Shakespeare's sugar packet, tore it open, and dumped it into her coffee. "But that's like true of anybody? The City's so small, everyone could walk everywhere."

"Oxford lived way the heck over here," I said, pointing, "in Covent Garden, with Cecil."

"I'll bet he had a family house too," Posy said. She fingered the index of Ogburn's biography. "He did."

Fuckin' Earl of Oxford. "Where?"

"By London Stone. Which is—" She swept up a salt shaker, held it hovering like a chess queen, and thumped it down on the map just east of Saint Paul's.

"Right here," she said. "Where he could walk to the bookstores too. Want to see where he lived?"

The London Stone was on Cannon Street. We went by it three times before we saw it, an ordinary-looking boulder set into the wall of a bank.

"Salters' Hall Court," I read the street sign at the next corner, "to Oxford Court."

At the end of an alley we came out into a little courtyard and a scrap of raised garden. That was all. Not a stone survived of the Earl of Oxford's house. Around the garden the back windows of offices looked down on us. Time had taken its revenge on Shakespeare pretenders.

"What a great garden," Posy said. "Who would think of something like this in the middle of the City?"

Posy led the way into the garden and stood under a magnolia, a pink spreading canopy in full bloom. Underneath her feet, beside the gravel path, white flowers starred the grass, and the iron fence was edged with holly and old roses. There were benches; Posy sat down. For a moment, pink under the magnolia, she looked like a little girl.

"It must get heat from the buildings," I said. "Or the Tube." I could smell the Tube smell, sweet like Cracker Jack.

"But it's so pretty."

I sat down beside her on the bench in the garden.

"Oxford's house." She sighed contentedly. "Do you realize that we could be like sitting where Shakespeare lived? And nobody knows but us?"

"Nobody knows but you, Posy."

She looked at me like I was rain on Sunday. "You know," she said, "we could get rich. We could write a book about finding the letter. Give lectures. And that's just the beginning. The book. The movie from the book. I want," she thought, "Spielberg to direct the movie. Ben Affleck and Cate Blanchett to play us. I want to be published in forty-seven languages and sell millions and millions of copies worldwide. More than *Memoirs of a Geisha*. I want to be interviewed on Oprah *and* the Beeb. I want a house in London with a garden like this. What do you want?"

I wanted Dad's teeth fixed and his future looked after and money in the bank. Money to come to London. Money to research Shakespeare's life. I didn't say anything.

"Let's sit here and read for a while," Posy said. "I'm getting more coffee. You want some?"

She brought back coffee, "real English watery coffee." I yawned and drank it—I was finally losing steam—and looked up at the magnolia, and watched Posy read, and started reading too.

⌒

In 1920 a schoolteacher named J. Thomas Looney decided Shakespeare couldn't be Shakespeare. From reading the plays, Looney figured that Shakespeare sympathized with nobles, knew law and languages and so on, most of the things Posy mentioned, so he had to be noble himself. Then Looney more or less picked Oxford out of a hat.

Oxford's family came to England with William the Conqueror. The de Veres were hereditary Lords Great Chamberlain of England and had been Earls of Oxford since 1142. The only family black sheep, Robert de Vere, the ninth earl, was the homosexual lover of Richard II.

("He's not in Shakespeare's play," Posy said. "He would have been so perfect but Shakespeare left him out.")

The de Vere men were all soldiers, Ogburn said—handsome, athletic, courageous, finest chickens you ever saw. John de Vere was so brave he was stupid; he once killed a wild boar single-handed with a rapier. Wild pigs go two, three hundred pounds and their tusks are knives. It'd have been like trying to kill a bull with an icepick.

"*Two* of Edward de Vere's aunts married poets. John de Vere's sister married Henry Howard Earl of Surrey?" Posy turned the page down to mark it. "And John de Vere kept a company of actors? So even in his childhood Edward de Vere would have seen plays."

"Everybody in England saw plays."

"You know what I mean."

What Ogburn didn't say, but I knew, was that crazy, courageous John de Vere was doomed. Read Lawrence Stone. The de Veres were earls of the old medieval school, little tin kings upcountry. On paper John de Vere was a great man; he owned three hundred castles. In real life he was like a dairy farmer, rich in land, rich in cattle and servants, but at the mercy of the bank. The Tudors needed gold, not service, and they wanted no private armies they couldn't control. The Tudors went after men like the Oxfords.

Ogburn tells a story about King Henry VII, the first Tudor king. Henry Tudor came to visit the Oxfords' family seat, Castle Hedingham. The Earl (John de Vere's father or grandfather or something) lined up all his retainers and servants on either side of the road to do his king honor. Henry enjoyed the show, and then slapped him with a huge fine for having more retainers than an earl was entitled to.

John de Vere married twice. His first wife died young, leaving a daughter. For his second wife, he made an unusual choice, not an heiress, but—

"John de Vere's second wife was Marjorie Golding. Sister of Arthur Golding," Posy said triumphantly, standing up and doing a little dance on the garden path. "Arthur Golding, translator of Shakespeare's favorite, most-often-quoted book, Ovid's *Metamorphoses*. Arthur Golding, Oxford's tutor while Golding was translating the *Metamorphoses*. Arthur Golding, Oxford's *uncle*. Which, if Shakespeare was Oxford, totally explains why Shakespeare knew the *Metamorphoses* in *both* Latin and English. Give it up for Oxford."

"Everyone read Ovid," I said grumpily.

As if Posy would listen. She chalked a point in the air with a wet finger and dog-eared another page.

Edward de Vere, born in April 1550, spent his first twelve years at Castle Hedingham. He would have had tutors in Latin and Greek, oratory, astronomy, mathematics, and philosophy. He'd have learned to ride and hunt with dogs and hawks, to joust, and to fight in the old tournament way with great horse, broadsword, and armor, or in the modern army way with light armor, guns, and épée. He'd have been trained to sing and play instruments, dance, and translate poetry. He would have seen his father's servants acting, perhaps got training in dancing and speaking from them.

"Most of this'd be an actor's education too," I pointed out. Posy rolled her eyes.

Ogburn headed off into a long section about how William Shakespeare knew music and dancing and so forth, which was about as convincing as saying Doris Kearns Goodwin was Kevin Costner because they both knew baseball. I skipped a handful of pages and got back to the de Veres.

In August 1561, Queen Elizabeth visited Castle Hedingham and stayed three days. She was twenty-eight. Edward de Vere was eleven. He'd probably read romances, knights and fair ladies. Heck, being eleven is all it takes to get a crush. He would be Elizabeth's man all his life.

When Edward de Vere was twelve years old, his father died.

Oxford's mother remarried right off. ("The funeral baked meats / Did coldly furnish forth the marriage tables," Posy quoted from *Hamlet*. "And the new husband was like a total nobody named Tyrrell, the name of a murderer Shakespeare uses. 'A murderer and a villain, / A slave that is not twentieth part the tithe / Of your precedent lord—'")

("Yeah, yeah," I said.)

Sir William Cecil had just been named Master of the Court of Wards, guardian of all the fatherless nobles of England. The new twelve-year-old Earl of Oxford became William Cecil's first ward.

And that's the first time we actually see Edward de Vere, because somebody wrote down an eyewitness account of his arrival in London. He rode down the Strand toward Vere House in Oxford Court by the London Stone, at the head of one hundred and forty retainers. One hundred and forty men, all in mourning black, the most expensive and difficult dye, riding on one hundred and forty horses behind a twelve-year-old boy.

"Is that amazing or what?" Posy said.

I got up from the garden bench and walked back down the alley to Cannon Street. I could see them in the road: one hundred and forty horsemen all alike, three or four abreast, a double exposure over the taxis and the red buses.

Uniforms barely existed in Elizabethan England. Even in the army, men wore their own clothes and supplied their own armor. And Edward de Vere, twelve years old, had come to London with a retinue more than half the size of King Henry's private guard, larger than Elizabeth's escort when she'd entered London before her coronation.

I was willing to bet that he'd brought every retainer an earl's entitled to.

I could imagine the faces of the men, bearded and experienced and not letting on what they were thinking. The boy in the front, the boy who wasn't Shakespeare, was less clear. Full of pride and hurt and mourning, full of himself, and an asshole because of it. A kid whose dad had died so he was showing off, riding with older men, to say not who he was but what he wanted to be. In East Bradenton he would have got a tattoo, lied about his age, and joined the army.

Hubris. The great wheel. Edward de Vere was doomed, like his father. He was going to wave his money around, spend too much of it— But he was the Earl of Oxford, and whatever else he had, he'd always have that.

The very last man in the world who would write as another man.

In the afternoon I'd planned to go to the British Library and see the manuscript of *Sir Thomas More*, but Posy put her foot down. We went back to the Gould apartment, and I took one of Posy's pills and tried to get some sleep.

Melatonin or not, I was still too wired, and I started looking at Oxford's poetry in Ogburn.

Mistake. Ogburn said folks called Oxford a great poet, but he also quoted a couple of Oxford's surviving poems. Big mistake. Oxford couldn't write without needing to wipe himself afterward.

> *Framed in the front of forlorn hope, past all recovery,*
> *I stayless stand, t'abide the shock of shame and infamy. . . .*

Ka-*thump*, ka-*thump*, like a wet parka and a pair of sneakers rolling around in the dryer.

Shakespeare's poems are meant to be heard. Almost to be sung; a Shakespearean line glides on its vowels, makes a sweet shape in the mouth. Shakespeare enjambs his lines, running a phrase on from line to line. *Tomorrow and tomorrow and tomorrow Creeps in this petty pace from day to day To the last syllable of recorded time* . . . You don't want to stop reading Shakespeare's lines, you can't, the breath goes on and on.

Oxford was completely different. He knotted his lines together in the old-fashioned Anglo-Saxon way, with consonants. The Anglo-Saxons got away with it because their vowels were long and heavy and mouth-filling, like Shakespeare's. Oxford hadn't a notion what vowels were for. "Framed in the front of forlorn hope," I muttered. Ff-ffft-ff. Thufferin' thuccotash. You could barely spit it out.

So Oxford didn't have the skill or the style to write like Shakespeare.

He also didn't have the time. Shakespeare was born in 1564, came to London around 1587, published *Venus and Adonis* in 1593; by 1598 he'd probably written about sixteen plays. Dating Shakespeare's plays is a contentious business, and all we really have is Francis Meres's list and the dates of first performance or publication; but by the time Oxford died in 1604, Shakespeare probably still had about twelve plays to write, including *Lear*, *The Tempest*, *The Winter's Tale*, and the late collaborations with Fletcher.

Ogburn had a fancy-footwork explanation; all the plays had to be written much earlier. *Hamlet* had to date to 1589 or before. *Henry VIII*, which Henslowe called a new play in 1613, had to be written at least a decade earlier.

Hah.

I turned out the light and lay awake in the unfamiliar bed, wondering whether Posy was reading the same thing I was, and whether it was discouraging her any.

I slept right through until the next morning. Yup: Posy'd been reading the biography overnight too. Nope: she didn't see anything to discourage her.

"His sister accused him of being a bastard," Posy said.

We were eating breakfast. Nobody else was up yet and we had the egg-white omelets and the fruit to ourselves.

"Imagine he was," I said.

"I mean a real bastard. She said his father never married his mother. If she'd won the suit, Oxford would have lost his title and the money and everything and even his *name."* Posy opened her eyes wide. "Joe, his life is like so *Dickensian."*

"Don't you feel sorry for him."

"All those bastards in Shakespeare's plays," Posy said. "Shakespeare's so sensitive about his 'good name,' and Oxford wrote a poem about the loss of *his* good name—"

"Yeah, Posy, Oxford's sensitive poetry? I've read some of it."

" 'Framed in the front'? Your poetry would suck too if you were thirteen or whatever Oxford was when he wrote it."

"It was published in 1576, which made him twenty-six and old enough to know better—"

"Oh, good morning, darlings."

Posy slammed Ogburn shut, put it in her lap, and mouthed "Shut up" to me.

The woman in the doorway looked like Princess Diana, if Princess Diana had lived until fifty and worked real hard on the bulimia. She was about size minus two, you could have stood her in the yard for Halloween, and she was dressed way more than natural for this time of day. Black-and-white checked suit. Hat. Gloves.

"Hello." She smiled, showing lots of big scary teeth. "I'm Silvia, with two I's." I thought about making a joke about two eyes—Silvia was goggle-eyed, with an asphalt road of eyeliner on each lid—but I figured I better not. "And you are?" It was *who the fuck are you sitting at my breakfast table,* dressed up for company.

"Joe Roper. Friend of Posy's."

Posy nodded, silent for once.

"Oh yes, a friend from *Harvard."* Silvia said it like it was kindergarten.

"Um, no, ma'am, I'm from Northeastern."

"Oh." She made the one syllable last about fifteen minutes. Not

Harvard. I might as well have said, I'm the man here to piss on the rug. "Well. Charmed to meet you, I'm sure. You're staying with us?" She turned to Posy. "Darling, you're not dressed."

Posy was in a T-shirt and a long skirt. She looked great. "For what, Silvia?" Posy said, innocence with a sharpened edge.

"*Church,* darling!" She explained to me. "Ted and I always go to services at the Abbey. It's such a civilizing influence, don't you think?"

"Couldn't say, ma'am. This is my first time in London."

"You've never been to the *Abbey?*" Silvia shrieked charmingly. "Well, we must intro*duce* you. Fifteen minutes, Posy darling."

Silvia served herself a tablespoon of egg-white and three strawberries. Posy and I silently hefted our books and made tracks.

"Bitch," Posy muttered under her breath in the hall.

"That's the girlfriend?"

"Girlfriend," Posy whispered and broke into giggles. "She would kill you. She's Daddy's *mistress.* She actually introduces herself like that, 'I'm Ted's mistress,' she's so modern and forward-looking. Lady Saliva."

"Is she going to make you go to church?"

"You don't have to go to church."

"She going to bitch on you if we don't?"

"Like she won't if we do."

I had a notion Posy was Jewish. "You call it, Posy."

"Sure," Posy said dangerously. "Let's go."

Ted Gould and Silvia-with-two-I's showed up fifteen minutes later, dressed to impress. So did Posy; she wore a fluorescent orange top, a green skirt, and a red feather boa and she carried her big pink plastic purse. Her jewelry, nose ring included, was purple plastic. Inside her purse was a hefty lump that looked to be Ogburn. I saw what she was getting at, so in the taxi I did the whole V'mont act for Silvia, ayuh, couldn't a' been more V'mont if I'd brought the cows. I told Silvia I was looking fohward t'hearin' the choiah, I used t'be in the Univussity of V'mont choiah. . . . Ted Gould looked from me to Posy to his mistress. We were amusing him. I wondered again what family story I'd stepped into.

The choir was wonderful. I'd heard them on CDs, but in their space, where they'd sung for hundreds of years and knew the echo by its first name— They wore Elizabethan neck ruffs. Men and boys like these had sung for Elizabeth. In this church, they'd sung these anthems. I looked up to the vault, lost in the lace of stone, knots of gold, Tudor portcullises, and roses. The preacher had a voice like old diamonds; you could polish it on your sleeve and carry it in your pocket and admire how the light shone through the vowels. His vowels were like East Bradenton: *wuds of my mouth, meditation of my haht*. I felt at home. The morning light shone through the old stained glass, casting blue patches on Posy. Blue was about the only color she'd missed. She was a true church quilt, Posy was; Posy didn't do things by half.

After the service Ted Gould went off to a meeting, but Silvia was determined she'd show us round Westminster Abbey, as if Posy couldn't do it. Silvia dragged us round to the Coronation chair, the choir, the Tomb of the Unknown Warrior, the Royal Air Force Chapel. She showed us monuments. Dead people in marble, lifting their eyes to Heaven. Dead people on clouds. Dead people with only money enough for a tiny misspelled tile: *O rare Ben Johnson;* I could have cried. Shakespeare got no monument here until the eighteenth century, but it was here now, a full-size statue of him, the biggest thing in Poets' Corner.

"And these are my people," Silvia said finally, grandly, showing us into a side chapel like it was a decorator apartment.

Right across from us was an Elizabethan monument the size of a two-story house, looking as fresh as the day it was painted. On the tomb two red-gowned women lay side by side, their hands pressed together in prayer. One was old, one young, they both had the same big sharp nose: mother and daughter. Three girls in blue were kneeling behind them: daughter's surviving children, all daughters. No male heirs, bad news. Around them, covering the whole wall, was an enormous black-and-gold Latin epitaph long as a Baptist funeral.

"Mildred and her daughter the Countess," Silvia said, making introductions. She hadn't mentioned the family name. I figured I was expected to know it. "My branch of the family descends through a daughter in the eighteenth century, but one feels such a *connection.* Do you have anyone distinguished in your family, Mr. Roper?"

My grandmother could knot cherry stems with her tongue; that was the best I could think of. I tried to make out the Latin. Mildred and the Countess, yeah, but I couldn't find a clue of a family name.

"Who are the girls?" I asked to gain time.

Silvia frowned. "Lady Elizabeth, the eldest, married the Earl of Derby. Lady Bridget married a nobody. Whom did Lady Susan marry? — I cannot bring it to mind, one goes quite stupid as one grows older."

"You certainly come from a distinguished family, Lady Silvia," I said desperately, hoping for a hint.

"Oh yes," Silvia said, triumphing. "I have it. Susan de Vere married the Earl of Montgomery."

"De Vere?" *Shit,* I thought. Oxford? Elizabeth. Bridget. There they were, two girls in blue, kneeling. Two women who didn't marry a Mr. W. H.

"Appalling story. Their father was that horrible man, the seventeenth Earl. I think he's buried out in the suburbs," she said as if he was planted under a pile of tires in the puckerbrush and it was pure charity they hadn't left him at the dump. "The Cecils wouldn't have him near them after what he did to his wife."

⌒

"Who was Oxford's wife and what did he do to her?" I asked Posy.

Lady Silvia went off to recover from church with a martini, but Posy and I stayed at Saint Nicholas's Chapel.

"You read the Latin," Posy said. "I'll read what Ogburn says."

Oxford had married William Cecil's favorite daughter. William Cecil, Elizabeth's spymaster, Oxford's guardian. I worked out the epitaph on the back of today's order of service. The epitaph was written by Cecil himself, the first piece of his writing I'd seen. Cecil said the right things about his wife, the older woman on the monument, and then got down to his real business, his mistreated daughter Anne. Cecil let his hair down near to his toenails about Anne. She was his favorite daughter, and she was slandered and betrayed by her heartless roadkill pond-scum of a husband. And what's more—Cecil wasn't even warmed up—Oxford had left his three daughters as good as orphaned if it weren't for their grandfather and the Queen:

> Lady Elizabeth de Vere . . . is 14 years old and grieves
> bitterly and not without cause for the loss of her grand-
> mother and mother, but she feels happier because her

most gracious Majesty has taken her into service as a
Maid of Honor. . . . Lady Bridget is . . . hardly more than
four years old. . . . It is not true to say that she was left an
orphan seeing that her father is living and a most affec-
tionate grandfather acts as her painstaking guardian. . . .
Lady Susan . . . is beginning to recognize her most loving
grandfather, who has the care of all these children, so
that they may not be deprived of either a pious education
or a suitable upbringing.

Right here in church. William Cecil was washing his family
linen right in front of the congregation, splashing suds every
which way. And the monument was freshly gilded, too. You'd
think after four hundred years they'd let it fade. —I remembered twelve-year-old Edward de Vere riding into London to
conquer it, with his army of black-dyed homemade storm troop-
ers behind him. Sort of man who would make enemies. Well, he
had.

"Listen to this, Joe. Cecil set spies on his children and the
wards. He made them spy on each other. —Lady Silvia goes
through my underwear."

"They must have had no end of interesting times together, Cecil
and Oxford."

"Excuse me?"

A man was standing at Posy's elbow. Middle-aged man, wild
gray hair around a bald spot, big graying beard, American by the
sound of him, but he was wearing a choir robe—no, close to it
but not quite. He had a badge. Tour guide.

"Are you talking about William Cecil? Are you interested in
him?"

⌒

Don Cannon introduced himself. He was a bookseller when he wasn't volunteering as an Abbey guide. He had moved to London a couple of years ago to take care of his crazy American aunt, who had moved here because she believed in the Earl of Oxford. He wasn't an Oxfordian. "Eighty percent of the Oxfordians are insane and the rest are misguided," Don Cannon said while Posy and I looked at each other self-consciously. "But I sell mysteries on the Internet, and that whole thing's a good conspiracy."

Like Posy, Don Cannon was studying Cecil.

"William Cecil's an incredible character. As sly as his son Robert. I'm writing a biography of William. Conyers Read is completely inadequate." He shoved his fingers vehemently through his beard to show how wrong Conyers Read was.

"Are you *that* Don Cannon?" Posy had read an article by him.

An American tourist came by to ask where Queen Elizabeth and her husband were buried. Don Cannon pointed impatiently toward Elizabeth's tomb. "Her *husband,*" he told Posy. "You can't imagine what a pleasure it is to talk to someone who's even heard of Cecil, much less cares." He beamed at Posy. I figured Posy was affecting Don Cannon pretty much the way she'd hit me.

"What's wrong with Conyers Read?" Posy asked him.

"Good on the politics, don't get me wrong, but he makes Cecil an utter cipher. My theory is that Read discovered the kind of man Cecil was and decided he'd better not talk about it. You remember the story he tells about Cecil as a boy? Cecil and the ghost?"

"That's so *typical.*"

I had no idea what they were talking about.

"When William Cecil was a boy at school," Cannon told me, "he bet another boy one of his schoolbooks and lost. That night, the other kid was falling asleep and heard a ghost in his room. 'Ooooooh, you have to give back the booook, betting is *eee*vil, thiiink of your immortal soul,' and so the kid was terrified and gave the book back."

"The ghost was Cecil," Posy explained to me.

"Cecil was one of those men who has to be right," Cannon said. "And he loved money as much as he loved Elizabeth. So he kept putting his enemies in situations where they were crazily wrong and Cecil was right and rich. Take fish on Wednesdays as a very small example— No. Take Amy Robsart," Cannon said. "Alison Weir has to be right; Cecil had Amy Robsart murdered."

"Totally," Posy agreed.

"And if you understand Cecil murdering her," Cannon said, stroking his beard like a man warming up to a story, "understand how Cecil thought, you'll understand what he did to Oxford."

~⁀◦

I knew parts of the Amy Robsart story; Cannon told us the rest.

Amy Robsart was the wife of Robert Dudley, Earl of Leicester, Elizabeth's favorite and probably her lover. "Robin" Dudley and Elizabeth had known each other since they were eight. She let him visit when she was in bed, causing no end of gossip. When she created him Earl of Leicester she tickled him on the neck. By 1560, two years after she'd come to the throne, rumor had she wanted to marry him. But William Cecil wanted her to marry a foreign prince.

The only advantage Cecil had was Amy Robsart. As long as Amy Robsart was alive, Dudley couldn't marry Elizabeth.

"But you're saying Cecil murdered her?" I said. "Makes no sense."

"You don't understand William Cecil's mind."

A couple of tourists paused to listen, thinking we were talking about the women on the monument. "What do you want?" Cannon barked. They wanted to know where Shakespeare was buried. "Stratford," Cannon snarled and pointed them toward Poets' Corner.

"Let me lay it out like a mystery novel," he continued. "September 7, 1560, Elizabeth went out riding with Dudley. She came back and told the Spanish ambassador, de Quadra, she'd heard that Amy Robsart was dying, 'dead or nearly so.' De Quadra was trying to get Elizabeth engaged to Philip of Spain, so this worried him.

"The next day de Quadra visited Cecil to get the facts. Cecil was usually cautious and completely loyal to Elizabeth. On that day he seemed to act completely out of character. He told de Quadra he thought Elizabeth would marry Dudley, gave vague hints, said he wanted to resign over it but expected he'd be sent to the Tower. Then he was incredibly indiscreet."

Cannon paused to point a kid toward the Shakespeare monument.

"William Cecil," he said, "told the Spanish ambassador, *the Spanish ambassador,* that Queen Elizabeth and Dudley were plotting to poison Amy."

"He said this about the Queen?" I said.

"Yes, and Read utterly misrepresents it. De Quadra was so amazed he wrote down what Cecil had said: Elizabeth and Dudley 'had given out that Lady Dudley was ill but she was not ill at all, she was very well, and taking care not to be poisoned. God, he trusted, would never permit such a crime to be accomplished, or so wretched a conspiracy to prosper.' "

Incredible as it was, that sounded like Cecil on the monument.

"Read thinks that Cecil was sending a message to Elizabeth," Cannon said. "Which is ridiculous. But the point is that Amy did die, at almost the same moment Cecil talked to de Quadra."

Posy nodded.

"September 8 was a Sunday. Amy Dudley acted as if she were expecting an important visitor. She insisted her servants leave her house and spend the afternoon at a local fair. Forced them to go. Everyone agreed later that she was acting wholly out of character too. When they came back from the fair, they found her lying at the bottom of a flight of stairs, dead of a broken neck."

"So Agatha Christie!" Posy said.

"Now watch how Cecil worked. Cecil defended Dudley, publicly. At great length. Very publicly. Went to visit him. Made it clear that the Queen knew Dudley was innocent, but that anyone who really wanted to indict Elizabeth's favorite shouldn't feel the slightest hesitation."

"Oh, like right," Posy said. "So everyone thought Dudley had her murdered."

Now I got it. "And Dudley was screwed to the wall. He couldn't marry Elizabeth."

Cannon nodded. "If he'd tried, he would have been accused of murder—and Elizabeth with him."

This was sly, I thought. If this was true, it was really sly.

"Cecil was just one lucky politician. All his enemies were crazier than shithouse rats. Can you imagine Dudley trying to pull the Queen into a murder plot? Insane."

"And Elizabeth never married," Posy said soberly. "She never got the man she wanted. Dudley left her a pearl necklace and she wore it all her life. It's the big one in the late portraits."

She fingered her purple necklace.

"So then what happened with Cecil and Oxford?" I asked.

Cannon gestured up at the tomb. "You can see the tone of it right there. Cecil saved Elizabeth, so he got the mastership of the

Court of Wards as thanks. His first ward was Oxford. And before long Oxford started acting as crazy as a shithouse rat too."

On the tomb, the three little girls in blue stared down as if they were hearing their father's story for the first time.

Oxford got a good education at Cecil's house. From there he went to Cecil's old college, Saint John's, Cambridge, and to Gray's Inn, where he had special training in law.

"He studied law," Posy said contentedly.

He seemed headed for a brilliant career until, when he was seventeen, he killed a man.

"For no known reason," Cannon said. "Again, just like with Amy Dudley, nobody knows what happened. Again Cecil stepped up for the defense. Cecil got the charge reduced, got Oxford off, and made sure everyone at court knew every sordid detail."

The victim was Thomas Bricknell, an assistant cook in Cecil's household. According to the verdict, Bricknell "died as the result of his own crime" by running onto Oxford's sword. "Cecil says in a letter that he tried to have the jury find that Oxford acted *se defendendo*, in his own defense," Cannon said. "Which no one would believe. Attacked by a *pastry cook?*"

"Yeah." Everybody was going to say it all stank and Oxford was where the stink came from. I remembered Oxford's portrait, the dark pissed-off face and angry eyes, the twelve-year-old with his private army. You could believe Oxford spitted a servant with a sword. Whatever Oxford's problems had been, I didn't figure Cecil had caused all of them.

"To this day," Cannon said, "all the anti-Oxfordians point to that episode and say Oxford was out of control from the beginning. But the cook probably died accidentally. Some big brawl in the Cecil household, and 'Why came you between us? I was hurt under your arm.'"

"Shakespeare jokes about *se offendendo* in *Hamlet,*" Posy put in.

"Shakespeare obviously knew Cecil family gossip and was targeting Cecil in a way Elizabethans would have recognized. Polonius's name in the bad quarto is Corambis, 'divided heart'; Cecil's motto was 'Cor unum,' undivided heart. Hamlet calls Polonius a fishmonger; among other things, that's a reference to Cecil's Fast, an unpopular bill Cecil sponsored to support the fishing industry. Cecil set spies on his children and on Oxford; Polonius sets spies on his children and on Hamlet. Polonius's advice to his son is taken from Cecil's 'Certain Precepts,' written to *his* son Robert."

"And Oxford is Hamlet?" I said.

"Oxford could have been another Dudley. He was exactly the sort of young man Elizabeth liked. Talented in writing, if you believe the people who praised him. Talented in music. A patron of the arts. A soldier; he was in his first military campaign at nineteen. And an incredible athlete. Three-time jousting champion of England."

"Cecil wouldn't have trusted him," I guessed.

"Maybe he wasn't trustable. Elizabeth called him 'my Turk'," Cannon said. "Which could mean any one of several things, a pagan, a great soldier, a man successful in war and love. Or someone even she couldn't control. Anyway"—Cannon looked up at the monument to dead Anne Cecil—"Oxford was rich and had a good title. So Cecil forced Oxford into a political marriage with his daughter. And it all went incredibly wrong."

⁓

Oxford became engaged to Cecil's favorite daughter, Anne, in the summer when he was twenty-one. Anne was only fourteen.

"Juliet!" Posy murmured.

"Cecil says in a letter that it was Oxford's idea, which clearly isn't true. It may have been Elizabeth's idea. Oxford had money and social position; Cecil had money and street smarts. Oxford would settle down. Cecil could control him. And Cecil's grandson would be the Earl of Oxford."

"But Oxford so wanted to settle down with a fourteen-year-old," Posy guessed.

Cannon nodded. "Oxford didn't go along with the marriage at all. Cecil actually had Elizabeth come to his house one day to give the bride away, and Oxford didn't show. But then—"

"Excuse me," said a fat man, tugging at his sleeve, "who's the most famous person buried in the Abbey? Is it Shakespeare?"

Cannon got a weird look in his eye. "Sir Cloudesley Shovell, sir. Right that way." He pointed the fat man helpfully in the wrong direction and smoothed down his indignant beard.

"But then," Cannon went on, "Oxford committed high treason. Or—" He paused, looking at both of us. "Or Cecil said he did. And after that, Oxford had to do what Cecil wanted."

In 1571 Thomas Howard, Duke of Norfolk—the only duke in England, the highest-ranking noble—secretly agreed to marry Elizabeth's Catholic rival, Mary Queen of Scots. Norfolk thought this would provide a good English marriage for Mary and neutralize her. But William Cecil figured the combination of a Catholic queen and one of the treacherous Howards would drive Elizabeth from the throne. So Cecil had them both arrested. Mary Queen of Scots would be in prison for fourteen years. Thomas Howard was marked for death.

Oxford was Norfolk's first cousin: Thomas Howard was the son of Henry Howard, Earl of Surrey, whom Oxford's aunt had married. Norfolk was twelve years older. He was Oxford's hero. They had been friends all Oxford's life.

"Now," Cannon said, "watch Oxford begin to act crazy. Oxford tried to rescue Norfolk from the Tower. Or—and this is important—or Cecil said he did. Again, the same way as with Amy Dudley, we don't know quite what happened. According to a rumor at the time and a Privy Council minute three years later, Oxford bought a ship and offered a captain two thousand pounds to take Norfolk to Spain. The story may be true, but the bulk of the evidence comes from the Privy Council, which Cecil controlled."

"Cecil framed Oxford for treason?" I said.

"You have to remember," Cannon said, "Cecil always knew he was right. And he thought Oxford should marry Anne."

Cannon paused to give directions to a family that, for a wonder, didn't want to find Shakespeare; they were looking for the restrooms.

"Again, Oxford was in trouble, insane trouble. This time he could have been arrested for treason and beheaded. Again, Cecil came to the rescue."

"Cecil's just so always there when you need him," Posy said.

"And Oxford so clearly needed to be controlled. So Cecil staged a big wedding and Queen Elizabeth gave the bride away. A ward can't marry the daughter of a commoner so Elizabeth created Cecil Lord Burghley. Was this a trade for Oxford's life? Or a reason to ennoble Cecil?"

"And Norfolk died—"

Cannon tilted his head back and drew a line across his throat, below the beard. "The peers tried him in Westminster Hall. Oxford had to be there, voting. His father-in-law condemned his cousin to death for threatening his queen."

"And Oxford had to vote yes," Posy said. "Because he knew law. Because that's what the statute said. That's *awful.*"

"The prime part as far as Cecil was concerned?" Cannon said. "Norfolk was the only duke in England and there were no marquesses, so the earl with the oldest title was the highest-ranking nobleman in England. That was Oxford. Cecil had just dealt himself a trump card, if he could control Oxford."

"You're making Cecil into a real villain."

"No," Cannon said. "He was a moral man. A good man with a mission. There's nothing worse. —You should see something here," he said. "To understand Cecil. Come on."

He led us away from the school groups and tourists, down a narrow corridor, past more monuments, and up an ancient flight of stone stairs. He took out a key ring and unlocked the door at the top of the stairs.

"This," he said, "is Cecil's England. This is what Cecil thought he was fighting for."

It was another chapel, a locked chapel, raised up from the Abbey floor level. It was small and plain, very quiet, and very, very old. In the middle loomed a Moorish-looking block of stone, battered, with the marks of old decoration stripped away.

Don Cannon closed the door so no one else would come in.

"The tomb of Saint Edward the Confessor," he said in a low voice. "King Edward of England. Henry V is over there, at his feet." Henry V. Shakespeare's Prince Hal. "Can you feel what the kings were? What they are, here? This is what Elizabeth meant to Cecil."

"Like the Madonna," Posy half-whispered.

"Not 'like.' England had got rid of the Pope and the Church. What they had was Elizabeth."

We stood in front of the Confessor's tomb for a few minutes. Around us rose the upper parts of pillars; stone was springing up around us, delicately arching toward the fan vault. Like jets of water, and as evanescent as fountains in comparison with this rock. Three trefoiled Moorish arches were cut into the lower part of the Confessor's tomb, the height and width of a person crouching down, and the bottoms of the niches were scooped and smoothed from hundreds of years of people kneeling there. Butted up against the side of the block was an altar, but it looked like an afterthought. The altar was the rock itself.

Don Cannon opened the door again and led us out.

"For Cecil, Elizabeth was holy," Don Cannon said at the foot of the stairs. "Whoever she was, whatever she did, she was England. For her Cecil would commit crimes so large no one would believe they could exist. But he would do it out of reverence. That's what makes him so terrible."

At the end of the ancient corridor we saw exuberant light: Henry VII's chapel, a riot of carved seats and banners, of stone exploding upward into tracery as delicate as palm trees. Its altar was high and square too. A rock.

"Oxford is not just some totally random nobleman who's supposed to be Shakespeare," Posy said. "He's, what, Elizabeth's second cousin, and he may be Elizabeth's lover, and Cecil's son-in-law and Cecil's prize chess piece and the senior nobleman in England? This is like incredible stuff. Your aunt knows people who are Oxfordians? I really want to meet your aunt."

"You don't want to meet my aunt," Cannon said nervously.

"I *do*."

"They're having a meeting tonight," Cannon admitted. "But they're all crazy. I want you to know that."

"Where's the meeting?" said Posy, unstoppable.

"I do think it's possible Shakespeare *knew* Oxford," Cannon said, backpedaling. "The court wasn't that large, and Oxford was well known. Perhaps Oxford was even Shakespeare's patron at one point, though there's no record of it. Oxford was the patron of quite a few literary men. I think Shakespeare put at least one in-joke for Oxford in *Hamlet*. Would you like to see that?"

He took us round a final corner into another chapel, this one much darker and crowded with tombs. Cannon gestured at a tomb like a big, old-fashioned stone table. The table legs were four kneeling soldiers in Elizabethan armor. One of the soldiers was right up against a pillar, forever with his face to the wall, like an Oxfordian who couldn't see anything but his obsession. Underneath the table was stretched out an effigy of a soldier in veined marble, with his feet crossed and resting against a little boar.

"Horatio and Francisco," Don Cannon said. "Act I scene 1 of *Hamlet*."

It took me a moment to make out the names on the tomb: Horace de Vere. Francis de Vere.

"Oxford's other favorite cousins," Cannon said.

"So," said Posy, "where can we meet the Oxfordians?"

～

"Oxford's so like a puzzle piece that fits where Shakespeare doesn't fit," Posy said to me as we walked back toward Covent Garden. "I don't see why you don't see it."

Under a sapphire sky, Queen Elizabeth's standard was flying

over the roof of Buckingham Palace. The sun was out. Posy's purple earrings made dancing purple glints on the sidewalk.

"What Cannon was telling you is that Shakespeare looked at Oxford and saw *Hamlet*. You want Oxford to have written *Hamlet*. He couldn't have."

"It just makes so much sense to me, though. *Hamlet* is like Oxford's life coming out right. His mother loves him, she wishes she hadn't married the other man, he gets rid of the girl, he kills Polonius—"

"He dies?" I suggested.

"My mother," she said. "My mother is an economist at the Fed. She hangs around with Nobel Prize winners and university presidents. She is so totally serious and accomplished, and the last three times I went to see her in New York? She had to fly off somewhere else, every time. You've met Daddy. He hangs around with Steven Spielberg. He so wants me to be a producer. Like I'm expected to be rich and famous, on his terms?"

I was getting some of the story. Not Shakespeare's story, hers. "Uh-huh."

"Daddy so doesn't know about literature," she said. "Did you see his stupid book collection? He probably thinks David Selznick wrote *Gone with the Wind*. He reads about Shakespeare because he wants to understand what I do, but—I understand what it would be like to have to be Oxford if you wanted to be Shakespeare," she said. "I used to write like tons of stuff where I was tall and thin and blond and beautiful, and I always like wrote about things I know, skiing in Switzerland and premieres and stuff, and whenever I didn't know how to end it I'd kill myself off and have my parents cry total swimming pools of tears and read my stories and love them. William Shakespeare of Stratford would have written about *gloves*."

You're not Shakespeare, I thought.

There were beggars stationed at the edge of the park, and a guy in a ragged parka came up to rich American Posy, holding out a dirty hand. "Got the price of a cuppa, miss? Price of a cuppa?" She gave him money, smiling at him. "Oh, thank you, luv, thank you." The beggar actually closed his hands together flat over the coins, like he was praying. I caught his eye, and for a moment we gave each other the hairy eyeball. The beggar's eyes were blue and cynical. You know and I know this is all shit, the eyes said, but she can spare it and I have to look grateful, don't I? The beggar turned away, still thanking her.

"No," I said. "I don't think Oxford could be Shakespeare any more than you could." Oxford had money, Oxford had position, Oxford went to Harvard and his father-in-law knew Ronald Reagan. Everything that happened to Oxford had to be important. If he gave money to a beggar, the beggar had to ooze thanks. If he wrote a poem he had to be Shakespeare. "You're just too— You've got too much, Posy." I wasn't saying this well.

She stared at me, really hurt. "You don't have a right."

"Yeah, I do. I know things you'll never know about." The grocery store. When Dandee Foods closed. When the only fucking grocery store in East Bradenton closed, when I looked down Main Street one night and realized the only store with lights on was Dad's. "Shakespeare didn't have to be a genius," I said. "But he was in a lot of dark places, and I think they taught him to notice what was going on. Oxford never needed to look around him, watch where he stepped. If he got shit on his boots Cecil would wipe it off."

"And blame Oxford."

"Sure, but that didn't necessarily teach Oxford anything."

"You want to make everything into this big deep rich-against-poor thing," Posy said. "You don't want earls to be people, you don't want me to be a person, you don't want me to understand thing one, because I go to Harvard and Daddy makes movies. I really hate being just Daddy's daughter and nobody caring who I am. —I want to be noticed," Posy said. "I. Want. To be. *Noticed*. But not for Harvard. Not for Daddy. For who I am. For me. For Posy Gould."

I glanced at glimpses of orange and green under her black lamb jacket, purple sparklies at her ears, the pink purse.

"Posy," I said, "people notice you."

I didn't mean it for a compliment. Beauty, luck, riches make people oblivious. They have admirers and not relationships. Shakespeare probably never wanted to be noticed. But she took it as a compliment. After a moment she reached out and took my hand. Her fingernails were short, as if she somehow bit them under the polish.

"Shit," she said. "What are we fighting about?"

"Shakespeare," I said.

"Shakespeare."

⁓

Lady Silvia'd made it clear we should be at the apartment for Sunday dinner, so we weren't. We escaped to a half-deserted Italian restaurant on Shaftesbury Avenue, ordered ourselves spaghetti and what turned out to be a bad, bad red wine, and took turns reading passages from Ogburn aloud to each other.

Oxford didn't get on with his fifteen-year-old wife or with his new father-in-law. Cecil complained Oxford was a spendthrift (like everyone else at court, including Cecil). Oxford was bored and found himself a biker gang to join. In May 1573, "by the highway from Gravesend to Rochester," Oxford and three men

staged a mock robbery, firing on two former servants of his—
who ran and complained to Cecil.

"*Henry IV* part 1, act 2, scene 2?" Posy said. "Falstaff and three
of Prince Hal's friends rob some travelers at Gad's Hill? On
guess which highway? And Shakespeare says the robbery takes
place in May in the fourteenth year of Henry IV's reign. Henry
IV died before May of his fourteenth regnal year, but Elizabeth
didn't, and May of *her* fourteenth regnal year was May 1573."

"Shakespeare heard a story about Oxford acting out," I said.

"Shakespeare," Posy said, "was *nine years old* in 1573. I so win
on that one."

Oxford wanted to go on a Grand Tour, or to fight Spain in the
Low Countries. Elizabeth wanted to keep her pet knight in crimson velvet and engraved armor, mock-fighting in tournaments.
Oxford needed her permission to leave the country—all nobles
did—and she refused it.

So he committed treason again. (It was a sort of cruel fun
watching this guy bollix up his life, like watching a cat fight duct
tape.) Oxford left England without permission and went to Brus-
sels, where some of the noble Catholic exiles were living. This
time, though, he got away with it: he let himself be hauled home,
Elizabeth forgave him, and over Cecil's objections she let him go
abroad.

"You thought Shakespeare went to Italy, the Goscimers
thought he went to Italy, *Oxford* went to Italy, duh."

By March 1575 he'd just reached Paris and had been presented
to the king of France. Then Cecil, who didn't like letting his son-
in-law out of his sight, wrote and played his trump card. Anne
was pregnant. Oxford ought to come home.

But Oxford didn't.

. . . thereby to take an occasion to return I am off from that opinion; for now it hath pleased God to give me a son of my own (as I hope it is) methinks I have the better occasion to travel, sith whatsoever becometh of me I leave behind me one to supply my duty and service.

" 'No way am I coming home; I'm gone,' " Posy summarized with her mouth full of spaghetti.

Get someone to take over the hardware store, I thought silently. Or close it. Let me be. I need this.

"And he beat feet out of Paris before Cecil could collect him. He said he was going to Italy to try to see military service," Posy said. "But he didn't. He visited Padua. Genoa. Venice. He wasn't like doing the Famous Whores of Italy tour or the Big Battle-fields, this was Advanced Renaissance Culture. And he went where Shakespeare plays are set. Verona. Rome. Naples. *The Taming of the Shrew, The Merchant of Venice, Romeo and Juliet, Two Gentlemen of Verona, The Tempest,* the Roman histories?"

"Shakespeare set a play in Rome, Oxford went to Rome, there-fore Shakespeare is Oxford?" I made a gesture like balling up a piece of paper and throwing it away. "Nothing is better than God and peanut butter is better than nothing, but Posy? Peanut but-ter's not better than God."

Posy pointed around the restaurant. The walls were decorated with posters, the Leaning Tower of Pisa, the Blue Grotto, the Roman Coliseum. "Have you ever read like one of those really bad paperback romances where they have a scene in the Coliseum and you know the author got the details off the Internet? Shakespeare is so not like that. That whole swimming scene in *Julius Caesar?* 'Upon a raw and gusty day, The troubled Tiber chafing with her

shores'? You have just got to find some way to get to Italy in winter and look at the Tiber, because that is *totally right.*"

The University of Vermont choir, where I sang, went to Italy in
March my senior year. I remembered a day by the Tiber, looking
at gnarled yellow water gnawing bridge pilings. You'd have to be
crazy to swim in the Tiber in winter, which is the point of the
scene in *Julius Caesar.*

"Maybe Shakespeare went to Italy," I said. "I don't have trouble with that, he had seven years to do it in. But I'd have to prove
it before I could say it. And 'Shakespeare went to Italy, Oxford
went to Italy, so Shakespeare is Oxford,' shit no."

"We don't say Shakespeare is Oxford," Posy said, "the letter
says that."

"The letter—" Oh, forget it.

Meanwhile, back to Oxford and the Cecils: Deserted and at
her father's house, Anne Cecil had her baby, a girl, the Elizabeth
de Vere who would be engaged to Southampton. According to
what we'd seen on Anne Cecil's tomb—according to Cecil's evidence—Elizabeth de Vere was born on the second of July 1575,
nine months after the last time Oxford had slept with Anne. But
Oxford heard about the birth only in late September, and Elizabeth was baptized only in September, which had to have raised a
few questions in his mind.

It did in everybody else's.

He didn't come home until the next spring, and as he got close
to England, in Paris in April, he started hearing gossip about his
wife.

"Again, all sorts of Shakespearean parallels." Posy ticked off
points on green glittery fingernails. "One, Oxford rushes back to
England and gets attacked by pirates in the English Channel.

They let him go but take his baggage. The same thing happens in *Hamlet* for no reason at all.

"Two, when he gets home, it's a scene right out of Shakespeare," Posy said. "How many plays did Shakespeare write about women who may have cheated and the man's in agony because he doesn't know? *Othello, Antony and Cleopatra, The Winter's Tale,* hello—"

"Cheating women are an old story."

"People write about things that *disturb* them. —Oh wow," Posy said. "I have such an idea."

I bet she did.

"This is even better than Cecil murdering Amy Robsart. Who's sick of his son-in-law?" She spread her hands.

"Cecil," I said. "And I can't blame him."

Posy waved a hand dismissively. "Who was Oxford's guardian when Oxford's sister accused Oxford of being a bastard? Cecil. Who loved his daughter, who was married to this horrible man? Who knew how Oxford would react if someone told him Elizabeth wasn't his child and the whole court was talking about it?"

"Oh, come on, Posy."

"Who like totally did it *again?* I think Cecil *did.* I don't know Cecil killed Amy Robsart, and I don't know he framed his own daughter for adultery, but if he did one, why not the other? Oxford believes the baby isn't his for some secret reason that he hints at in his letters to Cecil. I'll bet," Posy said, "somebody brought Oxford one of Anne's handkerchiefs that some other man had been wiping his forehead with. Just like *Othello.*"

I shook my head wordlessly.

"And Cecil spread it all around the court. Haven't we heard this before? Cecil completely wins. Again. He has his favorite daughter back home. Everyone thinks Oxford is a total shit. Again. Anne loses," Posy said, "but who cares about Anne, she's just the girl."

"Forget producing movies," I said, "you ought to write 'em."

Posy unexpectedly gave me a big sweet smile, as if I'd complimented her.

"Oxford wins too," she said. "Sort of? He's got rid of his wife, who he thinks cheated on him. He isn't poor, yet. He's only twenty-five. He goes off and starts collecting writers for friends.

"And then," said Posy, "I wonder what Oxford does. Don't you wonder what he does?"

"You think he starts writing Shakespeare. In the 1570s." Twenty years too early.

"I *so* do."

~

The Blue Boar Society met at a big Victorian hotel in Russell Square. The corridor outside the meeting room looked like a minor-league version of a Modern Language Association meeting. Folding tables with fliers, pamphlets, books for sale. I'd figured the Oxford crowd would be snobby effete types, sucking up to earls, but the Oxfordians had the look of weekend farmers at a cattle auction. The ones in front of the table were looking carefully at the books, checking hooves and teeth, trying to separate out the decent milk and meat and the cow good for another calf or so. The good stock wouldn't come up in a sale like this, these were auctions for folks who just liked the look of a cow in a field, but nobody was running down anybody else's stock. Might want to sell a cow of your own someday.

Most of them were men, and the women in the audience ran to blue rinses and sensible shoes. As Posy shrugged off her jacket and showed off her glittery thin-strapped blouse, guys' jaws dropped all over the corridor like transmissions falling out of cars.

Don Cannon was standing by one of the tables, talking to an old lady almost as colorful as Posy. Cannon grinned all over his face and came forward to take Posy's arm.

"Let me introduce you round. This is Miss Posy Gould, from *Harvard*."

She might as well have been the Earl of Oxford himself. Everyone not stuck behind a table crowded around her.

I was left with the woman Cannon had been talking to. Hair dyed bright yellow-red, salmon-pink dotted pants suit, orange scarf, and, behind thick 1950s cat's-eye glasses, slightly crossed eyes the color of cataracts: this had to be Don Cannon's crazy auntie, who'd moved from upper New York State to study Oxford on his home ground.

"I'm Betty Lou Cannon. This is *my* book. *Edward de Vere's Literary Career.*" She beamed and thrust a thin pamphlet at me. "Only five pounds! All proceeds go to the Shakespeare Oxford Society Endowment Fund! To establish the library and conference center!"

Who was it said, "Thank you for your book, I will waste no time in reading it"? I wished I had the nerve. "Yes, ma'am."

She was watching me like a cat watching a sardine. I moved a little away from her, opening the pamphlet for politeness' sake.

Aunt Betty Lou thought Shakespeare and Arthur Golding weren't the only guys whose works Edward de Vere wrote. No, after he left his wife, Oxford had written Gascoigne's *An Hundred Sundrie Flowers of English Poesy,* Lyly's *Euphues* and its sequels. . . . Aunt Betty Lou had him writing everything but "Columbia, the Gem of the Ocean."

And, still in the 1570s, he'd started writing Shakespeare.

All the plays Shakespeare adapted for the stage—why, Oxford wrote them. The *Ur-Hamlet. The Famous Victories of Henry the Fifth.* Aunt Betty Lou was a horrible example of the kind of creative redating the Oxfordians had to do, the same redating Posy was threatening to start on. Aunt Betty Lou had hauled Anthony Munday's *Sir Thomas More* all the way back to 1580 or so, and of course Oxford had written it all, not just the scene in Shakespeare's handwriting.

I looked up to see whether Aunt Betty Lou was still watching me. She was peering at the clock instead. "Bill Boyle and I are just about to talk about Elizabeth, Oxford, Southampton, and *The Glass of a Sinful Soul!*" she confided like she was inviting me to get baptized. "Bill has such revelations! Come listen. You can finish reading later."

Thankfully I managed to slip the pamphlet back onto the pile.

Everybody was settling down in the conference room on little uncomfortable chairs. Posy was in front, surrounded by big attentive Oxfordian men. She looked a little overwhelmed. Aunt Betty Lou fluttered up to the front of the room. She sat down behind the conference table next to a pleasant-looking middle-aged man and a young dark-haired man with thick eyebrows and a professionally cheerful expression. I took a seat in back, near the door.

"Good evening," said the young man, moving to the podium like he talked in front of an audience every day. "You all know who I am, I think. For the courageous young lady from Harvard in our midst tonight, I'm Henry de Vere, Earl of Bulbeck. My ancestor was William Shakespeare."

Everybody else applauded. *Shit.* That was who the guy looked like. Henry de Vere had the same mouth as Oxford, the mobile pursed lips of a man who talks easily, and the same snooty eyebrows.

"Tonight we have with us, also from America, a figure"—he said *figger*—"familiar to many of you. Mr. William Boyle is the well-known editor of the *Shakespeare Oxford Newsletter*, a member of the board of our American sister society, and a stalwart defender of our Cause. Bill is delivering a paper by Charles Boyle on a provocative new topic, Queen Elizabeth I's translation of Marguerite de Navarre's *Miroirs* and its relevance to the always vexed question of the Earl of Southampton's paternity. Miss Betty Lou Cannon has asked to comment—"

Aunt Betty Lou was gathering notes round her like an endangered bird building a nest. She beamed through her glasses at Bill Boyle, who stood up with a sheaf of pages and began to read.

"When Elizabeth I was just eleven years old, she made an English translation of Marguerite of Navarre's *Mirrors*..."

Elizabeth's *Glass of a Sinful Soul*, Boyle said, was about free love and spiritual incest. The audience perked right up at incest. I listened with half an ear, but around me folks were taking careful notes, just as if this was scholarship.

It made them feel important, I guessed. Even the Earl. *I am Shakespeare's descendant.* The Cause. The endowment fund. They had themselves a crusade—

"Elizabeth's young life was immersed in issues of incest, and in particular the politics of incest—" Boyle was going into a whole snarl of secret relationships. Southampton was the love child of Elizabeth and Oxford. Elizabeth and Oxford were half-brother and -sister, Oxford was really King Henry's bastard—Betty Lou jumped up to object, scarves fluttering agitatedly in all directions. No, Boyle had got it all wrong! Oxford and Elizabeth were secretly *married!* That's why Oxford signed himself king of England (he what?)—

"This is complete rot!" A frog-faced man, a professor-looking type, popped up like toast in the audience. "You lot shouldn't be allowed to read books! You are ignorant, stupid people motivated by snobbery!"

"Sit down," said the earl.

"Shakespeare was a great intelligence! Oxford was a frightful lightweight! Shakespeare was interested in the girls! Oxford was a roaring homo!"

"Sit *down*, sir!"

"Anne Vavasour was not the Dark Lady—"

"—was too—"

"—incest—"

"—conspiracy—"

"—you're out of order—"

"—it's a *metaphor*—"

"—*down*, Dr. Frowst—"

"—*Edward de Vere's Literary*—"

"—nonsense!"

This was fun, but I was ready to leave. Posy was stuck in front. There's some advantage to not going to Harvard. I faded out for a Guinness.

When I came back from the bar, they were still chasing Shakespeares in the conference room, so I stayed outside and cruised the books on the tables. Secondhand editions of the plays, a paperback *Cult of Elizabeth*, Alison Weir's biography, Bindoff's *Tudor England. A Hawk from a Handsaw: A Student's Guide to the Authoring Debate*, by Rollin de Vere. *"Shakespeare" Identified in Edward de Vere, Seventeenth Earl of Oxford*, by Thomas Looney.

Letters and Poems of Edward, Earl of Oxford. A thin paperback. I picked that one up.

"May I help you with anything?"

There was one woman still at a table, making sure the books didn't walk.

"Book?" the woman said. "Aspirin? Glass of wine?" She reached down toward the floor and set a fair-sized green bottle on her table. "You've been to the bar already, but after Betty Lou two drinks are much better than one. Here, sit." She patted the chair at the table next to her, filled a plastic glass brimful with white wine, and handed it to me. "Hello. I'm Katherine Darnell."

She was about sixty, big and vigorous and pink-cheeked, with crimped white hair and intelligent blue eyes. There was a big pin on her lapel, looked like it was made by a child. She wore reading glasses on a chain. I would have bet money she was a librarian, a teacher, something like that. Even if she was retired, I figured she still volunteered somewhere a couple days a week. She was a hefty lady, would have made two or three of Rachel Goscimer, but it was Rachel Goscimer I thought of. Darnell? I knew the name from somewhere. Maybe she ran something for the Oxfordians.

"Not a bad book really," Katherine Darnell said. "And I'm rather flattered you picked it up. Don't worry, though, I shan't make you buy it."

I blushed. There on the cover of *Letters and Poems of Edward, Earl of Oxford* was the name of the editor. Katherine Darnell.

"Have a look-through, though, if you like." Katherine Darnell wasn't an anxious author. She turned placidly back to the thick book she was reading. Like Rachel Goscimer, she read with a stack of index cards, scribbling as she turned pages.

I paged through the poems—more of the same sneakers in the

same dryer, ka-*thump*—and looked at the letters. Oxford's letters weren't any more promising than his poetry. There were barely seventy pages of personal letters, and many of them were about obscure court business, addressed to his brother-in-law Robert Cecil. "Again I know and well perceive how this escheat of Danvers shall be made a great matter to cross my good hap and to obscure the rest of the lands. . . ."

"So," I asked, "you believe in Oxford?"

"No, no, not at all," Miss Darnell said. "I'm a complete agnostic. I like a good fact, though, and the old edition needed updating."

Well, here was a fellow soul. "I helped to fact-check *In Search of Shakespeare*," I offered.

Katherine Darnell beamed and showed me the book she was reading.

"Well," I said, flattered.

"Splendid book," she said.

"Good people who wrote it," I said. "Not me, I mean."

She raised her glass. "To good writers. And good people who fact-checked it, I believe. I haven't found a single error."

I thought of Fulke Greville's father. "There's some stuff we should have put in, though." We sat in friendly silence for a bit, sipping the wine.

"So," she said. "Why are you involved in the Glorious Cause?"

"I'm just here with Posy. The good-looker from Harvard. How'd you get involved with doing an edition?"

"The Cannons live down the road from me. I like Don, and he and I both like a mystery. I do think your biography's splendid, but you haven't talked about my favorite Holmesian incident in Shakespeare's life. The poet who doesn't bark in the night-time."

"Bark?"

Her bright blue eyes gleamed. "A chance to sow agnosticism! Dear Mr. —"

"Roper. Joe Roper."

"Mr. Roper. I promise I shall not try to make you believe in spiritual incest and Oxford as rightful king of England. But I do believe poor Miss Cannon may be on to something when she talks about Oxford beginning to write in the 1570s."

"Gascoigne's *An Hundred Sundrie Flowers?*" I said.

Katherine Darnell picked up her edition and turned to the poems in the back. "Twenty-six of them." She riffled the pages with her thumb. "I honestly don't know what Oxford wrote, but I think he must have written more than this. So many people called him an accomplished poet and a playwright, it can't all have been flattery. Since I retired, I've started looking at the manuscript collections in the B.L. I hope to get through them by 2010 at the latest."

That was scholarly dedication; shame she was working on Oxford.

"I don't think I'll find much," she said surprisingly. "I think he began writing plays quite early, and one doesn't find many play manuscripts."

This was as good an excuse as any for not finding poetry. Katherine Darnell could call herself an agnostic, but she was leaning to Oxford's side.

"The dating's crucial, of course," she said. "Oxford had to begin writing the plays much earlier than they're traditionally supposed to have been written, perhaps as early as the 1570s. Otherwise the later plays were written after he died. But one can make that case."

"You can?" I said neutrally.

"Only circumstantially, but yes. The year after Oxford

returned to England, 1577, we hear of a play, *The History of Error,* performed at court, the first of a number of plays with titles similar to Shakespearean plays. For example, February 1580, *The History of Portia and Demorantes,* which might be *The History of Portia and the Merchant,* that is, *The Merchant of Venice.* Our Glorious Cause argues that Oxford began to write early versions in the late 1570s and early 1580s, when we know Oxford was patron to two companies of players."

I'd heard all of this but the companies of players. "I thought he had money troubles."

"Terrible money troubles, selling estates all the time, but he gave his name to a men's company and a boys'."

I knew men, divorced and poor from the child support, living in an old beat-up double-wide, but they had a good truck, a good hunting rifle, and a couple of eager-nosed dogs. All right: Oxford liked plays.

"There's internal evidence that some of the plays began, at least, to be composed very early. Quite small things," Katherine Darnell said. *"Love's Labour's Lost,* an early play, satirizes John Lyly's Euphuism. You Shakespeareans date it around 1594." I nodded. "But the height of Euphuism was in the late 1570s and early 1580s. In the same play Shakespeare refers to 'Monarcho,' one of Queen Elizabeth's fools. Monarcho retired around 1575 and was dead by 1580, when Thomas Churchyard wrote an epitaph for him."

Monarcho I hadn't heard of. "Uh-huh," I said neutrally.

"And the star in *Hamlet,*" Katherine Darnell said.

"The 'star that's westward from the pole'? What about it?"

"Have you seen the article on it? It was in an American astronomy magazine about a year ago."

I shook my head. A year ago had been just when Rachel

Goscimer went into the hospital; I hadn't been reading astronomy magazines.

"Shakespeare's exact about his astronomy," Katherine Darnell said. I nodded. "From the description in *Hamlet*, three professors in Texas worked out that the star must have been in Cassiopeia and visible after midnight in late fall. There is no bright star in Cassiopeia now, but in Shakespeare's time there was one. A nova, visible for about a year."

She rooted around in a suitcase-sized handbag and brought out a set of clipped Xerox pages. She settled her reading glasses on her nose.

" 'To the Elizabethan observer'," she read, " 'the new star was not only a memorable sight but an event with disturbing religious and philosophical implications. . . . fixed stars had been regarded as unchanging celestial symbols of security and order . . . the unprecedented new star shook people's confidence.' In *Hamlet* Shakespeare uses not only the star itself but astronomical imagery implying disorder. Eyes 'like stars start from their spheres.' The 'brave o'erhanging firmament' seems to Hamlet 'but a foul and pestilent congregation of vapours.' "

Right. "His use of *retrograde*."

"Exactly. Tycho Brahe discovered the star, and Shakespeare refers to Tycho several times in the play. The location of the play, Elsinore, is just by Tycho's observatory at Uraniborg; Rosencrantz and Guildenstern are names of Tycho's relatives, and the names appear in a famous portrait of Tycho. Shakespeare probably saw the portrait, either the engraved version or a copy owned by Thomas Digges, the astronomer."

Thomas Digges was the father of Leonard Digges, who contributed a preface to the First Folio. That was interesting. "Here's

a real event Shakespeare was thinking about when he was working on *Hamlet*."

"Precisely!" Katherine Darnell smiled at me.

"What year? Too early for when we think *Hamlet* was written?"

She nodded. "That's it. The traditional dating of *Hamlet* has him
writing it all in a rush around 1599–1601. But the star appeared
much earlier, and I'd suggest he started thinking about *Hamlet* in
connection with reading Tycho's description. He worked the star
into the play so thoroughly that he didn't want to take it out, even
though the play probably wasn't finished until much later."

The big question in dating *Hamlet* is whether the *Hamlet*
referred to in 1589 could be Shakespeare's *Hamlet*. Oxfordians
wanted the early dating. "I'll give you it feels like he was already
reading astronomy before he saw the star."

"Precisely. Feeling isn't evidence, but I feel the same way.
Shakespeare had an interest in astronomy, he'd read in Aristotle
that the stars were fixed, and now here was a new star! So, Mr.
Roper, when do you think the nova occurred?"

During those years in his early twenties, reading at Richard
Field's shop. During the lost years. "After 1584, '85. How about I
guess 1587." That still gave her the 1589 *Hamlet*.

"It was 1572," she said.

"What?"

"November 1572."

"Let me see that."

She handed me the article. It gave a perfectly good case for
Shakespeare. Digges wrote about the nova in a book that went
through seven editions, the last in 1605. The Tycho Brahe portrait was reproduced in Digges' book. Holinshed and Camden
described it too. It was famous.

"This doesn't prove anything about the date of *Hamlet*."

"Not for Shakespeare," Katherine Darnell said. "But in 1572 Oxford was twenty-two and studying astronomy. His father-in-law consulted Thomas Digges about what the star might mean, Elizabeth was so perturbed by it. I do think the date would fit Oxford well."

I shook my head, not convinced. "Is that your dog in the night-time?"

"Not yet. More wine?"

I still had a half glass. "No, thanks. Just tell me."

"Perhaps my pet dog won't impress you." She helped herself to wine. "Let us consider an aspiring Elizabethan literary man," she said. "Call him Will Stephens. Stephens comes up to London from Noplace-upon-Avon. He's not got a penny, of course. He has no library unless he knows a bookseller or a great man."

"Richard Field," I said.

"Yes, Richard Field. Our Mr. Stephens reads at Richard Field's shop when he's not holding horses or being a barman. And when he begins to make a success of himself, what does he do? He writes a poem, doesn't he, praising Richard Field as a great man and a patron of poets."

I went through college on a patchwork of scholarships. I'd written quite a few thank-yous in my time. "He publishes his poems with Richard Field," I said.

"Certainly, and Field makes a nice profit. But our Mr. Stephens never thinks of doing what so many other poets did. He never writes a poem to thank Field, or any of his literary friends."

"He thanks Southampton."

"Southampton was no literary man. —The fact is we have rather a lot of Elizabethan thank-you poems," she said. "Even if they weren't published, the families always kept copies. Put them on the top shelf in the library, or the muniment room, and kept them because they were dedicated to Granddad. When the family turned the library into a billiard room, they shipped the lot over to the Bodleian or the B.L., and there they still are. Shakespeare should have written some thank-you poems from before he was famous, and we should still have them."

"I have a theory about him," I said. "Not thank-you poems, bad poems. He must have written some mediocre stuff when he started out. Parts of plays, and poems, like before he becomes a carpenter a man has to have made bad boxes in shop." I'd been looking for them in the Kellogg, and had been disappointed that Frank Kellogg had collected mostly letters and not poetry. "I want to find a bad box."

"A bad box, I like that. Have you found anything?"

"Not a thing."

"Let me send you the list of manuscripts I've checked. —I haven't found a single possibility either. So far the dog doesn't bark. The poet is silent. Will Stephens, who writes so movingly about friendship, doesn't thank his friends."

"And Oxford does?" I said.

"My dear man! Poems from him and to him. Dedications. Thirty-three books were dedicated to him. John Lyly, Anthony Munday, Angel Day—and of course Oxford wrote dedications himself, as well as paying for publications. You should look up his prefatory letter to Bedingfield's *Cardanus Comfort*. No, better, I shall read it to you."

She pushed her reading glasses up on her nose and found the place in her book. "Bedingfield sent his translation to Oxford privately," she said, "and Oxford had it published, and said why:

for in your lifetime I shall erect you such a monument
that . . . you shall see how noble a shadow of your virtuous
.life shall hereafter remain when you are dead and gone.

Shakespeare said, 'You shall not be/The grave of your deserving.' "

"So did a lot of other writers," I objected. "You're sounding like you believe in Oxford."

"Oh no," Katherine Darnell said. "I really don't. Because one shouldn't depend on belief. I do, I very deeply do, believe in Shakespeare, the man who wrote the plays, who is the only important person in this story. And I believe in Shakespeare's audience. I believe that even just after his death, when the traditional view is that no one particularly cared about the plays, someone knew how important he was, someone cared deeply. I believe that if there is a secret about the authorship, someone wrote it down, someone referred to it, someone left a record. And I believe that for four hundred years, whenever someone has found that record, he's kept it, because it's about Shakespeare. Somewhere, on a top shelf, in a box, in a dusty pile of papers—"

"Heminge and Condell," I said. "Heminge and Condell were the ones who believed in him and they collected the plays for the First Folio. I'm glad you're doing the work, but all you have is bits and pieces that don't mean anything."

"Yes," she said, "I'm prejudiced, I suppose."

Yes, she was; but I didn't hold it against her.

"It's a bad thing in a scholar. So are the Stratfordians— I try to keep an open mind, when I see Oxfordian evidence— That's no excuse. It motivates me, I suppose, to think I might find something new and fine. Do you know how William Blake's manuscripts were saved?"

I didn't.

"One thinks everyone always has known about such an enormous genius as Blake, but he wasn't popular at all in his lifetime. He was just one of those funny little men whom artists take up. After his death, his wife, who deeply believed in him, packed up his manuscripts in a trunk and gave them to the British Museum. There they sat for years. British Museum guards aren't very well paid, and one of them came across the trunk and said, 'Right, here's this lot, never be missed,' and sold it out the back door of the British Museum with Blake's papers still inside. Do you know who bought that trunk?" she asks. "Dante Gabriel Rossetti, possibly the one man in London who could know what Blake was about. That was miraculous. —I shall tell you what I believe. I believe God is a librarian. I believe that literature is holy, Mr. Roper, it is that best part of our souls that we break off and give each other, and God has a special dispensation for it, angels to guard its making and its preservation."

She took off her reading glasses and made almost a bow with them.

"If it is important to know who wrote Shakespeare's plays, if it is important to find lost plays or poetry by Oxford, I believe there will be a record, and by some miracle someone will find it. Perhaps— I am sixty-eight with a good pension. My mother lived to ninety-five. I reckon I may have twenty years to go hunting." She laughed at herself, pink-cheeked, and lifted her glass. "I am really nothing but a tiddly old lady with delusions of grandeur, and I talk too much. I do not really believe in Oxford. He would be too—different from any Shakespeare one can imagine. But I do believe the hunt is worthwhile."

The doors of the meeting room banged open, interrupting us. The square-faced man shot out first, followed by a whole group of people waving Xeroxed papers at each other. Aunt Betty Lou was talking up her pet theory to Posy. Posy looked worn out.

"Oh dear, here they come. Mr. Roper," Katherine Darnell said, "I am going to give you a present." I protested, but she wrote in a copy of *Letters and Poems of Edward, Earl of Oxford* and handed it to me. "Thank you for listening," she said.

Angels and ministers of grace defend us, she had written. "Thank you. Hope you find something, Miss Darnell."

"I shall send you my list. And if *you* should ever find anything—the slightest thing—anything odd—and most especially if you should ever find something *wonderful,* I should dearly like to know. Oh, take this too." She handed me a copy of the astronomy article, gave me one last smile and a handshake, and turned back to selling copies of her book.

"Let's go," Posy said.

We escaped and waited outside the hotel for a taxi. "That was totally embarrassing," Posy said.

"Yeah," I said.

"They've never read *anybody.* They haven't studied *anything.* You actually bought a book?"

"I talked with the editor a while," I said. "She gave it to me."

"G-d, no *wonder,* she couldn't sell it. Unbelievable. They're like UFO freaks. Taxi!" She waved one down. "They are such fucking *idiots!*"

I sat back in the taxi, looked at Katherine Darnell's edition and the astronomy offprint, and thought about Hamlet's star.

That night, alone in Ted Gould's garden room, I read the offprint again.

The star appeared in November 1572. Tycho Brahe saw it on the sixth of November, but whether England was under a weeks-long cloud cover then or what, Holinshed gave a different date for the first sighting in England, "the eighteenth of November in the morning."

The astronomy people didn't know this date was important, but it was. "The eighteenth of November in the morning" was after midnight of Accession Day, November 17, the anniversary of Elizabeth's coming to the throne.

It was the beginning of Elizabeth's fourteenth regnal year. She was thirty-nine, getting old for marriage and heirs. The previous year, the Pope had excommunicated her and put a price on her head. And a new star was rising glaring in the sky. She was so disturbed by it that she sent Cecil to consult astrologers.

Oxford was twenty-two then, Elizabeth's pet tournament knight. He would have seen Elizabeth pacing up and down, still in her party clothes from the Accession Day fireworks, wringing her long fingers, demanding Cecil tell her why her stars were changing.

The times are out of joint.

In 1572 Shakespeare was eight years old. When he was thirty-six or so, around 1600, he went back and created *Hamlet*, and for some reason one of the pervasive metaphors in the play was a star that he saw in 1572.

Of course Shakespeare could have remembered the star. It must have impressed him. It impressed other people. But the date would have fit Oxford well, Katherine Darnell had said. Yes. She and I had both thought Shakespeare was already reading astronomy when he saw it.

I read the article a third time, and took my glasses off and fiddled with them, and stared blurrily at the daffodils under the Gro-Lites, and finally, frustrated, I dabbed one finger at my closed lips and drew a small, a very small, a dry and tentative point in the air.

⟶

Monday morning Posy and I printed out a copy of *Sir Thomas More* from the Internet and went, at last, to the British Library to look at Shakespeare's one possible manuscript.

The new British Library was up on Euston Road. Outside it looked like a giant Chinese restaurant, brick with red-and-green trim and a sort-of-Thinker statue where the gilded dragon ought to have been. Inside, it was a handsome place with a huge central hall, vistas and staircases and bookshops. Dominating it, in the place of honor right by the stairway, stood a big marble statue of Shakespeare.

Posy had a library card already. I presented my credentials as Goscimer's researcher and got mine. I took the card out into the big central hall, sat down on a sculpture like a bronze book, and just cradled my library card in my hands a moment. The British Library.

There are books in the British Library that don't exist anywhere else in the world. "Thank you," I said to Posy.

"Come *on*," Posy said, rolling her eyes.

Sir Thomas More was in the Ritblat Gallery, where the British Library was having a millennial exhibit of its treasures. The gallery was a low, dark maze, separated into areas by illuminated engraved glass. Science. Politics. Literature. Science meant Szilard and Einstein's letter to Franklin Roosevelt about the atom bomb. Politics meant the Magna Carta. I wandered around with my mouth open. Even Posy, who'd been here before, didn't say anything.

Shakespeare had a case to himself. In the center of it was the manuscript of *Sir Thomas More*. Posy and I leaned over the glass, and through faint reflections of ourselves we squinted at what might be Shakespeare's handwriting.

The manuscript of *Sir Thomas More* was beat to shreds. It was written on long thin paper burned brown with time, half eaten away. The ink from the back had wicked through to the front. Words were crossed out and interlined in teeny-tiny handwriting. There were blots. There were scribbles and score marks all up and down the page.

"Does this look like the same handwriting as the letter?" Posy whispered.

No one's even sure it's Shakespeare's handwriting on the manuscript. In Shakespeare's day any number of playwrights would work on one play, like scriptwriters do now. The principal text of *More* was written by Anthony Munday (yeah, the Anthony Munday who spied for Cecil and wrote *The English Romayne Life*). He probably wrote it before 1590. Several other poets revised it, and one, Hand D, could have been Shakespeare. What Posy and I were looking at, through the thick glass of the case in the Ritblat Gallery, was the material written by Hand D.

Hand D was quick, flowing, steady. Surreptitiously Posy fished a Xerox of the letter out of her purse and we compared the handwritings. The trembling in the letter could have been the difference between a young man's handwriting and an old one's. Or between Shakespeare's and a forger's. The letters were shaped more or less the same.

"Well?" said Posy.

"This is why we need Nicky," I said finally.

Posy tucked the Xerox away and pulled the *Thomas More* printout

out of her purse. We looked between the printout and the hand-writing, making out the big famous speech Shakespeare was supposed to have given More.

For to the king God hath his office lent
Of dread, of justice, power and command,
Hath bid him rule, and willed you to obey;
                                          . . . What do you then
Rising gainst him that God himself installs
But rise against God? What do you to your souls
In doing this? O, desperate as you are
Wash your foul minds with tears and those same hands
That you like rebels lift against the peace
Lift up for peace, and your unreverent knees
Make them your feet to kneel and be forgiven . . .

"Is that totally Shakespeare or what?"

"The knees and the feet, that's pretty bad. 'Souls' is a tad religious for Shakespeare. Could be Shakespeare though."

Shakespeare talks about the power of a king. Shakespeare enjambs phrases, running the sense on from line to line. *Not all the water in the rough rude sea Can wash the balm off from an anointed king.* Shakespeare's lines glide on long vowels like these. Shakespeare does the same violent zigzags between abstract and specific, *wash your foul minds with tears.* Shakespeare repeats words, turning the sense around. *Lift against the peace/Lift up for peace.* Shakespeare always uses the word *unreverent*, not *irreverent.* Could well be Shakespeare.

"This manuscript doesn't feel right, though?" said Posy. She pointed at the page in the case. "It doesn't feel like manuscript?

You know, when you look at Dickens's manuscripts or whatever, how he's like always intertweaking and scribbling stuff on the margin and you can practically see the ideas growing? This looks like a copy. There are like just a couple of changes."

I knew what she meant. "Shakespeare never rewrote, though. Jonson said so."

"I don't know," Posy said. "Nicky would be like, it hasn't got the Shakespeare nature?"

"Harvard ought to throw you out the door if you can't do better than that."

"O fucking K then, *be* uptight, I'm just trying to say how I feel. What do you want to do, then, since we don't have anything from Nicky?"

"Fulke Greville's biography." I was still burned that Nicky knew about Fulke Greville's father and I didn't.

"Oh, come on, you can read that anywhere."

But this was the British Library. "Posy, I just want to hang around here for a while."

"It's London outside," Posy coaxed. "You're just trying to get ahead of Nicky."

Sure. "You read Ogburn," I said, "I'll do Fulke Greville and Hand D."

"Until lunch," Posy said, "and then we go to the Tower?"

"Why the Tower?"

"A guy from one of Daddy's movies is in town doing a demonstration. I was going to surprise you. He's talking about jousting, it's pretty cool. —Joe. It's London. Take like a breath?"

I guessed she was right. "Fine. Okay."

"Okay." She handed me the printout of *Sir Thomas More*. "I'm going to read in the café. I'll meet you in the lobby at one?"

The catalog was out in the front hall, on the big landing halfway up the stairs. Readers in jeans and mufflers were clicking away at the online catalog. I drifted, mesmerized, toward an unused terminal.

A soothing businesslike screen, grey-blue, grey-yellow, SEARCH. Simple search or advanced? ADVANCED. I'd seen the B.L. catalog before; it was on the Web. You could search on any combination of title, subject, author, date, even publisher, up to six of them.

For millions of books you needed a search engine that fine.

I tried SUBJECT, Sir Thomas More, AND SUBJECT, Shakespeare, and got seventeen titles. Seventeen titles. On one aspect of one play.

"How do you get books?" I asked the girl at the next terminal.

The Humanities 1 Reading Room was the most elegant library I'd ever been in: low-ceilinged, full dim indirect light, with rows of big solid desks and wide comfortable chairs in blond wood. I made a note of my seat number and went over to the order terminal to start requesting books.

SUBJECT SHAKESPEARE AND SIR THOMAS MORE. *Shakespeare and Sir Thomas More. The Shakspere Signatures and "Sir Thomas More." Shakespeare's Hand in the Play of Sir Thomas More, with the Text of the Ill May Day Scenes*. I'd read some of these, but I'd take another look at them. SHAKESPEARE AND HANDWRITING. *Shakspere's Unquestioned Autographs and "the Addition" to "Sir Thomas More." Shakespeare's Handwriting: A Study. Problems in Shakespeare's Penmanship*. I ordered them all.

While I was waiting for them, I tackled *Sir Thomas More*, which I'd never read.

Act I. Scene 1. London. A street . . .

Munday was no genius and *Sir Thomas More* wasn't a good play.

It started with some standard Elizabethan clowns pushing and shoving each other. "Compel me, ye dog's face!" The verse was plodding iambic pentameter with a rhyme now and then, way below Shakespeare's level:

To save my life, it is a good adventure:
Silence there, ho! Now doth the Justice enter.

But *More* wasn't all Munday. As Sir Thomas More entered, a breath of good verse blew across the page—a bit, I guessed, that Shakespeare might have written.

'Tis strange that from his princely clemency,
So well a tempered mercy and a grace
To all the aliens in this fruitful land,
That this high-tempered insolence should spring.

Lame verse again as the clowns decided to rebel:

Force now must make our peace, or else we fall;
'Twill soon be known we are the principal.

But then things started going weird.

I had never seriously read about *Sir Thomas More,* but I thought I knew Shakespeare had written only the Ill May Day scene in the early part of the play. As I read past that, the "Shakespearean" verse didn't stop.

Now I can perceive it was not fit
That private men should carve out their redress

Which way they list . . .
What though I be a woman? that's no matter;
I do owe God a death.

This was Munday? We owe God a death, says Feeble in *Henry IV,* part 1. It's one of Shakespeare's most admired puns. If it was Munday, Munday was good enough that Shakespeare stole from him.

I took a moment away from *Sir Thomas More,* looked up Munday in the B.L. catalog, and put in requests for a couple of his plays.

There were almost two separate poets here. Bad Verse didn't like Thomas More and was trying to turn him into a clown. Good Verse was making him a hero. Good Verse seemed to be writing Surrey's lines as well as More's:

In hope his highness' clemency and mercy,
Which in the arms of mild and meek compassion
Would rather clip you, as the loving nurse
Oft doth the wayward infant, than to leave you
To the sharp rod of justice . . .

Hand D must have finished his work on the manuscript by now, but the voice kept on right to the end, that second poet who could write in the same sweet fluid way.

. . . France now hath her full strength,
As having new recovered the pale blood
Which war sluiced forth . . .
Swords should decide the difference, and our blood
In private tears lament his entertainment.

Shit, this was familiar. Blood as water, blood as tears. It was a metaphor Shakespeare used all the time. It was the sort of thing that made people think Hand D was Shakespeare.

Great men are still musicians, else the world lies;
They learn low strains after the notes that rise.

"Else the world lies" was rhyme filler; but the rest—

I leaned back in my chair and stared at those two lines. It's harder to come down from a high note than rise to it, that's what the poet was saying. True; I knew it from singing in the choir. But whoever wrote this had made singing a metaphor, packed the meaning so tight it fit into two lines even with the filler. Great men always have to come off their greatness like a singer off a high note, harder than they climbed. Giving up takes more grace than getting.

That was a lot to fit into a line and a half.

Shakespearean is a word. But there was more Shakespearean poetry in *More* than Hand D had written.

"Earth to Joe?"

I looked up, blinking. Posy was a blur of black and yellow, like a bee. "I haven't even got my books yet, Posy."

"I knew it," she said. "From like the total absence of books on your desk? Come get lunch, they'll be at the order desk when you get back."

We ate lunch in the library café. "You can work till two, then we have to see the guy at the Tower, I phoned Daddy we would. Daddy's inviting some people to dinner. Silvia," Posy smiled cattishly, "Silvia won't be there. I think they had a fight, I hope I hope I hope."

"You ever read *Sir Thomas More?*" I asked.

Posy shook her head. "Ogburn thinks it's all Oxford's," she said.

"It's not all anybody's," I said. "It reads to me like two guys wrote most of it between them. Ever read any Anthony Munday?"

"Just *The English Romayne Life.*"

"Good writer?"

Posy shrugged.

Munday could write lyrics, I'd read some, but lyric poets weren't spare on the ground in Elizabethan times. What there weren't, until Marlowe and Shakespeare, were fine dramatic poets, people who could make recognizable human speech into great poetry and great characters. The second poet of *More* was a dramatic poet. I left half my sandwich and went back to find out about Munday.

The manuscript of *Sir Thomas More,* I read, was written by six different people. Munday wrote the fair copy. The other handwritings were Hand D, the playwrights Dekker and Chettle, and two unidentified other guys, one of whom was probably only a copyist. Dekker and Chettle I knew about; you couldn't mistake them for Shakespeare, not even Chettle on a good day. But Munday? Could Munday have written More and Surrey's other speeches?

Munday's best play was supposed to be *John a Kent and John a Cumber.* I went hunting in it for that second voice, the voice like Shakespeare.

It took me an hour because eventually I was looking on every page. *John x 2* had clowns, and jokes, and men dressing up as other men, all the uninteresting stuff in *Sir Thomas More.* There was a play scene, like in *More.* There was most of a nice lyric. But here was the best speech:

When twice two hours the daughters of the night
Have driven their ebon chariot through the air,
And with their dusky wings breathed calmy rest
Upon the eyelids of each living thing,
The silver shining horned lamp doth rise,
By whose clear light we may discern the path,
Wherein, though lamely now I seem to plod,
Yet will I guide ye safely to the spring
And for your coming at the back gate wait.

That just wasn't good enough. "Back gate wait." *Ack retch retch,* a cat harfing hairballs. And what was Munday saying? "Four hours after dark when everyone's asleep, I'll lead you to the spring by the light of the moon." It was pretty words, not poetry, it wasn't that breathless fine compression like "Great men are still musicians."

The rest was just fucking awful.

Can you, my Lord, and you, and you, and you,
Go to the venison for your suppers drest,
And afterward go lay ye down to rest? . . .
Why then, I pray ye, be content to go
And frolic cheerily, for it shall be so.

Could the same man have written that and More's speeches? Or Surrey's speeches, or even the clown's verse? No. You could bet your entire pink ass the same man who wrote this had written *To save my life, it is a good adventure: Silence there, ho! Now doth the Justice enter.* And thought it was good.

"Two o'clock," Posy said.

"I need to look at something first. Can you order me up more Munday?"

"If it's for tomorrow," Posy said. "What do you want?"

"Everything. Start with the plays."

While she went off to the order terminal, I read why Munday was supposed to be the author of *More*. It wasn't because the play sounded like Munday, but because from time to time, while he was transcribing the text, Munday had made author's changes to it.

> That Munday was the author of part of what he was transcribing can be proved by the occurrence of certain passages in which the text was obviously altered *currente calamo* . . .

"Currente calamo" means while he was writing it down; which meant that Munday was the author of at least part of what was in his handwriting.

Except it fucking didn't read as though he'd written it all, did it?

> . . . *currente calamo*. The theory that those corrections might have been dictated to him by an author standing at his side may be dismissed as grossly improbable.

I looked at that sentence. I read it two times, and three times, and I knew I'd found what I'd been looking for.

I could see them. Two men in a room, one at a table copying rough draft, the other standing looking over his shoulder: Tony Munday and his friend Bill from Ass-end-on-Avon, two young writers whacking out a play. Tony'd done the clowns and Bill had written most of More and Surrey. Now Munday was making a fair copy, patching it all together, and Shakespeare was reading over his shoulder, kibitzing, saying "Let's have it go this way."

It wasn't just a thesis, it was a good one. Maybe somebody had said it before, but I didn't think so. I had in front of me most of what'd been written about *More*, and everyone who'd written about *More* had been mesmerized by the handwriting; they thought Shakespeare had to have written *only* what's in Hand D.

No, I thought. No.

Writing this thesis would mean learning about stylistics, taking a good long look at exactly what was in whose handwriting, looking at Dekker and Chettle's contributions, I could do that, I couldn't get too excited about it, not yet, not yet, I had to talk to Goscimer—

It would mean learning a heck of a lot about Munday, because if Munday and Shakespeare collaborated on this play—

I had more than a thesis.

If Munday and Shakespeare collaborated on this play, they had to have done it together; it was written like that. And if they were in the same room together at the same time, with Shakespeare looking over Munday's shoulder making corrections while Munday wrote—

Munday knew Shakespeare.

Anthony Munday knew William Shakespeare.

I knew for sure no one had ever suggested that.

I had something that could start me on my path to writing Shakespeare's life.

I leaned back in my chair, staring at the book lying open on the blue-gray leather-covered desk in front of me. Anthony Munday knew William Shakespeare. Anthony Munday and Will Shakespeare sat in a room together writing a play.

I'll find out whispered through my head.

"How much Munday did you find?" I asked Posy.

"A ton. They're on your card for tomorrow. You're looking smug. What?"

"Tell you when I know more. I've got to read Munday." Did Munday say anything about Shakespeare? Did he write anything down? Someone knew how important he was, Katherine Darnell had said. Someone cared deeply. Someone left a record. If Munday was Shakespeare's writing buddy, did Munday talk about him? Or write about him?

"So we're going to the Tower? Finally?"

"Sure," I said. "Let's have fun."

We will be famous, Posy had told me. We might at that.

But not from Oxford.

The Tower of London was terrific. Anything would have been terrific that day, but it still was. The ravens, huge, sleek, mad-eyed, stalked around like feathered velociraptors. Posy and I craned our necks up at the massive Tower walls. Oxford tried to rescue Norfolk out of here? Insane.

We saw Sir Thomas More's cell. It was misty, cold, but it wasn't the cold that kept me shivering; it was sheer nerves, wondering at my luck. *Sir Thomas More.*

Posy led me to the Tower Armory, a big dim building with hollow steel men standing all around. One steel man wasn't hollow: he had his helmet up, talking to an audience of schoolkids.

"Knights in shining armor, fair ladies' favors, King Arthur's round table?" the knight was saying. He was a big young blond guy who looked like he did his jousting in Malibu. "No way, dudes. Jousting is fullbacks on horseback."

The English kids looked questions at each other. They had no idea what fullbacks were.

"These guys were major athletes." The knight passed around an armored glove so the kids could feel the weight. I hefted it too; just the one glove weighed more than *The Mysterious William Shakespeare*. "This armor I have on weighs about a hundred twenty pounds, plus the padding. When I fight in a tournament, it takes two guys a couple of hours to bolt me into my armor. Knights gotta have muscles like Superman."

I was impressed. I'd played freshman football at UV, and hockey of course, and bitched about ten or fifteen pounds of padding. The knight flexed his muscles in the armor, which creaked and clanged. All the little English boys goggled. They were deciding to be knights.

"After I have my armor on, I get winched onto my horse, which is like one of those Budweiser horse dudes? The horse has got armor on too."

The knight clumped over toward a long glass case in the middle of the Armory. The schoolkids followed him like ducklings, and so did Posy and I.

"This is the kind of lance I carry in tournaments." The Tower Armory has the only surviving example of an Elizabethan tourney lance. The knight stood a good respectful distance from the case. "In the movies, we carry balsa-wood lances with spaghetti inside them, to look like splinters when the lance breaks. This is a real lance. I would guess fourteen, sixteen feet long, weight depends on the wood, maybe thirty-five pounds. It's hollowed out and fluted to cut down the weight. These lances are meant to break and splinter, and they're very, very dangerous."

The schoolkids' eyes got wide and they smiled.

"In a tourney," the knight said, "my horse and I are on one end of this field, the tiltyard, and there's another knight at the other end. We gallop at each other and try to ram each other off our horses with our lances. We aim for the head," the knight said, "because that gets us the most points."

Guys whacking at each other's heads with giant railroad ties that were going to explode into splinters on contact? Fuckin' A. Cecil was right. Oxford was crazy.

"Do knights ever die?" a kid with glasses asked.

"You can get hurt, if your horse falls on you or you get dragged. Not in the movies," the knight added quickly for the kids' sake. "Our armor is thicker than Elizabethan, not so brittle. But a guy could get real badly hurt if a splinter went through his eye slit."

"Dead," a kid with a froggy voice supplied. "Fookin' dead is what you'd be, mister."

"What's the worst thing that ever happened to you?" a girl asked.

"We were filming in the summer and I was wearing black armor? Got so hot they had to hose me down between takes. When the water hit that armor, it steamed."

"And jousting is a good idea why?" Posy asked the Malibu knight.

"Hi, Pose!" said the knight. "Well, it's a great way to impress girls." He sidled toward her hopefully. His armor creaked.

Jousting. Like fighting a three-hundred-pound wild boar with a ten-ounce rapier.

"The knights could give a speech before the tournament," the knight went on to the kids. "Here I am, I'm about to risk my life?

I get a chance before the tournament to stand up and tell the audience why I'm there, what I'm fighting for. Like I can say, 'King, you ought to fight France,' or 'Drink Coca-Cola,' or whatever? That's my moment. This is why you got to learn to write in school. So you can write your own speeches."

"It's a pageant," Posy said to me. "Almost like a play? I was reading about one of Oxford's tournaments. He wrote a famous speech for one of them, the Knight of the Tree of the Sun speech."

Never heard of it.

" 'Ow much does it cost to be a knight?" a little black kid squeaked up.

"Big money, dude."

" 'Ow tall d'you 'ave to be?"

Tournament armor was expensive. And it wasn't just the armor. It was the horse, the devices and mottos, the painted shield, the herald's speech, everything that went into the entertainment. William Cecil didn't fight. He ran the government while the nobles farted around, hitting each other with two-by-fours to impress Elizabeth.

Posy and I wandered out onto Tower Green. A chain fence, like the chain around an old-fashioned cemetery plot, showed where the headsman's block had stood. A marker gave the names of people beheaded here: Posy touched the name of Oxford's cousin, the Duke of Norfolk. It began to rain, heavy dark spatters on the concrete like ghosts of blood.

We went inside the Beauchamp Tower and up the stairs to a kind of parlor for noble prisoners. Posy found the signature of one of the Mary Queen of Scots conspirators scratched into the wall; I found Robert Dudley's ragged staff and IANE, Jane,

Lady Jane Grey. Across the mantelpiece someone had carved ARUNDEL foot-high, a signature made by a man with the rest of his life to do it in and no other way to say he was still alive. Arundel was a Howard family title; this must have been another Howard in trouble. From the windows we could see the headsman's block on Tower Green.

I wondered where Thomas Howard had been held. Here, where he could look out at the scaffold? The Tower walls were high and thick and heavily guarded. Did Oxford really try to jailbreak his cousin out of here? What could Oxford have done? A tournament knight in crimson velvet, spurring his horse toward the walls of the Tower, armed only with a breakable lance and a speech?

Before dinner I checked *Letters and Poems of Edward, Earl of Oxford* to see whether the tournament speech was in it. No. There was nothing about the tournament in Ogburn either. People seemed to have missed this, which made me more curious about it.

It was a minor thing beside Munday and Shakespeare.

⁓

The guests Ted Gould had invited for dinner were Don Cannon and his aunt. When I came upstairs, Ted Gould was showing Cannon his library of movie books. Don Cannon's eyes were so wide tears were just about running down his cheeks. Aunt Betty Lou was all dressed up in a long pink dress and a rhinestone necklace with the gold coming off. Gould's glass-and-steel Los Angeles decor turned the two of them into a joke, Cannon with his wild hair and beard, Aunt Betty Lou in her Fat Old Barbie getup. I was wearing my good jacket and best blue shirt, but I didn't feel all that well dressed myself. Posy hadn't come down yet.

Ted Gould served us all drinks. Aunt Betty Lou ordered "a

teeny Martooni." Cannon stuck to Coke. "Try the Laphroaig," Gould suggested. It was a good idea.

The dining room was all dressed up, decorations on the glass table, little cast-aluminum flowerpots, one by every place, filled with tied bundles of cinnamon sticks matched for color and size. The cinnamon was tied with gold ribbon and the napkins were gold with silver threads at the edges. The candles and the candlesticks were the same silver and gold. Fancy.

"Daddy," Posy said, "who are we expecting, Martha Stewart?"

Posy looked gorgeous. She was wearing some sort of slinky dress that changed colors as she moved and a glow-in-the-dark circle for a necklace. But something had happened since this afternoon; Posy's transmission was stuck in bitch. "That's really kind of you to invite my friends to dinner," she snarled at her dad. "I really appreciate it."

I pulled her aside a moment. "Anything the matter, Posy?"

"You're going to *hate* this," she whispered.

"Well," Posy's dad said heartily, "let's have dinner."

What with the napkins and all, I'd expected there'd be extra forks and spoons and stuff, and there were. Dinner was little tiny individual chickens, birds, parakeets — I hoped they weren't pigeons — on rice that slithered in every direction. I did my best and watched how Ted Gould ate, feeling like a dog at an etiquette lesson.

The wine was great, though, and Aunt Betty Lou chuffed down a couple big glasses and got pretty well lubricated. And about the time the parakeets were being cleared, Ted Gould started asking her about her Oxford theories.

She got going. Incest. Secret pregnancies. Forced marriages. Ted Gould drew her out with a big lawyerly smile. Betty Lou said she thought Oxford was Elizabeth's second child; his sister Mary de Vere was her first. "The Earl of Southampton was her second son, by Oxford!" Aunt Betty Lou said earnestly.

"By Oxford," Ted Gould said. "That's pretty hard to believe." He kept smiling.

Across from me, Cannon was kicking his aunt's ankle under the table. Posy was pushing her food around with her fork. I didn't know what was going on, but I didn't like how Posy's muscles were all tight in her jaw.

Oh yes, Aunt Betty Lou explained. The Sonnets! It was all there, so clear! "And her *third* son was the Earl of Essex."

"Betty *Lou,*" Don Cannon said. "I told you—"

"You don't need secret marriages to link them with each other," I said, trying to steer the conversation off Aunt Betty Lou's craziness. "There were only twenty-six earls, they were all each other's cousins—" But no one was listening to me.

"My silly nephew doesn't believe any of this," Aunt Betty Lou was telling Gould happily. "But a powerful man like you, Mr. Gould—you know we have *many believers* among the entertainment industry, but *you,* with your connections, I am so glad you have an *open* mind—"

She was practically incoherent with pleasure. Crazy Aunt Betty Lou, blinking her half-blind eyes behind her cat's-eye glasses. She was a slow old-lady cat at a dog show, thinking all the dogs were admiring her because they were looking at her.

"Lady," Ted Gould said, and then his voice changed, "do you really believe all this crap?"

Aunt Betty Lou's mouth dropped open. Cannon flinched. Across the table, behind the gold candles, in the green glow of her necklace, I saw Posy. Her mascara and lipstick were standing out on her white miserable face. Posy had expected this.

Ted Gould was taking out a little notebook. "This Shakespeare thing? I had one of my girls do some research. Bacon was also supposed to be Shakespeare. The Earl of Derby. Queen Elizabeth, when the Virgin Queen wasn't busy having children. Oxford was an asshole. Lost his money, mistreated his wife, murdered people, betrayed his own family—"

"I can explain that," Aunt Betty Lou quavered.

"Lady, if you can explain Oxford being Shakespeare, you can explain anything. But—" Posy's dad turned a page. "Why don't you explain yourself? You're an ex-librarian, right? You used to work in a place called Bolton, up near Albany?"

Don Cannon sat up straight. Aunt Betty Lou's shoulders hunched.

"You were asked to retire after you kept telephoning the Bolton police that men were following you on the street and looking in your window? You lived on the ground floor?"

Aunt Betty Lou shook her head, no.

"The fourth floor, wasn't it? Was there a balcony? No? You had some other complaints against you at the time, right?"

Aunt Betty started to shake her head again, then nodded, yes. "Listen," Cannon said, "Gould, listen—"

"What sort of complaints?" Ted Gould's voice was insistent but friendly, encouraging, playing good cop.

In a tiny voice, Aunt Betty Lou whispered, "I bought books."

"My aunt's no business of yours, Gould," Cannon said.

"My daughter believes in this Oxford crap, so you people are my business, you know what I'm saying?"

Underneath the table Aunt Betty Lou's fingertips were scratching against each other so hard she was scratching her pink polish off. The glass table was cruel. There was nowhere to hide.

"They said you bought too many books?" Gould went on. "I don't understand that, how could you buy too many books? You're an educated woman, you must have been buying history, biography, that sort of thing?"

Aunt Betty Lou was crying. Her nephew handed her his handkerchief. "Gould—"

"I phoned your head librarian. *Flowers in the Storm* was your favorite, you bought ten copies, for one little branch library. A plain but educated woman rescues an earl and restores him to his rightful place, just like you, Miss Cannon. Look," Gould said to Cannon, "I'm sorry for your aunt, obviously she's a nut, but this Oxford thing is shit, am I right?"

Aunt Betty Lou gave one tremendous hiccup of a sob and looked up imploringly at her nephew. Posy stared through the glass table, the thousand-yard stare. Cannon stood up.

"Look, you son of a bitch—"

"You're telling me you believe this?" Gould didn't stand up. He spread his arms wide, innocent, looking up at Cannon. "You're telling me you *believe* this? You're a smart man. You believe this Oxford shit?"

Cannon looked at his aunt, back to Gould. He was trapped between the two of them, between obligation to his own sense of history and obligation to his aunt.

I stood up without really thinking about it. "Let them alone," I said.

Ted Gould turned toward me. "*You* believe this?"

"No," I said. "I don't. But the point isn't whether Miss Cannon bought too many romance novels. Lay off her."

"This is bullshit, Gould," Don Cannon said. Aunt Betty Lou was still looking at her nephew, pathetically waiting for him to defend Oxford. "Come on," he said roughly. "Come on, Auntie, let's get out of here."

White-faced Posy stood up. "I hate it!" she screamed at her father. "You try to walk in to whatever I'm doing and take it over! I hate it when you spy on me! I'm not yours! I'm not *yours!*"

Her plate hadn't been cleared yet, and she picked it up and threw it, bird and rice and all, at Ted Gould.

It hit him right on his tiepin and splattered: all over him, on his suit, on the glass table and the white carpet. Aunt Betty Lou shrieked. Cannon pulled her away toward the exit.

"Wait," Posy said to them. They looked at her like she was her father. "I'll get you a taxi. Coming?" she asked me.

"Posy," I said. I wondered if this was where Posy got her education in grace, cleaning up after her father. And herself. Right now I'd seen more of the Gould family story than I cared to.

"All right, stay here, I don't care!"

Cannon and his aunt were already leaving. She stormed out after them, leaving me alone with Ted Gould.

⁓

For a while neither of us did anything, just stood there. Finally Posy's dad picked up one of the crumpled gold napkins and started wiping his face with it. Grease and bits of bird were all over him, all over his perfect tailored suit and silk tie and custom-made shirt.

"You want some water for that?" I asked. What do you say.

"Forget it."

I set Posy's overturned chair upright. I didn't want to be here.

"Leave all that crap, somebody'll pick it up, forget it." Gould looked at the napkin, threw it down on the table among the spilled food, and stared at it.

"You'd think I could do something right for her," he said after a while. "I love my girl more than anything else on earth. I'd do anything for Posy. I *love* her," he said and looked up at me. "You'd think once in a while she'd appreciate that. But I just can't win for losing. You got kids?"

I shook my head.

"You got a father? You throw food in his face?" Gould asked. "Never mind. Forget it. I got my problems, you got yours."

"You ought to get that grease off," I said, for something to say.

"Yeah." Gould picked up the napkin again, blotted at his tie. "I liked this tie."

Posy and her Daddy. Big hugs and big expectations. Presents and screaming fits, and love that took a person over, and grace, and the need for grace. And Posy acting like a maniac, alienating Cannon, who was working on Cecil.

"Nicky Bogue told me about the letter," Ted Gould said. "Posy must have been crazy, she thought he wouldn't tell me, I spend enough money with him."

So much for *Nicky adores me.* "You're a collector?" I said.

Gould waved a hand toward the library door. "That's nothing, in there. The good stuff, the autographs, the manuscripts, they're in L.A. I got Griffith, Billy Bitzer, Selznick— What about that letter?"

"I think it's a forgery."

"You don't want it to be real?" Gould said, looking up at me. "You don't want to get rich and famous?"

"Not that way."

"No kidding? You don't think Shakespeare is Oxford?"

"Not Oxford, not Bacon, not Queen Elizabeth," I said.

"How you ever going to get ahead, then?"

How was I going to get ahead? I had *More.*

"She gets these ideas," Gould said. "Posy. Harvard, I don't know from Harvard, they're all old women, what I think, they went to L.A. they'd get eaten alive. She reads these books, she gets ideas. I tell her she should get somebody else to read her books for her. You really think the letter's crap?"

"Shakespeare is Shakespeare."

"Posy hasn't talked you round?"

"She's tried," I said, heartfelt.

"Ain't that the truth." He sounded a little proud of her. "Yeah," Gould said. "I ought to change the suit. Come on upstairs."

Gould's bedroom had a king-size bed and a walk-in closet as big as a room. He showed me his wardrobe. Two hundred, three hundred shirts. And this was just his London apartment; he lived in L.A.

"You need a shirt," Gould said, washing his hands off. The man had a washbasin in his closet. "I always buy too many shirts here, I'm crazy for London shirts. Turnbull & Asser, Thomas Pink? Your shirt is cheap crap, you should excuse me for saying so."

He went down the row of shirts, picking out one, two, three.

"What I'm saying to her," he said with his arms full of shirts on hangers, "it's all about the brand. You want to make an impression, you don't buy from J. C. Penney, you should excuse me. You buy Turnbull & Asser. Harvard, I don't know what she's doing at Harvard, but she wants to make an impression there? She should stick with the brand. Oxford is J. C. Penney. Shakespeare is Shakespeare."

He pushed shirts at me. "Take 'em," he said. "I love her. She's got this crazy idea in her head. She won't listen to me, why should she listen to me, I don't know from Shakespeare. Get this crazy Oxford idea out of my girl's head, and shirts? The shirt off my back you can take. Anytime."

~

I went out looking for Posy and found her in a Covent Garden café having one of her sweet coffees. She looked cold and a little red around the eyes.

"I hate him spying on me," she said.

It was raining still, cold and raw. Posy had wrapped a long red scarf around her hair and neck and she was hunched into a long dark coat. She looked small and frail and sulky.

"Now Daddy's going to sic Saliva on me," she said, "and she'll take me shopping to distract me, and he'll take me out to dinner and tell me how to be a success and I should drop out of Harvard and get into the real world and if I like stories I should produce them and I really fucking *hate* it, you know?"

"He cares about you," I said.

"He told you how stupid I am and how dumb Harvard is," Posy said, "and then he gave you a shirt."

I laughed unhappily.

"Make him give you a jacket. I'm worth it. You want some coffee?"

"And something to eat," I said. "What were those birds?"

She ordered chicken and artichoke pizza, at least it wasn't anchovy. I ate my way around a couple of pieces before I said anything else.

"He's right," I said. "Oxford won't get you anywhere."

"He is so wrong."

"No. Posy, do you go to Shakespeare Association meetings?" She nodded. "Look at the Oxfordians. You called them idiots. There are a couple of reasonable people there, this woman I met is reasonable, but basically you called it, they're nuts. People in the Shakespeare Association, the Folger, they're not nuts. It's not just because they're right. They're right the right way. They do *scholarship*. When it comes to scholarship, the Oxfordians lose."

"I'm Oxford," Posy said, "I am Oxford. You know that whole thing Cannon was saying to us, shithouse rat? That's what Daddy does to me. At least Oxford could go to fucking Italy? If I went to Italy, Daddy would be on the next plane."

"You're smart. You can make a success at Harvard. Just do the work, stick with Cecil."

"You know what I do? I know stories," she said. "Joe, I can tell a story. I just can't believe in the story of William Shakespeare of Stratford, everything his biographers say is just so dumb and dull. But Oxford? I know I'm right about this."

"Then prove it. Learn to read secretary hand, go to the library, go to Hatfield, look at the Cecil papers."

"You think the Cecils would have kept anything?" She leaned forward over her coffee cup. "Let me tell you the saddest thing I ever heard, Joe, and you said it. The Goscimers believed Shakespeare went to Italy. They knew it. And they lied. They went back to those tired old stories about William Shakespeare holding a horse in front of the playhouse. Because if they hadn't, everyone would have laughed at them. And so," she finished quietly, "and so they never found anything new. They never did anything really big. The proof of Oxford isn't in the Cecil papers. We have it. Nicky is looking at it now."

I thought of Rachel Goscimer, dying in the hospital. *Shakespeare did go to Italy.* Posy had no right to judge what the Goscimers had done.

Her hazel eyes glowed. "And we have me, Joe. I look good on

camera. I'm going to do more with my life than write scripts people buy because of Daddy."

"Well, you fucking do that, Posy. You do whatever you want, you piss off people right and left, like you did Cannon tonight. You decide you don't need to do the research, you ignore Rachel Goscimer spending her whole life doing the research. You kiss off four hundred years of Shakespeare scholarship, and see where it gets you. Want to be noticed for yourself? That's what you're going to be noticed for."

She stared at me. "We have the *letter*," she repeated.

"Which Nicky is going to say is a forgery, because it is. Unless he says it might not be because you want it and he *adores* you. Don't you respect yourself at all?"

She burst into tears. She put her hands up over her face and cried. A man at the next table looked at me indignantly. Let her cry, I thought. Let her cry, and then let her start doing the work. Ah shit. I passed over my paper napkin for her to use as a handkerchief. Then I moved over to the chair beside her and she leaned against my shoulder and cried.

"She thinks I'm a spoiled brat," Posy said finally. "Lady Silvia."

I didn't say anything.

"Why did he have to leave Mom for Saliva?" She wiped her eyes. "I never cry," she said. She hiccupped, half a laugh. "I never cry about anything, and I'm only a bitch when I want to be, and I'm not as stupid as he thinks I am, and I'm not the dumb little Valley girl she thinks I am, and *I'm not going to work in fucking Hollywood for Daddy.*"

Neither of us said anything for a while. "S'all right, Posy."

"You're right. They're stupid people. I guess that makes me stupid."

"Nope."

She never cried, I thought, and no one had ever taken her to feed the pigeons. I remembered her throwing grain into the air in Trafalgar Square and the pigeons whirling around her. And I'd never been to London. I'd never got up my courage to go to London, maybe never would have got there, never read *Sir Thomas More,* if it hadn't been for Posy.

She wasn't a dumb Valley girl. Why did she act that way?

"Posy," I said, "I got something for you, something to tell you. I found something in the British Library."

The couple next to us were just leaving. I waited while he helped her on with her coat and they left a tip and threaded their way past empty tables. It was late; we had the café pretty much to ourselves.

"I think Munday knew Shakespeare."

She was looking at me strangely. "You've found something that *says* that?"

I explained: Shakespeare did Surrey and the good More character, Shakespeare looked over Munday's shoulder while Munday wrote the good draft. "I'm pretty bowled over by that. If Munday knew Shakespeare, that'd be my thesis and a lot more."

Posy's moment of vulnerability was over. "Duh," she said, "Munday knew Shakespeare, of course he did."

Now I didn't understand her. "Posy, I fact-checked Shakespeare's life and nobody's ever thought Shakespeare and Munday wrote *More* at the same time."

"Do you know who Munday is?" she said.

"Playwright. Cowrote *The History of Sir John Oldcastle,*" which was a knockoff of Shakespeare's Falstaff. *"English Romayne Life.* And his plays suck."

She shook hair out of her face impatiently. "I know who Munday is, because I 'neglected the British Library,' as if I haven't been there before, and read Ogburn. In *The English Romayne Life* Munday talked to a patron who told him to go to Italy but didn't have the money to send him? You know who that was?"

"Who?"

"Oxford."

Oh shit, she was back on Oxford again. "So?" I said defensively. "So Munday knew Oxford."

"Shut up and let me finish. When Munday came back to England, Oxford hired him as one of his secretaries. Munday is Oxford's *secretary,*" Posy repeated. "Of course he's writing fair copy, because he's Oxford's *secretary,* that's what secretaries *do.* And you know what else Munday is? Oxford has two companies of players. Munday and John Lyly run them. You know what I think? I think you just found *another* piece of evidence proving Oxford is Shakespeare."

My lips went numb. For a moment I couldn't breathe. My thesis. *Sir Thomas More.* The thesis that was big enough to make me noticed and small enough I knew how to do it, and was nothing to do with authorship or Oxford— I swallowed and got my breath back. "Fuck that. Munday's running Oxford's players? Okay. Players need plays. Munday's going to find cheap young talent. Shakespeare."

"Daddy's doing it to you too," Posy said. "He's saying I'm not going to get anywhere believing in the letter, and he's giving you his fucking *shirts.* But all the time, the evidence is building up—"

We were sitting in the corner of the café, at a cold table by a window. Posy wasn't wearing any gloves. Her hand was little, cold. She laid it on mine. She looked around her, past me, out the window, and then she turned back to me, hooked me under the chin, and pulled my face down and kissed me. It was a kiss as if she thought someone was watching and she wanted to show she didn't care. Her lips moved against mine.

"Let's not be safe," she said. "Let's not believe what everybody else believes. Let's be great. Together."

⁓

Great. Together. I hadn't any interest in that kind of great. Gould was gone when we got back to the apartment; a couple of silent Spanish women were washing the table and cleaning the food off the rug. I went into the library and pulled a couple of biographies of Munday off the Net.

Anthony Munday was one of those minor Elizabethans who always appear somewhere in a list of playwrights, but are never important enough to be first. He was born in either 1553 or 1560. His father was a London draper. He was an actor before he was six-teen, maybe a boy playing women's parts, then was apprenticed to a printer, but only lasted a year. In the late 1570s he started writing.

He dedicated some of his early work to Oxford. Oxford told him he should go to Rome to study the Renaissance. Munday did, and when he got back, Oxford hired him as a secretary. Munday eventually moved on to work as a playwright, court messenger, editor, and producer of pageants for the London guilds. He's best known for editing a revision of Stow's *London*.

I wasn't finding out much about him and Shakespeare—of course; who knew that?—but between the lines, I was finding out only too much about him and Oxford.

Munday had saved Oxford's life.

In 1580, Munday had come back from Rome and was working for Oxford. Oxford had been separated from his wife four years.

He was living in a bachelor apartment, probably leaving his socks on the floor and drinking out of the bottle. He had started hanging around with a bad crowd headed by Lord Henry Howard, the Duke of Norfolk's literary younger brother.

He'd fallen in with real bad guys. Henry Howard was spying for Mary Queen of Scots, who was still trying to get the throne. Charles Arundel, another of the group, was on his way to being an open traitor in the pay of Philip of Spain.

Under their influence, Oxford had apparently become a secret Catholic. Which would get him imprisoned, maybe tortured, maybe killed.

Now here was Munday, just back from pretending to study for the Jesuit priesthood in Rome. In 1580, the first of a wave of Jesuits were coming from Rome to England in disguise. Some of them, like Mary Cat's favorite, Edmund Campion, were priests pure and simple. Some were organizing a Catholic rebellion and planning the Queen's assassination, with men just like Henry Howard.

Some of them had been Munday's classmates.

Anthony Munday, who still had his English College sweatshirt in his closet, knew these guys' agendas.

I figured Munday found out Oxford was Catholic.

There were any number of ways this story could have played out. Munday could have been spying for Cecil, one of those family spies Cecil liked. But Munday and Oxford stayed friends for life. So it was more likely that Munday was what Oxford had always been short of, a friend he could trust.

How did Munday get the message through to Oxford? Maybe he took a big chance, just laid it on the line. Maybe he asked Oxford out for a drink and worked up to it, or volunteered to clean up Oxford's library some Saturday morning, showed up in

blue jeans and old English College sweatshirt, started reminisc-
ing to his employer about priest-spies. I could only imagine all
of this.

But however it happened, for once Oxford didn't act crazy,
didn't screw up, *did the right thing*. He went to the secret service,
confessed he'd been a Catholic, renounced it, and told Cecil's
men that Henry Howard and his associates were traitors.

That much I found out from the Internet and Ogburn. By now
it was two in the morning and cold, but Katherine Darnell had
printed Oxford's testimony against Howard and Arundel, and I
wanted to read it. I huddled down under the tasseled covers in
the guest room, slung my parka over my shoulders, and, for the
first time, read the authentic voice of Edward de Vere.

December 1580, just after Christmas. Oxford was being interviewed by Cecil's men. An ordinary Catholic would have been
interrogated under torture. But Oxford— I could practically see
him, sitting on the edge of someone's desk with one well-tailored
leg swinging, talking scornfully and as fast as the secretary could
take it down.

> Item, to be demanded of Charles Arundel and Henry
> Howard: What combination, for that is their term, was
> made at certain suppers, one in Fish Street as I take it,
> another at my Lord of Northumberland's, for they have
> often spoken hereof and glanced [at it] in their speeches.

Oxford knew the value of words, and he skirted neatly around
how much of the conspiracy he knew. If he was Catholic he must
have just gone through a ball-wrencher, choosing between his
country and his conscience. But he wasn't going to let on; any

mixed feelings he had, he just took out on Henry Howard and his friends. He field-gutted them and left their entrails for the ants:

> Item to Charles Arundel: A little before Christmas at my lodging in Westminster, Swift being present, and George Gyfford talking of the order of living by money, and [the] difference between that and revenue by land—he said at the last that if George Gyfford could make three thousand pound, he would set him into a course where he need not care for all England and there he might live more to his content and with more reputation than ever he did or might hope for in England, and they would make all the Court hear wonder to hear of them, and diverse other brave and glorious speeches. Whereat George Gyfford replied, "G-d's blood, Charles, where is this?" He answered that if you have three thousand pounds or can make it, he can tell the other. . . . That speech finished with the coming in of supper.

"Diverse other brave and glorious speeches." "Combination, for that is their term." Oxford had a dead accurate memory for the words people used. I could see him picking up their words with silver tongs, examining them, and tossing them aside. He let his cousins stumble over their own tongues; they weren't only Catholics but sheer bare-ass idiots, little men using words too big for them.

I looked ahead in Ogburn and saw Oxford in a couple of brawls with the Howards. No surprise there. But for the first time I kind of liked the guy. Oxford was finally taking something seriously, whether you could be a good Catholic and a good Englishman too, and he'd chosen his side.

It was way past time to go to bed. I was brushing my teeth, groggily, in the bathroom full of mirrors when I remembered Mary Cat's Edmund Campion again, and something she'd said about him.

"Edmund Campion," I said out loud and grinned at myself in the mirror. *"Edmund Campion."* I knew where Shakespeare had been in 1580, and I knew where Edmund Campion had been. Mary Cat and I had talked about the coincidence: our Elizabethan heroes could have known each other.

In the winter of 1580, Edmund Campion had been in England in disguise and working on a major treatise. He had stayed with a scholarly Catholic Lancashire family, the Hoghtons.

When Shakespeare was sixteen, in 1580, he may have left Stratford for a year and worked as a servant.

For a Catholic Lancashire family.

The Hoghtons.

And Munday had known Edmund Campion and his associates in Rome.

I was trying to connect Shakespeare with Munday? Here it was. Shakespeare, Campion, Munday.

I stood in the bathroom with my toothbrush dripping and my teeth foaming, grinning at myself like an idiot.

If Shakespeare were at the Hoghtons', he would have heard discussions about whether a Catholic could be a good Englishman; Campion had always argued that merely being Catholic wasn't treasonous. And a few years later, when Shakespeare had come to London, when Munday was writing a play about Sir Thomas More, the Englishman who most represented the conflict between religion and loyalty, who would have been a natural collaborator? Shakespeare. . . .

It was all fitting together like gears. Shakespeare had been a servant. When Shakespeare came to London, he wouldn't have held horses; that was for people who couldn't do anything else. He'd have wanted to be in a household, well paid and well fed, where he could read. Munday was Oxford's secretary. Munday and Shakespeare had known the same people and thought about the same things.

Were the Stratfordians and the Oxfordians really getting at the same truth? Shakespeare could have gone to see Munday, and Munday could have recommended him to—

Shakespeare could have worked for Oxford.

Posy had said she was Oxford. I was Shakespeare, Shakespeare the servant, watching family fights, being allowed to read books, being given secondhand clothes—and hearing stories. I lay awake in the darkness, and then rolled over and set the alarm for early, so I could get to the library as soon as it opened the next morning, and then turned on the light again.

By the desk was a London phone book, in four volumes. I looked up the number for the hostel of the Society of Saint Mary on Docklands Road. Mary Cat probably didn't want to hear from me. But if this panned out at all, I was going to call her up and tell her about it.

That'd teach her to give up on graduate school.

⁓

By the next morning my half-formed toothpaste ideas were turning into a research strategy. There were no cheap restaurants serving early breakfast in Covent Garden anymore, but I found one up near Holborn. I ate a big British breakfast while I worked my strategy out.

If Shakespeare knew Oxford—was Oxford's servant or one of his actors, or if Oxford was Shakespeare's patron when he started writing—it would explain away a lot of the "problems"

Oxfordians found with Shakespeare. Shakespeare knew family things about Oxford? No problem, because he worked for Oxford. Shakespeare knew books Oxford knew and men Oxford had patronized? Sure, because Oxford patronized men just like him. Whatever else you could say about Oxford, the man supported writers. He would have noticed Shakespeare. If there was a household in England where a servant could have sat around reading Montemayor's *Diana*, Oxford's would have been it.

So could I find any new connections between Munday, Oxford, and Shakespeare? What would they look like if I found them, and where could I look? I decided to look at all of Munday's work from the 1580s, and the work of other people Ogburn said had hung around Oxford in the early 1580s, and any existing writing by Oxford, and see if I could find traces of Shakespeare.

And I found them. It was easy.

The first thing I found was tournaments.

The tournament where Oxford had been the Knight of the Tree of the Sun was a lot more important than anybody had made it. It had taken place only three weeks after Oxford had betrayed Henry Howard to Cecil, it was about whether a good Catholic could be a good Englishman, and it was a political spectacle to rival a presidential convention. Henry Howard's nephew, the Earl of Arundel, started things off by inviting other knights to join in combat with him "in mutual honour and affection" for Elizabeth. (Translation: I'm not a traitor like my uncle.) Oxford appointed himself the leading challenger. (Translation: I'm more loyal even than Arundel.) Before the jousting, Oxford gave a speech to Elizabeth, and then he beat up everyone else, including Arundel, and won the tournament.

Arundel and Oxford were doing trial by combat, fucking unbelievable, trial by combat, two guys hitting each other upside the head to prove their loyalty; but it was art too, and no knight had ever been more artful than Oxford:

> By the tilt stood a stately Tent of orange tawny Taffeta, curiously embroidered with Silver, & pendents on the Pinnacles very sightly to behold. . . . From forth this Tent came the noble Earl of Oxenford in rich gilt Armour, and sat down under a great high Bay-tree, the whole stock, branches and leaves whereof, were all gilded over, that nothing but Gold could be discerned. . . . After a solemn sound of most sweet Music, he mounted on his Courser, very richly caparisoned, when his page ascending the stairs where her Highness stood in the window, delivered to her by speech [Oxford's] Oration. . . . 'As there is but one Sun to shine over [the Tree of the Sun], one root to give life unto it, one top to maintain Majesty: so there should be but one Knight, either to live or die for the defence thereof.' Whereupon, he swore himself to be the Knight of the Tree of the Sun, whose life should end before his loyalty.

Golden armor, golden tree, golden-tawny tent, Elizabethan pretties: this fight was also a play. A political play. It was about who was loyal and who was not, and whether Catholics could be true Englishmen.

The same subject as *Sir Thomas More*.

Yes, there would have been discussions of Catholic loyalty at Oxford's house. Munday would have been talking, and so would Oxford.

And who else? Shakespeare?

To read Anthony Munday and the other people I wanted, I had

to go to the Rare Book Room. Sunlight hovered around a row of windows far above, but down where I was, there were nothing but dim religious reading lights; I could barely see my penciled notes.

Payday again—Shakespeare seemed to know Oxford's friends and Oxford's friends noticed Shakespeare early. Gabriel Harvey, admirer of Oxford, wrote about Shakespeare. Shakespeare admired the Euphuistic literary movement before he parodied it; John Lyly, Oxford's secretary, invented Euphuism in a book dedicated to Oxford. Shakespeare used Robert Greene in several plays; the 1589 *Hamlet* was referred to in a preface to a Greene book; Greene dedicated works to Oxford. Maybe I was just playing six degrees of William Shakespeare, but none of this discouraged me from thinking Shakespeare had lived in Oxford's household.

I found something pretty cute in a book by another of Oxford's secretaries, Angel Day. In 1586 Day put out *The English Secretorie,* a collection of sample letters with a long and unintentionally funny preface defining what a letter was, in six parts, in Latin. Brevity was the soul of a letter, Day pontificated, so he had to define brevity. I thought of Holofernes dissecting a letter, or of Polonius.

My liege, and madam, to expostulate
What majesty should be, what duty is,
Why day is day, night night, and time is time
Were nothing but to waste night, day, and time.
Therefore, since brevity is the soul of wit
And tediousness the limbs and outward flourishes,
I will be brief . . .

This wasn't discouraging either.

What I really wanted, though, was more links between Shakespeare and Anthony Munday, so Munday could have introduced Shakespeare into the household.

Munday was a trial; he wrote every kind of thing in the world and did it badly. I read his plays first. *The Downfall of Robert Earl of Huntingdon* and *Death of Robert Earl of Huntingdon* didn't contain any references to Shakespeare, though it sounded as though whoever wrote them might have read some Shakespeare once. Munday's pageants for the London guilds were horrible. *Chryso-thriambos: The Triumphes of Gold*.

Munday's work wasn't always bad, but it wasn't good. It was in that slidy area between not bad enough to make you laugh and not good enough to make you laugh, or think, or cry. I'd start one Munday piece after another, and about a page in, I'd realize I wasn't reading anymore, my eyes were just sliding down the page like skiing on flat ice, no texture to it, no purchase, no thrill, I was just waiting to get to the end.

There was nothing that sounded like Shakespeare, nothing that referred to Shakespeare. What I wanted (okay, what I was fantasizing about) was another collaboration, Munday and Shakespeare again, but I wasn't finding it.

During lunch, while I chewed my sandwich in the library café, I leafed through Ogburn, seeing what Oxford had been doing when I wanted him hiring Shakespeare.

I hit the lottery. He'd been buying a house.

And not just any house.

Oxford had gone through a really bad patch after he turned Henry Howard in. The Howards had turned on him, either because of Henry Howard or, more likely, because he'd got the wrong woman pregnant.

She was a Howard cousin and a Maid of Honor, and her name

was Anne Vavasour. (The Oxfordians thought she was the Dark Lady of the Sonnets. In 1581? No.) At almost the moment Oxford was eating Arundel's lunch in the tiltyard, Anne Vavasour was giving birth to the son Oxford's wife hadn't given him. Elizabeth was furious, Cecil was furious; Elizabeth sent Oxford to the Tower; and when Oxford finally got out, he was banished from the court.

Money and power came from the court; he lost both. Elizabeth probably fined him. He was paying bills for the Knight of the Sun's golden armor and golden trees. Anne Vavasour had gone off to have affairs and become somebody else's mistress; Oxford's bastard son was being raised by the Howards. Anne Vavasour's uncle, Thomas Knyvet, blamed Oxford for her ruin, attacked him in the street, and almost killed him. Knyvet's men and Oxford's men started a gang war on the streets of London; people got killed on both sides. Oxford recovered, but slowly, and he was lame.

Cecil had got him out of jail, so he owed Cecil too. Oxford went back to living with his wife.

He must have had a miserable time. Cecil wrote that the Oxfords had only three servants, which for an earl was like living in a refrigerator box. Ogburn quoted the letter, and I could just see Cecil smiling nastily:

> My Lord of Oxford is neither heard nor hath presence either to complain or defend himself. And so long as he shall be subject to the disgrace of her Majesty (from which God deliver him) I see it apparently that, innocent soever he shall be, the advantages will fall out with his adversaries. . . . [God] knoweth best why it pleaseth Him to afflict my Lord of Oxford in this sort, who hath, I confess, forgotten his duty to God.

All of Cecil's enemies were wicked. Praise be, they never got away with it.

But in 1584 Oxford did get away with something. He bought a house in London.

Oxford still owned Vere House in Oxford Court. He could have stayed with the Cecils. When he was restored to Elizabeth's favor he would have to spend most of his time at court.

But he bought Fisher's Folly, which was his own.

> There is [in the high street from Bishopsgate and Hound's Ditch] a . . . large and beautiful house with gardens of plea-sure, bowling alleys and such like, builded by Jasper Fisher. . . . It hath since for a time been the Earl of Oxford's place. The Queen's Majesty Elizabeth hath lodged there. . . . This house being so large and sumptuously builded . . . was mockingly called Fisher's Folly.

On Mary Cat's Elizabethan map I found what had to be Fisher's Folly, just outside London Wall. It was a huge house with lots of outbuildings, halfway between a farmstead and a palace, and completely misplaced. It should have been by the river with the other great houses; but it was right next to the tenter fields where London's washing was laid out to dry. The Earl had found himself lodgings by the laundromat.

Oxford was pissing in Cecil's eye.

I clasped my hands behind my neck and looked around the B.L. cafeteria. The cafeteria was right by the King's Library and I was sitting as close as I could, to get the benefit of the bindings and the famous titles through the glass.

Ogburn thought Oxford invited all his writing friends to stay there. Reasonable theory. Ogburn thought Oxford and his friends locked themselves into their writing closets all day, scribble, scribble, scribble, and then got together for dinner and wrote high-toned dedications to each other. Ogburn was a clean-living polite Southern guy, worked for the State Department and wrote 892 pages of biography in his spare time. I figured they drank breakfast and went bowling in the backyard, made bets who could write his whole name in piss and whether if you threw salad at the ceiling it'd stick. They talked about their Harleys and their horses and their women problems, smoked a lot of J and nursed hangovers, and occasionally maybe they hawked out a poem.

Oxford gave up tournaments about the time he bought the Folly. He was thirty-four, getting old for head-banging on horseback and way too poor to buy armor. Cecil was still treating him like a ward; about the same time he bought the Folly, Oxford was giving Cecil a ration of shit because Cecil had spied on him again:

> I pray, my Lord, leave that course, for I mean not to be
> your ward nor your child. I serve Her Majesty, and I am
> that I am, and by alliance near to your Lordship, but free.

No man's free. Oxford still thought he could say so. I am that I am, free as G-d. When he rode into London, twelve years old, he'd been at the head of a hundred and forty men, he'd owned three hundred castles. Now he had a house and a gang of drinking buddies. Free.

Ogburn thought Oxford was Hamlet, but it sounded to me like Oxford was getting to be Falstaff, drinking sherry out of a beer mug, calling princes by their first names and embarrassing them. Short of money, and not as young as he used to be. But free of his obligations. Free by having less and less to lose.

In 1584 or early 1585 Shakespeare would just have been leaving Stratford for London, and Oxford would have been just setting up Fisher's Folly. He would have needed servants.

Books? Fisher's Folly must have had books. Court info? Legal training? Sports, tournaments, falcons, hunting? Poetry? Drama? Oxford had two companies of players, for shit's sake.

And in the corner of the room somewhere, maybe one of Oxford's players, maybe less than that, maybe just a servant, there he would have wanted to be, somebody who cleared the plates and fed the dogs and scraped the salad off the ceiling, twenty years old and up from Stratford to escape Anne Hathaway the way Oxford was escaping Anne Cecil. Free. Will Shakespeare. Listening to the writers talking around the table. Repeating John Lyly's curlicued phrases under his breath. Hearing Anthony Munday talk about Italy and Catholic politics, or Gabriel Harvey on law and Latin quantitative rules and English poetry and the value of long vowels. Shit, they would have talked about everything, talked and quarreled, and then they would all have climbed on the outhouse roof and tried to piss on the laundry.

Where was Shakespeare's library, his university, his patron? Where did Shakespeare spend his lost years?

At the corner of Houndsditch and Bishopsgate, at the big house by the laundry fields? At Fisher's Folly?

I slammed Ogburn shut and went back into the Rare Book Room to read what Munday wrote during the Fisher's Folly years.

It took me until late afternoon, but I found something, and it was about Catholicism. In 1584, the year Oxford bought the Folly,

Munday had sketched out the entire plot of Shakespeare's history plays in a book called *A Watch-Word to England:* "The great division of the two noble houses of *Lancaster* and *York,* which cost so much English blood, that there remaineth no house of high or mean Nobility, that hath not smarted for it." This went on for about two pages, and it sounded like Shakespeare's treatment of the Wars of the Roses in *King Henry VI,* his earliest history play. This wasn't any smoking gun. The Wars of the Roses had been the big war of recent English history; two English writers could have used it the way two American writers could have used Vietnam, with no communication between them. Munday was thinking of the Wars of the Roses as anti-Catholic propaganda; by the time Shakespeare wrote the great history plays, he would be pitting English against English, one good reason against another. But it was another thread tying Shakespeare and Munday.

Angel Day at Fisher's Folly. Munday at Fisher's Folly. Gabriel Harvey, Robert Greene, John Lyly. Catholicism and the Howards and the Knight of the Tree of the Sun. All from the 1580s.

From the lost years.

I got up from the desk and stretched, stiff, hungry, and exultant. I knew what I wanted to see, now, before it got dark.

~

Where Fisher's Folly used to be, at the corner of Bishopsgate and Houndsditch, there was a branch of the Halifax Bank, a square prosaic gray building with scaffolding over it. The bank was renovating for the new millennium, like everything else in London. The scaffolding advertised its dot-com address.

It was late, twilight. I stood in the doorway of the bank, with my back against the chill stone, and looked out on Bishopsgate.

The street was a grubby East London commercial drag, offices and retail space mingled. Even in Elizabeth's day Bishopsgate had been a road to somewhere else. Traffic lights were slicing the dusk in both directions. A furniture truck ground and clashed its gears, going toward the north.

And here was where it had been, the big house by the laundry fields.

Looking across this street, Shakespeare would have seen the gates of Bedlam Hospital, the gardens and grounds and the sprawling buildings of the biggest madhouse in London. He would have heard the inhabitants screaming and laughing and seen them at the gates, looking out at him. Insanity amused Elizabethans. Kings kept fools as mock counselors, and the rich visited Bedlam as if it were a zoo. Shakespeare wouldn't have been able to get in by himself, but if Oxford went, Shakespeare could have gone with him.

Fools and Lears, melancholic Hamlets, guilty Lady Macbeths, suicidal Ophelias, right across the street.

And up the road—

I pushed at the door of the bank. A red-haired kid on the other side was just fumbling the lock closed.

"Sorry, sir, come back tomorrow—"

"I'm not trying to do any banking. I wonder if you know how far away the Theatre was from here."

The banker was about my age, a friendly wisp of a guy in a cheap suit. "Is it the cinema you mean?"

"Richard Burbage's Theatre." I unfolded Mary Cat's Elizabethan map and pointed at the Theatre. "Richard Burbage was the first Hamlet. His building, the Theatre, was near here—"

"Mr. Singh?" the kid called.

Mr. Singh was the manager, a plump turbaned man with gold rings and gold teeth, and he knew a good deal about the neighborhood, but he didn't know where the Theatre was. "Now if it were to tell you the location of a very good chip shop, sir, or the old vaudeville, that I could supply without difficulty. Perhaps the former London County Council or private citizens have placed a Blue Plaque. But it has never been my fortune to see it."

"Blue Plaque?"

Blue Plaques, Mr. Singh told me, were signs put on historical buildings. "You will see an example opposite commemorating Saint Mary's of Bethlehem, the very famous asylum. Regrettably Labour no longer favors such historical displays."

I'd found another history buff. "I think Shakespeare might have worked here," I said. "I mean— So far it's just a theory."

"In this very spot? Here, where we are standing?"

Here. Where we were standing.

"If it is confirmed I very much hope you will write to me here. Out of my own pocket, if the Halifax Bank would not do it, I would sponsor a Blue Plaque."

By now, March in London, it was deep dusk. Shops along Bishopsgate were lighting their display windows. This wasn't tourist London; there was no stencil in the crosswalk reminding foreigners to LOOK RIGHT; it was an older and shabbier and deeper-rooted city. SHOP FITTINGS, TAILORING, KITCHEN SUPPLY, places for men who worked with their hands, commercial suppliers, not dependent on passing trade and already rattling down their shutters. Here the city really looked foreign; the sign painters wrote with curly white letters on black or with yellow letters on green, old-fashioned signs, exotically English. I walked up the road, stopping at the edge of the sidewalk to look up for Blue Plaques. Nothing.

On Mary Cat's Elizabethan map, the Theatre was near the Curtain and they were both near Shoreditch, the street that was the continuation of Bishopsgate. On the modern map there was a Curtain Road not far beyond Liverpool Street Station, and I headed into the maze of streets behind Bishopsgate to look for it. I passed old-fashioned small shops, tobacconist and newsagent, butcher, rat-catcher with an old-fashioned swinging sign, a painted star of rats with their tails tied together. The streets were too narrow for delivery trucks, almost too narrow for cars.

Whether or not Shakespeare worked at Fisher's Folly, as soon as he touched foot in London he would have walked these streets. He could have tended bar anywhere from Southwark to Westminster, held anybody's horses—but for shit sure he'd have gone to the Theatre.

Here at least was Mr. Singh's old vaudeville house. It was a Victorian building faced with elaborate dark red tile, with curlicues round the doorway, and to the left of the doorway was a tiled tan scroll, probably the theater name. I squinted at it curiously, trying to make the ye-olde writing out in the light of the streetlamp.

"Near this spot stood the Theatre."

Here. I was close enough to the main road to hear the echo of traffic. I made a note of the cross streets and walked back to the rush-hour streams of cars. This was Shoreditch, I saw from the white enameled street sign. But it was the same street as Bishopsgate, and down the road I could see the Halifax Bank.

Fisher's Folly.

Four hundred years melted away under my boot soles. My knees felt rubbery, disconnected. Cross the street halfway, look for traffic, cross to the other side, walk down the road: that's how far away the men at Fisher's Folly were from Shakespeare's stage.

Those good old boys at Fisher's Folly could have got up at two-thirty in the afternoon, drunk as walruses, had a good scratch and a piss and slopped down their tankard of breakfast beer, and still have made it to the Theatre by three.

I hadn't any proof at all they saw plays. (But they did, of course they did.) I had no proof Edward de Vere ever hired William Shakespeare as a servant, a player, a secretary, anything.

Only the hairs standing up on my arms, which was no proof.

But he was here. Shakespeare was here.

I called up Posy at the apartment, wanting to talk to her, see what she thought, maybe just show off, but she was out with her father to dinner. Making up, maybe. Learning a little more about each other, learning to get out of each other's way. I wanted to rewrite her life, give her a better biography. Do it for both of them.

Some of that remote feeling around my knees was probably sheer hunger, so I found an Indian restaurant in honor of Mr. Singh and tucked into an enormous plate of tandoori chicken, because it wasn't messy and I could think and write while I ate.

I couldn't see anything wrong with the idea, from either Shakespeare's side or Oxford's. Oxford had a lot of books and a lot of culture. If his poetry was anything to go by, he couldn't write. But he was a good patron. He liked to hang around writers. If he couldn't write, he could watch. And help.

He'd sponsored Thomas Bedingfield's *Cardanus Comfort*, John Lyly's *Euphues* novels, probably Robert Greene's continuation of *Euphues*. He'd even given encouragement to Angel Day—Day's persnickety preface was grateful to Oxford. He'd hired Lyly, Day, and Munday as secretaries.

And Will Shakespeare was just the sort of guy Oxford liked to help. Munday was a draper's son; Will Shakespeare was the son of a glover. Hand D is a secretary hand, and Shakespeare's signatures are consistent with his writing a secretary hand. Shakespeare could even have been one of the Earl's secretaries.

As an aspiring literary man, Shakespeare would have been looking for a patron; Oxford would have fit him. In a well-run Elizabethan household the servants got one afternoon a week off. But if Oxford sympathized with Shakespeare's ambitions, Shakespeare could have got a lot more time. Right down the street was the Theatre, sucking in men his age from all over London. Man, the people he could have met just at the pub—

And Shakespeare got it. He got it all. The talk at Fisher's Folly, the books in the library, the foreign languages and reminiscences of Italy. Yes, Shakespeare went to Italy during the lost years; yes, he had a noble's education and experience of the court; yes, he studied law—*but not firsthand*.

He got it through Oxford. He watched Oxford and Oxford's friends.

And he saw plays. He paid his penny at the Theatre and stood down with the groundlings. He saw young Richard Burbage, dark and sturdy and deep-voiced, acting in ridiculous plays with hobblehorse verse. He went backstage, and one day he introduced himself: Will Shakespeare, one of Lord Oxford's men, living right down the street, could he try his hand at rewriting an old play? He started doctoring plays with Munday or for the Burbages, started using the voices he heard at Fisher's Folly, turning them into the voices he heard in his head. Greene or Chettle, whoever wrote *Greene's Groatsworth,* said Shakespeare stole old material. "And with his *Tiger's heart wrapped in a Player's hide* he thinks himself the only Shake-scene in the country."

Oxford wasn't Shakespeare. He was Shakespeare's material.

Shakespeare stole Oxford.

⁓

I was beyond being proud of myself. I was just happy. I walked back all through London, for the sheer pleasure of it, and got back to the Gould apartment late. I rang the bell and Posy came downstairs to answer it.

"Come outside," I said. I didn't want to talk to her in her father's apartment. She got her coat and we walked down Floral Street toward the market.

"Wow," she said, looking up at me. "What'd you find? Where have you been?"

"Fisher's Folly. The Theatre. You get to talk with your dad?"

"Never mind him. You're like a neon sign, I FOUND SOME-THING. Tell me?"

I told her while we walked through Covent Garden. It was late; the stores had shut down, the market buildings were dark. We stood looking at the portico of Saint Paul's Church, the actors' church, unchanged since Wren's day. I thought I could smell vegetables, fresh loam, the smell of the past. We sat down on the steps of one of the market buildings.

"First off, Munday and Shakespeare. Shakespeare may have known the same English Jesuits Munday knew," I said. "In Lancashire."

"Honigmann's theory?" she said.

"Yeah. Campion was at Hoghton Tower too, same time Honigmann thinks Shakespeare was there. Munday knew Campion and his group. Munday and Shakespeare would both have known how complex the Catholic issue was. When Shakespeare came to London, I think Munday introduced him to Fisher's Folly," I said. "I think he was working for Oxford. There are the same issues, Catholicism and loyalty, all through."

"Wow," she said. She frowned, but as if she were thinking. "What about the first Sonnets? Is Shakespeare working for Cecil?"

I thought. "Is he writing for Oxford? Does that make sense?"

"Yes," she breathed. "Shakespeare's saying, 'Marry my patron's daughter,' and Oxford's protecting Shakespeare, and that's why Cecil can't touch him?"

"Shakespeare knows everyone who could have been around Fisher's Folly," I said.

"Wow."

"This is big," I said. "Posy, this could be the lost years."

"As big as the letter?"

"Real," I said, and then put it another way. "I want the truth. I'm going to go after the truth of this. What do you want? You want Oxford and a story, or you want the real thing?"

"The real thing," she said, and took my hands. We looked into each other's eyes. "The real thing," she repeated.

"You'll get noticed," I said. "You can have that, Posy. It's going to happen."

"This is all your stuff," she said. "It isn't mine."

"Uh-uh. Cecil and the Sonnets? That's yours. There's enough for you and me both. There's enough for a lot of people." I thought of Mary Cat. So much, and a good researcher going wasted.

"The lost years," she said.

"Going to be a good story," I said. "And I'm going to need you to tell it. Hick from V'mont, I won't know how."

She was still looking into my eyes. "You're something else. You're giving me like this totally original theory, and you still think you're a hick?"

I thought about that. "Like you're a dumb Valley girl, Posy?"

We were something else, because of being together. We sat for a while in silence, walked back in silence, wondering what we were. We held hands in the elevator. I laced my fingers into her slim fingers, ran my thumb across her bitten nails.

"You want to do something?" Posy said as we stepped out onto the white immaculate carpet.

"Find out more about Munday and Shakespeare. I know there's going to be more, I haven't half read Munday yet."

She looked up at me, suddenly defensive again. "Like that is not what I meant?" Defensive and Valley Girl. She stood on tiptoes, tilted her face up toward mine. "You're too tall." She tugged at my jacket to bring my face lower; her lips brushed against mine.

Oh. You want to do something.

"Yeah, uh— I was being stupid."

"You don't want to do something?" she said.

Posy's bedroom was next door to her father's; and if I didn't want to talk to her in her father's house, I sure as heck didn't want to sleep with her there. Did I?

"I don't want to sneak around with you, Posy," which was pretty talk for I was acting like a jerk. What I was doing was figuring in what her father wanted, making her father the same big presence in her life she thought he was. What I was doing was being a hick from East Bradenton, not knowing what to do with a girl like this.

She looked up at me. "Whatever. Forget it."

Posy started up the steel-and-glass circular staircase. I watched helplessly the back view of her, round little behind, squared shoulders. Down below where I was, it was almost dark; at the top of the stairs a modernistic-looking dim light made a glow. It caught her hair from the back, a halo of burning red.

Oh she doth teach the torches to burn bright —

Shakespeare always gets it right. I could have stood here with her all night. I didn't want her to go away. But it wasn't because I wanted her, though I did, it was because as long as we held hands, for that moment, I knew her and we were safe together on the same side. Parting is such sweet sorrow.

"Posy?" I said.

She turned.

"Just wanted to look at you," I said. "And tell you I'm not forgetting anything. It's just— There's time."

She rolled her eyes, shrugged, half laughed. *"So* dumb." She stayed there for a moment, leaning over the railing, as if she was going to come back down again. But she just said good night, and turned, and disappeared upstairs, and I looked after her until she'd gone.

Parting is such sweet sorrow . . . Good night. Good night.

~~~

The next morning Ted Gould and Lady Silvia were both at the breakfast table with us. We couldn't talk. Lady Silvia wanted Posy to go to some show. "Go to the B.L. for me," Posy said, giving me a long look. I went back to the B.L. to look for connections between Munday and Shakespeare.

In the fourth or fifth book in my stack, I found them.

It was a fat musty little volume, three smaller books bound

together. The book I'd ordered the volume up for was *A Gorgeous Gallery of Gallant Inventions,* preface by Munday, and it included a version of Pyramus and Thisbe that Shakespeare had almost certainly used in *A Midsummer Night's Dream.* It was awful—it's the version that actually uses the word "pap"—and Shakespeare had pounced on it like an Iron Chef on roadkill. The stuff in *A Midsummer Night's Dream* that everyone thinks is Shakespeare being brilliantly ridiculous had been Shakespeare stealing with both hands, from a book his friend Munday had probably shown him. I wondered if this book—if, maybe, this copy of this book—had been in the library at Fisher's Folly. I imagined this book in Shakespeare's hands.

Back in this time books had been published unbound, and often two or three like-minded ones had been bound together to save money. *A Gorgeous Gallery* was bound with two other books, and the other complete one at least had an Oxford connection. *The Paradise of Dainty Devices* was where some of Oxford's poems, including "Framed in the front of forlorn hope," had first been printed. I'd had some vague idea that *Paradise* was a collection of poetry by noblemen. Nope; Oxford was the only living noble author in *Paradise.* Apart from Lord Vaux, who had died twenty years before, the other poets were commoners. One of them, Thomas Churchyard, actually had been Oxford's servant.

Oxford was keeping low company. Servant company. I pictured Shakespeare and the Earl hanging around together, talking about their rotten marriages, and Shakespeare taking in every accent of how his employer talked.

The third book in the volume was one of those pathetic little multiple amputees that people used to bind up at the end of other books. It was too small and too damaged to be a volume by itself; it was missing its title page, its dedications, and who knows how much at the beginning and end; but these two poems somebody had thought worth keeping. A handwritten note in the front said the title was *The Paine of Pleasure*, the author was Munday, and it had been published in 1585. Prime time for Fisher's Folly. I tackled the shorter poem first, "The Author's Dream."

Rankest dankest Anthony Munday.

Good L—d what fancies fall in sleepe, what wonders men shall see
That never like were seen nor heard, nor never like to be.
For proof, peruse this Dream of mine, and see what Fancies strange,
Me thought the world began to turn, unto a wondrous change . . .

It was short at least, only a couple of pages, which couldn't be said for "The Paine of Pleasure."

When I sometime begin to weigh in minde,
The wretched state of miserable man:
Me thinkes (alas) I presently doe finde,
Such suddaine harmes that happen now & then.
*   As everie way doe plainly seeme to show:*
*   That man dooth liue within a world of woe.*

"Life sucks and then you die," I muttered, earning a glare from an Orthodox Jew reading Arabic at the desk next to me. I looked forward to see if it got any better. Thirty-six pages of this, in black letter no less, and the ink had browned through and spread so it was a bitch to read. It looked like some kind of a religious poem, and Munday had found himself a moral: every mortal joy was but a toy, and in case you missed it, he repeated the rhyme every three or four stanzas.

I hoped it was time for lunch, but no, it was barely ten-thirty. *On*ward and *up*ward, gotta read every line, close your eyes and think of Shakespeare.

In childish yeeres, we first with cries begin,
To shew in age, such sorrowes as ensue:
In lustie youth, we dayly trauaile in
Such wicked wayes, as wicked age dooth rue.

I looked ahead at the chapter heads. Beauty. Riches. Honor. Love. All the dull abstractions.

Horses, Hawks, and Dogs?

Horses, hawks, and dogs: that was the fifth pleasure. The sixth was music, the seventh dancing. I glanced down the first page of "Horses, Hawks and Dogs" and fell on a bit about a horse that "snuffs, and snorts, and stands upon no ground"—printer's error for secretary hand "stamps upon the ground"?—which was way more elegant than Munday's usual line.

I took one deep ragged breath, settled my glasses higher on my nose, turned back to the beginning, and started reading *The Paine of Pleasure* line by line.

See then by love, what cost, what care, what woe
In getting first, and keeping then with pain:
In getting first, what daily griefs do grow,
In losing then, what more despite again.
*   Oh madhead man, to joy in such a thing . . .*

Look at those big wide vowels. Who was this?

> *For beauty first breeds liking in the mind,*
> *Liking breeds lust, lust lewdness, lewdness, what?*

It wasn't Munday.

Some of it was rough enough to be Munday, as if two men had collaborated on this poem too. The first sections were stiffer than the rest, and all the way through, whoever was writing this had to deal with the ABABCC rhyme scheme and the joy-toy rhyme. The good stuff really started only with the horses and dogs.

But oh my G-d.

After Munday, after all those shriveled little lyrics of his I'd been reading, this was wonderful.

The Paine of Pleasure was as long as a play, and after those first sections there was hardly a line of crap, it went down like cold soda on a hot day, you didn't know how thirsty you'd been for just this. Whoever he was, this guy was good. He played around with rhymes that would have fallen dead and putrefied for anyone else. He put in all the little bits of filler a bad poet would use, and he made me smile at them.

> *By larges and longs, by breves and semibreves:*
> *Minims, crotchets, quavers, sharps, flats to feign:*
> *Ut, re, mi, fa, sol, la and back again.*

And he loved words. Loved them.

> *By fencing grows our terms of the bravado,*
> *Our foins and thrusts, the deadly stab and all . . .*

The poem was full of technical terms, for tennis, archery, hawking, music, fishing, dancing, *byas, crank, snite, shotterel, dregge.* I
checked the *Oxford English Dictionary.* This guy was using every
term properly, and if *Paine* was written any time around 1585, four
or five of these uses were earlier than the first use the *OED* cited.
Often enough the first use was Shakespeare; Shakespeare had a
huge technical vocabulary, particularly for sports. I thought of
Will Shakespeare, clearing the dishes and listening to Oxford's
guests talk, weeding the cranks in the bowling alleys at Fisher's
Folly, watching the soldiers practice their archery at the butts.

> *What sport it is to see an arrow fly,*
> *A gallant archer cleanly draw his bow,*
> *In shooting off, again how cunningly*
> *He hath his loose, in letting of it go:*
> *To nock it sure, and draw it to the head*
> *And then fly out, hold straight, and strike it dead*
> *With other terms that archers long have used,*
> *As blow wind, stoupe, ah, down the wind a bow:*
> *Tush, says another, he may be excused,*
> *Since the last mark, the wind doth greater grow.*
> *At last he claps in the white suddenly,*
> *Then oh well shot the standers by do cry.*

Those were dramatic voices. Dramatic poetry, which is rare
before Marlowe and Shakespeare. And this wasn't Marlowe.

And for shit sure it wasn't Munday.

Whoever wrote this was taking the joy-toy rhyme and playing
with it, so that you'd anticipate it and groan to yourself and think,
shoot, here comes that rhyme round again, and then he'd twist it

into a new shape and hand it to you like a bouquet. He was doing really sweet things with the rhythm. "At last he claps in the white suddenly": you have to read that line with a pause between *white* and *suddenly,* a pause where the arrow hits, where the guy gasps and thinks to himself, I did it, and there's that little surprised silence before the bystanders applaud. Whoever wrote this was making poetry out of where the reader took a breath.

The point of the poem was supposed to be that the guy regretted everything he'd done; pleasures were nothing, the study of divinity was everything, every joy was but a toy. "Arithmetic doth number worldly toys/Divinity innumerable joys." But he couldn't stick to the point. He kept embroidering great little bits about how a man gets enslaved by learning and accomplishment, what fun it was to learn to sing, what a frustration and a pleasure. This was a poem about an education, about words, by a man who had not only a moral conscience but a heart and a brain.

And he remembered the very phrases the fencing masters used.

> *Lie here, lie there, strike out your blow at length,*
> *Strike and thrust with him, look to your dagger hand:*
> *Believe me, sir, you bear a gallant strength,*
> *But choose your ground, your vantage where to stand . . .*

Dramatic poetry. Voices.

This couldn't be Munday. Munday could fly before he could write this. This guy was not writing about the big Elizabethan subjects, love, drama, death; he was writing about training a horse and learning to climb. He was writing about nothing. He made it everything.

And the poem wasn't three or five pages long. A lot of Elizabethans could be interesting for five pages. But the difference between a lyric poet and a playwright is how long he can keep it up, and this was thirty-six pages long. It was clumsy, some of it was really bad, I hoped some of it was Munday.

The rest?

Yeah, I knew who it was.

It wasn't clearly Shakespeare, not the way you could argue *More* was. Yes, this man used enjambment and correct technical terms. He loved dogs, loved music and hunting; he called law a pleasure. His verse was dramatic; he took a lot of his effects from the way people actually talk. But he didn't have the same sure singing line as Shakespeare, the same complete command of long stressed vowels. He didn't have the same interest in government and the great man that Author Two in *More* showed, and he didn't use those brilliant condensed metaphors. "The pale blood/Which war sluiced forth": whoever wrote *Paine* wasn't capable of that.

But if he were Shakespeare a couple of years before writing *Sir Thomas More?* He wouldn't have the same techniques yet. He'd still be fumbling, writing poems instead of plays, on subjects he didn't really care about. He would have the talent to do voices and characters, but he wouldn't be taking full advantage of it. He'd still be making bad boxes.

My G-d, my G-d, I had found him.

I'd found one of Shakespeare's bad boxes. Written, probably, in collaboration with Munday. In 1585, right about the time Shakespeare came to London. When Oxford had just bought Fisher's Folly, when he was living in it, collecting servants and authors and going to plays.

In 1585, right when and where my theory had said it would be.

Except this was all moonshine. I couldn't prove the poem was Shakespeare's. It was attributed to Munday. And I didn't even really know when *Paine* had been written. All I had was the hand-written note in the front; 1585 would be convenient, but it needed proving.

I checked *The English Short Title Catalog*, the registry of rare books in English. *ESTC* listed *Paine* as published in 1583 by Henry Bynneman but cited "the unique copy"—the book at my reading desk, dated 1585 and with no publisher's name.

My mouth went dry. The unique copy. I'd only seen it because I'd been reading a book bound with it, and I'd only bothered to read it because I'd been reading Munday and because Rachel Goscimer had spent four years telling me to read everything.

God is a librarian. I shook my head as though I had a bug in my ear.

I didn't want 1583. It was too early, before Shakespeare could have come to London. I wanted the 1585 date.

There are ways to date a printed book. Elizabethan printers didn't have a lot of type; it was all hand-cast and expensive. They'd print a book or even a partial book, then they'd sort the type and use it again. The effect was that you could sometimes follow printer's type as it wore out from book to book.

The easiest to follow were unusual letters—ligatures, for instance, *æ*, *ff*, *fl*, which are one letter in type. They wore out in distinctive ways, like typewriter keys in old mysteries. One year the *æ* was nice and crisp; a few years later, weary; and finally it was gone, replaced by a new, slightly different *æ*.

The printer didn't have one *æ*, of course, but a whole box full of them. Sometimes he'd replace the whole box at once, sometimes not. You could date wear best with capital letters that printers had relatively few of, like *Æ*.

This was going to be trouble and a half, but I could look for distinctive ligatures in every dated book Henry Bynneman had published and try to make up a type wear pattern chart. This was outside my line of work — Nicky Bogue could probably do it better — and it was bitching slow, but I could do it.

If Henry Bynneman always used the same printer. If I could identify other dated books printed by the same man. If this book was even actually published by Henry Bynneman. I could look through every book printed by every printer in London for every year in the 1580s, there weren't more than about three hundred per year, that was three thousand or so, . . . Katherine Darnell had written her e-mail address on the offprint she'd given me. She might be able to tackle it.

But on the first page of *Paine,* I found a good trace-character right away. The printer who'd produced *Paine* used one ligature so distinctive I'd almost never seen it before, an Old English *ée.*

At this period in England, there were two sorts of type, Roman and Old English. Roman is modern type. Old English is ye olde black letter. Italian and French printers never used black-letter forms, and *ée* is used only in French, so you almost never see a black-letter ligature *ée.*

But it was here.

The man who printed *Paine* was using it instead of regular English double E. Every EE in *Paine* had an accent: *déepe, swéete, héere.*

And I'd seen this before. Recently.

Where?

Katherine Darnell would have been praising the research angels. I was trying to remember what the fuck the other book had been.

It was fresh in my head, so I hoped I'd seen it in the British

Library and not in the Kellogg Collection. I'd noticed the *ée* because it was odd, but I'd been thinking about something else, something more interesting —

Munday maybe, somewhere in Munday, that was where it *should* be if the theory was right, and I'd only looked at about forty of Munday's books, so *which fucking one?* —

I had to reorder ten books before I knew I wasn't hallucinating. Anthony Munday's *A Watch-Word to England*. Printed for Thomas Hacket, not Henry Bynneman. 1584. The double *ée*'s were all over it.

> . . . which side were true men, and which were Traitours, and for how many days or hours they should be so estéemed . . .

The same typeface, about the same degree of wear. So *Paine* had been published within a few years of *Watch-Word*. Before or after? Could I prove *Paine* had been printed after *Watch-Word* by studying the wear pattern on the double *ée*'s?

I took off my glasses and looked at the two books beside each other. Maybe microscopically I could. But how many times would the typeface have been used between the two books? Ten, maybe? Less? Two or three?

I had to have 1585. By 1585, Shakespeare could have been here in London, maybe have met Oxford through Munday, maybe have got Oxford to hire him. Shakespeare was twenty-one years old, reading in the Earl's library at Fisher's Folly, picking up how Oxford and his friends spoke, what they talked about, how they were educated.

Shakespeare. I couldn't think about him, not yet. Because the

poem had to be 1585, not 1583. In 1583 Shakespeare was still in
Stratford; he wouldn't have met Munday.

It struck me suddenly what I'd found and who I was. It was
like driving a car and finding new gears, sixth, seventh, eighth. It
was inventing a new tool. I was going to write Shakespeare's life.
I closed my eyes and leaned against the solid back of my British
Library chair, and for a moment I just let myself be. I was Shakespeare's biographer.

I needed the date of *The Paine of Pleasure*.

I took a deep breath, stood up at my desk, stared down at the
fat little book, turned the mutilated pages to where the title page
should have been and wasn't.

If God is a librarian He wasn't going to make the only copy of
Paine undatable. If God is a librarian, He was going to give me this.

The *ESTC* had dated this book 1583. Wrong. Maybe it was
wrong that this book was the only copy.

Let there be a second copy. Let it have a title page. Let the title
page have a date.

There are 147 major research libraries in the world. They have
hundreds of millions of books. But most of them have their catalogs online, and it's doable to look up a single book in 147
libraries. If the title of the book was really *The Paine of Pleasure* . . .
I put my books back on reserve and went downstairs to the Internet terminals, glared at a priest reading his email until he signed
off, and started checking catalogs.

The online catalog of the Library of Congress didn't list *The
Paine of Pleasure*. Neither did Harvard, Yale, Columbia, Prince-
ton, the New York Public Library, the Folger Library, or the
Bibliothèque nationale.

I had got halfway through my list of libraries before it occurred to me that I hadn't ordered *The Paine of Pleasure*, only the book with it, and I should check the B.L. catalog too.

~

The second *Paine of Pleasure* was black. It was a photoreproduction from a book at Cambridge University, made back when photoreproductions inverted black and white, so it was the negative of a book. Probably the Cambridge original still existed only because it had belonged to Samuel Pepys. The photographic copy was bound in old cardboard and smelled vinegary. I turned the slippery fragile pages over, comparing it to the copy I had. It was the same edition, the same poem.

Munday's name was on the dedication but not on the title page. That meant it was his collection but not necessarily his poem.

The book had its title page.

And the title page had a date.

I read the date. Twice. Three times. It was a clear date. It wasn't hard to understand.

I closed the book and brought it to the issue desk with the others.

"Do you do Xeroxing?" Yes, they did. "Can you Xerox a book this old?" They had special machinery; they could do it. I ordered *The Paine of Pleasure*, the poems and the ghostly black title page. Even after what I'd just read, I wanted the poem.

I could have the copy the next day.

I left off my other books at the issue desk, got my coat and my backpack, came up into the main hall by the big stairs, and turned and looked up at the marble statue of Shakespeare in the place of honor.

William Shakespeare. The greatest writer in the English language. The man who said such wonderful things, so well, that four hundred years later I would read him for the first time and know he was my future. I would sit in a pickup truck reading *Young Man Shakespeare* and know I wanted to spend my life writing his. I had known Shakespeare all my life. I had pretty much wanted to *be* Shakespeare. I looked up at the marble face, a statue's face. I had learned so much about him these last days. I had known where Shakespeare spent his lost years.

And I'd been almost right.

I turned and pushed the library door open and went blindly outside into the air. I leaned against the base of the crouching-man statue, the statue of Reason, and watched, above the court-yard, the gray clouds scud across the sky.

Shakespeare didn't learn his craft as Oxford's servant.

Oxford was Golding's student when Golding wrote Shake-speare's favorite book, and Golding never wrote anything like it again. Lyly was Oxford's secretary when he wrote what Shake-speare used, and he never wrote anything as good again. Angel Day was Oxford's secretary when he wrote his only book. Anthony Munday *never* wrote like he's supposed to have in *The Paine of Pleasure* except when he was Oxford's servant, or when he was writing *Sir Thomas More.*

It didn't have to be true. It shouldn't have been true.

But it was.

There was a man in London, in Shakespeare's time, and when they hung around him, people wrote good stuff. Everything he published under his own name was bad. But people said he wrote well. So what were they talking about?

Think of *More.* Think when it had to be written. Not 1586, not 1588. By 1586 the Pope had offered a plenary indulgence to who-ever killed Elizabeth, Philip of Spain was getting a loan from the

Pope to invade England, and Catholics were being fined twenty pounds a month, a huge sum. And by 1586 Munday was one of the best-known anti-Catholic writers in England.

I could see a timeline, and it was the wrong one.

1567, Oxford was being tutored by Arthur Golding while Golding was writing Shakespeare's favorite book. 1568, Oxford studied law, one of Shakespeare's pleasures. 1572, he sponsored the publication of *Cardanus Comfort,* a source for *Hamlet,* and he saw the nova, also in *Hamlet.* 1575, he went to Italy, full of sources for Shakespeare. He came back in 1576, the year the Theatre opened. 1577, plays with names like Shakespeare's began to be mentioned in the Revels accounts.

1578 or so, he met Anthony Munday.

1580, Oxford quarrelled with the Howards and denounced Henry Howard and Charles Arundel, using their own words against them, a dramatic trick.

January 1581, as the Knight of the Tree of the Sun he jousted with Philip Howard, the Earl of Arundel. The tournament was about loyalty, the same issue as *Sir Thomas More.*

March to July 1581, Oxford was in the Tower—where Sir Thomas More was imprisoned and beheaded, where Oxford's cousin Surrey the poet was beheaded—with nothing to do but think and write. Could he, or he and Munday, have written a play about More then?

1582, although he was poor, Oxford was sponsoring players, and Munday was helping him.

1584, Oxford bought Fisher's Folly, a ridiculous house down the road from the Theatre, and started a writers' colony. His secretary Munday was talking about the Wars of the Roses as a current political lesson.

1584 or 1585, the first moment that Shakespeare could have moved from Stratford to London. 1585, the first moment that Shakespeare could have collaborated with Munday on *The Paine of Pleasure.*

1585 or 1586, the first moment Shakespeare could have collaborated with Munday on *Sir Thomas More.*

And *The Paine of Pleasure* was written—?

The title page gave the very day it was published.

October 17, 1580.

An autumn day in London. Shakespeare would have been sixteen. He wouldn't have been in London collaborating with Anthony Munday. He might have been still at school, or apprenticed to his father, or a servant in the Hoghtons' household in Lancashire where he might have just been meeting the people who would introduce him to Munday.

William Shakespeare of Stratford would have been sixteen.

*O*ne dusk in March when I was two months old, my mother went out on the Norton road and walked in front of a truck. By the time I was old enough to start wondering about her, I knew she was dead, and I sort of knew she had committed suicide, but Dad kept the details from me. Then one summer afternoon at the library I decided to look everything up in the old newspaper files. After I'd finished reading, I rode my bike out to the Norton road and I sat there, and I could see the truck and hear the brakes squealing, and I could see the truck like she'd seen it, the lights coming down on me, and the wheel treads at the last. I felt like my bones were breaking.

When Dad and I talked about it, he told me, "She just didn't know what was real, son. She saw things. Maybe she just didn't think the truck was there."

You have to have imagination. Rachel Goscimer was right about that. You can't recognize where a puzzle piece fits if you can't imagine the finished puzzle. But sometimes you don't know whether the picture's real or you're making it up, and you sit there, at the side of the road, seeing the truck all jackknifed into the tree and a smear on the windshield and a smear on the asphalt, and you don't know which is worse, making it up or not, and you might not even be sitting at the side of the road, you might be roadkill and dying and not know it.

I walked. I headed toward the City and got myself lost and just kept walking. I don't know where I went. Through streets of ugly brick-fronted buildings, by electronics stores, through a garden with dirty gravestones lining its walls, past office buildings. In a garden I would never find again, I saw a monument to Heminge and Condell and the First Folio. At the top of the monument was a bust of Shakespeare, looking like Marley's ghost, disapproving and dead.

I wasn't going to talk with Posy. Posy would think it was a great idea that Shakespeare was Oxford. I didn't want it to be easy for her. I wanted both of us to be thinking more about evidence.

I wanted us sitting on the steps at Covent Garden, holding hands and not knowing anything.

But you could make a good case that *Paine* was Oxford's. Oxford was just about to renounce Catholicism and the Howards; the subject of *The Paine of Pleasure* was repentance; a lot of Oxford's extant poems used the ABABCC rhyme scheme; the good bits were better than Munday could do; Munday was Oxford's secretary. The poem was describing a nobleman's education. The poem hadn't even technically been published under Munday's name.

And if *Paine* was Oxford's, Oxford wasn't a man who wrote a few bad lyrics. In 1580, he was writing a play-length poem that shared some characteristics—not all, but some, and not the easiest—with Shakespeare. And publishing it in a way that it could be taken for another man's.

I had just better hold on, have something to eat and think about it some more, get another handle on it and try to *explain* it.

Because Oxford couldn't be Shakespeare.

I reached the river. Between the brick buildings and the gasworks, on the south bank, I saw a thatch-roofed building as quaint as a bandstand in a park, and I knew where I wanted to go.

I already knew who I needed to talk to.

I found a telephone. "Mary Cat? Yeah. I'm in London. Can I talk to you?"

She could get away from the hostel in an hour, she said. She'd meet me at the New Globe.

Even in March, the New Globe was solid with tourists, elbow

to elbow, waiting to get in. I paid my ticket, huddled into the warm middle of the crowd, and listened to the guide. "William Shakespeare, greatest genius of the English language, was born 23 April 1564 in Stratford-upon-Avon." The guy was so certain. Solid as the oak and stone and horsehair plaster they'd built the New Globe from, solid as oak beams. And that's what I wanted; that certainty; the Shakespeare I'd known all my life.

The Shakespeare I'd built my life on.

The thing was, though, the guy was certain, but—Shakespeare could have been born on April 23, but all we know is he was christened the twenty-sixth. We think he went to Stratford Grammar School. We don't know.

What I'd been dealing with, these last days, was a man who I *knew* had been in a lot of the places where Shakespeare should have been, I *knew* had got the education Shakespeare should have got, I *knew* had known the men Shakespeare did.

He wasn't Shakespeare. He couldn't be. Shit, an earl. A fucking *earl*.

But he remembered words. Remembered every word Henry Howard and his friends said. *Diverse other brave and glorious speeches.* I'd told Posy Oxford was too rich to notice anything like that. Well, he hadn't been rich. Cecil had farmed him like the north forty. He'd been frustrated, and poor, and wrote a little, and had friends in the theater.

That didn't make him Shakespeare.

But had he written this poem?

A datable poem that sounded like Shakespeare. Some. Not a lot, but some. And was too early for Shakespeare. But not for Oxford.

I went into the Globe itself, stood down among the groundlings, eye-height to the stage. The stage was covered in scaffolding. No one knows exactly what the Globe looked like; Theo Crosby and John Ronayne had designed this one between 1994 and 1997, and just this winter, after three years of performing, they'd realized they'd got things wrong and had ripped the stage apart and reworked it.

Mist, not quite rain, drifted down on us groundlings' heads.

The original Globe wasn't a new building; it was the Theatre. The Burbages had owned the Theatre but not the land under it. The landlord had thought he had the Burbages by the short and curlies and had raised the rent, so the Burbages and their friends had snuck up on the building one night with sledgehammers and had hauled it beam by beam to Southwark.

That was the Globe. Slum theater. Theater for servants avoiding work, for pickpockets and whores. For shithouse rats and guys with Harleys who lived next the laundromat. For groundlings. Not for earls. Earls wrote for Elizabeth.

Oxford had bought Fisher's Folly because he liked plays. He'd published poems in *Paradise* as "E. O.," sharing the pages with men who'd been his servants. But what he hadn't done, what he couldn't do, what no one in the world could imagine him doing, was what Will Shakespeare could have done so easily: "I'm the Earl of Oxford's servant. I want to try my hand at rewriting plays. I want to sell you a play for five pounds," what Oxford might have paid for a pair of gloves.

Forget it. Oxford died in 1604. Shakespeare kept writing until 1613. Shakespeare had to be Shakespeare.

On the stage hangings of the New Globe, Atlas was holding the world with New Zealand facing forward because New Zealand had donated the hangings. "This is exactly like the original

Globe," the guide was saying. But nothing in the year 2000 was what it had been in 1599. It was a good approximation, you had to be grateful, and it was teaching us lots, but it was a new theater.

Downstairs, in the Undercroft exhibition space, I didn't see anything about Cecil or the Howards, Edmund Campion or Anthony Munday. The New Globe people stuck to talking about theater: Elizabethan theatrical costumes; music; staging; special effects, ghosts and hanging and demons. You could make a quill pen, try on costume armor, create your own edition of *Hamlet* from the bad quarto and the good one. I listened to a recording of an actor giving speeches from *Hamlet* in an "authentic" Elizabethan accent.

How did they know it was authentic? In the Undercroft exhibit there was a timeline of Shakespeare's life. They said he came to London via the road through Oxford. They knew how long it took him. How did they fucking know?

I wasn't going to find facts about the Elizabethans here. The New Globe was great for what it was. But it didn't do all-male versions of the plays because they were authentic; it did them because this theater had been built after Stonewall and Gay Pride and political correctness, and male actors wanted to experiment with playing women. (Twelve-year-old female impersonators? Not this millennium.) The New Globe didn't spread plague, or scatter hazelnut shells on the ground to keep off fleas. The New Globe had bathrooms. It knew how to keep authenticity in its place.

The New Globe had William Shakespeare, just as good a Shakespeare as it needed. And all it needed of him was here, quill pens, quotations, recordings of plays, photos of famous actors. Famous voices wafting like scent through the air. Words. Famous words. Comfortable words.

The New Globe had William Shakespeare of Stratford.

Which is what every single academic in English literature had too. William Shakespeare of Stratford wrote Shakespeare's plays. We were sure of it. William Shakespeare of Stratford dealt in wool and grain and lent money at interest and kept back grain during a famine, which didn't sound like Shakespeare the playwright, but that wasn't important. We were sure of it. Some of what we know about Shakespeare fitted Edward de Vere like a glove, but Edward de Vere was an impostor, we were sure of it. Shakespeare was Shakespeare was Shakespeare was Shakespeare, a man holding a quill pen, writing the plays: a mask for anybody's face. In the lost years he could have been in Tibet studying levitation with Sherlock Holmes. It didn't matter. Because we knew it didn't matter. We were sure.

And if I said anything else, I never could teach, I never could write. Not in any reputable college in the world. Roland Goscimer wouldn't give me a recommendation. Shit, he wouldn't even let me write a thesis.

But who Shakespeare was was all over his plays. All over them. It was too late not to know that.

So what was I going to do?

I wandered into the store. Most of the stock was gift-shop stuff, Globe magnets and Globe dishtowels and china statues of Hamlet and Sir John Falstaff, but the books were good. Lots of material on staging. Whole books debating the shape of pillar bases and whether the Globe had twenty sides or twenty-four. *Tudor and Stuart Monarchy*. Roy Strong's *Cult of Elizabeth*. John Southworth, *Fools and Jesters at the English Court* —

Thomas Churchyard. Monarcho.

Katherine Darnell had said something about Churchyard

writing the elegy of a fool named Monarcho. I did the bookstore thing, retreated behind a counter and opened Southworth quickly to scan the index.

Thomas Churchyard, Oxford's former servant—Thomas Churchyard, who'd been in *Paradise* with Oxford—had written an elegy for the fool Monarcho in 1580. Not too hard to believe Churchyard had presented a copy of it to his old employer.

And Monarcho showed up in Shakespeare.

Ah, fuck, it was little things. It was iron filings on a sheet of cardboard, all moving in the same direction, rising and arching. I could ignore it. I could say anything. I should be saying the things that English departments knew how to hear. I could keep quiet until I was on my deathbed, like Rachel Goscimer.

"Joe?"

Mary Cat didn't look much different: kerchief over her curls, little gold cross and penitential Salvation Army red parka. The parka looked worse than ever; it had got a rip in the elbow, and she'd patched it, but feathers were oozing out from the patch.

"What a surprise! What are you doing in London?" She took a second look at me. "Joe, are you all right?"

"Yeah, fine." I was thinking about myself connecting Shakespeare and Munday and Campion, glibly promising myself I'd show off in front of her.

"Have you found something in the Kellogg after all?"

I didn't know how to answer this.

"Something for a thesis?" she asked.

Fuck, no. "I don't think so."

She smiled at me. She looked tired. Not as happy as I'd expected. "You miss Boston?" I asked.

"I miss you, Joe," she said. "What is it? You sounded so worried."

214 / SARAH SMITH

If I told Mary Cat, she'd tell me to talk to Goscimer. Who, I realized, was just about to get to London too; shit, he was going to be here by Sunday to talk on the BBC. About *In Search of Shakespeare*. Oh *shit*.

"The thing in the Kellogg is nothing, I'm just here to make sure it's a forgery."

If the poem was real, I thought, the letter wasn't a forgery. If the poem was real, Nicky Bogue was going to say the letter was real.

How many days did I have until he did?

She was peeling off her wool gloves. The yarn clung to her rough hands. "You—you do look worried," she said, frowning up at me, "but you don't look as though it's a forgery, you look as though it's good. I mean," Mary Cat said, "you look— You look— *Extraordinary*, Joe. You look as if the most extraordinary thing has happened."

Extraordinary. Amazing. And I was biting on it, like I'd bit on the Shakespeare letter in the Kellogg. "It's nothing." How I hoped it was nothing.

"Well," Mary Cat said. "It's brought you to London, anyway."

"Yeah, London's great. I need to get out of here," I said. I was going to get angry at Mary Cat just for acting cheery, just for talking when I was panicked. "I keep seeing what's wrong with this place."

"Have you seen the Globe?" said Mary Cat. "I mean the real one? Or the Rose?"

"No," I said. "No, I haven't." You can't see the Globe anymore, I thought; you can't see the Rose. They're gone, with the Theatre and the Curtain and Fisher's Folly and Anthony Munday and Oxford and Shakespeare and everybody who fucking knew who wrote that poem.

"Let's go. They're right round the corner," she said, "and I think they'd do us good."

~

The Rose was the first theater built on the Bankside. Shakespeare's *Titus Andronicus* and *Henry VI*, Part 1, premiered at the Rose. Christopher Marlowe wrote *Tamburlaine, The Jew of Malta,* and *Dr. Faustus* for the Rose; Ben Jonson and Thomas Kyd had plays performed there. Edward Alleyn, the great Elizabethan actor, was the house leading man, and Philip Henslowe was the manager. Remember Ben Affleck in *Shakespeare in Love?* Edward Alleyn. And the theater? The Rose.

In 1989, an old warehouse on Bankside was being torn down for a new office development. During the winter building lull, when it was too cold to pour concrete, a Museum of London archaeological team was allowed onto the site. And on one cold winter day, they unearthed the first pilings of the Rose.

God is a librarian.

The developers had built the office building—modified so the Rose could be excavated someday. Meanwhile they'd stabilized the excavations under concrete and a pool of water in the building's basement. You could see it from a viewing balcony above. Mary Cat and I looked down at blue lights on the concrete floor, outlining the walls of the theater. Dim floods shone down into the pool in the middle of the basement, and once our eyes adjusted, we could see an eerie rubbled outline, part of the stage. There wasn't much to see. To feel—

Edward Alleyn acted *here.* Alleyn, the first of his kind, England's first great secular actor. Shakespeare stood *here* watching his early plays being rehearsed. The water was brownish like tea or peat-water, clear, not very deep. Toward the back of the basement, behind the pool, was a set of iron stairs. I could see a man with a cloak slung rakishly over his shoulder standing on the stairs, gesturing as he spoke. He half-ran, half-slid down the stairs and waded into the pool, ignoring the water and the white sticks and anything but stage and audience, and for a moment the pool and the concrete were alive with faces, groundlings watching Edward Alleyn.

Mary Cat had been right. I'd needed to come here.

We stood for a long time in utter silence. We were the only two people on the balcony. The Rose doesn't get the crowds the New Globe does. From the little gift shop we could hear someone singing along with a radio. In here, speaking would have been wrong, like talking at the Confessor's tomb.

Good as it was, the New Globe was the lightning bug. This was the lightning. The hairs stood up on my arms.

Forget I'd ever seen the poem?

Shakespeare did go to Italy, I thought. He did. And I'd told Posy I wanted the real thing, and so did she; and fuck me, but I'd got it; and here was my friend Mary Cat, here when I needed to talk.

I cleared my throat finally. "I found something," I said quietly, so as not to disturb the Rose. "And it scares me. I got started thinking about—a problem—one way rather than another. And I keep finding things and everything makes sense. But it shouldn't. I don't want it to."

Mary Cat leaned on the pipe railing, looking up at me.

"You could tell me whether it's as strange as I think. Part of it's about Catholics, your Edmund Campion. And Anthony Munday. Shakespeare may have known Campion at Hoghton Tower," I said. "Munday knew him in Rome. Could Shakespeare have used that to make Munday's acquaintance?"

Mary Cat shook her head violently. "Munday *hated* the Catholics.

He testified against all of Campion's associates. He came to their executions, Joe."

"Why do you think he wrote *Sir Thomas More,* then?" I asked.

"The play Shakespeare was supposed to have had a hand in?" She shook her head. "I'd have to look at it. I didn't even realize it was the same Munday."

Like everybody else, she'd never read anything but the Ill May Day scene. I still had the printout of *Sir Thomas More* in my backpack. I took it out and handed it to her.

She looked down at her rough hands on the railing. "I don't know when I'll have the time to work on it, Joe." Her fingers were red and raw. I held it out to her anyway, kept it in front of her until she took it.

"What are you, Mary Cat?" I asked. "The scullery maid?"

"There's only three of us at the hostel."

"It's a waste of you."

"You install windows because you need the money. I scrub floors because I need God."

I clenched my fists around the pipe railing. I could see the scars on my knuckles. I could see Dad's missing teeth and the empty main street of East Bradenton. I didn't want to scrub floors, I didn't want to install windows, I needed Shakespeare.

"Joe," Mary Cat said, "what is it?"

I only shook my head. "Let's go to the Globe."

⁓

When the archaeologists found the Rose, that wasn't the end of it. That map of London showed the theaters in their relationship to each other. On one side of the street, the Rose. On the other side, the Globe.

218 / SARAH SMITH

Mary Cat and I looked through an iron fence at a cobblestoned yard between a new apartment building and some luxury condos. Here, in someone's parking lot, behind a fence, just a couple of feet away from someone's kitchen window, a new wide smooth curve of granite reflected the light, and two words were sand-blasted into it.

THE GLOBE.

It can't be dug up; there's a historical building over the site. But it's there.

We pressed our faces against the fence. The heavy river mist collected on my glasses. I wiped them on my sleeve and then stepped back to try to imagine Shakespeare's theater. I estimated the curve of the building and walked back down the street, one door, two. Now I was inside it, on holy ground. Somewhere under my feet was a wooden circle, the last remnants of the tim-bers from the Theatre that had become the timbers of the Globe, and four hundred years ago, in this place, here, servants and apprentices had stood crowded elbow to elbow in the rain, look-ing up at Shakespeare's stage. I looked up beyond the stage to three stories of massive timbers and white plaster, and then to the hut above the heavens, above that to the thatched roof and the painted playhouse flag, Atlas bearing the globe on his shoulders. I walked backward, looking up, seeing the gray mist, the Globe's black timbers and dripping thatch.

The cloud-capp'd towers, the gorgeous palaces,
The solemn temples, the great globe itself —

The real thing.

And I saw him, the way he would have looked when he'd first

seen the Theatre, when he'd first stood inside it. Not the fancy Italian-dressed boy Posy had showed me; he was thirty-four by then, a man with some mileage on his face. *Defeatured* is Shakespeare's word for it, looking old out of disappointment. The year he'd bought Fisher's Folly, he'd given up his acting companies. Everybody thought it was because he was poor. But that had never stopped Oxford.

You saw Burbage, I thought. You walked down the road and saw Burbage. Shit, you saw all of them, the best theater company in England, honed by playing to real audiences every day, and you couldn't have them. You couldn't buy them. You couldn't write for them. Thomas Churchyard could get five pounds for a play, Anthony Munday could, but you were senior earl of England, five pounds was what you paid for a pair of gloves, and there were some things you wanted it wasn't fitting for you to have.

Because you were an earl. A fucking earl.

Hamlet wrote a play. Hamlet brought the actors to his house and started talking with them, listening to them, telling them what he wanted. "Nor do not saw the air too much with your hand—"

He turned, the man in my imagination. He turned away from the building and looked at me. *Do you see now,* he said, *do you see that I did whatever I had to?*

Mary Cat was looking over at me, a little concerned.

"Mary Cat," I said, "did Dad ever talk to you about my mom?"

"No," she said in a way that might have meant no, but she'd figured it out anyway.

"*Her* mother had died in a car accident, and she was afraid of cars. After I was born, she started seeing cars that weren't there. She knew they weren't there, she was trying to ignore them. So one night she went out walking the Norton road and she saw a truck, I don't know whether she was being healthy-minded or what and saying to herself that truck's not really there, but anyway, it was." I wanted to make that story into a joke, or not tell it at all. It wasn't a joke. "I did a lot of research on hallucinations after I found that out, and there was this guy who wrote about his own hallucinations. He was a mathematician. He said the hallucinations came from the same place his math did." I see things, I didn't tell Mary Cat. I can smell Elizabethan London, no problem. I just saw Oxford. I could share a padded cell with Batty and Looney. "I don't think I'm crazy. I've got a good imagination but I know what's real. At least I always did. But what I've found is so fucking different from anything *anybody's* ever found. And if I were going to start hallucinating about anything, it'd be Shakespeare."

"It's about Shakespeare?"

I took a deep breath. "I found a poem today. Not in the Kellogg. In the British Library. Published. It's long, it's supposed to be Munday's, it isn't. It's good. Parts of it are really good, as good as Gascoigne. The sort of person you'd have heard more of."

"Shakespeare?" said Mary Cat.

I shivered all over. "I hope not. — It's too early to talk about it. I'll come back and look at it again and it'll be ordinary."

"You hope not?"

"Mary Cat," I said, "the date's wrong."

And I told her, told her the whole story from the letter onward; and I watched her not believe it. We had known each other for years, we had gone through papers and oral exams together, we'd studied together, we'd painted houses for Habitat for Humanity together, we'd cried for Rachel Goscimer together, we'd bitched and moaned over the Kellogg; and she'd watched me disapprove of her going off to be a nun, and not say as much as I could have, so she didn't say anything now. She just listened. But the freckles stood out on her face, and behind her I could see the Globe, Shakespeare's Globe, Shakespeare's stage, and she turned to look at it too, and I knew she felt like I was spitting on Shakespeare, right here at the Globe, because that was how I felt.

"1580," I said.

She shook her head unconsciously.

"You haven't seen it."

"But—*Shakespeare?* And you say it isn't very good. How can it be Shakespeare? How do you know?"

"It's not very good," I didn't know how to tell her how that poem had affected me, "but then for bits and pieces it's really good." Oh shit. "I don't know, I don't know, Mary Cat, if I knew I wouldn't worry about being crazy. Can I show you the poem? Look, it's okay if it's ordinary, it won't be Shakespeare, I just—" I shook my head. "I can deal with that, what I can't deal with is thinking it is. And I can't ask Goscimer. Not now."

"No," she said, "of course you can't."

"So will you look at it?"

"Me?" she said. "Joe, I'm just a graduate student, like you." She pressed her scoured-raw fingers together as if she were praying. "I'm not even that."

"I trust you," I said.

"I'd like to help," she said. She walked a little way away from me; she leaned her forehead against the fence, pressing against the iron bars with her long fingers. "Oh, Joe, never mind help, I'd like to *read* it. If you even *think* it might be Shakespeare's. But—" She turned back toward me, her face a mask of misery. "I can't. I shouldn't. Please."

"Why, Mary Cat?"

"I'm not a researcher. I don't do that anymore. —Joe," she said. "Joe, the sisters at the Society are trying to get me to go back to school."

Good for them, I thought.

"I know you'd like that," she said. "But don't, Joe, don't. They think just because I have most of a Ph.D. — They think I should be teaching. Joe, I want to be your friend, Joe, but I want to be a nun— I have to prove myself."

"Scrubbing floors instead of Shakespeare," I said flatly.

"Yes," she said.

They're right, I thought. "Yeah. Sure."

"I feel as though I'm not being your friend," Mary Cat said.

"Yeah, well, forget that. I understand."

She kept on looking at me, as though I could give her some absolution for not looking at my poem, not doing what she was good at. "You can say no, that's your decision," I said. "But you're not being your own friend."

She looked away from me for a moment, and then she did something I'd never seen her do in four years of knowing her. She reached up and pulled the kerchief off her hair. Her curls sprang out, unruly in the rain. And for a moment she wasn't a nun at all, she was just a stubborn unhappy woman with a little gold cross around her neck.

"You need me," she said, looking up at me. "I can see that. I know that. You need someone to talk to. A friend. And every-thing in me says I ought to do that for you, that that's the right thing to do. But— I have a chance to join an order, if I can prove myself, I know it's not all of what I hoped, but it is a chance." She looked up at me. "You must find someone else."

Yeah. Who else was I going to talk to? Katherine Darnell. She leaned toward Oxford; she wasn't an academic. Who else was I going to talk to, without going public, talking to some specialist?

Who else?

Duh.

"Yeah," I said, "I can find someone else. But Mary Cat? At least you ought to get your Ph.D."

"Don't tempt me, Joe, no one will ever let me teach. Make me feel better by saying you really have someone else to talk with?"

"Yeah," I said. "Sort of. I do." Don't tempt me, she'd said. That's not what someone says who's sure of herself. "Are you sure?" I asked her. "Is this really what you ought to do?"

She smiled sadly. "I'm sure I can't read your poem." Her face went still for a moment, the long stare of a soldier. She looked desperate and sad to me.

"Pray for me," she said.

I nodded. "Pray for me," I said, which wasn't my style at all.

"I will. Take good care, Joe. God bless you." She shook my hand, and held it for a minute, looking into my eyes, seeing something in my face, or wanting to say something. But all she said was, "Do you want to come see the hostel?"

"No, I'm staying with this girl, I've got to get back."

"Oh," she said. "A girlfriend?"

"I don't know. I guess. Yeah."

"That's nice." She smiled wanly, then with a sudden mischief, "Does she study the Elizabethans?"

"Yeah. She does."

"Good luck with her then, Joe."

And I wanted to say something too, I had a lot more questions to ask her, a lot more to say, I wanted to know what was going to happen to her. But she was already tying her kerchief back over her red hair, and putting back on with it her professional nun's cheerfulness.

"Goodbye then. Joe," she said, "be careful."

"Goodbye. You be careful too."

Mary Cat went off down Southwark Bridge Road. Wait, I thought, looking after her, but it was too late, she was just turning the corner; and whatever I could have said to her, we hadn't had quite enough time, it was too late.

⁓

"Nicky said he'll have the report by the end of the weekend," Posy said darkly. "I'm like going to totally kill Saliva before then."

"The end of the weekend?" It was Thursday morning at the Gould apartment. On Sunday afternoon, Roland Goscimer would be speaking on the radio, telling the world what Shakespeare did in the lost years. He would be in London tomorrow, I figured. Or he'd have arrived already. I had picked up my poem at the British Library early this morning and had had the Xerox Xeroxed again, three copies. One would be for Katherine Darnell; I'd e-mailed her asking for her address. The other two— Who? Steven May, maybe? He'd written the standard book on Elizabethan courtier poets. How could I talk to anybody without talking first to Goscimer?

"I made Daddy buy me a car," Posy said. "And I made Saliva spend like a whole day at car dealers with me. She was *so* bored. Do you want to go somewhere, or do we have to stay in the library? Have you found out more about Munday?"

I wasn't ready to go back and face Munday and that marble

mask of Shakespeare. I just wanted to cower under the bed and cry until I could talk to a sensible reliable person who wasn't an Oxfordian.

What I was going to have was Posy.

"*I* found something," Posy said.

"What?" I said touchily.

"I didn't have a lot of time, but we went past the London Library and I remembered something. Have you read *The First Night of Twelfth Night?* Do you remember Hotson gives a list of who was there?"

According to Leslie Hotson, Shakespeare wrote *Twelfth Night* for a gala party Queen Elizabeth gave on Twelfth Night, January 6, 1602. The Lord Chamberlain kept his party-planning notes and the invitation list. God is a librarian; it's the only record existing of an audience for a Shakespeare premiere. "There's a list of who she wanted in the audience, not who came."

"The same thing," Posy said. "She's the Queen, duh, you can't say sorry, I have to wash my hair? Guess who's on her list and who isn't."

"Oxford and Albert Einstein. I don't know."

"Oxford's wife is there. Oxford's daughter and son-in-law. Where's Oxford?"

"You think he's backstage?" I said.

Posy kissed her hand to me and handed me the book. Not only the Countess of Oxford and the Earl and Countess of Derby, but Oxford's sister and her husband and a fistful of Oxford cousins. In all, about a third of the audience were Oxford's family and friends.

One more thing, one more unimportant interesting thing, one more iron filing jumping in the air.

"I want to go to Castle Hedingham," Posy said. "Before any-body else knows. I want to be the first, the only one except you. Do you have to go to the B.L. today, or can you come?"

Shit, I didn't want to go to the library. "I want to go to Strat-ford," I said, and didn't know why, and then did. Stratford at least had really been Shakespeare's. I wanted to find him there.

"Boring."

"I want to go to Stratford." I wanted to visit Shakespeare, my Shakespeare. The Shakespeare I always thought I knew. I wanted to get my certainty back.

"Okay, but Hedingham first."

We could get to Castle Hedingham and Stratford both in one day if Posy drove, Posy claimed. So we got Posy's car, which was garaged in a bad neighborhood in North London. It was a snappy yellow '30s-looking Batmobile that looked way too high-powered for Posy or anyone else. Posy drove north on the high-way.

"So, what did you find out about Munday?" Posy asked me.

"You want to watch the road there, Posy."

I hadn't quite thought through Posy driving. She zinged along fast enough to make my teeth vibrate. I was in what would have been the driver's seat in America, but this was a British car, my side only had the radio on it, and it was like one of those night-mares where you're driving down a twisty highway with no steering wheel or brakes. When Posy swerved to the right to pass, I clutched at air.

"Let me drive."

"It's my car, it's your first time in the country, relax."

"Then get off the highway, country's what I want to see."

We got off at Milton Keynes, the city the British planned back in the sixties, streets all letters and numbers, everything concrete and gray. I expected to see little robots sweeping the streets. But outside Milton Keynes we crossed some sort of invisible dividing line into farmland. The roads shrank to narrow lanes, and it was spring. Oil spots from farm equipment dotted the road, the oil shining iridescent and lilac in the March sunlight. Shadows of clouds swept across a field, and in the sunlight the hedges were checkered with shifting light and dark greens. We passed through sudden scraps of village: a square-steepled church and a pub, a shop that sold seed in familiar twenty-pound bags, a shop that fixed motorcycles. Tiny roads headed off over rises, into woods. I'd seen roads like this in Vermont, heading across pastures and past barns, unpaved, unofficial, existing only because they had someplace to go. Pale blue signs pointed to High Garrett and Gosfield, Great Maplestead and Little Maplestead, Bird Pasture Farm, just off the road but unvisited, secrets in plain sight. I cranked down the window and smelled field grass, like home.

He was a farm boy, Oxford. A man from the country.

In the early afternoon we reached Castle Hedingham.

We came to the village first, perhaps fifty buildings around a church, sprawled in a valley as comfortably as a dog sleeping in the sun. Old brick, old black-and-white buildings, mossy tiled roofs, even a thatched roof or so, a bicycle shop, a tea room, a country hostel with two bikes leaning against the wall. There was barely room for a sidewalk between the road and the housefronts, and cars were parked haphazardly up and down the street. Behind the main street and the town square stood an ancient church guarding a green graveyard. A warren of lanes led up toward the castle, and the streets curved along the line of a disappeared curtain wall.

"Castle first," Posy said, "or lunch?"

I nodded at the Bell Inn.

Posy parked her yellow car by the inn, which was painted pink, somebody's favorite color I guessed. The building was bow-fronted with time. The yellow car shone in the sun. A crow fluttered down from bare branches to investigate. It perched on the hood, black against yellow. The valley was deeper than it looked, cupping the village like the palms of hands; Posy, pink-cheeked and warm, unhooked her black jacket and shook out her hair and the crow flew away.

I had to duck to get through the pub's low door. Inside, the decor was Couldn't Care Less, mismatched chairs and old tobacco smoke and beer smell, but old, old. Huge beams braced the walls like trees. What looked like half the people in the valley were lingering over lunch. The empty table by the window had a handwritten sign on it, "Reserved for Patrick 1:45." I gravitated to a table where a corner post met a bearing beam and ran my hand up and down the wood, oak rubbed by centuries of shoulders and elbows into a thick smoothness. In the crotch where the brace met the corner post, there was an ax cut, a logger's mark, still sharp-edged and almost splintery, as if it were new. I touched it the way Posy had touched Shakespeare's signature on the letter. When this had been made, the king of England had held his throne in fiefdom from the Pope and the earls of Oxford had owned this village.

The ploughman's lunch had Stilton cheese, the cream of parsnip soup made Posy and me both grin. "Patrick" came in, a shy man with a ZZ Top beard and a face-hiding cap, and the waitress brought him his food without asking, two beers and a pizza. I wanted to tell him to try the soup.

As we paid and left, Posy pointed out a handwritten notice on the wall: "William Cecil, Lord Burghley, stayed here with his party in 1592."

The Bell Inn had been here when Oxford was alive, and ever since, and now.

"No wonder the Bell never renovated," Posy said as we walked up toward the castle. "The villagers would totally riot if they ever shut down the kitchen."

"Shakespeare," I thought out loud. "I was looking at a mark on a beam. A logger's mark, what a guy makes to get paid for a tree he's cut. Must have been made when the Bell was built, it's in the frame. The guy who made that X probably never gave it a second thought, wham wham with the ax, his mark, on to the next tree. But nobody tore the place down, nobody renovated or painted or covered the mark up, so it's still there. And now who knows the guy who made it or his family or his friends or what he believed or how he looked? All we know is the mark. That's all we know."

"This relates to Shakespeare how?" said Posy.

"All we're judging from is marks on walls. Whatever's left from four hundred years ago."

"I think we just ate lunch in Shakespeare's pub," Posy said. "I think we've been where his house was in London, we know the books he read, we know where he got his education, we know who his secretaries were. I think there's like a ton of stuff we know. And we have the letter. Are you going to tell me about Munday?"

"Not now."

Through the trees we could see the castle.

In Oxford's time, Hedingham castle was almost a village, a maze of buildings like the Tower. In the millennium, only the Tudor bridge and the castle itself still existed. Hedingham was tall and plain and simple, a smooth-sided white cube with one remaining square tower. By the entrance the stone facing had fallen away, showing massive flint beneath.

Inside, it was cavelike and as functional as an Indian adobe house. Hedingham was five stories tall, one big room to a floor. A storeroom on the lowest floor, a hall and guards' room on the first. Above that, the two-story Great Hall with its half-round Norman arch and its minstrels' gallery; above that a dormitory. All the windows were carved with Moorish twisted-rope decoration. It was built by soldiers who had gone on the Crusades; it was comfortable, the kind of place that would have had couches to sprawl on and books and newspapers scattered around if it wasn't a museum, but a little exotic too; it belonged someplace where the natives spoke another language, in a hot desert under a holy sun.

"I totally love this house," Posy said. We climbed to the minstrels' gallery and looked down at the Great Hall, no bigger than a rich man's living room. Perhaps fifty or sixty people could have sat there comfortably, listening to music or watching a play. The arched recesses, the gallery, the stairs where the servants went up and down would have made good places for actors to wait for cues. A shouting group of schoolkids poured into the hall, pointing at the suit of armor and the helmets, pretending to sword-fight.

"This house was like four hundred years old when he was born. It would have been so great to grow up here."

One of the schoolgirls was leaning over the railing of the minstrels' gallery. "Oh Romeo Romeo, wherefore art thou Romeo," she said and dropped her hat over the edge like a water balloon.

"Wow," Posy said softly.

We looked out the windows. Outside on the lawn a man with a hawk was talking to more schoolkids. He swung his arm forward; the hawk exploded into the air, muscling up toward the tops of the trees, above us, spiraling high.

The top floor was a barracks. The retainers slept here with rugs hanging between them for privacy. The earl and his family had an alcove tunneled into the thickness of the wall. By Oxford's time the Oxfords probably lived in the Tudor buildings, but I stood at the entrance to the earl's alcove and wondered whether Oxford ever camped the night here, listening to the soldiers.

It hurt me to be here. I wanted Shakespeare to be the man I knew, Shakespeare from Stratford. But this place fit him too. A house full of history. Soldiers to listen to, ordinary farmers and villagers hanging around the Bell, servants and actors to mimic, and the fate of England being discussed every time his father's friends visited.

Outside, on the lawn, kids were galloping at each other, whacking at each other with imaginary swords.

The castle was on a little hill and the trees around it were full of crows. Crows have long memories for meat. Maybe they remembered that there had been crowds of men and horses here once, a long time ago, and scraps from feasting. From the window I could see the crows' big messy nests high in the trees, nine, ten, eleven in one oak; the birds were scolding hoarsely. *Light thickens, and the crow makes wing to the rooky wood.* There were other castles on hills in England, other woods and crows. But there they were, wheeling and wavering in the sky like iron filings.

"Come outside," I told Posy. "I want to talk to you."

Beyond the castle and the lawn around, beyond the Tudor bridge and the site of the tiltyard and the archery butts, there was a path around the lake. We took the path into the woods.

"Munday is the clue," I said.

The path whispered with dead leaves. By the side of it, a birch tree or some English tree with white bark had split a rock and was growing through it, clutching the two halves of the rock and spreading them apart with its roots. It looked like an Elizabethan emblem, something a knight would wear on his shield.

"All this is theory, Posy, I've got no proof. But I started with the idea that *Sir Thomas More* was written by two men at the same time, Munday and another man who I think sounds like Shakespeare."

I'd already told her this. I jammed my fists in my pockets nervously.

"Right," said Posy, "except Shakespeare was Oxford."

"You hold on here and let me talk. We know a lot about Munday's life. One of the authors of *More* makes fun of More, I think that was Munday. But Munday was strongly anti-Catholic; after the arrest of the first Jesuits, he probably wouldn't have written at all about Sir Thomas More."

"So you think *More*'s written before July 1581?"

"You *let me talk*. All I'm saying is *More* was *maybe* written around early 1581, and *maybe* a collaboration with another guy who sounded like Shakespeare. I would want some more evidence of that, and I'd look for two kinds." I held up one finger. "The other guy might write on Catholic loyalty again." Two. "Or Munday and the other guy might collaborate again."

"So?" Posy said. "Did you find anything? Which?"

"Both," I said.

Posy opened her mouth and said nothing.

"You remember the Knight of the Tree of the Sun?" Posy nodded. "You ever read the speech? I found it. The tournament was about Catholic loyalty. January 1581. Right afterward, Oxford got put in the Tower, where More had been held. It could have suggested things to him."

"Surrey too," Posy said. "Surrey was in the Tower too, wasn't he? I mean, he was beheaded?"

The Earl of Surrey. The second character that Good Verse wrote in *More*. The Earl of Surrey, first poet to use blank verse in English, first man to write sonnets in English. And Surrey was Oxford's uncle. Norfolk's father. Henry Howard's father.

How can you say who wrote the plays isn't important? How could you miss the importance of Surrey in *More?*

"Yeah. Oxford was up to his eyeballs in Howards. He got involved with Surrey's son, betrayed him as a Catholic, got involved in the Knight of the Sun tournament, which was a play about Catholic loyalty, got put in the Tower. He had nothing but time, started thinking about all of 'em. Reread Surrey."

"He thought," Posy said, "that Surrey was thirty when he died, and here he was, thirty, and like he'd done nothing?"

"He *hadn't* done nothing. He saved Norfolk's brother. And he did it with words."

Diverse other brave and glorious speeches. Oxford had described Henry Howard and Charles Arundel as clowns. He'd made them little jingling harmless fools with bells on—and Norfolk's brother had escaped the Tower.

Words. Who can object to words? Little things, poems, plays, no account to anyone? Plays are nothing, you put them on in houses after dinner, while the important people are sprawling on the couches digesting their food. Plays are just fun, and using the way a person talks to say something about him is just fun too.

But the right word is the lightning.

"I think," I said, "he realized he'd found something more powerful than Cecil. A way to end-run Cecil. I think," and I said it. "I think Oxford and Anthony Munday wrote *Sir Thomas More*. While Oxford was in the Tower, sometime between March and June 1581."

Posy put her hands up to her face. "Oh *wow*," she said, muffled, and unexpectedly began to giggle. "Oxford, in the Tower, with a quill pen," she said.

"What?"

"*Clue*. The game. Whatever. Oh, Joe," she was laughing at me, "you were the one who was like, 'Oxford's poems are shit.' "

"I found more, if you want to hear."

I'd brought one of the Xeroxes, rolled up and jammed in the inside pocket of my parka. I brought it out. She reached for it; I shook my head.

"This is a poem I think Oxford wrote most of. It dates from October 1580, when Oxford's maybe thinking about religious issues. It's a repentance poem that doesn't quite come off; he keeps drifting back to all the things he enjoys that he's supposed to be repenting. It was published under Munday's name, and there are parts of it I sort of hope Munday wrote, but some of it's better than Munday could manage, and it's about a nobleman's pleasures."

"It's *big*," Posy said. "And it sounds like who?"

"It's not so clear as *More*. Rougher," I said nervously.

"Well, yes, this is before he reread Surrey."

"Posy, we're making that up. All I know is I could argue a good case Oxford wrote the poem."

"Let me see that," Posy said.

I handed it to her.

Nobody is going to have an experience like that again: watching while someone reads a new Shakespeare poem. Posy read down the first page; she frowned; my heart skidded around in my chest. It's not Shakespeare, I thought. It's Oxford. Oxford sucked as a poet. Okay, fine. I don't have to risk my career.

And then she stopped, and she read a line again, and she went back a page. And then she began to read aloud to me:

O fond delight, oh grievous kind of joy,
Oh cankered coin, the cause of deadly pain:
Oh madhead man to joy in such a toy,
Oh greedy minds that so do grope for gain.
   Oh wretched wealth, whose joy doth breed such woe,
   Oh God forgive such fools as seek it so . . .

She wasn't reading just for me. She liked the lines. And through the branches of the wood, across the fields where the grass was just coming up green, there came something like a wind, and Posy tilted up her head and felt it, and so did I. There is a music to Shakespeare that is like nothing else. And I knew how dangerous it was, I knew how easily people bite at forgeries, because they want to hear that voice, that music, they want to hear the real thing even if it isn't there. Look at anything, call it Shakespeare, and it will be good. *Shakespearean* is a word, like *love*. But there it was.

"Wow," she said. "Is there more like that?" She began leafing through the pages. A Xerox of a Xerox of a blurred black-letter text. "Help me here. Show me something else like that."

I turned pages and we read together.

'Tis not the thing, but the delight therein
That makes or mars, delights or grieveth sore,
Then take good heed, when first you do begin
  To take delight in any kind of thing . . .

We looked at each other. We were perhaps two feet apart, elbow to elbow. Her hair was blowing in the wind. "What do you think?" I asked. "Too many *delights* there, doesn't sound all that Shakespearean."

"No such thing as too many delights," Posy said, and she put the Xerox down on the ground and her purse on top of it, put her arms around me, tight, and pulled my head down to her upturned lips and kissed me.

It wasn't a simple kiss, it was hunger and admiration and a little envy. Her mouth nuzzled against my lips as hungrily as a baby's. "You," she murmured. "You *did* it. Give it up to *you.*" Oh no, I thought, no, Posy, it isn't that simple or that fun, we don't know, this is so risky, betting everything— But all this time I was kissing her.

Give it up to me.

I took one quick look around to see whether we were visible from the castle and the lawn where the kids are playing; we weren't. I pulled her down behind the rock, onto the smooth English grass. She laughed and tugged at her skirt, pulling up its microscopic length. She was wearing iridescent tights. I ran my hand down the soft inside of her thigh. "Posy," I said, half asking her, but we already knew the answer. We both were shivering, not from cold though the grass was damp. The metal zipper of my jeans was castrating me. License my roving hands, and let them go/Before, behind, between, above, below . . . "Let me take this off," I said, "Yes," she said, "have you got—?" and Posy kicked her shoes onto the grass, stripped the iridescent tights away, the lamb jacket was a pillow under her head, the black sweater unbuttoned, the red bra unhooked, "Yes," she said, she was unbuckling my belt and pulling down my jeans, "Ooh," she said, "Oh girl," I said, and she said, "Oh, oh, Will Shakespeare," laughing, "Will Shakespeare!"

My soul doth tell my body that he may
Triumph in love, flesh stays no farther reason,
But rising at thy name doth point out thee
As his triumphant prize . . .

We lay on our backs, in the sun, under the blue English sky, smiling at each other. Her lipstick was all off and her mouth was naked and tender. I ran my forefinger along it. "You," I said.

"You," she said. "We're going to be famous."

"Never mind that, girl. We're famous now."

*I*n the car, we wiped off wet grass with Kleenexes from the glove compartment. "I so need a shower," Posy said, and looked at the Bell Inn speculatively and shook her head.

"We should get on to Stratford," I said, "if we're going to get back to London tonight."

She looked at me. I looked at her. She pursed her lips, not quite a kiss. I grinned. We weren't getting back to London tonight.

She started the car, getting it warmed up. I looked on the map for our route to Stratford.

"I was thinking how funny his name is," she said. "Will, you know, in British slang, like —?" She made the one-finger salute, "Will," and waved the finger. "Shakespeare."

"Posy, don't make fun of my guy."

"It's like all over the Sonnets, right? And isn't there that joke in the letter about where his name came from? Oxford must have thought the name was a hoot."

"Shakespeare's a common name in England."

Posy just put the car in gear.

"So what do you think of the letter now?" she asked me triumphantly.

"I don't have to think of the letter; that's what Nicky's for. But I think Oxford hired Shakespeare around 1585. As a secretary? Servant? Actor? He was only twenty, twenty-one. He couldn't have started out being the successor to Munday."

"So who is Shakespeare? Where does he fit in?"

"I don't know."

Castle Hedingham was already falling away behind us. I turned in my seat to look back at it. Thatched roofs, old brick red-gold in the afternoon light, sunshine, silence, and a white cube on a hill. If no one ever discovered who Oxford was, the village would always stay like this.

"How could Oxford stand to lose this house?" Posy said. "This was like *his*, his family's place. They'd had it for hundreds of years."

"He sold it?"

"Cecil took it. That, and Vere House, and that big place he'd bought, all at once, to pay his daughters' dowries."

"Fisher's Folly," I said, my lips a little numb. "Cecil took that away from him?"

The Armada summer, 1588, was the moment when Elizabeth became safe; it was also the year when her friends began to die.

In 1588, after years of cold war and intrigue, Spain invaded England. Philip of Spain threw an enormous fleet, the Armada, against the English coast. The English navy fought him. (Oxford was briefly part of the fighting.) They handed Philip his head on a plate, there was a storm, and barely a third of the Armada made it back to Spain.

Elizabeth had won.

But she was old. Fifty-five, too old for children. Robert Dudley, her Robin, died during the celebrations after the Armada. She sat for her Armada victory portrait wearing the rope of pearls he left her.

William Cecil was lonely too. In the Armada summer, the two women closest to him died, his wife and his favorite daughter Anne, Countess of Oxford.

Cecil buried his daughter in Westminster Abbey, with a long and bitter epitaph, and took over educating Oxford's children.

" 'Their loving grandfather who has the care of all these children' wanted to get Anne's daughters married to noblemen," Posy said, "and that meant like huge dowries. So Cecil basically strip-mined Oxford's assets for Anne's kids." Posy negotiated a narrow corner on the country road. "Cecil said that Oxford never paid the Cecils to marry Anne—that is such a crock—and now he wanted the money. Oxford had to sell Fisher's Folly. Cecil took Vere House in Oxford Court away from him, and in December 1591 Cecil grabbed Castle Hedingham too. Oxford had nothing."

"Cecil visited the Bell in 1592. He wasn't visiting Oxford?"

"He was gloating over his spoils."

"What did Oxford do?"

Posy shrugged. "Oxford got married to an heiress, Elizabeth Trentham. She and Oxford had a son, which totally pissed off Cecil. Cecil went after the *Trentham* money, if you can believe it, and Oxford spent a lot of time trying to keep his wife's money for their son. He was always poor. He ended up living in the suburbs in a house Elizabeth Trentham bought and just dropped out of sight."

"That's it?" I said. "He just faded away?" Oxford was only forty in 1590. It was only six years after he'd won his last tournament.

"Totally faded away," Posy said.

There was a silence in the car.

"Unless, of course," Posy said cunningly, "you think he was writing plays, and falling in love with Southampton, and all that."

~

So that brought us back to Southampton: Henry Wriothesley, newly at court in 1590, eighteen years old, standing hipshot in

attractive positions and toying with his long hair. Cecil had
wanted his grandson to be Earl of Oxford, and now he couldn't
have that, but there were other earls, and Southampton was
Cecil's ward. So Cecil bought the right to control Southampton's
marriage and told Southampton to marry Elizabeth de Vere.

By wardship law, if Southampton didn't marry Elizabeth, he
had to pay Cecil the value of the marriage. In modern money that
would have been about three million dollars.

Southampton was no fool; he'd been brought up with Elizabeth
de Vere like brother and sister, and he'd seen what had happened to
Oxford, but he didn't want to lose the money. He stalled like a '47
Buick, any number of ingenious and unpredictable ways, stalled
five years before he managed to elope with the girl he wanted.

Meanwhile he did love his pretty young self. He liked to have
poems dedicated to him, about beautiful men in love with themselves. (He had either no sense of humor at all or more than he's
been given credit for.) And in April 1593, while he was still
dawdling around with Elizabeth de Vere, a poem appeared, dedicated to him:

> *Even as the sun with purple-coloured face*
> *Had ta'en his last leave of the weeping morn,*
> *Rose-cheeked Adonis hied him to the chase;*
> *Hunting he loved, but love he laughed to scorn.*
> *Sick-thoughted Venus makes amain unto him,*
> *And like a bold-faced suitor 'gins to woo him.*

The poem was *Venus and Adonis,* and the author, making his first
known appearance in print, was William Shakespeare.

Shakespeare writes an aw-shucks preface, scraping his feet and knuckling one hand against the other and 'lowing as how he's no more but a poor 'prentice at this poem-writing business. He lies like a rug. *Venus and Adonis* is funny, sarcastic, gorgeously decorative (there's a great bit about a horse), and hotter than the Playboy Channel. What it isn't is deferential. Shakespeare takes chances you don't see other patronized poets taking, even with Southampton: he says Adonis is the passive partner in sex with Venus, he says Adonis wears hats to keep his pretty complexion.

Imagine Anthony Munday saying that about Oxford. Imagine any patronized poet treating his patron like that.

The poem doesn't have much of a moral—love sucks, you die, you get turned into a flower—but it occasionally deals with the same issue as the Sonnets: why a beautiful young man ought to get children.

> *Is thine own heart to thine own face affected?*
> *Can thy right hand seize love upon thy left?*
> *Then woo thyself, be of thyself rejected,*
> *Steal thine own freedom, and complain on theft.*
> * Narcissus so himself himself forsook,*
> * And died to kiss his shadow in the brook.*

It's the same argument as the first Sonnets. They both even use that same weird eating metaphor.

> *Upon the earth's increase why shouldst thou feed,*
> *Unless the earth with thy increase be fed?*

"Oxford was still a widower in 1590," Posy said. "He hadn't married Elizabeth Trentham yet. He was a total liability finan-

244 / SARAH SMITH

cially." Posy turned toward me and took her hand off the wheel
to make a point. "It would have been a big financial win for him
to get Southampton's money into the family. And Southampton
liked poems."

"Watch the road, Posy."

"Oxford started sending him sonnets," Posy said. "Maybe
because Cecil asked him to. Maybe because Philip Sidney's sonnets were just being published and Oxford really hated Sidney so
he was trying to outwrite him. When were Sidney's sonnets published?"

"1591. Watch the *road*, will you?"

"But then Oxford fell for Southampton. And Southampton
liked big poems," Posy said. She pulled over to the side of the
road, braked, turned toward me, pulled a lock of red hair over
one eye, and pouted flirtatiously. " 'Oh *Ned*,' " she said, " 'if you
really appreciated me like Kit Marlowe appreciates me, you'd
write me a *big* poem. Those shitty little sonnets probably take you
ten minutes, and I can't show them to anyone, they're so *personal*.' "

"He showed 'em around, or someone did," because a couple of
them were pirated.

"M'm," Posy agreed. "He would have. He was so totally vain,
and he was like no moral door prize? Shakespeare says the Fair
Youth slept with the Dark Lady *in Shakespeare's own house*."

"Depending on your reading of Sonnet 41—"

"Whatever. So would Oxford have written his boy a big poem?
When he wanted to show off to the boy?"

I nodded.

"But how did he feel about it? You be Oxford. I'm being
Southampton."

"I know how *I* feel about it. Southampton was engaged to Oxford's daughter." The fucking earl. I was staking my life on this man and he was writing love poems to his son-in-law.

"Well, sure, there's that, the shame thing."

"Yeah." You could call it that, the shame thing.

"You are so into shame," Posy said. "Believing that Oxford is Shakespeare. You're so *ashamed*. You're like so *awkward* with it. You wish you could go with it but sort of hide from being identified with it?" Posy looked at me, looked at me hard, as if she was writing my biography. "If the shit hits and you don't want to catch it, you don't have to? You can have an idea or have an affair, write a poem, but send somebody else out to take the heat, have somebody else do the interviews and the press conferences?"

"A front. An actor or a secretary."

"Ta-da," Posy said. "Somebody fast with the mouth. Somebody who can explain things. Whose daughter *isn't* engaged to Southampton. Somebody who could write but doesn't, that's totally key, because like you say nobody's going to believe Munday wrote some of the things he's supposed to once they read the things he actually wrote."

An actor would do, or a secretary, or a servant; especially if your friend trusted him, if you knew him.

"And the first time the name William Shakespeare appears in print," Posy said, "it's with *Venus and Adonis*. Totally ta-da."

~

I thought while Posy drove. 1590, Oxford met Southampton; okay, making no excuses for Oxford, Southampton was one of those people folks lost their heads over. Oxford had no youth left, no money, no son, no children at all; Cecil had snatched his daughters. All he had was a little talent for writing. Maybe it wasn't sexual, I thought. Maybe it was a father's affection for a prospective son-in-law. Maybe.

> *Devouring Time blunt thou the lion's paws,*
> *And make the earth devour her own sweet brood,*
> *Pluck the keen teeth from the fierce tiger's jaws,*
> *And burn the long-lived phoenix in her blood,*
> *Make glad and sorry seasons as thou fleet'st,*
> *And do whate'er thou wilt, swift-footed Time,*
> *To the wide world and all her fading sweets:*
> *But I forbid thee one most heinous crime . . .*

Impossible to have it come out right. Time doesn't stop, and young men get older, and old men see through them. Southampton was a narcissist. No one could love him like he loved himself. Not even Shakespeare.

An early dusk was falling. Posy flicked on the headlights.

Late 1591 or early 1592. Oxford got married again, for money, to dark-haired and lovely Elizabeth Trentham. Maybe she was the Dark Lady of the Sonnets. Maybe she was good to him.

Whatever else she did or didn't do, in February 1593 she gave him a son.

April 1593, *Venus and Adonis*, first appearance in print by William Shakespeare, making fun of Southampton.

May 1594, the second Shakespeare poem, *The Rape of Lucrece*, a much more sober and dramatic Roman poem about chastity, virtue, and citizenship. By 1594 the bulk of the Sonnets may have been written.

And while these private things were going on, *Venus and Adonis* was being reprinted and reprinted. Shakespeare was a success.

Sir Robert Cecil kept some of Oxford's business letters from these years, but there's nothing to tell what Oxford was thinking of William Shakespeare. Who was Shakespeare? A convenience got out of hand? A servant? A friend?

These, I thought, these were the lost years.

"Joe?" Posy said. "Where are we?"

We should have reached the motorway by now. I hadn't been keeping track. We were off course, in the middle of lanes with fields on every side. "Did we get turned around?" We found the number of the road by shining the car headlights on one of the road markers. But I didn't know whether we were going in the right direction. We drove through a village, but everything was closed, every window was dark. I couldn't find the village name on the map. It was a foreign country; even Posy didn't have the nerve to ring someone's bell.

"We're not lost," I said. "We'll be fine come daylight."

We pulled the yellow car off on a side road by a field and curled up together in the front seat, spoon-fashion, with my parka and the black lamb jacket over us. I gave her my flannel shirt and rested my chin on her shoulder. Posy twisted her head back over her shoulder to kiss me.

"Look at the stars," I said. Above the sleeping winter fields, the stars were thick as hope in the air.

"Our breath is fogging the windows. Like *Titanic*," Posy said, snuggling round to face me. "I wonder if you could do that in this car."

"We could try," I said.

"I should call Daddy," Posy said. "I didn't tell him I wouldn't be home." We were lost on some English dirt road, but she had her cell phone. She turned a little away from me and punched numbers. "Hello? Daddy? I just wanted to tell you, I took Joe for a drive and we've gone to Stratford. Yes, it's great. We're in this wonderful hotel. Yes," she said, "yes, of course, don't be *stu-pid*. Bye-bye. —Okay," she said and punched off her cell phone. "We're in Stratford, *but I didn't tell him the name of the hotel!*" As if it were a victory against spies.

"Posy," I said, wanting to ask her about her father; but she didn't want to talk, she kissed whatever I was going to say off my lips.

Yes, you could do it in the front seat of the car. Not easy, not warm, and we both got to know the gearshift pretty intimately; but you could do it if you wanted to, you could do it if you needed to, if you had to have someone to talk to and hold, if you were starved for just that, you'd try it anywhere and take it from anywhere. "It'll be so great," she said in a little whisper in my arms, "finally he'll notice me for me." That was the wrong reason; I was with her for all the wrong reasons, I didn't want to love her, only to talk to her about Shakespeare.

I held her tight.

You can't help it. They're just there, the beautiful wrong people; you come across them, you can't help it. Then they have you writing poems, they have you believing in things you aren't suited to believe, and the worst of it is you aren't going to come to your senses someday, your senses are here.

I held her in the dark and we lay there together, arms around each other, warm where we touched each other, cold everywhere else.

By the mid-1590s Oxford was happy. He had been married to Elizabeth Trentham for several years. His young son Henry was a healthy boy. The Oxfords bought King's Place in Hackney, a house in what was then the countryside, with about two hundred acres of grounds, an easy ride away from the Theatre.

In 1595 Oxford's daughter Elizabeth married a more suitable man than Southampton. William Stanley, the Earl of Derby, was rich and titled enough for Cecil; but he was also a musician and a playwright. A few years later, a Jesuit spy would describe William Stanley as too preoccupied to support the Catholics because he was writing "comedies for the common players."

Apparently for just this marriage, between Oxford's daughter and a playwright, Shakespeare created one of his loveliest comedies. It has a marriage, and a play within a play; a quarrel about a boy; a transformation of a man into an ass because of it. *A Midsummer Night's Dream* has lovers' misunderstandings, and magic, and forgiveness.

A gift for a marriage; a father's gift, and a poet's.

In 1598 William Cecil died. Oxford had outlived him. Queen Elizabeth was still alive, old but not giving up, needing plays to see her through the dark hours.

Shakespeare wrote them, one after the other, lights for the dark, histories for England and comedies for its queen.

~

"Shakespeare(TM)," Posy said, holding up two curved fingers for the trademark sign.

We drove into Stratford early in the morning, tired, crick-necked, and ravenous. I don't know what I'd expected, but Stratford was fucking shameless Disneyland, from the swans floating under the willows in the artificial-looking Avon to the Stratford Tour buses running at fifteen-minute intervals. The best part was the public bathrooms, clean and opulent, with free public showers. "Thank you, Shakespeare," Posy said and emerged from the shower a long twenty minutes later, looking warm and clean and Posylike again. The place where we ate breakfast took Visa, Mastercard, Barclaycard, and American Express. The ham omelet was called a Hamlet. Tourists were wandering around with blissed-out looks on their faces, like they couldn't believe they were here. There was no litter on the street, anywhere. Stratford wasn't a place, it was one great big souvenir.

"I wonder what they read in Stratford?" Posy asked innocently. She led me into in the bookshop on the main street. If you believed the books at the front of the store, they didn't read anything but Shakespeare; at the back, though, Stratford read Jeffrey Archer, Danielle Steel, and a bin marked "Great Bargain Literature."

A row of Harleys was parked near the bookshop, hogs at a garden party.

We did the tour. We saw the inn where Shakespeare and his friends *probably* drank and the house where Shakespeare's daughter Judith *probably* lived: "This 16th Century building houses 3 floors of Traditional Gifts, Classic English Characters and Collectors Items." At the John and Susannah Hall House, we looked at Dr. Hall's medical notes and an exhibit of medical instruments. Dr. Hall was the first full-time physician in Stratford. He recommended curing whooping cough by eating a roast mouse. I figured his patients wanted to get well. "Those medical instruments are *nineteenth century,*" Posy pointed out gleefully. "These people are *shameless.*" Downstairs at the bookstore, Posy bought me a Shakespeare-Man-of-the-Millennium mug with a cartoon sketch of Shakespeare, his hands clutched over his family jewels. Around the rim was a quote from *Hamlet*. "We know what we are, but we know not what we may be."

"I know what *you* are," Posy told Shakespeare as she handed me the mug.

The Shakespeare Tour Bus was coming down the road. "Anne Hathaway's cottage," Posy read. "I just can't stand it. It's a random cottage in Shottery that's the right era. That's so lame."

Shakespeare's schoolhouse was real, still in use four hundred years later. We looked wordlessly through a fence at an ordinary playground. Posy had bought a tour guide to Stratford; we turned to a picture of the Elizabethan schoolroom. "Nursery of greatness," Posy said.

"Abe Lincoln got his start in a one-room schoolhouse."

"Abe Lincoln isn't Shakespeare."

"No," I conceded. I was looking for Shakespeare. But lightning bugs, that's what I was finding; no lightning at all.

The millennium had reached Shakespeare's Birthplace; they were renovating too:

> From the beginning of September 1999 work starts on an exciting new project to re-display Shakespeare's Birthplace to be completed for Shakespeare's birthday, 23rd April 2000. . . . Inevitably there will be a certain amount of disruption during some stages of the refurbishment operation. . . .

"It's so authentic they have to update it every few years," Posy explained to me.

The Birthplace was Shakespeare's real house. The guide showed us the room where Shakespeare was probably born, furniture similar to what would have been in a house of this sort at that time. "What do you think of the Shakespeare authorship controversy?" Posy chirped to the guide. "I don't think of it at all, miss." The guide smiled with well-practiced charm. Posy smiled right back.

In the Shakespeare Visitor Center we walked through a series of dioramas. Shakespeare's boyhood in Stratford. Shakespeare's journey to London. The Elizabethan stage. The court. The playhouse. "Shakespeare's plays were so profitable that they allowed him to buy the second largest house in town, New Place." I put my finger on the sentence and scowled.

"Totally," Posy whispers. "Are they dumb or totally lying or what?"

Nobody had got rich off plays, or even off acting. Ten pounds was the going price for a court performance. A rip-roaring success in the popular theaters could take in two pounds a day. None of that went to the playwright, and not much to the actors. Edward Alleyn, rich enough to found Dulwich College, made his money from what the old biographies delicately call real estate. (He owned brothels.) Richard Burbage, landowner in London, major theater owner and leading actor, died worth three hundred pounds. William Shakespeare, landowner, wool dealer, moneylender, minor theater owner, and supporting actor, was rich enough to invest four hundred pounds in a single day.

"So where'd he get his money?" I whispered.

"This woman named Diana Price thinks he bought and sold costumes. Don't look like that," Posy whispered back, giggling, "it makes sense. Costumes were the most expensive part of the production. Edward Alleyn had a cape worth twenty pounds. Shakespeare only put down sixty pounds for New Place."

At the end of the exhibit we saw a reproduction of Shakespeare's will and a copy of the bust on the monument. He stared out at us, a round-faced accountant-looking sort of a man with an irritable upturned mustache and a goatee. He looked as if he'd been interrupted; *What,* he was saying, *Hamlet?* His right hand held a quill pen, his left rested on a piece of paper. The hands were different in style and color from the face. They had been restored in the eighteenth-century; the accounts say they were only repainted, but they didn't look Elizabethan. Eighteenth-century restorers gave statues fig leaves, new fingers, whole new arms and heads, like eighteenth-century stage productions made *King Lear* end happily.

"Let's see New Place," I said.

New Place had been Shakespeare's trophy mansion, the badge of his success. He'd bought it in 1597 when he was thirty-three. After he died it had been some other family's house, and then a shop; and in the eighteenth century, before Garrick made Shakespeare into an idol, it had been torn down. Now the Shakespeare Trust owned the site. We sat on a bench with a little memorial plaque, looking out over a giant lawn and twentieth-century gardens, sitting where Shakespeare had lived and written, if Shakespeare was my Shakespeare; and I felt a complex mixture of recognition and sadness, and beyond that just a sense I was wasting my time.

"This was Shakespeare's house," Posy said. "He never had a house in London, right?"

I shook my head wordlessly.

"And any time before 1597 he would have been living in lodgings in London, or he would have been staying in the house where he was born. With his wife, his kids, his mother, his father, *and* the servants?"

"Yeah."

"Sonnet 41," Posy said. "The one where Shakespeare complains that the Fair Youth has got it on with the Dark Lady and slept with her in Shakespeare's own house? 'But yet thou mightst my seat forbear'? Like there would have been *room* in his house?"

" 'Seat' might mean the Dark Lady," I said. "Or his wife."

"Mrs. Shakespeare, what was she, like nearly forty when Shakespeare bought New Place?"

"Over forty."

"And Southampton got it on with her, right there on Henley Street, and nobody noticed? I mean, *Southampton?* But at Castle Hedingham—"

"Yeah."

"Cecil went to Castle Hedingham in 1592. What do you bet he brought Southampton along, 'all this can be yours,' that sort of thing? 1592 would be a good date for Sonnet 41 if they're in order and start in 1590 and the sonnets just after 80 are about Marlowe, who dies in 1593."

"We could check if Southampton stayed here, whether he stayed at any of Oxford's houses." I didn't want to check anything. I wanted to curl up someplace quiet and dark where I could be sad about Shakespeare. I wanted to be sad in a dark place and have sex with Posy.

"We're so good," Posy said.

Holy Trinity Church was at the end of an alley of gnarled and ancient-looking limes. They'd been planted in 1993–94, full-grown when they were planted. For Shakespeare, there was all the money in the world.

Inside the church a gift shop sold busts of Shakespeare, snow globes of the Birthplace, and mottos from the plays. At the end of the chancel an old man sat by a wooden fence, taking a pound coin from anyone who wanted to see Shakespeare's monument. Inside the gate, velvet ropes and a brass rail protected the flat stone that marked Shakespeare's grave.

Shakespeare was buried near the altar with his family. The graves were lined up one next the other like slabs in a sidewalk: Shakespeare's wife; his daughter Susannah and her husband, Dr. Hall; their son-in-law; and in the middle the man himself, with the plain epitaph he chose.

Good frend for Jesus sake forbeare,
To digg the dust encloased heare:
Bleste be the man that spares these stones,
And curst be he that moves my bones.

Poets don't always give themselves big grand epitaphs. John Keats's is "Here lies one whose name was writ in water." Charles Baudelaire was buried with his parents; his whole epitaph reads "and their son Charles." Shakespeare's epitaph, like theirs, made no claims.

The monument on the wall was another story. Below the bust stretched a long gilded epitaph in Latin and English, claiming Shakespeare was the best thing since nail guns and Wonder Bread. It reminded me of Anne Cecil's monument in Westminster Abbey, with William Cecil's inscription. Epitaphs don't always tell the holy truth.

The old man at the wooden gate had a hearing aid and was reading a newspaper. The only other people in the church were down the other end of the building, visiting the gift shop.

"I think the whole thing was a conspiracy," Posy whispered to me. "The First Folio, this monument, Ben Jonson's poem . . . Jonson *knew.*"

"So Shakespeare, this man here, was the 'Stratford monument' that time was going to destroy?" I muttered back.

I looked up past the big gilded epitaph to William Shakespeare of Stratford, the bust, colorful as a can of beans, with his real quill pen poised in his stone hand and his round annoyed face.

Even in March, four wreaths were hanging on the wall below the monument. On April 23 the whole front of the church would be full of flowers. Every year, April 23, Saint George's Day, patron saint of England, there was a procession all through Stratford to the church. From all over the world actors and ordinary people brought wreaths and bouquets of flowers, and someone from Stratford replaced the quill pen. It was a religious festival, celebrating Shakespeare like people used to celebrate Elizabeth's Accession Day, like a saint's day. Saint William of England.

Posy was looking up at the monument. "Like I feel *sad,*" she said. "I want to believe? I want to be, oh, here's *Shake*speare, like I'm right *here* and this is the real thing?"

She stared at the monument glumly. I put my arm around her, looked up at the monument, doing my own mourning.

After a while, standing there began to feel like picking at a scab to see how badly it could hurt. I went off and started looking round at the rest of the church to see who else had been buried here around the same time Shakespeare had, and what their monuments looked like. I couldn't find Richard Field, but I did find a woolen draper named Hill, who'd died in 1597. He had a big elaborate epitaph in English, Latin, Greek, and Hebrew. The

Stratford Grammar School looked pretty promising if it had produced this, until I looked twice at the Latin.

Hic nutritus erat, natus nunc hic jacet Hillus
Hic que magistratus famater munere functus
Cum que bonos annos vixiscet septuaginta
Ad terram corpus sed mens migravit ad astra

"Isn't that like really bad Latin?" Posy asked.
"Yeah." It even tried to rhyme.

Heare lieth intombd the corps of Richarde Hill
A woollen draper beeing in his time
Whose virtues live whose fame dooth flourish stil
Though hee desolved be to dust and slime
A mirror he and paterne mai be made
For such as shall suckcead him in that trade.

"Whose epitaph does that remind you of?" Posy said.
Good frend for Jesus sake forbeare . . .
"John Combe's?" Posy said. "The usurer? The other epitaph Shakespeare was supposed to have written? 'Ten in the hundred doth the Devil allow'? I wonder if we have an authentic Shakespeare poem here."
"Lay off that, Posy," I said uncomfortably.
"Just practicing being offensive," Posy said brightly, and then went on seriously. "You know you're going to have to take a stand on Oxford and stop caring what people say about you. Because like half the world is going to think you're Charles Manson for not believing in Shakespeare, and I don't want to be doing the

bitch thing all alone while you're making nice with people?"

"Yeah." It was a point. "I'm still not sure what I believe, Posy."

"Oh, come on, Joe. You know. You just don't like it."

"Let's not talk about it here." There was that old man by the wooden fence, making some sort of living collecting pound coins one by one. Because Shakespeare was Shakespeare.

"Then come on outside; are we done?"

⟳

Outside on the alley of limes, the ancient alley that was less than ten years old, Posy put her hands on her hips and tapped her foot. "Okay. Aggro time. Repeat after me: Oxford is Shakespeare and Stratford is crap."

"No," I said. "I'm not going to act wild-eyed, Posy. I've got some ideas, I've been finding evidence to back them up, but that's not the end of the story. I need to show that poem around—"

"But Nicky is going to be like 'This is a real letter' in a couple of days. And after that, Joe, we've just got to put the story out," Posy said. "We've got to be like, yes, of course Oxford is Shakespeare. We can't give people like a six-part logic puzzle with poems and more poems and tournaments and Anthony Munday and *maybe*. We have to put it on a button and pin it on their nose."

"Posy, this isn't a marketing campaign or something."

Posy waved her hand around: the alley of limes, the church, Stratford, the world. "This is not a marketing campaign? 'Shakespeare, Man of the Millennium'?"

"We don't know enough," I said. "All we can say is there's a lot of interesting stuff around Oxford, and I think he wrote *Paine*—"

"That's so dim. Say 'He *wrote* it.'"

"I'm a dim guy."

"People want to have fun," Posy said. "Look at all the people who are wandering around here going like *wow,* because they've got to Stratford. They want to feed the swans and buy souvenirs and do the Shakespeare nature, and if you say that Shakespeare doesn't exist, you have to give them something else. It's all about the myth. Print the legend, you know?"

"How about questions?" I said. "How about 'Shakespeare is the most important guy in English literature, and we don't know who he was but maybe we can find out'?"

"People don't want unsolved mysteries except on TV," Posy said. "Get the message on a button and— Oh *shit!* Look!"

At the end of the alley of limes, by the wrought-iron gate, a group of people were setting up lights and a camera. "Making a film?" I guessed.

"It must be TV with that setup, but look who's there."

I took a second look, past the lighting girl and the cameraman and the man with the boom mike to the interviewer and his subject, a small, frail, happy figure, an old man in a raincoat, holding up a thick book.

It was Roland Goscimer.

It was too late to avoid him. He'd turned and seen us, he'd seen Posy at least, who could avoid seeing Posy? He waved at us tentatively, then again. I set my shoulders and walked down the alley of limes toward him.

"Joe! What are you doing in England?"

"Is this the BBC interview?" I asked. "I thought that was radio on Sunday."

"This is Germany," Goscimer said happily. "They're very fond of Shakespeare in Germany." The cameraman, the lighting girl, everybody smiled at me. *"In Search of Shakespeare* is doing wonderfully, Joe. My editor says they're even pirating it in China."

"Shakespeare is one of our greatest authors," the German interviewer said. *"Sein oder nicht sein, das ist die Frage.* I have read him since from I was a kid."

Goscimer introduced me; I stuck out my hand and muttered something. "And this is Miss Posy Gould from *Harvard,"* Goscimer told the interviewer, who grinned and shook Posy's hand a little longer than necessary.

"You come with us," the interviewer offered. "We are filming inside the church. Inside the velvet rope, yes? You see the big man up close."

"What are you both doing in England?" There was a moment of silence and a complex three-way look, Goscimer to me to Posy. I could see Goscimer wondering whether I'd just got lucky or whether—

"Have you *found* something?" he asked me.

I had wanted to avoid telling him about the letter since I'd found it. I'd taken the letter to Nicky so I wouldn't have to tell him. Thirty-five years he'd worked on this book. Would I have wanted to know, if I'd been him? Or to learn I'd been wrong, to find out later my student had known I'd been wrong and hadn't told me? And what about the poem?

"Yeah. Maybe."

"In the Kellogg Collection?"

"I want you to take a look at something, when you have time." How much I wanted him not to have to hear this, not now, not for weeks or months or years. But Nicky wasn't going to sit on the letter.

Just in time, Goscimer was needed for the filming.

"So are you going to tell him?" Posy hissed to me.

I'd tell him I found a letter. I found a play, and a poem. I'd lost—I looked back through the avenue of limes toward Holy Trinity—I had lost the Shakespeare religion. And what would Goscimer hear? That he was wrong and he had wasted his life.

Or that I was wrong.

I knew which I'd believe if I was Goscimer.

The crew was filming him being interviewed. The lights turned the March dusk into a summer afternoon; the grass gleamed luminescent pale green and the bare branches of the lime trees were blurred in the background. The director asked the two men to take off their coats. It was a better picture that way, an English-speaking girl with a clipboard explained to me. The Germans would dub in the interviewer's questions and Goscimer's answers in German and would optically replace the cover of the book with the German edition. The mike waved over the men's heads, out of shot; the sound man high-stepped over cables; behind the cameraman the tourists crowded around curiously. A crewman held a piece of cardboard with circular cutouts in front of one of the lights and moved it gently. I looked into the monitor and saw Goscimer and the interviewer talking in dappled shadows, a summer afternoon in a quiet English village, and in the background a suggestion of ancient trees.

"He defined the genius of the English language," Goscimer said, looking happily into the monitor where the words were rolling out for him. "And here, in this quiet Warwickshire town, Shakespeare's genius was nurtured—"

I watched miserably, my hands in my pockets.

It was dusk and damply chill by the time they were ready to

film inside the church. The lights were steaming. The filmmakers talked to each other in German. Goscimer took my sleeve and steered me away, back toward the darkened gift shop.

"Have you really found something, Joe?"

"Nothing I can swear to."

"Tell me."

The interviewer, Ulrich, was waving to get Goscimer back. "It'll take too long. This isn't the time."

"Yes, of course, of course. . . . When? Is it something good, Joe?"

I felt like my heart was being wrung like a washrag. "What's your time like?"

He was going back to London with the Germans this evening. He had an interview in the morning and a panel in the afternoon, and two signings. "Simon & Schuster is doing *very* well by me, Joe." He was happy.

It was no good wishing I could put it off.

"You got tomorrow evening free?" I said.

"Come by my hotel, Joe, they let me order whatever I like from room service," Goscimer said. "You come for dinner, you and your," he paused and looked at Posy, expecting me to supply a word, but I didn't, "you and Miss Gould."

"I'll come after dinner," I said. I wasn't going to tell him while I was eating the man's food. Oh *fuck* it.

The verger, a tall thin man, moved the velvet ropes aside, being helpful, really enjoying all this tourist stuff. Ulrich called Goscimer again and they went off to film.

"Did you tell him anything?" said Posy, low-voiced.

"No."

"So he gets to say stupid things all over German TV because

you're afraid of hurting his feelings in the middle of his tour?"

I looked at Goscimer under the lights, talking away about Shakespeare's genius. Maybe the Germans could fix what he said. Maybe they could digitally replace Goscimer's whole life. Thirty-five years. He was speaking to the camera again, talking about Shakespeare's monument. He looked fragile but excited, smiling, even after all the filming he'd already done this afternoon. Funny that he wasn't afraid of the camera the way he was of lectures. He had found his element, something he was really comfortable with.

"You know the worst part?" I told Posy. "He had the right idea when he wasn't any more than my age. He knew Shakespeare went to Italy. I'm seeing him after dinner tomorrow. I don't know how I'll tell him."

"Tomorrow," Posy said as if it were too early or too late.

He was speaking about Rachel Goscimer. "She cared for facts. For truth." I remembered a worn face on a pillow. *Did you find anything wrong?* She'd been happy when I had—not often. Rachel Goscimer wouldn't want me to tell him but she would know I had to. And then she would get that wan look, thinking of the Professor having to face it all alone.

He wouldn't be facing it alone. No, shit, I'd be getting broiled right there with him. Me. Looking and talking like Cletus the Slack-Jawed Yokel, and happiest with a question when I had two or three days to chew my tongue and think up an answer. Ayuh.

We'd have Nicky. And Posy. Posy could do all the TV, be the front. I could stand in the background somewhere and mutter. "Uh huh, yup, found this letter." Found this poem. Found this *Thomas More.* How could I tell him when I was barely sure myself?

"Can you get in touch with Nicky on your phone?" I asked Posy. "Get him to come tomorrow evening, Durrant's Hotel, and bring the letter. We're going to need the letter."

"You're really going to tell him you don't believe in Shakespeare?"

"No," I said. Just evidence, suggestions, timelines, *The Paine of Pleasure, Thomas More.* "Yeah. Pretty much."

Goscimer had finished his speech and there was only one shot left to go. The cameraman looked at his clipboard and began moving his lights so they would shine on the monument and the grave. The Professor fumbled inside his jacket for a moment, brought out his wallet, and took something from it, something yellow and faded and flat. "Will you hold this for me for a moment? Hold out your palm—"

It was a yellow chrysanthemum. It had been pressed in a book; the petals were the color of parchment, the stem a dusty faded green. "This was in her Shakespeare," he said.

It was one of the chrysanthemums I'd brought her, that last day.

Shakespeare *did* go to Italy, she had said. And I had said *I'll find out.* And I had. I had. She and Goscimer had written the very best book they could. And then she'd got Mary Cat and me the Kellogg Collection, so if we all were very lucky, their lifework would be proved wrong.

She meant us to surpass them; that was the gift she gave with the Kellogg Collection. And I knew for the first time what it meant to be a scholar, that even when we'd done the best we could, we'd always have to want to be surpassed, outdated, wrong. And I knew I had to tell Goscimer, whatever it cost him or me.

Goscimer was being filmed. He was holding a bunch of fresh

flowers, yellow chrysanthemums. He knelt down slowly by the grave, supporting himself with his cane, until he was on one knee. He laid the flowers next to the epitaph. He stayed for a moment, still on one knee, his head bent, his hands folded on the round knob of his cane. The Germans made the little stir that meant they'd stopped filming, but Goscimer was lost for a moment, kneeling like a knight's page in front of his master.

He raised his head and looked around for me. I handed him the flower from Rachel Goscimer's book. He held out the fragile ghost of it, and then hesitated and gave it back to me.

"She loved you," he said simply. "Give this to Shakespeare, Joe, from all of us."

He struggled to his feet and stood aside. I looked up at the monument. Shakespeare. From below I could see his goatee, an expanse of red waistcoat, the white pen, the sheet of paper, Shakespeare's nostrils. They had a sucked-in look, as if the bust was modeled from a death mask. Hamlet might start a fight at a funeral, but I wasn't going to. I knelt down and laid the flower on the grave. *Curst be he that moves my bones.*

"We expect great things from this young man," Goscimer said, looking up and patting my shoulder. "Mr. Joseph Roper." Like an introduction. I scrambled up, embarrassed.

The Germans were packing up. Hans and Ulrich asked Posy and me to dinner in London. I made excuses. "We're staying in Stratford tonight." Goscimer smiled, drew me aside again. I thought he was going to ask about what I'd found, but what he said was, nodding at Posy, "Does she really have a tattoo—?"

I'd forgot to look. What with one thing and another.

Goscimer leaned on his cane and looked up into my face. "Remember you're young, dear boy. I spent so much of my life in libraries." He looked over my shoulder toward Posy and sighed. "The unlived life is not worth examining. But I shall be glad tomorrow night, shan't I?"

"Yeah," I said. "Tomorrow night."

The lights went out. The Germans started coiling up cables and fitting the equipment into its cases. Posy was standing by the grave in the sudden shadows, her hands stuffed into the sleeves of the black lamb jacket, her chin tucked down. She looked cold. I went over and put my arm around her. Her shoulders tensed.

"Something I did?"

"Praying to Shakespeare," she whispered sarcastically, and looked up at the monument. "Hi. *I'm* Posy Gould."

"What was I going to do? Tell him right then?"

"Sure," she said. "Kill Shakespeare on German TV. Would they run that segment or what? I just hope you tell him sometime, that's all."

"Tomorrow night," I said. "Did you reach Nicky?"

"I left a message."

"I want him to be there."

"What if Nicky says the letter's fake?"

"You think he will?"

Posy shook her head.

⸺

I brooded at dinner, brooded as we walked back by Bridge Street toward the hotel. We stood looking at the enormous nineteenth-century statue of Shakespeare surrounded by his characters, and I brooded some more. "You're right," I told Posy. "We have to have a story for Goscimer." A new story he could start thinking about instead of all this grand myth that wasn't Shakespeare; something that would give him somewhere to go, something to live for.

"We so have a story," Posy said.

"We have a poem that's possibly Oxford's and sounds a tad like Shakespeare. *More* and Munday and Fisher's Folly. A reason why Shakespeare wrote the first Sonnets. We have hints and bits and pieces."

"What was it you said when you told me Oxford couldn't be Shakespeare? 'All the plays have to be redated.' Well, *Hamlet?* And did you know *All's Well That Ends Well* is like full of topical references to 1578?"

"Still a lot of thinking to do about redating." Years of thinking and research and work. But— "Henslowe calls *Henry VIII* a new play in 1613, but he may mean that Fletcher had newly revised it," I thought aloud. "It never read like a late play to me."

"Totally not," Posy agreed.

"And the 1605 double eclipse in *Lear* could be the double eclipse of 1601."

"And the 1609 Strachey Bermudas letter is so not the only possible source for the shipwreck in *The Tempest.*"

We started walking back along the Avon toward our hotel. "It's not enough," I said.

"It's enough to talk about."

"No. Why the mystery? Why not call Oxford Oxford?" On the dark Avon, the swans were floating asleep, smudges of white on black. "Sure, Oxford could have wanted a front. He could have got William Shakespeare of Stratford, William Shakespeare the actor, to publish *Venus and Adonis* under his name. Sure, they could have decided to keep it up when the poem made some money. But why not shut down the whole sorry mess once Oxford was dead?"

Posy looked at me expectantly. "Well?"

I shrugged. "I don't know."

"You think they were ashamed of the Sonnets?"

"They didn't publish the Sonnets." They didn't publish any of his poetry in the First Folio, only the plays.

"Shakespeare of Stratford wanted to keep being Shakespeare?"

"They wouldn't have cared what he wanted."

"Mm," Posy agreed. "So why?"

"Why not give Oxford his due? And the obvious answer is Shakespeare wrote everything all along."

We walked back to the hotel in a brooding silence.

Sex with Posy on cold wet grass had been a fine affair, sex with Posy and a gearshift had been okay, sex with Posy in a comfortable bed ought to have made me a happy man. I thought I'd been properly appreciative until Posy pulled away from kissing me afterward and accused, "You're *thinking.*"

She fell asleep; I didn't. The years from Elizabeth's death to 1623 had been in my part of Shakespeare's biography, the part I'd fact-checked, and I ought to be able to think up something, some odd fact about Shakespeare, that—

I put the bedside light down on the floor, slid my arm out from under Posy, and pulled *In Search of Shakespeare* out of my backpack. I rested it on my chest and began reading, looking at the whole period again, searching for something, a date, a clue.

Well, yes, I thought finally. There had been *that*— And the longer I thought about that strange moment just after Elizabeth's death, the stranger it was. The dog that did nothing in the nighttime. The dog that licked the burglar's hand. What Robert Cecil had done for Shakespeare.

Posy woke up as I eased myself out of bed. "Whuff?" she said. "Joe? What time is it?"

"I need an Internet connection. I need to check the exact day something happened."

The hotel had an Internet connection downstairs. I shivered from the night chill while I searched on King James and the King's Men. The hotel was serving early coffee by the time I found everything I wanted. I stumbled up the stairs to our room. Posy was curled up in bed. On my side of the bed were scattered Ogburn, Katherine Darnell's edition of the letters, *In Search of Shakespeare*, notes, and the ruins of the room service menu, which I'd torn apart for bookmarks.

"You didn't bring me coffee," Posy accused, opening one eye.

"I know why Shakespeare had to stay Shakespeare," I said. "Posy, I know when it happened. Within a couple of hours. I know where it happened and who did it. And I know why nobody said a word."

Posy drew the sheet up above her breasts and glared at me from under her eyebrows.

"And I'm sorry I didn't bring you coffee. But Posy, people ask why everybody always said Shakespeare was Shakespeare? *I know.*"

"Well?" she said after a moment. "That's three beats, enough with the portentous pause. You're going to tell me?"

"I can show you," I said.

When you're really important, they build the railroad station by your house. Robert Cecil had made the Cecils that important.

Posy drove her yellow car through the enormous wrought-iron gates opposite Hatfield station and up the long, long, wide road toward Hatfield House. Partway up the drive a sign pointed us toward the tree where Elizabeth sat waiting for her courtiers to tell her she was queen, and we stopped to look at the ruins of an enormous oak.

Elizabeth would have seen the courtiers coming up the long drive. She would have been ready, in her black-and-white Protestant dress, with her improving book between her long fingers, sitting under a tree that could be pointed out later, waiting to close the book and hold out her hand for the ring that wed her to England. I stood by the oak where she had sat, looked down the drive. Four hundred years ago. The story had probably never happened, but Elizabeth hadn't needed reality. She was a myth even then.

There were only a few cars in the parking lot by Hatfield House. Posy parked the yellow car by the steps, and we stared at the sheer enormous wall of five-hundred-year-old brick and granite. Hatfield House looked like one of the sketched great houses on Mary Cat's map of London, cubes of brick and white stone cornered with towers, but it was huge. We couldn't see it all at once; we had to turn our heads to take it in.

"We're here why?" Posy whispered.

"Visiting the mythmakers," I said as Posy waved her father's plastic at the ticket taker.

Robert Cecil's house felt like a tomb, like a museum, gilded and elaborate and chill. Through an enormous carved arch we went into the Marble Hall, Cecil's great hall, maybe four times larger than the hall at Castle Hedingham. Below the famous tapestries on the wall hung the famous portraits, the two women whose fates had been intertwined with Robert Cecil as they'd been with his father: Elizabeth and Mary Queen of Scots. I hiked down to see them, my boots squeaking on the cold stone floor.

Elizabeth on the wall was timeless; but by the time brilliant, hunchbacked Robert Cecil joined her Council, she was old. Her teeth were blackened and gone. Her red hair was a wig. But she had fought death since she was a child, fought sickness and the headman's ax and the Pope himself, and she had always won. Myths don't die. It was treason to say Elizabeth would. She was the Madonna. She was England.

In 1601 Robert Cecil made the family's enduring fortunes by committing treason. He started a secret correspondence with the son of Mary Queen of Scots. For two years Robert Cecil counseled James. Wait, he said. Wait and trust me. I can bring you the throne.

James Stuart was no mythic figure. From damage in childbirth, his legs were weak and spindly, and he drooled. At thirty-seven, he'd never been out of Scotland. He believed in witches. He fell in love with handsome, stupid men. Worst, he was rumored to be Catholic. But James was happily married to the understanding Protestant Anne, and they had sons. There would be heirs for England.

In the early part of 1603 Elizabeth began to die.

One day, she had herself lifted into a low chair. When she found herself unable to rise from it, she commanded her attendants to help her to her feet. Once in that position, she remained there unmoving for fifteen hours, watched by her appalled yet helpless courtiers. . . . By 18 March, her condition had deteriorated alarmingly; . . ."she appeared already in a manner insensible, not speaking sometimes for two or three hours . . . holding her finger continually in her mouth, with her eyes open and fixed to the ground."

Myths die hard. On March 23 Robert Cecil and two of his allies went to see her. She could no longer speak. According to what Cecil reported later, he asked Elizabeth who should succeed her. Would it be James? According to Cecil, Elizabeth made with her hands and fingers a crown above her head, to signify James should be king.

The Cecils have always been lucky. Elizabeth died that night. One of Cecil's men removed from her finger the ring that twenty-five-year-old Princess Elizabeth had been given under the oak tree at Hatfield, and galloped away through the rain toward Scotland to give it to James.

Today it was almost raining. In the gloom Posy and I looked at the portraits of Elizabeth in the Marble Hall. There was the enameled betrothal ring on Elizabeth's living hand. She was herself again, a queen, triumphant, immortal, surrounded by emblems and metaphors of herself: virgin-white ermine, pearls, eglantine, a rainbow, a serpent of wisdom, a dress embroidered with eyes and ears to signify she heard and saw everything; dressed in herself, surrounded by herself, signifying herself, Elizabeth. Mary Queen of Scots, on the end wall, was only the heir's mother, a woman in mourning black, her chin falling, her nose sharpening, frozen in wariness like a hunted old deer.

Royal presents to the Cecils glittered everywhere: Queen Mary's posset set, portraits of King James, King Charles's cradle. Queen Elizabeth's silk stockings, gloves, and gardening hat, left behind on a visit, were preserved in a case in the library. The gloves were magnificent, long-fingered yellow kid with little tin mirrors. Elizabeth's hands must have glittered in the sun.

Ten thousand gilded spines shone from the library walls. Somewhere on these shelves, probably, was every book William Cecil ever owned. I thought of the schoolbook he got back by pretending to be a ghost. The guide lifted fabric covers to show manuscript treasures under glass, prizes as magnificent as those in the British Library's treasure room, the sort of manuscripts Frank Kellogg had only dreamed of. Letters from Queen Elizabeth and Mary Queen of Scots; the rough draft of the warrant for Mary's execution. A lot of Oxford's surviving letters were here. Over the fireplace, from a two-story-high mantelpiece like a tomb, the picture of hunchbacked Robert Cecil presided over what was probably, even now, the greatest private collection of books and manuscripts in England.

"This is the most magnificent house. All this great stuff."

A house full of power, of things, of greatness. "Cecils were collectors," I said. "Collectors, mythmakers, storytellers, you think that's fair?"

Posy nodded.

"Think what they must have thought of Oxford. He wasted things. He sold his castles. He was the Earl of Oxford and he didn't put it in a case like a treasure."

We went out into the gardens. Above us, bruised purple-and-blue clouds were blowing and the tops of trees were thrashing, but the paths were lined with thick close-limbed bushes and our breath hung almost motionless in the air. Round the corner, across the lawn, stood the last surviving wing of the old Hatfield, Elizabeth's prison-palace in its formal gardens. We looked through the door into the old banqueting hall, a barn in comparison to the gilded riches of Robert Cecil's house. Behind the palace we walked down a narrow village street of outbuildings, sheds, greenhouses. A man in rubber boots was trundling a wheelbarrow down the path; another man was leaning against a garage, smoking a cigarette.

The Tudor outbuildings at Castle Hedingham would have looked something like this; Hedingham's Great Hall would have been roofed like this with plain oak beams. Outworn, unimportant, those plain buildings; since they were built, the Age of Elizabeth had flowed through England like a great golden river and swept all the plain things away.

And now Elizabeth's time was done too, and James was king and Robert Cecil was his right-hand man, and there would be even better times. Better and better, forever and ever, like the new millennium.

"Come in the knot garden," I said.

Among the enlaced green shrubs of the knot garden, daffodils jerked intricately in a shower of rain. We took shelter by a wall under a topiary arch. The bitter smell of boxwood stung our noses.

"It was the week of Elizabeth's funeral," I said. "She'd been buried on Monday, April 28, 1603. King James had been working his way down from Scotland, and all Elizabeth's old courtiers except Cecil had gone north to meet him. James had been having himself a circus, riding in triumphal processions and getting keys to cities and creating knights and nobles left and right.

"Of course the man he wanted to meet was Robert Cecil.

"On May 3, the Saturday after the funeral, James came to visit Cecil. Robert Cecil gave James's retinue lunch and sent them off to bowl on the lawn, and he took James by the elbow and went off with him to the knot garden, and they talked for two hours alone."

The rain was getting heavier. The flowers nodded their drenched heads. I could see two men walking down the paths arm in arm, each helping the other, short Robert Cecil with his cloak looped over his crooked back, tall James with his dripping lips and thin legs. Ugly men know each other's selves without being told. James would have trusted Robert Cecil.

"Cecil listened to James," I said, "watched him, gave him advice." Shakespeare's hunchbacked villain was a king, but hunchbacked Cecil hadn't needed to sit on any throne; he could move faster behind it. "James was a generous man, and he would have asked, 'What do you want?' I think Cecil asked him for something and told him to do something."

Posy just nodded, looking up at me.

"What he asked for was Oxford's pension. Queen Elizabeth had given Oxford a pension of a thousand pounds a year. The Oxfordians say it was for writing plays, and James said later it was because Oxford was ruined. Anyway, Cecil asked the King to continue it. Which he did. But not until July. Cecil kept Oxford hungry a while."

"And the advice?"

"Cecil advised James to become the patron of an acting company."

"Sure, the Lord Chamberlain's Men," Posy said. Shakespeare's company.

"Yeah. Did it ever strike you as funny, that Robert Cecil did a big favor for Shakespeare after Elizabeth died? He'd had all kinds of trouble with Shakespeare. Southampton and Essex had used *Richard II* as a rallying cry in the Essex Rebellion. Shakespeare had made fun of Robert Cecil's father. But now—" I looked back at Robert Cecil's great rich house, the house of the most important man in England. "Now I think Cecil told James to become patron of William Shakespeare's company."

"*Cecil* did?"

"He did the paperwork himself. And that was just the beginning of it. About ten days after James reached London, the royal family took over all the acting companies. The Lord Chamberlain's Men became the King's Men. Queen Anne got a company too, Queen Anne's Men, combining Worcester's Men with a new company Oxford had started. The Admiral's Men, who played at the Rose, became Prince Henry's Men." The most favored company was the new King's Men. James gave them money for scarlet cloth for uniforms, and they marched in his coronation procession, all of them, Burbage, Kemp, and the actor William Shakespeare. "Goscimer never knew why; we had to call it *unexpected*."

"So why?" Posy said.

"James liked plays," I said. "His whole family did. But he liked spectacles. Circuses. Things coming down from the sky, ship battles, Inigo Jones sets. A different kind of play than what Shakespeare had written for Elizabeth. No history plays. No *words*. Queen Anne liked to act in private so she wanted masques, singing and dancing and costumes, things she could appear in, with not too many lines to memorize. In Elizabeth's time people used to say they were going to 'hear' a play. Starting in James's time, they 'saw' one."

"Masques," Posy said. *"Star Wars."*

"That kind of play, yeah. Elizabeth had liked the Shakespeare plays. What I think Cecil found out, that day in the knot garden, was James wouldn't like them so much." The rain was falling around us, but I moved out of the shelter, looked back toward the house of the king's advisor. Rain blew against my glasses and blurred house, gardens, everything. "Lunchtime, May 3, 1603, in the knot garden," I said. "I think Cecil realized he could tell James that the poet William Shakespeare was a glover's son from Stratford and James wouldn't know any different, or care."

"King James?" she said. "Cecil lied to *King James* about Shakespeare?"

"James had never been out of Scotland." He didn't know the Howards or Oxford or any of the old Elizabethan nobility. Shakespeare's identity could have been a open secret at Elizabeth's court, the way the authorship of *Astrophil and Stella* had been an open secret. But James wouldn't have known.

And James was king, but Robert Cecil was the king behind the throne.

I took my glasses off and wiped them on my sleeve, and put them on to see Posy looking across the gardens toward the Old Palace, back toward Robert Cecil's great rich house.

"Who was going to say Shakespeare the playwright wasn't Shakespeare the actor when Cecil said he was?" I said. I could see the two of them, the shambling Scotsman and the brilliant little Englishman. Cecil laid his fingers reflectively at the side of his mouth, the way his father had, and looked up at his new king. *William Shakespeare,* he said; perfect silver English vowels. "So, Posy? Cecil took every acting company there was and gave them patronage from the royal family. What actor was going to jeopardize that? Actors got their best money from royal performances, they got costumes, they got sets. Oxford couldn't move from the Lord Chamberlain's Men to write for the Admiral's Men. He didn't even have Oxford's Men. He didn't have actors."

He didn't have Shakespeare.

I unzipped my parka and swiped my glasses across my flannel shirt. The cold rain ran down my neck. My throat hurt.

"The Lord Chamberlain's Men started getting in trouble," Posy said. "And new Shakespeare plays stopped being published. And in 1604, William Shakespeare of Stratford retired from acting and went back home."

"And Shakespeare stopped reading after 1603."

"Yes," Posy said, "because he died."

~

We ducked back to the shelter of the boxwood arch. Posy looked through the arch to the big house. "He could do it," she said, half to herself, understanding it, turning the idea over. "Cecil could do it."

"You have the booklet about the Cecils?" I asked. I turned pages with rain-sticky fingers until I found the Cecil pedigree. "Robert, 1st Earl of Salisbury, K.G.," and his wife and his children, and their children, and their children, down to right now, twelve generations on.

"Cecil probably told himself Shakespeare was politically dangerous," I said. "But I think it was about family." His dad. His sister. It was about *my seat forbear.* " 'Keep your hands off my sister, my name, my family, my honor.' " Oxford had dissed the Cecils, he'd used a private letter, he'd mistreated Cecil's own big sister. He'd screwed up the marriage with Southampton and written poems about it.

"Robert Cecil felt he *deserved* to control Shakespeare," Posy said, "the way William Cecil deserved to control Oxford. And he could."

"William Shakespeare never should have happened. Cecil just put things back the way they should have been."

"Nobody ever has any business being themselves," Posy said soberly. "And Cecil had no clue about Shakespeare, that Shakespeare might be important or something—" She ran her fingers across the leaves of the enormous old boxwood arch, stirring its chill acrid smell; she stared through the rain at Hatfield Palace, toward the windows through which Elizabeth must have gazed while she waited to be queen, to be manipulated, to be loved and used and turned into a myth. "So Robert Cecil just did it. Like his father had. And got away with it. Again, and again, and again."

"Yeah," I said. "Except—"

The garden was deserted; Hatfield had been almost deserted. If this were Stratford, it would have been jammed, rain or no rain.

"Except this time," I said. "Even Cecil couldn't get rid of Shakespeare."

⁓

"I found something," I told Goscimer.

The rain that fell on the knot garden at Hatfield was still falling outside the windows of Durrant's Hotel. Goscimer looked good. Being taken care of, even on tour, agreed with him; people had been feeding him, and he'd bought a new suit. I looked down at my own scarred hands and out at the darkness beyond the hotel window.

I'd spent the past two hours walking around London in the rain, wondering what I could say to him. It couldn't be Shakespeare, not the letter, not the poem. I had to start with—

I took a breath. "Yeah, I found something in the Kellogg Collection. There's a guy going to come here with it tonight, and we can both take a look at it. But I don't want to start there. I want to talk about *Sir Thomas More.*"

"You found something?" said Goscimer after a moment. "Rachel would be so proud— What *is* it, Joe?"

More would be my strong point with him. "Let's start with *More,*" I said. "I read it a couple of days ago, the whole thing. You've read it?"

"Well, a long time ago, Joe, I recall it was terrible. Except for Shakespeare's part, of course."

"A lot of speeches are good. I don't think Shakespeare wrote only the Ill May Day scenes. I think he wrote most of More's serious scenes and the speeches of the Earl of Surrey." I'd printed out another copy of the Internet version of *Sir Thomas More.* I pulled it out and read:

France now hath her full strength,
As having new recovered the pale blood
Which war sluiced forth . . .

Goscimer fingered the printout. "This isn't a scholarly edition, Joe, and no one has ever argued that Shakespeare wrote anything but the Ill May Day scenes."

"I know. I'm arguing differently."

"How does this connect with the Kellogg?"

I sat on the edge of the bed like a criminal in front of a judge. "I started reading Munday. He could have written the comedy scenes in *More,* couldn't have risen to that Surrey speech"—with a balloon tied to his ass, I thought—"Munday didn't have the poetic talent. I think Shakespeare and Munday collaborated, not

Shakespeare rewriting Munday the way Fletcher probably rewrote *Henry VIII* but a true collaboration, writing together and at the same time."

"I would want to see your argument," Goscimer said doubtfully.

"I'll have to develop it more. But I wanted to know what you think. Because there are some problems with Munday writing a play about Sir Thomas More anytime when he's supposed to have."

"Remind me when that was," Goscimer said, impatient, wanting the Kellogg.

"1590 or before. But England was still jumping at Catholic spies, Jesuits, from 1581 well into the 1590s. Father Garnet? John Gerard? And Anthony Munday wrote against the Catholics starting in 1581."

"So you don't think Munday wrote *More?*" Goscimer said, puzzled.

"No, I think he did. And collaborated with Shakespeare. But I think there's a problem with the date."

"Joe, excuse me, what did you find in the Kellogg Collection?"

I looked at the clock. "You'll see it soon. When the date began to bother me, I wondered if I could find anything else that looked like a collaboration between Munday and Shakespeare, and I started reading him. And I think I've found one. A poem. But there's a problem with that date too."

"A poem," Goscimer said, stunned. "You think you've found *a new Shakespeare poem?* No one finds this much all at once." This wasn't praise.

"I know. But once I got to Munday—" Once I'd got to Munday it had been like following a string.

"How long is this poem? Is it a sonnet, or— Was it in a manuscript?"

I pulled one of the Xerox copies of the poem out of my backpack and handed it to him too.

It was too much. Thirty-six pages, black letter, blurred Xerox off a Xerox, on top of *Sir Thomas More*. He had sixty pages of *More* in his right hand, *The Paine of Pleasure* in his left; his hands were weighted down with works I was identifying as Shakespeare's. Nobody finds this much. If *Paine* had been a sonnet, he might have read it all, thought it over; in two or three hours he might have been willing to consider a sonnet. But I had given him too much.

"This must be in LION," he said. "Let's see what LION has to say about it."

"It'll say Munday wrote it," I said, but he was going to the authorities, LIterature ONline, the big database of English literature; I couldn't blame him.

Goscimer's battered old laptop was on the desk: no, I realized, it was a new one, thin and sleek, almost as up-to-date as Posy's. I helped Goscimer plug his computer into the phone jack; Goscimer settled his reading glasses on his nose and typed in his username and password for LION.

"It's here," he said.

Lines of text sprang up on his screen. Goscimer read a little. He looked up at me, frowning, his lips drawn down. "It doesn't start well," I said nervously. "That's Munday. Sir —" I hadn't told Goscimer the half of my argument, but Goscimer was paging through the black stanzas, reading slowly down the screen between each button-push.

He looked up. "Joe," he said gently.

"It's not all that good. But look at what he chooses for content, look at his technical terms —"

"I am, Joe."

Yet doe I not forbid to clime at all,
For some must clime, and those I well allow:
But yet I wish the best to feare a fall,
And those that clime at all, to clime, but how?
When neede requires, and then so carefully,
As that they come not downe too hastily.

"Joe," he said. "That is not Shakespeare."

"Here," I said, pointing out " 'Tis not the thing, but the delight therein."

" 'Delight, delight,' " Goscimer said, " 'delight' three times. It is a clumsy commonplace. Not Shakespeare. Look at this couplet, just below it, here. 'For I would have it used for exercise/In some cold mornings, and not otherwise.' You cannot possibly say this is Shakespeare."

"It's not all good," I said. "I didn't say it was good."

"This is a waste of time. Joe, if you had looked on LION at first, you would have seen *The Paine of Pleasure* was published in 1580. It is far too early for Shakespeare."

Goscimer thriftily disconnected from LION and raised his thin index finger. "You should have known to check," he said. "You of all people. Why bring up this nonsense now? —Tell me about the Kellogg. I hope the Kellogg item is not nonsense like this, Joe."

I had no way to avoid this. I'd never had. He was going to react like I'd reacted to Posy at the beginning.

"I know about the date," I said.

"You *know?*" Goscimer said, squinting up at me. "1580?"

"I know," I said. And there was no avoiding it anymore. "What I found in the Kellogg Collection is supposed to be a letter from Shakespeare."

"Oh, dear," Goscimer said under his breath. "Another letter from Shakespeare."

"I wouldn't mention it to you if I thought this one was a forgery; I wouldn't waste your time. The letter says that Shakespeare, William Shakespeare born at Stratford in 1564 — Shakespeare went to Italy," I said. "You were right. But the man who went to Italy — the man who collaborated with Anthony Munday on *More* and maybe on *The Paine of Pleasure* — the man who wrote the plays — he wasn't William Shakespeare of Stratford."

"You are not talking about *the authorship question?* You know that is nonsense."

I took a breath.

"And who is he?" Goscimer said, taking off his reading glasses, folding them with shaking hands, suddenly angry. "Who is your Shakespeare, Joe? After Rachel and I worked for many, many years on Shakespeare's life, and found nothing of the sort, *nothing,* who is this man whom you find so easily, in the *Kellogg Collection?*"

"You never considered him," I said, "and neither did I because nobody believes in him. Edward de Vere. The Earl of Oxford."

"Oh, Joe," Goscimer said. That was all, but the word carried such a weight of anger and disappointment, it made me flinch with shame.

"I know what you're thinking. I thought so too. I didn't want to believe it — I don't. But it's there. All this stuff is there."

Goscimer stared at the glasses in his hand, not up at me. "You have been at the Kellogg Collection too long," he said. "I never thought you were gullible — Joe, go away and *think.*"

"Sir. Professor Goscimer —" I had brought a printout of my scan of the letter. All my pieces of paper, too much to give him, too much to ask of him; I held it out to him anyway. "I never wanted," I said, *"never,* to find anything to get in the way of your book. Shit, don't you think I hate this too?"

Goscimer took it, but he didn't even look at it. "The *Kellogg Collection,* Joe." Still looking at me, he tore the printout of the letter in halves and in quarters. "Joe, this is laughable, but it would destroy any possible career you might have, any chance of a career."

The telephone buzzed. On the desk, by the phone, were an ashtray and matches. Goscimer balled the pieces of paper into the ashtray and answered the phone.

"Miss Gould?" Goscimer said. "Come upstairs." He hung up the phone, put the ashtray carefully down on the room service menu, and lit a match. The paper puffed up into a little smoke and flame.

"I am very surprised Miss Gould could take the authorship question seriously."

We waited in a raw silence the time it took the elevator to rise to Goscimer's floor. I answered the knock.

There were three of them, not two. Posy, Nicky Bogue — and Ted Gould.

"Good evening, Professor Goscimer," Nicky Bogue said, limping to center stage. "I can see Mr. Roper has been speaking to you. May I say, by the way, Professor, how thoroughly I enjoyed *In Search of Shakespeare?* But you won't want to hear that now. You'll want to know about the letter."

"I have no patience with any letter," Goscimer said.

Nicky Bogue was carrying a flat leather portfolio. He moved the laptop carefully aside. His narrow closed-in face was Robert Cecil's at Hatfield, keeping his own counsel. He opened the portfolio, and on the desk he spread the manila envelope, the eighteenth-century envelope, and finally the letter.

"The outer envelope, 1930s," Nicky said, indicating it with one long finger. "The eighteenth-century envelope, authentic. The handwriting's meant to be David Garrick's, and it may actually be; that interests me, but it's not our issue this evening. The letter— I'd like to turn down the lights a moment."

Ted Gould, at the doorway, turned off the overhead lights, leaving nothing but the dim light at the door of the suite. Nicky turned off the table lamp and took from his jacket pocket what looked like a Maglite. He clicked it on. Out of the duskiness, shapes glowed ghost-blue: the cuffs of his tailored shirt, Posy's purple jewelry and lipstick, and the letter.

"UV told the story in five minutes. Sodium hypochlorite on the blank leaf of a folio," Nicky Bogue said, bored. "A common enough forgery. More modern than I thought. Probably not more than fifteen years old."

In the dark I thought Posy looked across at me, but when Ted Gould turned the light back on, she wouldn't meet my eyes.

"Mr. Roper hadn't bothered to check it under UV," Nicky explained. He tossed the letter down on the desk.

My face flamed.

"I could have told you instantly. I admit, I let you dangle. You too, Pose my dear. You were rather cocksure of yourself, Mr. Roper, and Posy has been very fond of the unorthodox explanations of Shakespeare. I wondered if you might convince her otherwise." Nicky's mouth twisted. "But I seem inadvertently to have provided an object lesson that, when it comes to famous men four hundred years ago, it's far too easy to believe anything at all."

"You didn't *test* the letter?" Gould said to me.

You think it's real. Come with me to London. I looked across at her. *Posy.*

"I didn't test it," I said. "But what I found doesn't depend on the letter."

"Oh, really," Nicky Bogue said, bored.

"The Earl of Oxford," Goscimer said under his breath. *"No one* believes in the Earl of Oxford."

"So," Ted Gould said to me. "You had fun. On my dime. I'm not complaining. The money's not the point, I've got it, I can spend it. The point is what you were doing to my girl."

I didn't say anything. I just looked at Posy, and she wouldn't look at me.

"I worry about my daughter. You were feeding her crap," Gould said. "She gets these ideas, I'm not saying she doesn't get ideas." Posy's cheeks were as white as they'd been at the dinner table with Don Cannon. "Harvard, whatever, I don't understand it. But the point is," he said, "the point is, she's going to Harvard, she should be a success at Harvard, she's not going to be a success believing this crap, am I right?" He turned to her. "Am I right, Posy?"

They looked at each other, Daddy and daughter. Throw something, Posy, I thought. Go to Italy, go to Fisher's Folly, get away from him; you have a chance to escape; it's now.

"I never *believed* it," Posy said to all of us or none of us. "Joe—" For one moment she looked at me, and her eyes were wide and dark the way they had been this afternoon at Hatfield looking out on the rainy knot garden. *"Shakespeare* wrote Shakespeare."

"And the Cecils always win," I said. "Do they?"

"I don't know what you're talking about."

"Give me the letter." I went over to the desk and picked it up.

"It's yours," Nicky said. "Northeastern's. Take it, and the report."

"I'm paying for that report," Gould said. "I don't mind."

"And sign the receipt, please, I want the thing off my hands."

Rag-stock paper, the same; iron-gall ink, the same. On one corner the letter had been eaten away to lace, the same. The writing was piss-poor, barely legible; the lines straggled down the page painfully, shakily, irregularly, blotted with sweat. The same. But the smell, that four-hundred-year-old smell of wood fires, of horses, of fog and smoke and time and neglected shelves in libraries, it was nothing now but a little cinnamon, a little sweetness and a mustiness.

Nicky Bogue was smiling at me wryly. "Does it look different?" he said. "They always do, once you see it."

"It smells different," I said.

Nicky painted that for me himself, Posy had said about her good-looking portrait of William Cecil. Nicky adooores me. Nicky had asked Posy, Are you sure you want to be involved with the Oxfordians? I looked into Nicky's eyes, Robert Cecil's ice-blue eyes.

Would Nicky Bogue have stolen a Shakespeare letter and substituted a forgery? Even for love of Posy, or of Shakespeare?

"Yes, that smell," Nicky said. "It was a good touch, wasn't it? It dissipated over the week."

Between ten and twenty million dollars—

"One does want to believe in the letter," Nicky said. "One— gets excited. It's natural. Don't feel badly over it. It was very good of its kind."

"You want to be careful what you think," Ted Gould said. "Right?"

Had Ted Gould investigated me too, the way he'd investigated Betty Lou Cannon? Had he learned about Mom?

"You don't want your imagination to get away from you," Gould said.

Crazy as a shithouse rat. Crazy doesn't mean that your imagination is wrong, it means you don't know whether you're wrong or right, and it's killing you. You don't know if your wife is true to you or not, if your daughter is really yours, if the truck headlights are really glaring into your eyes and the airhorn really blaring, if the wheels are really crushing you, if you are really dying. Crazy and wrong, and Nicky and Ted Gould and the Cecils are always right. "Posy?" I said. But Posy was looking down at her hands, chipping at the polish of one fingernail. The Cecils were always right, whatever they did, whether they did everything or nothing at all; and Posy was going to be right too.

"This is embarrassing," Ted Gould said. "Shit happens sometimes, everybody screws their feet to the floor once in a while, you'll get over it. Look, Joe," he said, friendly. "I booked you into a nice hotel. You're gonna want to rest up, do a little R&R, you know what I'm saying? Relax. We brought your luggage, some cash for you, Posy said she was paying you. Have yourself some fun, forget all this crap, and your ticket's in your luggage for when you want to go home."

"Joe," said Goscimer, "everyone is wrong sometimes. Oxfordianism is an attractive—fable. None of us"—he looked around the room—"none of us will say anything, I'm sure. Come and see me when we are both home."

I still had the letter in my hand.

"You will bring everything back safe to the Kellogg," Goscimer asked me, "with the rest of the forgeries?"

I nodded.

They let me leave with it and nobody cared. My backpack was downstairs at the concierge's. Everything was in it, all my clothes, folded and clean, my notes from the B.L., the address of the hotel where Gould had booked me, and my ticket home, first class. I even had the CD with the scan I'd done of the letter.

I sat across the street on a bench in the square, watching the front entrance of the hotel. It was still raining. After a while they all came out. Ted Gould came first, and behind him walked Posy with Goscimer on her right and Nicky Bogue on her left. The doorman flagged down a taxi. Nicky reached out to take Posy's arm; she drew away and wrapped both hands round Goscimer's left arm. That was the last I saw of her, a toss of hennaed hair in the rain, a flash of purple earring, green fingernails on Goscimer's sleeve, a ghost of face turning behind the window as the taxi drove away.

I left my backpack at the hotel and went out to get drunk. On a Saturday night in a city full of bars, I figured I could get pretty fucking monumentally drunk, and I tried. I drank Guinness at a pub in Queen Square. I tried overpriced Jack Daniel's at a trendy bar in Soho and switched back to beer at an American-style joint filled with tattooed skinheads. I got into a shouting fight about whether Devo was a fecking good band or nowt better than fecking Liberace. I met some Aussies, big Dave and little Colin and Colin's Chinese girlfriend. The Aussies said Aussies could drink better than anyone. Dave threw up in Leicester Fields. I threw up too, being companionable, spreading a bush with everything down to the lint on the inside of my socks. I told the Aussies about Robert Dudley, framed for the murder of his wife. We agreed it was a bloody fucking shame. Dave fell asleep on a park bench. Colin and the Chinese girlfriend and I wandered down toward the Thames. The Chinese girlfriend had some licorice-tasting stuff in a hip flask. We took turns drinking it, warm from the girl's thigh. I cried a little, thinking about Posy. "We supposed put water in," the Chinese girl said, giggling nervously. By the time we got to the river, the streets were moving around me like glowing fog. "Where you want to go, mate?" Colin asked me. "You want to go home? You got someplace to go, mate?"

They sat me on a bench in the park below the London Eye. I looked up at the neon pods, circling up into the sky. I could see people entering the bright pods one by one. William and Robert Cecil. Anne Cecil. The Earl of Southampton, his long hair spilling out from beneath a hat, his complexion white in the neon glow from the Eye. Thomas Howard, Duke of Norfolk, beheaded. Anthony Munday. Edward Alleyn, Richard Burbage. Red-wigged Elizabeth. Shambling King James. Edward de Vere and William Shakespeare. Kings and queens, bikers, poets, courtiers, spies, they all went up into the glowing clouds, but none of them came down.

"This too weird," Colin's Chinese girlfriend said. "He see things? I go home."

"Right," said Colin. "Sorry, mate."

I saw more people riding the Wheel. Dad, younger, with all his teeth, holding hands with my mom. Ted Gould, Lady Silvia, Nicky Bogue, Goscimer, Posy. The wheel has come full circle. I am here.

"You could have left a manuscript," I said aloud. "Fuck you. You could have written thank-you poems. Fuck you. You could have said where you were in the lost years, you could have let somebody see you write, *fuck you*—"

But no one was answering me.

I had a lot of money to spend and no idea to spend it on. In the early morning, hung over, I stared at the letter for a long time again, and then I looked through *Time Out* for the most wasteful, millennial, un-Shakespearean thing I could find in London. I went to the Dome.

The Millennium Dome was supposed to be the quintessence of England in the year 2000, greater than the Ritblat Gallery exhibit, greater than the London Eye. In the Body exhibit, I shuffled with the Sunday crowds through a plastic intestinal tract. I saw play blood gushing through plastic veins. *How weary, flat, stale, and unprofitable/Seem to me all the uses of this world.* I stood numb with boredom under the pastel lights of Faith, listening to a piped-in Om, the sound of nothingness. In the England's Self-Portrait wall, I saw Shakespeare on the wall of the glories of England along with *The Full Monty* and the butty sandwich.

In Peter Gabriel's Millennium show, dancers and acrobats circled, embraced, high in the enormous blue-and-white-striped circus tent, coming to weightless pretend-orgasm. The kids watching the show kicked their heels and poked each other. They'd seen Gabriel's videos, they'd seen R movies, this new century was old hat to them.

King James would have liked Peter Gabriel. What could Shakespeare have done against big sets and explosions and people on wires having sex in midair? Shakespeare was a couple of guys onstage talking about men the new guys at court didn't know. *Shakespeare was sooo 1590s,* I heard a familiar ghostly voice say, and told myself to stop it. *Shakespeare was so totally not like the millennium?*

What could Shakespeare have done when his time was over? When all the acting companies belonged to the royal family,

Burbage and Shakespeare belonged to the King and Edward
Alleyn to Queen Anne? Retire? Enjoy his big house?

He could die.

I thought about Dad, and Mary Cat, and I went to Docklands
Road instead.

⁓

Docklands Road was a dead-end street of gray, boarded-up
buildings, warehouses, a betting shop, a thrift shop, a pub. Saint
Mary's Hostel was a three-story brick building painted a faded,
flaking orange. Outside, men were leaning against the wall,
smoking in the misty rain. Inside, the air was full of smoke too;
homeless guys shuffled around, coughing up lungies, setting folding tables with paper plates and plastic spoons. Sunday dinner-
time.

I asked a tiny Irish nun if I could speak to Mary Cat. "She's out
for the moment. Will you not have some dinner in the meantime?"

"Sure." I felt homeless enough.

I helped set up folding chairs and brought stuff out of the
kitchen. There were only two nuns doing everything. Yeah, they
needed her. The little Irish nun moved down the row of paper
plates, sliding big dollops of stew onto them with a spoon. I
stirred my stew around on my plate and drew shapes in it. The
old guys and I turned our chairs around, sang *holy holy holy*. My
head hurt.

I looked at the windows on either side of the door.

The glass was near falling out of them.

"I'll fix your windows," I said.

I was still working on windows at four o'clock when
Goscimer's program came on the BBC, and I listened to

Goscimer talking about Shakespeare. In Shakespeare's lost years, Goscimer said, he was living in London.

He did go to Italy. But you have to have more than belief. You have to have proof. You have to check your sources, not go farther than they do, not find too much too fast, not have too much imagination. I went outside, pretending to have a cigarette, but I don't smoke; I just stared.

Come to see me when you come home. Sure. I could go back to the Kellogg, finish up cataloging all the forgeries, and find some thesis to write. Do an edition maybe. I could take my inspiration from the Goscimers, who had said that Shakespeare never went to Italy.

At five o'clock Mary Cat came in, shaking rain off a second-hand plaid umbrella. She went past me, not noticing me.

"Mary Cat?" I said.

She looked like a lightbulb somebody had turned off. "I can't talk now." She almost ran off into the kitchen.

"Mary Catherine will have had a disappointment," said the little Irish sister, looking after her. "Mother House told us by the phone. If you're a friend of hers, you might stay and talk with her a bit."

"What's happened?"

The Irish nun shook her head. "*I* would have let her stay! I suppose that's why I'm not in Mother House." She looked after Mary Cat with helpless kindness.

So I knew what had happened. I went into the big half-deserted kitchen. She was at the sink, scrubbing at the dishes, her back to the whole world. I silently started cleaning things, working my way around from stove to sink until I was elbow to elbow with her.

"Want to get a cup of coffee or something?"

With the cuff of her rubber glove she wiped her hair out of her eyes, or maybe she was wiping her eyes. She nodded without speaking.

We finished the dishes and got our coats. Outside it was freezing. On the corner the pub was brightly lit, the only place around.

"You okay with going there?" I said, nodding at it.

"I think I'll have a beer," Mary Cat said.

Okay, yeah, I couldn't criticize. "You do that."

Inside, Mary Cat got us seats in a dark corner. I got her a light beer and me a Coke.

"So?" I said.

Neither of us said anything for a bit. I drank my Coke. Mary Cat hadn't touched her beer.

"You want to talk about it?"

She shook her head.

"They won't let you stay?" I said. "Even here?"

She put her head down on her arms.

I put my hand out and covered her hand, for friendship. I could have told you, I thought. But that was the one thing I had never said to her. I had told her, You should teach, and You've grown out of wanting to be a nun, and You're a good researcher, and everything but They'll never let you. Because Mary Cat had done a courageous thing in India and ruined all her hopes, and I'd been hoping that someone would see it as much as I'd been hoping she'd decide not to be a nun all the same.

She'd been seventeen, just graduated from high school. She'd gone to India to join a teaching order. They'd sent her to a little town on a truck route, to teach the women to read. You know how

AIDS spreads in India? Along the truck routes. The truckers gave it to the prostitutes, and from there it went to the husbands, the wives, the babies. Three of Mary Cat's women students died during her first eight months in India, and five of their children.

So she'd got her mother to send her boxes of condoms, and she'd started giving them out.

Now nuns were beginning to give out condoms and conduct sex education—only now, seven years later than Mary Cat had. Their bishops were fighting them. And so whenever Mary Cat applied to join an order, someone higher up would always decide to send a message and say no.

"Did they tell you you should teach instead?" I said.

She shook her head, which was still resting on her arms.

"Just told you off?"

She raised her head and wiped her eyes.

"It's my fault," she said, her voice thick with crying. "Joe, the bishop asked me if I was sorry, and did I know how deeply I had offended God and Mother Church. And I do." Her voice broke in a hiccup. "And then he asked me if I would do the same thing again. And, Joe, even for the love of God, I had to say I would."

You'll find someplace, I'd said before. Someone will believe in you. I'd thought someone would, because it had happened to me once, because an old woman with imagination had looked at a hick undergraduate from Vermont and seen a biographer.

I could go back and see Goscimer, and write a thesis, and get a Ph.D., and teach, and never say a word about Shakespeare's biography again.

"The worst is," she said, "I'm crying because I'm angry. There is so much good there, the Church has so much that is truly good to say about the sanctity of love. But Joe, I feel bitter about the one thing I think they have wrong, I focus in on my little piece of righteousness, and I say snippy things to myself about people who use sanctity as an excuse for never thinking a thought that hasn't been stamped by Holy Father— Here I'm doing it again. Oh, Joe," she said, "pride, pride. I have so much false love of my little spark of a notion. And I am ruined entirely."

Pride, pride. I could never speak about Shakespeare's biography again. I could get out the letter, early on a lot of mornings to come, and think about whether it had been real. I could do editions. I could teach freshman English in a community college. Maybe get to teach the Shakespeare plays. But if anyone ever asked me who Shakespeare was, what would I say?

Mary Cat looked into my face and wriggled her hand free and put an arm around me, and I put an arm around her. Not a hug, because even if Mary Cat wasn't a nun, she wanted to be. Just shared misery. Shared fear.

"What happened, Joe?" she asked.

"We were talking about you."

"It's your turn, I've bled enough for now."

"I've screwed up," I said. "Ah, fuck it, Mary Cat, I've screwed up. I talked to Goscimer. I'd figured out more," I said. "I had a whole theory, Robert Cecil, King James. I thought the letter was real. I thought he'd find out within a day or so anyway. So I talked to Goscimer. And the letter turned out to be forged."

Mary Cat didn't say anything, just looked at me, eyes wide.

"I don't know what's real anymore," I said. All of a sudden I wanted to bawl like a baby. I had to jam my fingers in the corners of my eyes. "The way Goscimer read the poem, it sounded like shit. Maybe he could dismiss it that fast. But he didn't really take a look at it, he looked on LION and saw Munday and 1580 and that was it for him. He only cared what edition of *More* I'd read."

"And you hate him," Mary Cat said. "It isn't worth it."

"I don't, I understand him. Pride," I said, swallowing, "yeah, I know pride, I know why I did it. I wanted to be proud of myself, I wanted something to tell me, 'It's all right for you to go study Shakespeare, you're not a hick from East Bradenton, you don't belong in the hardware store.' I believed in it to make me important," I said.

"Oh, yes," she said. "You and I both, Joe. I was going to be a heroine, and instantly too. Knowing exactly what I was doing, so I wouldn't have to suffer."

"Pride and stupidity," I said.

She gave a little moan of laughter. "Stupid, that was the word I was looking for. Oh, Joe, aren't we a pair. At least you don't have the burden of being even a little right."

I didn't say anything.

She looked up at me. "Joe?"

"You want to know my worst?" I said. "I keep thinking I could be right. I think the letter I found could have been real, and the guy who was looking at it could have made a copy of it and stolen it. I just want to be right, just want to be right— He had the letter for a week. When the letter came back, it was forged, but I don't know what it was when I gave it to him. And *I* gave it to him. *I* took it out of the library and gave it to him with my own hands, and the only care I took of it was I got a receipt."

"Joe," Mary Cat said—

"Pride, sure, I know. I want to keep on being important and right, fucking Joe the Man Roper, Great Shakespeare Biographer, so I want to turn Nicky into a forger, stealing the letter to sell to Ted Gould. But—" I didn't know how to put this. *But it's all true* was the bottom of it, and I didn't know that.

"The paper had a smell," I said.

The smell. The bar was full of the smell of beer and old tobacco smoke. For a moment I was back under the high-school football bleachers, smelling beer and urine and the faint smell of char from where some asshole back in the 1960s had lit a fire under the bleachers and almost burned them down. Smoke is one of those smells like cat piss, once it gets on something you need dynamite and prayer meetings to get it out. The smell of smoke had hung on thirty years under the Bradenton Regional bleachers.

I'd seen the letter on Nicky Bogue's desk, in a clear plastic archival envelope. Archival envelopes keep air out. And smells in. For shit sure a smell would have survived a week.

And what could I do if it were true? I was the guy who'd lost Shakespeare's letter. I'd have to get it back and I had no fucking idea how to do it, because I already had it, didn't I?

I looked into Mary Cat's horrified eyes.

"You think I'm going crazy?" I said. "I do. And the worst thing is I'm not sure of it. I'll never even know."

~

I acted normal; I didn't know how else to act. I went back to the hotel Ted Gould had chosen for me. I took a bath and went to bed. I lay staring at the ceiling.

In the early morning I went out to a copy shop and got another printout of the letter. I went to a teashop, sat by the window, got out the letter and the printout, held them up together against the window. They matched. So if they'd forged the letter, they'd scanned the forgery and replaced my CD.

I could go crazy over this.

I went and stood outside the British Library, and didn't go in. What would I read about? Shakespeare's life?

I went in, finally, and sat at a desk. I didn't order any books. I had the printout with me, and I looked at it, stared at it, two hours maybe, until I could begin to see in it traces of a modern hand. I had the Xerox of *The Paine of Pleasure* with me too, and I read it again, leafing back and forth through the black-letter lines, and sometimes it seemed like nothing, an ordinary dull midcentury poem; but then a line or two would flare into light. I went out and got the magnified scans printed out and read what I could. William Shakespeare of Stratford wrote to Fulke Greville that the Earl of Salisbury was dead, Robert Cecil was dead, and that once, long ago, he had held a nobleman's horse and said he wanted to wear satin.

Come to London, the Earl had said.

Who is a man? He's what he can imagine. Carpenters imagine staircases, poets dream poems. Nuns think up ways to serve. Biographers make up lives. I'd made up Shakespeare's, and mine with it. Joe Roper, the genius biographer, the big man. And maybe I had been right, and maybe I had been taken by a forgery, but everything I was doing now, sitting in the library reading, all that was a forgery.

William Shakespeare, actor, poet, playwright. Born in Stratford, son of a glover. It ought to be easy to imagine, shouldn't it? Everyone could imagine it. Educated at Stratford Grammar School. Patron saint of lost causes. Married at eighteen, escaped Stratford at twenty-one. Wrote poems to eighteen-year-old Southampton at twenty-four, perhaps; wrote *Venus and Adonis* at twenty-six. For four hundred years people have imagined that life.

I couldn't imagine it anymore.

So, the last thing I would do in London, I said goodbye to being a biographer.

There'd been a place in London to see London Wall and the bookshops by Saint Paul's, to watch Edward Alleyn and to look up at the cloud-capped towers of the Globe. There was a place too to say goodbye.

I took a printout of the letter and a Xerox of *The Paine of Pleasure*, and my library card, and a box of matches. Some things, like goodbyes, you need to do more than get drunk for.

It was a long bus ride to Hackney Central. In Oxford's time, Hackney was out in the country. Now it was in North London. Grubby in the late afternoon, the McDonald's by the bus stop rubbed shoulders with Venus Big Foot Dry Cleaners, Afro International, a restaurant advertising curried goat, and a storefront lawyer with a cardboard sign in the window, "We Welcome Asylum Seekers."

Only the tower was left of Saint Augustine's Church, where Oxford had been buried. The churchyard was a few old gnarled trees, a tuffety lawn scattered with dandelions, and some flat tombs that more or less marked where the church had been. The grave markers had been moved back to line a low brick wall.

The flowers on the two magnolia trees were battered and browned. Most of the gravestones were unreadable, the names rubbed off.

Oxford died in June 1604, just over a year after King James's family took over the actors. His widow lived at their house here, King's Place, until 1609, and was buried here with him when she died in 1612. Old descriptions of Saint Augustine's mention an elaborate granite tomb that may have been theirs. The tomb disappeared long ago.

I wandered through the damp grass, looking at the surviving table tombs and the monuments propped against the garden wall. I went inside the bell tower and looked at the remains of a Gothic window netted against the pigeons.

There was nothing here to worship. This wasn't Stratford. There were no carefully tended monuments, no quill pens replaced yearly, not even a Blue Plaque. Believe in Shakespeare and you got BBC interviews, glory of Britain, Man of the Millennium. Believe in Oxford and you got the Halifax Bank where Fisher's Folly used to be; the garden in Oxford Court. Here.

Nothing. You got nothing. No undiscovered Shakespeare poem, no brilliant reworking of Shakespeare's entire career, no career, no job, no thesis, no letter, no proof: nothing.

Across the street, by the dry cleaner and the McDonald's, were a pharmacy and a hardware store. In one of them, I knew, I could buy Drano or razor blades or a lot of aspirin and solve my problems. I could step out on some fast-moving street, some street where a lot of trucks were going to the north and there was no stencil on the pavement saying LOOK RIGHT.

No longer mourn for me when I am dead.

And I couldn't do that either. I thought of Dad, and of Mary Cat.

I would do some good. I would take Ted Gould's money and get Dad's teeth fixed. I'd apply for the assistant manager's job at Coleman's Ace Hardware at the mall. And I'd endure, like Dad and Mary Cat endured. I wouldn't write biography about people who were standing in front of me, or people too far away to know.

I knelt down in the damp grass by a gravestone, one with an

elaborate design of skulls and an hourglass and the trumpets of judgment, well-carved, Oxford would have appreciated that. I balled up the printout of the letter and the first sheets of the poem and set them alight, and laid the rest of the poem on top of it and my card from the British Library on top of that. It was a poor excuse for a funeral pyre; the grass was wet, and the card was laminated and only got sooty and browned on the edges. In the end I left the card half-wedged into a crevice in the stone.

> *. . . Now I want*
> *Spirits to enforce, art to enchant;*
> *And my ending is despair . . .*

I wasn't going to despair. I was going to do my best.

I lowered my head against the cold wind, left the graveyard, crossed the street toward the bus stop. I waited among a crowd of mostly black people, women with shopping bags gossiping about grandchildren and church, boys with British accents and American clothes, men coming back from work.

On the wall of the bus shelter was glued an ad for British Telecom. *Parting is such sweet sorrow, That I could say 'good night' till it be morrow.*

All my life, I knew, all my life I would be haunted by words from Shakespeare.

The bus was coming.

If I were a scholar, any kind of a researcher, I would go to see the site of King's Place while I was here. It was part of saying goodbye that I wouldn't. I had given up running after dead men. I was going to have a life. I was going to enjoy it if I could. I was going to get married and have kids and buy a house, and do all the things men do, and not care about Shakespeare.

The bus pulled up beside the shelter. I got my money out. I looked at the bus door, at the stairs up to the door. And I stood, motionless, with my money in my hand, and people jostled around me and pushed me out of the way, and I watched the bus pull away from me.

Rachel Goscimer told me always to look at everything. And sometimes all a man has is what his friends tell him.

"Excuse me," I said to the man next me, "do you know, is there a King's Place Street around here, or—" The house had been renamed Brooke Place by the time it was torn down. "Or a Brooke Street, something like that?"

"Brooke School, you want, man, or de housin' estate? Brooke Road you want." He pointed up past Saint Augustine's.

Brooke Road was an ordinary city street lined with cars. I saw the schoolyard first, shabby and overused, with a few leafless thin trees poking up among pavement. Behind it was the housing estate, four lean brown-and-orange blocks of bleak apartments, bad 1960s architecture, surrounded by a big parking lot full of cars.

I stared across the bleakness. It was almost reassuringly ugly. There was nothing left. I'd seen a picture of King's Place, a big ancient house, but it wasn't here anymore, I couldn't even imagine it. There was only the parking lot, the blocks of buildings, a few struggling shrubs planted by the pipe fence. It didn't matter. Everyone was dead. The Earl and Countess were buried in an unmarked grave across the street from a McDonald's; Robert Cecil was dead at Hatfield and Anne Cecil in Westminster Abbey with her mother. Young beautiful Southampton had died an old grey man. Oxford's only son, Southampton's only son, Shakespeare's only son had died young and left no children. Shakespeare's Mr. W. H., the one whose name would live forever because Shakespeare wrote about him—he was most dead of all, because no one really knew who he was anymore.

The rest is silence.

The housing estate was one of those places that tried to sprinkle a little fairy dust over itself by giving the buildings historical names. There was a notice board at the edge of the parking lot, telling which one of the apartment blocks was which. Hunsdon Estate, the board said. The Hunsdons had owned King's Place before Oxford. (It was already beginning to feel strange to me that I knew so many things about a time four hundred years gone.) The sign was half-covered with graffiti. I read the names under the blue spray paint. Hunsdon, Carey—

And another name.

It was like walls cracking down around me, like the sky opening and the sun coming out. It was like—it was—thousands of puzzle pieces falling out of the air into a single completed puzzle. It was Prospero giving away his books, freeing his captive spirits, as if all his books and spirits and angels had taken off in their freedom and then, in the air, hesitated and wheeled toward him, *We're back, we want to stay.* It was like when everything goes wrong in Shakespeare's late romances, when love fails and people die, and then Shakespeare says, You thought this was the end? No. This is only the end of the beginning.

If this was insanity, if this was forgery—

I was so surprised I began to laugh. I threw back my head and laughed the way I hadn't since—maybe for my whole life. A woman walking toward her car looked at me warily, wondering whether the white man was going crazy. "I know someone who lived here," I said. She pushed out her lower lip, *That's likely.*

"Is there a Hackney Archive, ma'am, or anything like that?" I asked. "The library. Tell me where the library is."

It was almost five o'clock. I ran. The library doors were just being locked. I pushed them open, stood panting over a thin scholarly man who already had his coat on to leave.

"King's Place," I gasped. "History of King's Place. Who knows—?"

"That would be me," the man said.

"Can you tell me," I said, "the housing estate— Why is there a building called Fulke House?"

And when the archivist had told me why, I went back to the churchyard of Saint Augustine's and stood in the middle of the neglected tuffety grass, among the table tombs and the nameless stones. God is a librarian. William Blake's manuscripts were bought by Dante Gabriel Rossetti, who thought he was buying a trunk.

And for the first time I wondered what Rossetti thought. Opening the trunk, seeing all those pictures, those poems, so utterly strange. Was he glad? Or was he afraid of it, stomach full of bats, sucked into the future without even an apology? Or was it everything at once, strangeness so new he felt glad and lost?

"Oxford," I said, just in case he was listening. "Fulke Greville. Poet, playwright, scholar. He wrote a letter to Shakespeare about you? Shakespeare wrote back. And it wasn't because Greville's father was honorary sheriff of Stratford. It wasn't even because Greville knew your daughter. No. It's because God is a librarian, man. Fulke Greville bought your house."

310 / SARAH SMITH

And I pried my library card out of the crack in the gravestone, and took the bus back to the British Library.

⁓

Biography is a horrifying thing sometimes. Shakespeare knew that too, how a good man becomes Othello, Hamlet, Lear. It's chance almost, tragedy and happiness. The gods pull off your wings, you die. You look at the other side of the housing estate, there's no sign there, you go home and spend the rest of your life managing a hardware store.

It's chance. Except not always.

Anthony Munday was a poor half-good writer, a wrinkled little soul who testified against Edmund Campion's friends and watched them being torn apart and wrote about it. But if I was right, on one imaginary Saturday morning in 1580, he pulled on his Jesuit College sweatshirt and told his employer to do the right thing. That wasn't chance.

Biography means a man's life matters. It matters who Shakespeare was, because it matters who we are. Every moment.

How you figure out who you are, how you live your life, that's the question. Shakespeare had it right there too.

At the British Library I found things; it took until they closed Tuesday night. Wednesday morning around Posy-wakeup time, I staked out the deserted garage in North London where Posy kept her car.

It was near dusk when she came down the shabby half-deserted street. She was wearing her black lamb jacket and the pearls; I remember thinking that was risky on a street like this. I followed her into the parking garage and waited until she was putting her key into the car lock before I came up behind her.

"Shit," she said. "Is this where I scream?"

Nobody would hear her if she did, I'd thought about that.

"Is this about your letter? You've got your letter, Joe. What do you fucking want?"

"We're going to Hackney," I told her. "Both of us. I'm driving. Get in."

"No," she said. "No way."

At the hardware store I'd bought a roll of clear window strapping tape and a box cutter. I brought the tape out of my pocket and showed it to her. "Posy," I said. "One way or the other you're going with me, so it might as well be the easy way."

Her eyes widened. She looked up at me, and I don't know what she saw, but she slid into the car.

I drove the car to Hackney by the bus route; I wasn't going to stop and ask directions. Posy hunched to my left, looking sidewise at me, then stared through the window at the traffic, the city, the sky.

"Nicky missed something," I said. We were behind the Hackney bus, breathing fumes. "You'd told him about the letter, and he knew it was addressed to Fulke Greville, but he was looking for Shakespeare, and he got the wrong connection."

"Basically I just want to know you're not kidnapping me or something," she said.

"You thought the letter was real the first time you saw it," I said, "so you told Nicky. What happened next?"

"You're making no sense," she said. "Nicky told you the letter's a fake."

"I could guess," I said. "You got Kellogg to promise you'd be able to publish the letter, you went off and read Oxfordians and passed your orals, and came back to collect your letter and found out the guy had died on you."

I so wanted to get first crack at the collection.

The bus swerved right and I followed it, keeping Posy's yellow car on its trail as we headed into North London.

"And, he'd left the collection to Northeastern," I continued. Because some dumb hick's thesis advisor's wife had talked him into it. Because Posy hadn't told him what the letter was. "Someone else was going to find the letter. Me."

She'd known it wouldn't work to say the letter was a fake. No. "I think this one is real," she'd said, and "We will be famous. I want the real thing." She'd made the biographer believe it was the real thing, and then broke his heart.

"The letter's not real," she said. "Nicky said so."

"So what I'm going to do," I said, "is tell you the rest of the story of the letter. The part you don't know."

Ahead of us, I could see Hackney: McDonald's, Venus Big Foot, and the scabbed neglected tower of Saint Augustine's. "That's where Oxford's buried." We passed Saint Augustine's without stopping and turned off onto Brooke Road. Across the road from the Hunsdon Estate sign, I pulled raggedly into a parking place and shut off the engine.

It was dusk, cold, late enough so that the people who lived in the housing estate had gone inside to their warm dinners. It wasn't a bad neighborhood, just poor, but I saw the place with Posy's eyes. The parking lot, the housing estate. Deserted. Scary. The end of the world.

I got out of the car and went over to Posy's side. I opened the door and jumped back as she tried to kick me.

"Okay," I said. "Look at that sign over there."

She wedged herself in the car, arms crossed, sullenly. I held the keys up in front of her. "I've got 'em, Posy."

"Fuck you," she said. "You've got the letter, it's a forgery, Nicky even told me I was stupid to believe it was anything else, what do you want from me?"

I had brought a flashlight. I pointed it toward the Hunsdon Estate sign.

She got out, reluctantly. I locked the car and put the keys in my pocket. Her eyes followed the keys. She trailed behind me at a sullen distance. I shone the flashlight on the sign, the blue graffiti, the name. *Fulke House.*

"Greville bought Oxford's house," I said. "That's what you didn't know."

In the blue dusk, half lit by the flashlight, I saw Posy's profile, her white face and henna hair. Her mouth opened; she shook her head slightly. She didn't say anything.

"Greville bought the house around early 1609. Oxford had died in 1604. Since 1604 there hadn't been any new Shakespeare plays printed. And from 1609 until 1619, there wouldn't be any. But in 1608-09, just about the time Greville bought the house, three new plays and the Sonnets appeared. *Troilus* was pirated from foul papers stolen from some 'noble possessors.' The Sonnets, pirated from who knows where. The 1608 *Lear* didn't say where it had come from, but it's longer than the acting text, and from all the misprints Okes corrected while he was printing, he probably set *Lear* from Shakespeare's foul papers. Something was going on around the time the house changed hands," I said, "and it involved manuscripts.

"Oxford's wife moved in a hurry. She had already bought another house. I think she did what people always do. She left things behind."

I could see that chest Elizabeth Trentham left as clearly as I could see the bikers on the outhouse at Fisher's Folly, or the little duck of the head and grin the British Museum guard gave Rossetti as he pocketed the price of a trunk full of worthless papers. The chest would have been maybe the size of one of those old-fashioned oak carpenter's boxes, around two feet by two by three. Painted, black and white diamonds, Elizabeth's colors, with Oxford's coat of arms in the center; the Earl had liked things handsome. The paint would have been a little dusty and chipped; the Earl had been dead four years. The box would have been sitting off in a corner somewhere. In an attic. A bedroom. The library. An outbuilding. And it would have been stuffed so full of papers that the whoreson was heavier than a dead minister and not worth moving.

I could see a man opening the chest, wondering if it'd do for something if it was repainted. *Wonder what —* And running his eyes down lines of scratched-out and interlined manuscript, and muttering *holy fucking SHIT who IS this* and sitting down to read.

"In 1609," I said, "one of Greville's plays was pirated too. A servant stole the manuscript of Greville's *Mustapha* out of his library and sold it to Nicholas Okes and Nathaniel Butter. The same printer and publisher who pirated *Lear*. It doesn't prove the two manuscripts came from the same library or the same servant took them. But it's interesting, isn't it, Posy?"

She was looking away from me like she'd looked away from Nicky. Look at me, I thought.

"Another interesting thing about Greville," I said. "Supposedly he wrote three plays. Two of them survive. The third is just a title. The story is it was Greville's own play, but it might have been another writer's manuscript that someone saw in his library and thought was his.

"The name of the play was *Antony and Cleopatra.*"

And she reacted. She reacted, just a little. I sat down on the metal-pipe railing, not so close to her that she'd be afraid.

"Think who Greville was," I told her. "Think who he knew. He was Cecil's enemy. Cecil had stripped him of his offices. He was in exile in the country, writing *The Life of Sir Philip Sidney*. You ever read it? The title is camouflage; he was writing a history of the Elizabethan age. Robert Cecil wouldn't let Greville use the Cecil papers at Hatfield, so Greville was working with the Sidney papers at Wilton."

Something flickered in her eyes. Curiosity maybe, or recognition; or maybe just a trick of the streetlight.

"Yeah," I said. "Wilton, the Herberts' house. Where William Herbert lived, William Herbert, who was supposed to marry Bridget de Vere; and where his brother Philip visited with his wife, Susan de Vere. Oxford's youngest daughter.

"Susan de Vere," I said. "The court season she married Philip, almost every play at court was by Shakespeare. It never happened before and never would again. But through that whole season it was Shakespeare, Shakespeare, Shakespeare. And who was Susan de Vere besides being Oxford's daughter?" I said. "This one's in Ogburn."

Posy looked up at me; we looked into each other's eyes.

"She was an actor," I said. "Queen Anne liked plays, she acted in plays in private with her maids of honor helping her. Susan de Vere was in more plays than any other of them."

She was Cordelia, I thought. The youngest daughter. Her father's rescuer.

"And Susan de Vere knew Jaggard. A couple of years before Jaggard printed the First Folio, probably while he was planning it, he dedicated a book to her and her husband—mostly to her."

Posy's eyes widened and she shook her head.

"Let me finish," I said, "because this is the end, Posy, the last bit of it. Fulke Greville was at Wilton, Susan de Vere must have visited Wilton, I think Greville took the plays to her. And starting around 1612, after Cecil died, the Herberts began doing interesting things. In 1615 William Herbert got himself made Lord Chamberlain, which put him in charge of the King's Men, Shakespeare's company, and he didn't budge from the office until after 1623. The Herberts got the office of Master of the Revels too. Herbert friends and relations held it, Sir George Buck, Ben Jonson, Henry Herbert, and they kept it until after 1623, when the First Folio came out.

"The First Folio. It was a big expensive book. Posy, you're good with money. You want to explain to me why the King's Men put it out in folio instead of issuing the plays separately in quartos? Wouldn't the quartos have made more for them?"

Someone had wanted a beautiful book. An important book, a book to show off on the library shelves of big country houses *that in black ink my love may still shine bright*.

So the book had got published. The First Folio. With eighteen new Shakespeare plays in it, eighteen plays that had never been published before. They didn't call it Oxford's works. King James was still alive. Maybe James knew about Shakespeare by this time, maybe he didn't. Maybe he knew but no one wanted to remind him.

Maybe Shakespeare wrote them after all.

The Works of William Shakespeare.

It didn't matter what the book was called. Not then. Everyone who counted knew who Shakespeare was, just the way that

everyone knew *Astrophil and Stella* was about the Herbert brothers' uncle and Penelope Rich. They couldn't even imagine the
English Civil War, their playbooks tossed into fires, their names
dying out and being forgotten. They couldn't imagine the new
millennium, the housing estate and the parking lot, or Posy and
me.

Under the streetlights her rouge was too dark, her face too
pale. Bright colors, colors that in a few years would start looking
garish. Could I trust her? Did I have a choice?

"So that's where the letter fits," I said. "The letter Nicky told
me is fake. I don't know what he's told you. I don't know what
you believe."

I jingled the keys in my pocket, and thought about it, and
tossed them to her. They fell in front of her on the street. She
crouched, scrabbled for them, stood up awkwardly, and backed
away from me.

"Yeah," I said. "Go. And Posy? If you have the real letter, or
find it, you can publish it. The letter's yours."

She took a few more steps away from me, then turned, out of
range, ready to run. The streetlight shone behind her, making her
a silhouette.

"It's a fake," she said. Her voice was a rough whisper.

"If it was ever anything else," I said, "I can't prove it."

The silhouette of her shoulders tensed. I knew those squared
shoulders from looking at her with her father.

"What is this all about?" she said. "You think I stole this fake
letter and you're *giving* it to me? What is this?"

"It's not my story," I said. "I'm not telling a story here, I'm not going to imagine anything. I could make all kinds of speculations and accusations. Nicky stole it for you. Or stole it to protect you. Or your dad wanted it for his collection, or your dad and Nicky stole it for you because they'd do anything for you, either of them. I could say you stole it, because you didn't want to be second author to a graduate student from Northeastern, or because you didn't trust me to market a new kind of Shakespeare, get it all down to a slogan on a button and look good on TV. —You were right about that, I would have screwed it up."

"You could have got coaching or something," she said. "You just didn't care."

I wondered if this was a confession. I waited a moment to see if she'd say something more, but she didn't.

"Maybe I could have my letter looked at again. Maybe the CD isn't the same kind Northeastern uses. Maybe there's modern pollen from England caught in the ink. I could spend years thrashing myself over the head. I'm not going to. If the letter's real," I said, "it's yours. Take care of it. Be famous."

I couldn't see her face, just her long legs, ready to run. Legs I knew. A woman I hoped I knew.

"This is how you can do it." I said. "You figure the letter isn't just a forgery. Someone sold Kellogg a copy of a real letter. You find the real letter, in another collection you can publish from. Just find it, Posy."

"This is totally crazy," she said. "And I know why you're doing it. You think I'm going to give you back the letter, and it's going to be real, and you and I are going to be together again. I don't care about Oxford and I don't care about the fucking letter and I don't care about you."

"Care about yourself," I said. "Let me tell you another story, about another Cecil. All her life she did somebody else's business. Got married because her father wanted something, got unmarried because her husband wanted something else, got batted around like a tennis ball. Every once in a while, this past week, I kept thinking the people we were meeting were Cecils. Nicky was a little Robert Cecil, your father was William."

"And I was Anne?" she said out of the darkness. "I am *so* not Anne."

I looked for words and said it, finally, exactly as I'd thought it when she took the microphone away from Goscimer. "You have grace." I remembered her talking with me over coffee at Northeastern. *How did Shakespeare get to be Shakespeare? I want to know.* "You're smart, and you're curious, and you've got ideas, you've got the leverage with Nicky and your dad—" Her shoulders twitched impatiently. "If anybody does, you do. Maybe the Cecils always win, Posy. But if they do, don't you be Anne; you be a William or a Robert, one of them that wins; don't you dare be Anne."

So I left her. I turned and made myself walk down the street, not looking back, away from her.

And maybe, I thought, the letter was fake all the time. Maybe what I'd done was get Daddy's little girl to run after a will-of-the-wisp, a forgery. Elizabethans went in for revenge; maybe this was mine, making her as uncertain as me. *What you believed is real.* It would be worthy of a Cecil, messing with her head that way, getting the letter back, or getting back for the letter, the only way I could. On the other hand—I thought of Posy tackling Nicky, who adooored her, and telling Daddy off; of Posy working in real archives, finding the place where she could squirrel away the letter.

She might learn secretary hand.

At the corner of the street, I turned back, once, and saw her under the streetlight, standing with her arms crossed, her head on one side, looking at the Hunsdon Estate sign. She shrugged and tossed her red hair, and turned away, and then turned back; and when I made myself turn the corner, she was still there, under the streetlight, still gazing at the sign, a red-haired girl in black and pink, against a background of little tenacious shrubs struggling into green.

A girl to be noticed.

What are you going to do?" Mary Cat asked me yesterday.

There's a kind of story that a biographer can make out of a life after it's finished, a story with beginning and middle and end. But even if the facts are good, the story's no more guaranteed to be true than any other, because the story is always the biographer. The biographer's never finished; he can break off parts of himself into chapters, books, plays, but the story he tells is still just his storytelling, he's always crossing out and interlining, scribbling the moment between past and future where anything can happen, where a man can find a letter or meet a girl, have an adventure, act or write or think *I am*.

God is a librarian. He'll know where to file me and Posy, all bound up and cataloged and judged. I don't know. This story isn't finished.

Last night, I checked my mail at a bookstore with an Internet connection, and Katherine Darnell had left her phone number. I made an appointment to meet with her today, Friday, the first of April, the first April Fools' Day of the new millennium, in Stratford.

So that's what I'm doing. Betting the farm. Sure it's stupid. I'll go back to Boston and propose to Goscimer that I do an edition of *More*. If he approves it, I'll read Munday and try to date *More*, and if my theory doesn't work out, that's fine and I can teach after all, but if it still sounds to me like Shakespeare was at work all through it, I'll say so. Then what happens, happens. I'm pretty sure I won't make it in academia, just the way Mary Cat isn't going to make it as a nun. Even what I'm going to do today would get me drawn and quartered if Goscimer knew I was doing it, and all I'm going to do is give that Xerox to Katherine Darnell.

I can always install windows.

The thing about window installation, it's good pay, and it's seasonal. In January, February, when the fares are cheap to London, there's almost no work at all. I figure I can do installing in the summer, researching in the winter. If it comes to that.

Being a manager at a hardware store isn't seasonal, though, and last night I called Dad. I told him I wasn't going to come back and work at the store, however things worked out with teaching. He was surprised I'd even thought of it. I guess I was the one had always wanted to think I might go back home to Vermont. I hung up and started thinking about him, that he might be doing what he's doing because he likes it— Well. It's okay between him and me. It's fine.

"What are you going to do?" I asked Mary Cat.

Mary Cat and I have been doing some talking. Mary Cat's coming round to the idea that maybe no order will ever take her. She's been trying out all sorts of other lives on me. She's going to teach in India. She's going into AIDS nonprofit work. She's going to produce comics about AIDS. (Mary Cat, Sister Mary Catherine, who I thought I knew, spent her whole high school drawing comics before she discovered Mother Teresa. Last night she drew me as Library Man, flying over the B.L.) I figure some of this is real and some of this is just her leftover seventeen-year-old talking. She's got some catching up to do.

So that's my story. Don't have a girl, don't have a job, still have to finish sorting out the fucking Kellogg Collection. But Mary Cat's coming back to Northeastern to finish her degree.

"You are going to help with the Kellogg again?" I ask her.

We both make faces.

"Still going to work on Edmund Campion?"

"I think so. I like him. He's so Elizabethan. Have you read 'Campion's Brag'?"

We sit in companionable silence, watching the green English fields out the bus window. I get out the Xerox of *The Paine of Pleasure*, start reading through it again, still seeing a confusion of clunky lines and good ones. I don't know what to make of it. "Think you could read this poem someday?" I ask Mary Cat awkwardly.

"I'm a bit short of certainty in my life, Joe, don't deprive me of Shakespeare too."

Yeah, I know the feeling.

Mary Cat hesitates, about to say something.

"You don't have to," I say.

She sighs, and picks up her backpack and opens it, takes a paperback out; after a moment she hands it to me.

"If you're determined to look twice at Shakespeare, I should give you this," she says. "I found it in a bookstore yesterday."

I look at it. *Family Life in Shakespeare's England*, a book published by the Shakespeare Birthplace Trust and written by a woman I haven't heard of, Jeanne Jones. I figure it's going to be one of those sentimental books full of Elizabethan woodcuts of people feasting and line drawings of Elizabethan furniture.

"Read it," Mary Cat says, in the voice of a person who's read it already.

I start leafing through. It's about wills. Jeanne Jones went to the Stratford town records and looked at all the wills and inventories between 1570 and 1630. She lists everything Shakespeare's neighbors' wills say about them, their occupations, how much they were worth when they died, the contents of their houses.

They were farmers, tailors, glovers, butchers, weavers, drapers; they brewed beer. The majority couldn't sign their names to their own wills. There was only one large documented library anywhere near Shakespeare's Stratford. It had 186 volumes, mostly sermons and joke books. Nobody has ever described Stratford this way before.

I'm reading so hard, Mary Cat has to tell me we've arrived in Stratford.

The Stratford Tour buses are still running from the monument by the bridge, bringing tourists closer to the Shakespeare nature. Mary Cat looks at them, looks at me; I look at her.

"I've been to Stratford," she says. "Let's see what isn't on the tour."

A few blocks beyond the cute little inns and expensive clothing stores, beyond the Hamlet omelets and the Shakespeare souvenirs, Stratford turns into an ordinary small town in the Midlands. There's a TV repair shop and a computer store, a grocery or two, a sports shop that sells soccer equipment, a couple of pubs, three or four farming-supply places, and a couple of thrift shops. There are empty storefronts, too. Not so different from East Bradenton.

What would happen to this place without Shakespeare?

We stop in front of an Oxfam thrift shop. Battered pots and pans are piled carefully on the sidewalk. In Shakespeare's time, Stratford men wove wool and made gloves. The clumsier-patterned English gloves were being forced out by Italian imports; wool was falling out of favor. By 1590 Stratford had 33 percent unemployment. Most of the Stratfordians who worked had two or three jobs: tailor, farmer, wool dealer, moneylender, brewer. Which means, take it from me, nobody was making enough to live on from one job.

"When I was in India," Mary Cat says, "everyone did odd jobs in the little towns. The men went off to the city and sent money home to their wives. The wives couldn't read or write. They could farm a little, or bring produce to market, but most of the cash they got was what the men sent home."

"A smart kid," I said, "they would have talked about him. They would have treated him different." I was a smart kid in East Bradenton. People were always asking me what book I'd read.

"There was a boy in my village," Mary Cat says. "He was so bright."

"What happened to him?"

Suddenly she grins. "We found him a scholarship. He's at school in Delhi."

Outside the thrift shop is a pile of 50p paperbacks, and there among them, what else would be in Stratford, I see a battered familiar volume, *Young Man Shakespeare.* I pick it up and leaf through it, falling under the spell of it again for a minute, that romantic story of two young scholars falling in love and going to Italy to find the true Shakespeare. Roland and Rachel Goscimer's version of Stratford is full of interesting literate people and university men.

"How big would the library be in an Indian town, two thousand people or so?" I ask Mary Cat.

She waves a hand at the pile of paperbacks. "That size. Thrillers and romances and comic books, and the worse the better, if you know what I mean. A couple of good books. Rajat, my student, had got through the lot by the time he was eight."

Did you find anything wrong? I can practically hear Rachel Goscimer's voice, almost see her out of the corner of my eye.

Yeah, plenty.

I turn to the last page of the book. The Goscimers have come back from Italy; they're in London, holding hands on Tower Bridge, looking toward the site of Shakespeare's Globe. "And then we went back to Boston," I read, "and began to write."

Young Man Shakespeare wasn't about Shakespeare, I tell Rachel Goscimer's ghost. It was about you. It was you both talking about Shakespeare until the sun came up. It was *Romeo and Juliet* with libraries, a 1950s movie with Audrey Hepburn and Cary Grant; it was hands interlaced over the leaves of some four-hundred-year-old book.

I put the book down. Rachel Goscimer is fading away, smile last. *Read everything,* she says one last time. *Use your imagination.* I look past her toward Mary Cat.

And there is a transformation going on, while I watch. Ever since I have known her, Mary Cat has worn that same penitential parka, leaking feathers until it's limp and almost flat. Now she's inside the Oxfam shop, looking through a rack of jackets.

One of them is a black lamb vintage jacket. As Mary Cat touches it, I hold my breath. Red hair, black jacket, they're nowhere near alike, the two women, but for a moment I think something more painful to believe even than Oxford, that I was infatuated with Posy between Mary Cat and Mary Cat.

No.

Mary Cat is trying on a green wool jacket that suits her fine. "That's good," I say, "look at yourself in the mirror." She hesitates, and looks, and stands looking a long time, not like a girl who's admiring herself. Like someone looking at a future she can't quite imagine yet. Nuns never use mirrors.

We're between lives, both of us, Mary Cat and I.

"Maybe?" I say. "Maybe that kid Rajat was the reason you

were in India. Maybe your job was to get him to school in Delhi."

She turns and smiles at me. If God is a librarian, I think, He's not going to lose track of Mary Cat.

"Want to go to Holy Trinity?" I ask her.

A couple of blocks brings us back to tourist Stratford, to the Avon and the big monument near the bridge, to prosperity and Shakespeare and the millennium. We stroll down the riverwalk past the theater toward Holy Trinity Church to meet Katherine Darnell.

Stratford is rich now. In 1590, a third of the town was out of work. Suppose a man were to come home to a place like that, Stratford, or East Bradenton, from—say Hollywood—and say he was a screenwriter. All most East Bradenton folks would know is that he had money. My, ain't he rich, did'ya see his car.

Shakespeare brought the money home to Stratford and spent it there. You can't ask more of a local man.

Today the alley of limes is dappled with sunlight. In Holy Trinity Church, I pay the old man at the gate, and I wonder again what he'll do if the tourists ever go away. This time we have to stand outside the velvet ropes. Mary Cat and I look up from a distance at the bust of William Shakespeare.

Well, man? I ask him.

No answer. Shakespeare is looking past me, out the window, with his pen in his hand.

What really happened?

There's a sudden inundation of children at the door, a tour group of schoolchildren. They pour down the aisle; a harried lady waves a bunch of tickets at the gate man, and the children tumble past him. A little brown-eyed Indian boy, a round-headed African girl, a gangly thin-legged African boy with big cheekbones, a Scots or Irish girl with kinky red hair and freckles, one kid in a wheelchair, two twin towheads, a snub-nosed boy with a buzz cut.

What were you? His servant, his front, his Anthony Munday, his best friend?

The statue isn't saying anything.

Were you all in it? The Earl, his daughters and their husbands, the Earl of Derby who wrote plays, Pembroke and Montgomery, John Heminge, Henry Condell, Arthur Golding, Munday, Ben Jonson — Who did what?

Shakespeare doesn't have a word for me.

Or isn't this your story at all; is it just my story?

I move aside and watch the kids. Their teacher is lecturing about Shakespeare, but they aren't listening. They're looking out the windows or squinting at the statue. The wheelie kid is whispering to the kid next to him and they both break into toothy giggles. And one little kid, a girl with a wild head of hair working up to be dreads, is staring up raptly at Shakespeare. Mary Cat is looking at her, smiling.

Each one of them has their own story about Shakespeare. A bus driver in a peaked hat has come into the church, and a trendy-looking Italian couple, and an old lady with a walker. I step back to give the old lady a chance at Shakespeare. Near his grave are some memorial tablets. J. O. Halliwell-Phillips, the nineteenth-century critic. The tablet for the soldier actors who died in World War I, with Kipling's epitaph.

We counterfeited once, for your disport
Men's joy and sorrow; but our day is passed
We pray you pardon all where we fell short
Seeing we were your servants to the last.

Every one of them has a story, a piece of Shakespeare that they call their own. "Cry God for Harry, England, and Saint George!" "To thine own self be true/And it must follow as the night the day/Thou canst not then be false to any man." "Angels and ministers of grace defend us." "To hold the mirror up to nature." "To be or not to be . . ." "We know what we are but know not what we may be."

I look up at that inexpressive bust on the wall. Maybe, I think, we needed somebody like you more than we needed the Earl. Shakespeare, who said things so many people recognize as part of their lives—maybe, so we could recognize ourselves in you, you had to be as blank as a mirror. My Shakespeare, the Goscimers' Shakespeare, David Garrick's. You fit us all. Will we recognize ourselves in the Earl?

The sun is just hitting the bust on the wall, and I can see again its surprised expression, its astonishment. *What, are you people still here after four hundred years?*

The kids are leaving. Mary Cat touches my arm. "I'll wait outside for your Miss Darnell." I nod, still thinking.

Did you know what you were? Either of you? Any of you?

But that's the one thing no one will ever know, what Shakespeare was. History is a point of view, over the same city, perhaps, but from a thousand eyes, not one. Wait five minutes, the light has changed, a wall has been demolished, a new window set in place, and from the top of the wheel another set of eyes are looking out over a different city. There's no one map, one story, one way to get to one truth; there is no single London and no single Shakespeare, no fact as sure as a story.

Maybe even Shakespeare never knew what he was. Maybe, like the rest of us, he just had moments when he thought *I am,* or acted, or wrote, and felt like he might know.

Out on the avenue of limes, I stand people-watching. The schoolchildren are streaming back toward their bus. The old lady is pushing her walker slowly past. They all look happy, exalted, as though they've found something. What are they imagining? *Family Life in Shakespeare's England? Young Man Shakespeare?* William Shakespeare, patron saint of lost causes? Saint William of England? In the fading afternoon sunlight, I watch all the people coming to and fro from Trinity Church, looking for Shakespeare, looking for Shakespeare, communing with the Shakespeare nature.

Will Shakespeare ever be only one man? Not while more than one person reads him, or wants to tell his story.

Down toward the end of the avenue of limes, by the gate, Mary Cat is standing under a tree, watching for Katherine Darnell. The sunlight catches her hair and turns it bronze and gold. Princess Elizabeth, I think. Princess Elizabeth under the tree, waiting, but no one is coming to get her, no mythmakers are going to torment her; free. No one is free. I walk on down the avenue toward her.

"Sorry I took so long."

"Oh," she smiles, "you were thinking."

"Thinking we'll never know. It's been four hundred years."

But somewhere, I thought, in someone's attic, in someone's library— What happened to Fulke Greville's papers, are they still at Warwick Castle? The Herbert family papers were decimated in the Wilton fire, but the papers of the Earl of Derby? Katherine Darnell will know.

"I've been thinking too," Mary Cat says suddenly. "I want to read your poem."

"You don't have to."

"No, I'll do it now—"

I get it out of my backpack and hand it to her, and watch her begin to read. I can tell she's not much taken with the first bits; her nose twitches a little.

"Shakespeare's still the most interesting person in the story," I say nervously. "William Shakespeare of Stratford. If he wasn't the one who did it, he made it possible."

Maybe I will never care for Oxford the way I care for Shakespeare.

But, whoever he is, I will write on Shakespeare.

The almost right word is the lightning bug; the right one is the lightning. The almost right life is nothing at all. The right life is dangerous, open-ended, more questions than answers, a map to undiscovered countries.

No one will believe me. I'll end up just another Oxfordian, one of those guys who look like they can take apart truck engines, spouting my theories to meetings of the Blue Boar Society. I'll end up owning a window installation company and doing Shakespeare research in my spare time, and being pretty fucking laughable.

Shit, lightning burns, doesn't it? Never mind. That's what lightning's for.

"Mr. Roper? Is that *it?*"

Katherine Darnell is coming through the gate, pink-cheeked in a blue coat, focusing right in on the Xerox. "Your bad poem?"

"Yeah—" I want to say something about the poem. But no good, Katherine Darnell is already leaning over Mary Cat's shoulder, looking at it too.

I watch their faces as they try to make out the black letter. They're reading together, the two of them holding either side of the page as if they're singing music. The light is going out of the sky. Mary Cat digs a little flashlight out of her pocket, shines it on the page. The glow reflects back from the paper. Mary Cat's face is full of light, as if she is watching lightning.

Someday we will know whether the play we are in is tragedy or comedy or farce. Someday we'll look back on this moment and know its meaning, say, "What a bad poem that was after all," or "Do you remember when we read it first? Do you remember the moment?" But day by day we only live, making do, step by step, imagining and acting and writing out our lives.

We know what we are, but know not what we may be.

We know what we are. Maybe.

We know what we are.

Apologies and Acknowledgments

Why write on the Shakespeare authorship controversy anyway? Obviously they're all nuts. . . .

I first heard about the Oxford authorship theory from my friend Joanna Wexler, who determined to point me at the mystery of Shakespeare. "There is no mystery," I said kindly. "Shakespeare wrote Shakespeare." Joanna loaned me a book, then another, then another (as I write, this I have two large bags full of Joanna's books in my office), and 95 percent of it seemed like sheer guff, but some tiny remainder was mildly interesting. It might make an academic comedy.

God has not only a large card catalog but a sense of humor. I decided to do a little research while I was in England for the British publication of *The Vanished Child*. And, much to my surprise, I began finding things myself.

So the book ended up being about how imagination meets research, how one believes what one believes—and how, rightly or wrongly, someone with decent academic credentials and an open mind might take the Shakespeare question seriously.

The modern characters are either fictional or, if actual, used in a fictional sense. Don Cannon appears thanks to his generosity in supporting Bouchercon; his friends would probably like to know he hasn't moved from L.A., doesn't have an Aunt Betty Lou, and is neutral on the authorship question.

Anything said about any historical character is speculative. It's worthwhile to say this specifically in the case of the Cecils. A conspiracy needs a couple of mustache-twisting villains, and

nothing said about William and Robert Cecil here is entirely outside historical possibility, but the Cecils were and are far more
than Posy and my fictional Don Cannon make them. They have
been major figures in the shaping of modern England, making
contributions in politics, history, and literature—facts reflected
here very inadequately. My apologies to them, and to the modern
descendants and families of the other Elizabethan figures discussed here.

The letter is made up; there's no letter and no Kellogg Collection at Northeastern. The rest of the evidence is factual, though
sometimes simplified. (See the notes at www.chasingshake-
speares.com.) *Hamlet*'s nova did happen in 1572; Shakespeare's
favorite book was translated by Oxford's uncle; Fulke Greville
bought Oxford's house; "The Paine of Pleasure" is a real poem;
and so on and so on. Some of the evidence is well known, some
known in other contexts; a few pieces are new.

For all this evidence, I am indebted to the scholars and independent researchers who have worked in this area before me.
Some (most, though not all, orthodox Stratfordians) are eminent
in their field, and among these I am particularly grateful for the
work of Harold Bloom, Donald Foster, Marjorie Garber,
Stephen Greenblatt, Parke Honan, Jeanne Jones, David Scott
Kastan, Irvin Matus, Steven May, Alan Nelson, Samuel Schoenbaum, Gary Taylor, Daniel Wright, and my own teachers,
William Alfred, Northrop Frye, Harry Levin, and Robert Lowell. Among independent researchers, I am particularly indebted
to the work of Mark Anderson, Charles Boyle, Stephanie Hop-
kins Hughes, David Kathman, Diana Price, Terry Ross, Joseph
Sobran, Roger Stritmatter, B. M. Ward, Richard Whalen, and—
above all—the decades-long work of Charlton Ogburn Jr. and

his parents, Charlton and Dorothy Ogburn. Others too numerous to mention have contributed to the authorship discussion, and many of them have become my friends; I am grateful to all of them. The invaluable Alan Sutton published several books that were extremely helpful to this project, including John Southworth's *Fools and Jesters at the English Court* and Jeanne Jones's *Family Life in Shakespeare's England*.

For those who are interested in the evidence in more detail, there are footnotes, a bibliography, and more material, including other evidence on both sides, on the Web site for this book, www.chasingshakespeares.com. There's also a genealogical table showing all the relationships among the Elizabethans, an edition of "The Paine of Pleasure," and a lot of fun stuff.

My heartfelt particular thanks to: Andy McKillop of Arrow Books; Simon Master, chairman of Arrow Books; Anastasia Cox, who went way beyond the call of duty to Xerox and send the front and end matter of "The Paine of Pleasure"; Joe Blades of Ballantine Books; Donald Maass; Kenneth Rendell; Evan Holzwasser; Professor Laurence Senelick, for reading the manuscript, giving me an excellent discussion of the authorship controversy, and agreeing to appear as a character; Christopher Dams of the De Vere Society of Great Britain; Greer Gilman; Dr. Elaine Sternberg, guide, philosopher, friend, London host, and cotraveler on a memorable trip to Hackney; Knight Boyer, fellow traveler to Castle Hedingham, and Chris, Siobhan, and all the dear Boyers; Martin Taylor, Senior Assistant Archivist, Hackney Archive Department; Charles de Vere, Earl of Burford (not to be confused with the fictional Henry de Vere); Kelly Link; Robert Wyatt, who makes the Internet sit up and do his bidding; Mrs. Maggie Edwardes, Headmistress of Bilton Hall School; Barry and the window installers at Lifetime Home

336 / Apologies and Acknowledgments

Improvement; Ken Smith, Carroll Rowan, and Mau Rowan, who measure twice and cut once; Bernard Barrell, a delightful and helpful man, expert on William Cecil's funerary monuments; Justus Perry and the gang at BF/VF for digital video tricks; Matthew Renner, twenty-one-year-old professional hog hunter and guide in Texas (and my very cool nephew; boarsoftexas@aol.com); Diana Donoghue of Castle Hedingham; Penny Doe and Kylie Turkoz-Ferguson, landladies of the Bell Inn, Castle Hedingham; Simon Daw of Castle Hedingham; Hilary Austin, for rescuing Nicky; and Catherine Penn, Bursar of Holy Trinity Church, Stratford-on-Avon (and thanks also to her husband, Nigel Penn, Verger of Holy Trinity, who appears uncredited in the filming scene).

Also the warders of the Tower of London and the librarians of: the British Library, London; the Widener and Houghton Libraries of Harvard University; the John Carter Brown Library of Brown University; and the Brookline Public Library, Brookline, Massachusetts. Special thanks to Dr. Charles Flaherty, director of the Brookline Public Library, and to Gabriela Romanow.

William Boyle and Charles Boyle of the Shakespeare Fellowship have been unfailingly generous with their time and research. Bill very kindly allowed me to use him as a character; the speech he gives at the meeting of the fictional Blue Boar Society comes from Charles Boyle's article, "Elizabeth's Glass," published in the *Shakespeare Oxford Newsletter,* 36, no. 4 (winter 2001), used with Charles Boyle's kind permission.

Thanks to my first readers: Steve Popkes, Alex Irvine, Dora Goss, Alex Jablokov, David Smith, Shariann Lewitt, William Betcher, James Patrick Kelly, Mary Tafuri Ross, Deborah Manning, Hallie Ephron, Kate Flora, Ellen Kushner, and Delia Sherman—who, by the kind of coincidence that wouldn't work at all in fiction, is actually the modern editor of the anonymous pre-Shakespearean play *King Leir*.

Special thanks to Mariah Perry Nobrega, excellent and much-loved daughter, who read the draft at the last minute; Christopher Schelling, extraordinary agent, sensitive reader, and uncrowned king of compilation CDs, who not only helped to shape the manuscript but sent it to the right place; my wonderful first editor, Rosemary Ahern, who found the weak spots and made them better; and Luke Dempsey, who has shepherded this project to publication.

The leftover bad bits are all mine.

About this Guide

The suggested questions are intended to help your reading group find new and interesting angles and topics for discussion for Sarah Smith's *Chasing Shakespeares*. We hope these ideas will enrich your conversation and increase your enjoyment of the book.

Many fine books from Washington Square Press feature Readers Club Guides. For a complete listing, or to read the Guides online, visit http://www.BookClubReader.com

A Conversation with Sarah Smith

Q: To what extent do you use your background as an English scholar in your writing?
A: As little as possible, really. When I was in grad school, everything was hugely theoretical—my thesis advisor invented the idea that the writer's biography didn't matter. The things that worked for me in grad school were reading everything, reading the unimportant books—that was considered a very dull thing to do.

I had the great luck to take Shakespeare from Robert Lowell. He would sit in front of the class and read the play aloud, very slowly, in a rumbling deep voice with that New England accent, and every once in a while he'd stop and say "Hamlet was mad," or "Falstaff was mad," or "That's a good line." He taught me to hear the music. He told me my final paper for the class made him cry, which is the best praise I ever got in grad school.

I suppose, come to think of it, Joe's way of speaking comes from Robert Lowell.

Q: Joe seems an odd choice for the main character of an academic mystery. How did you come up with him, and why did you decide to make him the man he is?

A: Joe was the hardest character to write. When you're writing a first-person story, the story has to matter to the main character more than it could ever matter to anyone else in the world. What goes wrong has to be utterly wrong, utterly destructive, the end of the world. Who would have complete faith that Shakespeare is Shakespeare, and who would be completely devastated if he wasn't?

Joe Roper is a young man like Shakespeare, with even fewer advantages than Shakespeare. He comes from a nearly dead town in Vermont; his father runs a hardware store. When he was nine years old he started reading Shakespeare by accident, and he fell in love with Shakespeare and wanted to know who this man was. He's bootstrapped his way up through the University of Vermont, he's working his way through graduate school at Northeastern by installing windows, and somehow, somehow, he wants to get good enough to write Shakespeare's biography. He's been given the chance of cataloging a collection of Elizabethan materials, and in it he finds a letter—supposedly from Shakespeare, saying Shakespeare didn't write the plays.

Q: And is he devastated?

A: At the beginning, he's absolutely sure the letter's a forgery and he locks it in a drawer and tries to forget it. But enter Posy Gould, another grad student, from Harvard and Hollywood via Victoria's Secret. Posy's seen the letter too. She believes it's real and she's *so totally* going to tell the *Times* about it. So Joe has to become a literary detective and prove the letter's a forgery, because he's Shakespeare's man.

**Q: That letter's fictional, but most of what they find is histori-
cal evidence. Can you talk about how that happened? Did you
find all this evidence yourself?**

A: A lot of people have written about the authorship controversy
and I stole from them. But I did find a couple of things, and one big
thing, which I can't really talk about until you've read the book.

**Q: In the book, Katherine Darnell says, "If it is important to
know who wrote Shakespeare's plays, if it is important to find
lost plays or poetry by Oxford, I believe . . . that by some miracle someone will find it." How did you find your big thing?
Did you deduce it had to be where it was, or was it a miracle?**

A: You have no idea. What Joe does in *Chasing Shakespeares* is
more or less what I did. He starts reading works by a minor playwright who might have worked with Shakespeare. He comes
across a volume from the Elizabethan era, three smaller books
bound together. He reads two of them, and they're awful, and
he's tempted to give the volume back to the librarian without
reading the third; but he grits his teeth and keeps reading. And
he finds something.

I gave the book back.

I gave the book back, it was past lunchtime, I was tired, and
then thought, "Naah, you know, I'll never find this anywhere
else, I'd better take a look at it." And, my goodness. I asked the
British Library if I could get a Xerox of it, and, bless their hearts,
they Xeroxed this Elizabethan book for me.

I didn't get to read my prize until I was on the plane going back
to America. We were trying to take off from Heathrow, into the
middle of an enormous storm, winds something like 90 m.p.h.
driving rain. The plane was skittering down the runway like spit
on a griddle, and I was reading what I'd found to take my mind
off things, and I put my hands together and prayed, "Don't let me
die, don't let me die, I have to tell someone about this."

Q: Is what you found Shakespeare's?

A: That would be hard to say. I talk about whether it is on the Web site for the book (www.chasingshakespeares.com). I would bet significant money it's Oxford's.

Q: What you're saying is, it could be a smoking gun linking Shakespeare and Oxford?

A: I'm very carefully not saying that. First, Joe's passion is my passion; I adore Shakespeare. I think if one's going to say something so radical about him, one should prove it again and again and again, and one should keep an open mind until then. The more one prepares one's mind to see every argument, the better one sees.

What do *you* think it is?

Q: With all this new information, why did you write a novel, not a Shakespeare biography?

A: As if I could. But the real answer is that the Shakespeare story isn't only about Shakespeare's life; it's a much more complex story that includes Shakespeare the man, Shakespeare the idol, Shakespeare the genius, our readings of Shakespeare over the past four hundred years. As Marjorie Garber has said, she doesn't want to know too much about Shakespeare's mere life because she wants to leave him sufficiently blank to hold the rest of the story.

To tell a huge, complex story like Shakespeare's, you need a big group of characters, each holding on passionately to his or her own Shakespeare and denying all the rest. You want them dissing each other's ideas and betraying each other and stealing manuscripts and doing all the stupid things that keep us shaking our heads and laughing.

The most magical moment of a story is when one character says something, and it's true, and another character criticizes it, and that's true too. Novels leave room for all those layers of truth, and that's why I had to write a novel.

Questions and Topics for Discussion

1. *"Shakespearean* is a word, like *love,"* Joe says, a word that everyone understands in his or her own way. Why are readers fascinated by Shakespeare? What is the essence of "Shakespeare" for you?

2. "Print the legend," Posy tells Joe. She's quoting from John Ford's film *The Man Who Shot Liberty Valance.* Shakespeare's traditionally accepted life is a powerful myth of genius, an ordinary man like us creating great poetry. Is the traditional idea of Shakespeare as important as "the truth"? Is it part of the truth, or the whole truth?

3. "God is a librarian," says Katherine Darnell, and tells the extraordinary story of the discovery of Blake's manuscripts. The story isn't all true, and the story about Elizabeth waiting in the park at Hatfield probably isn't true, but Sarah Smith uses both legends in *Chasing Shakespeares.* Do these legends have anything to do with the traditional idea of Shakespeare?

4. A big theme in this book is parents and children. Joe Roper and Henry Roper, Posy and Ted Gould, Posy and her absent mother, Edward de Vere and his father, Edward de Vere and his father-in-law William Cecil, William Cecil and Robert Cecil, Edward de Vere and Susan de Vere, and even, possibly, Oxford and his potential son-in-law Southampton. Of all the characters, only Mary Cat doesn't have a family life; she has a "mother house" instead. Why the theme, and why is Mary Cat an exception?

5. God, fate, coincidence, and that other kind of deus ex machina, genius, play big roles in *Chasing Shakespeares.* Does this bother you? Why or why not?

6. Does it make any difference that the evidence Joe gets is supposedly real evidence? Is *Chasing Shakespeares* a historical novel? Is it a mystery? Is it "true crime"?

7. Who do you think wrote the plays? Is it important who wrote them?

8. Do you think Joe actually found a new work by Shakespeare? Does what you think make a difference to what you think of the book? Joe argues that what he found wouldn't sound like Shakespeare. Do you agree?

9. Do people change fundamentally from age to age? Are the concerns of national political figures like the Cecils fundamentally different from those of entertainers like the Goulds? Can we understand the Cecils through the Goulds?

10. In *Chasing Shakespeares*, there's a lot of moving from place to place, in trucks and automobiles, on planes, by foot, and even up into the sky, as Joe, from the Millennium Eye, sees Elizabethan London emerge from the London of the present day. Why do you suppose Sarah Smith does this?

11. In the last scene of the book, Joe says that the Goscimers have seen Stratford through the eyes of post–World War II intellectual Boston. Joe himself sees Stratford, and Shakespeare, through the eyes of East Bradenton, Vermont. Can you ever really see a historical period through eyes "not your own"? How?

12. Who should Joe end up with, Posy or Mary Cat (or neither)?